Melissa Bank's first book, *The Girls' Guide to Hunting and Fishing*, was published by Viking in 1999. She lives in New York City.

THE WONDER SPOT

MELISSA BANK

PENGUIN BOOKS

PENGUIN BOOKS

Published by the Penguin Group
Penguin Books Ltd, 80 Strand, London WC2R ORL, England
Penguin Group (USA), Inc., 375 Hudson Street, New York, New York 10014, USA
Penguin Group (Canada), 90 Eglinton Avenue East, Suite 700, Toronto, Ontario, Canada M4P 2Y3
(a division of Pearson Penguin Canada Inc.)
Penguin Ireland, 25 St Stephen's Green, Dublin 2, Ireland (a division of Penguin Books Ltd)
Penguin Group (Australia), 250 Camberwell Road,
Camberwell, Victoria 3124, Australia (a division of Pearson Australia Group Pty Ltd)
Penguin Books India Pvt Ltd, 11 Community Centre,
Panchsheel Park, New Delhi – 110 017, India
Penguin Group (NZ), cnr Airborne and Rosedale Roads, Albany,
Auckland 1310, New Zealand (a division of Pearson New Zealand Ltd)
Penguin Books (South Africa) (Pty) Ltd, 24 Sturdee Avenue,
Rosebank, Johannesburg 2196, South Africa

Penguin Books Ltd, Registered Offices: 80 Strand, London WC2R 0RL, England

www.penguin.com

First published in the United States of America by Viking Penguin 2005
First published in Great Britain by Viking 2005
Published in Penguin Books 2006
1

The story "The Wonder Spot," appeared in different form in *Speaking with the Angel*, edited by Nick Hornby, Riverhead Books, 2001.

Grateful acknowledgement is made for permission to reprint excerpts from the following copyrighted works: "Highway 61 Revisited" by Bob Dylan. Copyright © 1965 by Warner Bros. Inc. Copyright renewed 1993 by Special Rider Music. All rights reserved. International copyright secured. Reprinted by permission. "Shake and shake the ketchup bottle" by Richard Armour. By permission of the Estate of Richard Armour. "Another Reason Why I Don't Keep a Gun in the House" and "The Rival Poet" from *The Apple That Astonished Paris* by Billy Collins. Copyright © 1988 by Billy Collins. Reprinted with permission of the University of Arkansas Press.

Printed in England by Clays Ltd, St Ives plc

ISBN-13: 978-0-141-02184-3
ISBN-10: 0-141-02184-5

For my sister, Margery Bates

CONTENTS

BOSS OF THE WORLD

You could tell it was going to be a perfect beach day, maybe the best one all summer, maybe the last one of our vacation, and we were going to spend it at my cousin's bat mitzvah in Chappaqua, New York. My mother had weeks ago gone over exactly what my brothers and I would wear; now, suddenly, she worried that my dress, bought particularly for this event, wasn't dressed-up enough. She despaired at the light cotton, no longer seeing the tiny, hand-embroidered blue flowers she'd been so charmed by in the store. She said the dress looked "peasanty," which was what I liked about it. Maybe tights would help, she said; did I have tights? "No," I said, and my face added, *Why would I bring tights to the seashore?* When she said that we could pick some up on the way to Chappaqua, I reminded her that the only shoes I had with me were the sandals I had on. I said, "They'll look great with tights."

"You don't have any other shoes?"

"Flip-flops," I said. "Sneakers."

My older brother came to my door. "Dad says we have to go."

She turned to Jack now and said, "Is your jacket small?"

If it was, I didn't see it, but my mother had already worked herself up into what she called a tizzy. "How is it possible for a person to outgrow a suit in a matter of weeks?" she wondered aloud, as though we had an unsolvable mystery or a miracle before us, instead of the result of Jack lifting weights and running all summer. He'd lost his blubber and added muscles where once there had been none; about once a day I'd put my hand around his bicep, and he'd flex it for me.

My father appeared in my doorway. "Just unbutton the jacket," he said.

Jack did, and my mother said a small, "Oh."

Then my father said, "Let's go," meaning, *We are going now.*

We followed our leader out to the driveway.

My little brother, Robert, was already in the station wagon, reading *All About Bats*, in his irreproachable seersucker suit. Beside him, our standard poodle sat tall and regal, facing the windshield as though anticipating the scenery to come.

When my mother tried to coax the dog out of the car, Robert said, "He wants to come with us."

"The dog will be more comfortable here," she said.

I thought, *We'd all be more comfortable here.*

Robert said, "Please don't call Albert 'the dog.' "

My father said, "Never mind, Joyce," and my mother said, "Fine," in the tone of, *I give up.*

I was about to get in the car when she said, "You're not wearing a slip." I'd decided slips were a pointless formality, like the white gloves my mother had finally given up asking me to wear. But she said, "You can see right through."

I was horrified: All I had on were white underpants. "You can?"

Robert said, "Just in the sun," and I relaxed; bat mitzvahs were seldom held alfresco.

My father said, "Everybody in the car."

I sat in the way back of the station wagon with Albert, farthest from my mother's tizzy and my father's irritation, though I would also be farthest from the air-conditioning, which would be turned on once my mother realized the wind was messing up her hair.

Until then, my brothers rolled their windows down, and Albert and I caught what breeze we could.

I had to close my eyes when we drove by the parking lot for the beach, but Robert turned full around at the tennis courts.

"Dad?" he said. "If we get home early enough, will you hit with me?"

I could hear the effort it took for my father to make his voice gentle: "We won't get home early enough."

Robert said, "But if we do?"

"If we do," my father said, "I would be delighted to play with you."

Robert was just going into fifth grade and would probably be the smallest boy in his class again, but he was almost as good a tennis player as my father. Robert ran for every shot, no matter how hopelessly high or unhittably hard; he was as consistent as a backboard. At the courts, he'd hit with anyone who asked—the lacquered ladies who needed a fourth, the stubby surgeon who kept a lit cigarette gritted between his teeth, the little girl who got distracted by butterflies.

. . . . .

On the Garden State Parkway, nobody spoke. My parents were miserable, probably because they'd agreed not to smoke in the car. Robert was miserable because they were, though he was the reason they weren't smoking. He was always begging them to quit, and they half pretended they had.

I was miserable because we were rushing toward the boredom only a bat mitzvah could bring.

Jack seemed oblivious; he was looking out the window. Maybe he was imagining himself away at college, which he and my father talked about nonstop. Whenever I reminded Jack that it was a whole year away, he'd say how fast it would go; I'd say, "How do you know?" a question apparently undeserving of a reply.

. . . . .

Rebecca, whose bat mitzvah we were going to celebrate, was hardly even related to me. Our mothers were distant cousins who'd learned to walk on the same street of row houses in West Philadelphia, and then when their families had moved to the suburbs, the cousins had gone to the same private school, camp, and college. I'd seen pictures of them as babies in sun bonnets in Atlantic City, as girls in plaid shorts in the Adirondacks, as young women in sunglasses in Paris. Both were petite, both had dark hair, and my mother said that both had gotten too thin during their phase of Jackie Onassis worship.

In my opinion, Aunt Nora was still too thin, and Rebecca was even thinner. She was a ballerina and kept her shoulders back too far and her head up too high; she would sometimes swoop into ballet jumps out of nowhere—when the four of us were trying to find the car in a parking lot, for example.

That winter she'd been the understudy for Clara in *The Nutcracker Suite* in New York City, and my mother had insisted we go. I said, "In case the real Clara breaks her leg?"

"We're going because it'll be fun," she said. "It's an enormous honor for Rebecca to be in the ballet."

"She's not in it," I said.

During the ballet I tried to be open-minded, but it made no sense to me; it seemed as likely for a girl to dance with a nutcracker as with a corkscrew or an egg beater.

During lunch, when Aunt Nora asked how I'd liked the performance, I said, "It wasn't my cup of tea," a phrase my mother had instructed me to use in place of *yuck* but which now seemed to affect Aunt Nora as my *yuck*s had my mother.

Flustered, I told Rebecca that I was sure the ballet would have been better if she'd been in it, and added a sympathetic, "I'm sorry you weren't picked."

I didn't realize my mistake until Rebecca scowled. Aunt Nora gave my mother a look, which was the same as talking about me while I was there.

On the train back to Philadelphia, my mother pretended that the four of us had enjoyed a splendid afternoon. She admired how thin and delicate Rebecca was. "Like a long-stemmed rose," she said.

I said, "She's more like a long piece of hair with hair."

I expected my mother to be angry, but instead she seemed almost glad—not that she said so. What she said was, "You might become friends when you're older."

I said, "I don't think so."

"Why not, puss?"

I shrugged. I told her that Rebecca had turned down a piece of gum I'd offered by saying, "I don't chew gum—it's not ladylike."

My mother saw nothing wrong with this; it was something she herself might've said. She repeated a ditty from her early life with

Aunt Nora: "We don't smoke and we don't chew, and we don't go with boys who do."

My mother told the same stories over and over—maybe twenty-five in all; if you added them up, there were only about two hours of her life that she wanted me to know about.

. . . . .

At a rest stop on the New Jersey Turnpike, we stretched our legs until my mother returned from the ladies' room.

When she did, Robert said, "You look great, Mom."

She did look great. The day before, she'd driven herself to Philadelphia to have her hair professionally colored, a wise decision, as her hair had turned orangey in the sun.

Back in the car, my father said he liked her dress, a mod print in yellow and pink.

I said, "It's a designer dress," which was what my mother had told me.

Now that the trouble seemed to have passed and the air-conditioning was on, I considered asking Robert to trade places with me.

My father, who could be what my mother called a reverse snob, said that all dresses were designer dresses; someone had designed them.

"Not Pucci," my mother said in a haughty voice.

"Ah," my father said, "putting on the dog," which was supposed to be a joke, but she didn't laugh.

I stayed where I was. I patted Albert's fleecy black coat. Looking into his sad eyes, I said, "I know just how you feel."

. . . . .

We were on the exit ramp for Chappaqua when my mother turned around and smiled in a way that had nothing to do with happiness. It was her way of saying, *Smile*, without risking the opposite, at least from me.

Before we walked into the synagogue, she said, "I'm so proud of all of you," like she was making a commercial about our family.

This synagogue was about twice as big as the one we went to, and the service seemed ten times as long, as it was almost entirely in Hebrew, a language I did not speak.

Finally Rebecca went to the podium, her toes pointed out. She seemed glad to be up there, in her chiffony pink dress, white tights, and black Mary Janes. She wore her hair back in a looped braid tied with a pink satin ribbon, though she might as well have been wearing a halo the way my mother gazed up at her.

For a second Rebecca looked out at the audience, at her family and her friends and her family's friends and all of the religious fanatics who had chosen to spend the most beautiful day of the entire summer inside. It occurred to me that she saw us as her public, and maybe she wished she could dance the part of Clara that she'd worked so hard to learn.

Then she looked down at the Torah the rabbi had ceremoniously undressed and unscrolled, and she began to read aloud. I kept thinking that she would have to stop soon, but I was wrong about that. She seemed to be reading the entire Torah up there.

Maybe she'd learned how to pronounce the Hebrew words, but you could tell she had no idea what they meant. She read with zero expression, as though reciting the Hebrew translation of a phone book or soup label, the only semblance of an intonation a pause at the end of a listing or ingredient.

In contrast, my mother, who was no more fluent in Hebrew than I, appeared utterly enthralled; she even nodded occasionally as though finding this or that passage especially insightful and moving.

Hebrew comprehension wasn't the only thing my mother was faking. When I pulled her wrist over to look at her watch and made a face that signified, *I'm dying,* she posed her mouth in a smile. Then she held my hand as though we were in love.

I couldn't see my father, but I thought he probably liked how long the service was. He'd become more religious since his own father had died. Before, my father had only gone to services on the major holidays with us, but now he sometimes went on Friday nights, too. He walked, as the Orthodox did, even though he was heading toward our

Reform synagogue, the least religious one possible. Usually my mother went with him, but one night he'd gone alone. I'd watched him from my window, and it was strange to see him walking down our suburban street by himself.

. . . . .

I was so relieved when the service was over that I let my mother kiss me. Then it was time to go downstairs to what was called a luncheon instead of lunch.

The catering hall was decorated with pink curtains, pink carpeting, and pink tablecloths; a pink tutu encircled each centerpiece of pink roses. Even the air seemed pink.

My mother found the pink place card with my name and table number; she announced that I was sitting with Rebecca and the other twelve- and thirteen-year-olds at table #13, as in, *Great news!* Like most adults, my mother seemed to believe that a nearby birth date was all kids required for instant friendship.

I told her that I hoped she got to sit with the other forty-one- and forty-two-year-olds.

I spotted #13 at the edge of the dance floor but took my time getting there; I circled tables, pretending I didn't know where mine was. When I did sit down, Rebecca didn't even look up; I imagined her saying to her mother, *Does Sophie have to sit with us?*

The boy next to her resembled the boy I liked at my school, Eric Green—blond, dimples—and he must have asked who I was; I heard Rebecca say the words *My cousin,* while her tone said, *Nobody.*

The bandleader called Rebecca's grandparents up to the stage to say the blessing over the candles; he said, "Put your hands together for Grandpa Nathan," while the band played "Light My Fire."

I felt free to eat my roll.

Then a girl wearing a gold necklace that spelled *Alyssa* in script said, "Where are you from?"

"Surrey, Pennsylvania," I said. "It's outside of Philadelphia."

"I've been to the Pennsylvania Dutch country," she said. "You know, the Amish?"

I'd been there, too, and was about to say so, but she turned away from me, as though living in Pennsylvania instead of New York made me less like her than the somber people whose beliefs forbade the driving of cars and the wearing of zippers.

To the table at large, Alyssa said, "Who's going to Lori's bat mitzvah?"

I felt a pang that I hadn't been invited to the bat mitzvah of a girl I didn't even know.

I was wishing I could get up and leave, but a second later there was no need; the band went from "Hava Nagila" to "Jeremiah Was a Bullfrog," and everybody at my table got up to dance. I saw that all the girls were wearing tights; they probably had slips on, too.

I ate my chicken and watched the dance floor.

You could tell Rebecca saw herself as the belle of the bat mitzvah, but the grace that served her so well in ballet deserted her at rock 'n' roll. Maybe she wasn't used to dancing with her heels on the ground; she marched like a majorette in a parade or, it occurred to me, like the nutcracker in *The Nutcracker*.

The boy who looked like Eric Green danced like him, too; he barely did anything except jerk his overgrown bangs out of his eyes and mouth the occasional phrase, such as, "Joy to the fishes in the deep blue sea."

He stayed in one spot while Alyssa go-go danced around him. I studied her, trying to memorize the way she shimmied and swiveled; then I remembered that I'd tried moves like these in front of the mirror in my parents' bedroom and discovered the huge gap between how I wanted to look when I danced and how I actually did look.

I got up to visit my brothers. But Robert was performing his disappearing-nickel trick for the children's table, and Jack was sitting between two girls. One with wavy hair and glasses was making him laugh, and the other, very pretty, was jiggling one high heel to the music. I wished that for once he would like the funny one, but as I stood there I saw him ask the other girl to dance.

I almost bumped into Aunt Nora greeting guests at the eighty-plus table. She wore a pale blue sleeveless dress and her hair up in a bun plus bangs. It seemed possible that she was trying to look like Audrey Hepburn, and she did a little; both gave the impression of fragility, though Aunt Nora's seemed to come from tension and Audrey's from innocence.

Aunt Nora made a kissing sound and squeezed my shoulder, which felt less like affection than a fact—not, *I like you,* but, *You are the daughter of an old friend.*

I knew there was some appropriate thing my mother wanted me to say, but I couldn't remember what and just offered the standard, "Thank you for having me."

She said, "Thank you for coming," which came out *cubbing;* Aunt Nora suffered from allergies.

I said, "You're welcome," and asked where my parents were sitting; she pointed.

As a judge, my father was an expert at making his face blank, but I could tell he didn't like the man who was talking to him. I cruised right over.

I heard the man say, "Am I right, or am I right?" and then my father noticed me and excused himself from their conversation.

In a low voice, he said, "How's it going?"

"Bad," I told him. "Very bad."

He stood up and put his arm around my shoulders; he walked me away from the table and said, "Want to dance?"

The band was playing "The Impossible Dream"; I said, "This one's kind of schmaltzy."

He said, "Do you know what schmaltz is?"

"I thought I did."

"Chicken fat," he said. He told me that people spread it on bread, and we needed to go to a Jewish restaurant so I could try some.

I said, "Could we go right now?"

He took my hand, and I let him move me around to the chicken-fatty music.

Back at the table, he told me to take his chair and went off to find another, leaving me between Mr. Am-I-Right? and the actress my mother had become.

"Hel-lo," she said, with the two-beat singsong of a doorbell. To the table, she said, "This is my daughter, Sophie."

"Hi," I said.

My mother said, "Are you having a good time?"

I said, "I am having a great time," and then just loud enough for her: "Everyone is more dressed up than I am."

Her smile disappeared, my goal.

She didn't realize that I was kidding until I suggested we drive around and look for tights.

My dad pulled up a chair, and he and I sat very close.

I asked if he was finished with his lunch.

He said, "Go ahead, sweetheart."

I snuck what was left of my father's chicken into a napkin when Aunt Nora came to the table and got everyone's attention: Did anyone want to dance "The Hokey Pokey"? My mother did. She and Aunt Nora walked off with their arms linked.

I spotted them with Rebecca on the dance floor as I made my getaway. The bandleader was singing, "Put your right foot in, and shake it all about," and the three of them did it along with everyone else, without thinking, as I did, *Why? Why would you put your right foot in and shake it all about?*

In the parking lot, I let Albert out of the station wagon and poured water into his bowl. "You're feeling sorry for yourself," I said, feeding him the leftover chicken, "but you don't know how lucky you are."

I was fastening his leash when I heard a voice say, "Hey."

It was the boy who looked like Eric Green.

I said, "Hi."

"I'm Danny," he said. "You don't have a cigarette, do you?"

"Oh," I said. A bunch of girls in my grade had tried smoking at a Girl Scout overnight, but I never had. I looked around the parking lot; we were alone. I said, "There might be a pack in the glove compartment." There was. "I don't see any matches, though."

"I have matches," he said. I handed him two cigarettes, and he held one and put the other behind his ear like a pencil.

He walked with me and Albert past the cars and along the grassy edge of the parking lot. He ran his hand along the bushes. I thought of the one afternoon Eric Green had walked me home from school, his finger through my back belt loop.

Now, Danny said, "Poodles are really smart, right?"

"I can't speak for the whole breed," I said, "but Albert is a genius."

"Can he do tricks?"

"Tricks are beneath him." I said that he'd been named for both Albert Einstein (Robert's hero) and Albert Camus (Jack's).

The sun was glinting off the cars, and in the bright light I saw that this boy looked less like Eric Green than I'd thought. It occurred to me that Danny was older, and I was right.

He told me that he was in eighth grade and his private school had already started. It always started early, he said bitterly, adding that he'd had to miss the last day of hockey camp.

I almost said, *That's too bad,* but it sounded like gloating.

As we walked, the bushes thinned out, and you could see a field on the other side. At a large gap, there was a path and Danny said, "You want to . . . ?" and I said, "Okay."

He took Albert's leash and cut through first. Then he reached his hand out for me. I took it, and he steadied me so I wouldn't slide down the hill, which was more mud than grass.

He said, "You okay?"

I nodded.

He seemed reluctant to let go of my hand, and when he looked at me, everything tingled—not the tiny on-and-off sparks of a foot falling asleep but single and continuous like flying in a dream.

The grass had been mashed down into a path. What had looked like a beautiful field turned out to be a vacant lot; a ratty blanket and rusted beer cans surrounded the ashes and burned sticks of an old campfire. Even so, the sun was lighting up the trees and weeds and flowers. There was the buzzing hum of insects in unison, loud and then quiet.

Danny lit his cigarette and said, "I can't believe summer's over," and I heard in his voice what I knew I'd feel in another week when my school started; it made summer seem less real now.

Danny blew a smoke ring. "Are you going out with anybody?"

I thought again about Eric Green, who had stopped talking to me. "Not at the moment."

At my feet, Albert was sniffing at what looked like a big finger of the flesh-colored gloves Jack wore while dissecting sharks in the basement.

I could feel Danny's eyes on me, and though we were in the shade, I thought of Robert saying that my dress was see-through in the sun. I suddenly felt queasy and nervous. "We should get back."

He didn't move; maybe he was hoping I'd change my mind. He used his first cigarette to light his second.

I got my voice to sound normal, but I felt the quiver underneath when I said, "Come on," to Albert.

I tried to pretend I wasn't hurrying, but I was, and Danny followed. Then we weren't on the path anymore; there wasn't a path. I was stomping down weeds. Pricker bushes were scratching my legs. Finally, I caught sight of the parking lot through the weeds. We'd wound up behind the synagogue, where only a catering truck and a maintenance van were parked.

I slowed down a little then; we walked side by side. In the distance, I could see guests leaving. A few wild children were running around while their parents talked. Rebecca's father, carrying a tutu centerpiece, was helping her grandmother into a sedan. I saw my father then; he was smoking near the station wagon.

On reflex, I crouched down behind a Cadillac, and Danny crouched with me. "That's my father," I said.

After a few minutes, Danny said, "You want me to see if he's still there?" He stood up. "What does he look like?"

"Tall," I said. "He's wearing a dark gray suit."

"I don't know."

I stood up. We were safe.

At the station wagon, I noticed that Albert's paws were muddy, and I wiped them with a rag.

Danny took the rag and wiped the mud off my sandals and pulled a blade of grass out from between my toes.

When he opened the door to the synagogue for me, I thought he was going to ask for my address so he could write to me, but all he said was, "Thanks for the cigarettes."

I was relieved and then disappointed.

In the hall, Alyssa rushed up to him and said, "My dad's here." She glared at me. I wondered if she was his girlfriend, or wanted to be; it was one or the other.

Danny didn't seem to care that she was angry. He said, "See ya," to me, and followed her out to the parking lot.

Downstairs, in the pink palace, Robert and Jack were sitting with my father at a table that had been cleared of everything, including the centerpiece.

My father said, "Let your mother know we're going, please," and I walked over to where she stood with a woman wearing a big-brimmed straw hat with a beige ribbon.

"This is my daughter, Sophie," my mom said, in her fakest voice of the day.

The woman said, "And how old are you?"

"Twelve," I said.

She cooed at this impressive accomplishment. "And when is *your* bat mitzvah?"

I was about to say that I wasn't having one when my mother cut in and said, "We're just planning it now."

I was shocked to hear my mother lie, but I didn't give her away. I remembered a cliché that seemed to fit: "Rebecca will be a hard act to follow."

The woman tittered, and said, "She's darling."

. . . . .

At the car, my mother told me to sit up front and didn't speak again until we were on the highway. "Where were you?"

"Walking Albert," I said.

"She was walking Albert," Robert repeated, in my defense.

Without turning around, my mother said, "I'm talking to Sophie, Robert." To me, she said, "You were gone for over an hour."

I was wondering what she suspected, and then I realized that she didn't suspect anything, she was just angry that I'd disappeared. "It wasn't like anyone missed my company," I said. "No one at my table would even talk to me."

She said, "That's not the point."

We passed three exits before she told me what her point was. I was a guest, she said; I was a member of this family. She kept talking, but whatever she was angry about wasn't making it into her lecture.

I knew that eventually I would have to say I was sorry, even if I didn't know why I should be and wasn't. Until I said it, my mother would go on talking and get angrier until she became tired and hurt, at which point my father would take over.

"I'm sorry," I said.

My mother kissed me. "I know you are."

It felt a little less crowded up front then. My mother said what a wonderful job Rebecca had done and then, almost to herself, said she hadn't even started to plan my bat mitzvah.

I looked at my mother. I looked at my dad. It had all been decided. I couldn't argue; I was supposed to be remorseful.

At a gas station, I climbed into the way back with Albert, where I closed my eyes and thought about Danny. I didn't remember being queasy or afraid. I remembered him taking my hand. I thought of him saying, "I can't believe summer's over," which I heard now as a declaration of love.

. . . . .

I came home from my first day of getting lost at Flynn Junior High to the news that I had been enrolled in the Hebrew class required of the bat-mitzvah bound. My mother was relieved; she'd been afraid we were too late, but there was room for me after all.

The topic that night at dinner was varsity football. Jack wanted to join the team. We were all surprised. He took photographs and painted pictures; he wrote stories and acted in plays; he'd played soccer, but only intramurally.

My parents objected—he would be too busy applying to college, they said—but Jack argued with reason and passion. For example, he said that joining the football team would demonstrate that he was well-rounded, etc., and might even strengthen his applications.

My father seemed glad to give in, and I thought now might be the right time to discuss the bat mitzvah I did not want to have. But his good mood shone down on Robert; my father suggested they hit at the public courts after dinner.

Robert got so excited that he jumped up from the table to change and was on the stairs when my mother said, "Robert?"

He stopped. "May I please be excused?"

My mother said, "Yes," and took this opportunity to ask me to get their cigarettes. She didn't like to ask in front of Robert, who regularly talked to my parents about their imminent smoking-related deaths.

They were supposedly limiting themselves to three cigarettes a day, the best and last of which they smoked together after dinner, with their coffee. They'd switched to Carlton 100s so they'd enjoy smoking less. And they kept them in the basement; the inconvenience was supposed to make them more aware of each cigarette, but I didn't see how, since the inconvenience was all mine.

I thought of this tonight and every night I went down the basement stairs and into what we still called the playroom even though we never played anything in there anymore except the rare game of Ping-Pong. The net was still up, but the table's identity was otherwise concealed beneath the junk that overwhelmed the rest of the playroom.

The cigarettes were stored in the refrigerator of my cardboard kitchen, and to get there I had to step over Jack's barbells and around boxes and books crowned with such unstackable items as an old telephone with its cord cut. Only my kitchen was left uncluttered and intact, which made me wonder if my mother hoped that one day I'd go back to whipping up imaginary cakes and pies for her and my father.

Upstairs, everyone was out on the porch, my parents on a chaise apiece and my brothers in the love seat, leaving an armless chair for me. None of the porch furniture was comfortable, though; it was metal, and when we stood up its diamond pattern was imprinted on the backs of our thighs like fishnet stockings.

Robert had changed into whites, but the excitement he'd had about playing tennis was gone; he sat silent and grim, all of his attention on the two cigarettes I'd put on the table between my parents.

When my father reached for his, Robert closed his eyes and said, "I can't watch this." His voice was matter-of-fact, as it always was, even when he discussed his future as an orphan.

My mother said a sympathetic, "Would you like to be excused?"

He nodded and rose, leaving his chocolate pudding behind in protest, and Albert followed him inside.

My father lit my mother's cigarette and then his. As though in reverie, he held the burned match a moment before putting it in the clamshell that served as an ashtray. I watched him take another puff, and then I began. I said, "I've decided not to have a bat mitzvah."

My father turned to look at me, one hand behind his head in a futile attempt at comfort. He was used to people pleading their cases before him, and he waited for me to plead mine.

Jack seemed amused, so I tried to pretend he wasn't there. He'd become a less reliable ally over the summer, when he'd begun to see himself less as a camper than a counselor, less the oldest child than the youngest parent.

My mother glanced from me to my father. I'd been fighting with her lately as I never had before—twice that week I'd sent her down to the cardboard refrigerator—and though she'd told my father, he had yet to witness this behavior himself. It occurred to me that she hoped he would now.

I kept my voice calm. "The only reason I'd do it would be for material gain." With a pang, I thought of the stereo my parents had given Jack for his bar mitzvah. "In conclusion," I said, "this seems wrong."

My father nodded for me to go on.

I thought, *Did you not hear my "in conclusion"?* But I nodded myself, as though deciding which of my many powerful points to voice next. "I don't know what I believe in," I said. "So I don't think I should go up on a stage and act like I do."

Robert's voice came from behind the screen door: Softly, less to us than himself, he said, *"Beema."* He knew the correct term for the stage in a synagogue because, unlike Jack and me, Robert had gone to Hebrew school since kindergarten. He loved it. The only reason he wasn't going this year was that he'd been chosen to tutor fifth-graders less brilliant than himself.

We all turned to look at him, a small figure in white.

He said, "Do you know what cilia are?"

My father sighed. "We're having a conversation here, honey."

Robert had written to the American Cancer Society and the American Lung Association for help, and often quoted from the brochures they'd sent. "Cilia are little hairs that keep your lungs clean," he said now. "When you smoke, you paralyze them."

My mother said, "Why don't you come out and finish your pudding?"

"Did you hear what I said?" Robert asked.

"We heard, honey," my father said and turned back to me, my cue to continue. I thought of saying, *Having a bat mitzvah represents everything I stand against.* But I knew my father would say, *For instance?* and I hadn't prepared examples. I was working up the courage to say, *My decision is final,* when my mother spoke.

If she'd wanted my father to witness my defiance a moment earlier, I could see that she didn't now. "You used to love Hebrew school," she said.

I said, "That was in first grade." It was true that I'd loved my teacher, Miss Bell, and songs like "Let My People Go," and stories about jealousy; but it was also true that I'd been so little that when Miss Bell had talked about God as Our Father, I'd pictured mine.

The four of us were looking at my father now. All that was left was for him to deliver his verdict. I didn't know what he would say. He could surprise you, because he really was fair.

He said, "I'd like to talk to Sophie alone," and Jack and my mother got up and followed Robert inside.

My father's cigarette was down to the filter now, and he took the last possible puff. In his face I saw that he was sorry about that; maybe he was already thinking of all the hours that separated him from his next cigarette.

He said, "You seem to have made up your mind."

I barely managed to say, "I've given it a lot of thought."

"Have you?" he said. "It's a big decision to make on your own."

I said, "I can understand that," which didn't sound right, and I realized that I'd just repeated a phrase he often used during discussions.

He looked right at me and said, "Having a bat mitzvah is an important part of being Jewish."

In his voice I heard the unexpected magnitude of my decision: It separated me not just from my mother but from him, too, and maybe even from my brothers. I thought of the story of Moses parting the Red Sea for the Jews, and I saw my family safe on the far shore, waving as I drowned with Pharaoh's soldiers in the unparting sea.

As though underwater, I could barely hear my father's words.

He said that a bat mitzvah was a rite of passage into adulthood. "I still remember mine. I didn't like studying for it," he said. "No one does."

I thought, *Robert will.*

My father's voice sounded more normal when he said, "Your bat mitzvah wouldn't have to be like Rebecca's."

He kept his eyes on me. "We won't make any plans until you say so," he said. "But I'd like you to try Hebrew school."

It was more of a request than a command, and I was lulled by his respectful tone. I said, "Okay."

"Good," he said.

Another moment passed before I realized that I'd agreed to go to Hebrew school.

My mother appeared at the screen door. "Would you like a piece of fruit or anything?"

"Yes," he said. "I'd like a cushion for this goddamned chair."

"Maybe next year," she said. Then: "Robert's waiting."

My father looked at me. He said, "Are we finished, sweetheart?" and I said that we were.

. . . . .

My mother gave me a lift to Hebrew school. She brought Albert along to make me feel better and said that she wouldn't mind a little music, meaning that I could tune the radio to a station I liked.

I said, "Thank you anyway."

We drove in silence. The sun was still strong and the sky a summer blue, and I thought of the vacant lot and of Danny saying, "I can't believe summer's over."

We turned up the long driveway. The synagogue was pretty if I covered my left eye and just saw the old mansion part, where the offices were, and not the ugly new addition—a submarinelike tunnel of classrooms plus the actual temple with its trapezoidal stained-glass windows.

At the entrance, my mother said, "You know, Aunt Nora and I weren't allowed to have bat mitzvahs. They were just for boys."

I turned a blank eye to my mother, informing her that her words were irrelevant to me.

"Well," she said, forcing a smile, "I'll pickle you up at five-thirty."

I said my most wretched, "Good-bye."

After I closed the door, she said, "Sophie?" and for a second I thought that maybe she would say something comforting, or even, *I don't want you to suffer: Let's go.* Unlike my father, she was capable of reversals.

She said, "Did you want to thank me for the lift?"

. . . . .

The classroom was brand-new and modern, with petal-shaped desks, a skylight, and Hebrew letters in fluorescent colors tacked above the blackboard—probably an attempt to make us think that Hebrew was groovy. Instead, the room reminded me of the Muzak version of a rock song. I took the last seat in the last row so I could be closest to the door.

The teacher was writing on a pad and seemed oblivious to the dozen twelve- and thirteen-year-olds who faced him. I exchanged silent greetings with the ones I recognized from regular school, even Leslie Liebman, whose hands were folded on her desk.

The bell rang, and just when it was getting strange for the teacher not to start the class, he stood. He wrote his name on the board and faced us.

Very slowly, he said, "I am Moreh Pinkus."

I'm sure we all thought that *moreh* was his first name and were surprised to hear him say it to us; it wasn't until the second class that we learned that *moreh* meant *teacher* in Hebrew.

He was probably in his early thirties but seemed much older, as the very religious sometimes do. He was almost bald, which made me wonder if he'd glued his yarmulke on. He seemed to shuffle because the trousers of his suit were too long. I would have thought he was Orthodox, but he didn't have long curls in front of his ears or the beard that I thought was required.

After introducing himself, Moreh Pinkus rummaged through his briefcase for what turned out to be the attendance sheet. He read it over, and even then hesitated before speaking; it occurred to me that he didn't trust or like his voice.

He called my name first: "Applebaum, Sophie?"

"Here," I said.

He looked up at me for a long moment, so long I wondered if he'd divined how much I didn't want to be there. But he did the same with the next person and the next—calling the name, studying the face—until he said, "Muchnick, Margie?" and there was no answer.

It seemed possible that she had dropped out or was in the other class, and I hoped that she had or was. Margie Muchnick was one of the girls who lived on or around Foxrun Road—the Foxes, they were called—and though I wasn't one of their main victims, nobody was immune; they'd nicknamed me Sofa and tortured me about Eric Green.

Moreh Pinkus repeated, "Muchnick, Margie?" and she walked in and said, "Here."

Inexplicably, she sat at the desk next to mine.

Margie was short and solid, dressed in a baggy sweatshirt, jeans, and black high-tops. She had a round face and wore her red hair in two bunches, big fat frizz balls. Her eyelashes and eyebrows were almost white, and she had the yellow-brown eyes I imagined a fox might have.

I didn't acknowledge her, let alone mouth, *Hi,* as I had to my other un-friends. I pretended not to see her, just as I did when I ran into any of the Foxes.

There was an embarrassing silence while Moreh Pinkus waited for her to apologize for her lateness; then he looked down at the attendance sheet and read the next name.

To make up for Margie's rudeness, Leslie Liebman helped Moreh Pinkus distribute our *Hebrew I* textbooks.

Margie flipped through the lessons and exercises. "Fascinating," she said.

At the blackboard, Moreh Pinkus wrote out the Hebrew alphabet; slowly, slowly, slowly he said the name of each letter, pronounced the sound it made, and waited for us to repeat after him.

It was hot, and Moreh Pinkus removed his suit jacket and draped it around his chair. When he returned to the board, I saw that he'd missed a belt loop. I noticed, too, that he wore a wedding ring, and I thought it might not be a bad idea for Mrs. Pinkus to look her husband over before he left the house.

I tried to focus on Moreh Pinkus, but it was hard.

Margie pushed her sleeves up, revealing a wristful of baby bracelets—seed pearls interspersed with tiny alphabet cubes on a chain that turned your wrist green—last year's symbol of friendship. I'd lost mine in the ocean, but now, just as Moreh's wedding band revealed that he was married, my bare wrist seemed to announce that I was friendless.

I kept wishing Margie hadn't sat next to me. I wondered if it would attract too much attention for me to change desks.

She herself solved the problem. She had a coughing fit—a loud one—and you could tell it was fake. I thought that she was trying to amuse herself or to get our teacher to turn away from the board. But she was just setting up the pretext for her escape: She left the room, as though in need of water.

I felt better as soon as she'd gone. With the rest of the class, I repeated after Moreh Pinkus, but the Hebrew letters refused to enter my brain. I fell into a bored daze, which I interrupted only to check the wall clock and will its audible minute hand to tick faster.

I pretended to take notes, looking up at the board and down at my notebook, while I wrote out the words to Bob Dylan's "Highway 61 Revisited." I lingered over "God said to Abraham kill me a son/Abe said, 'Man, you must be puttin' me on,' " which seemed pertinent.

It wasn't until I had to go to the bathroom that I realized how long Margie had been gone. *She'll be back in a second,* I thought. I wrote out all the words to "I Shall Be Released," until I was desperate to be released myself. I left the room.

Margie wasn't at the fountain or in the hallway; nobody was. To be safe, instead of going to the bathroom two rooms up, I went to the one across the temple, all the way down the hall, past the classrooms, the lobby, and the gift shop.

I opened the door to the powder room and tried to appear calm when I saw Margie. She was sitting sideways, her legs slung over the arm of one of the fat, maroon velveteen chairs that faced the mirror. "Well hello, Sofa."

I said, "Hi, Margie," and went through the second door, to the stalls and sinks.

I planned to say nothing as I passed back through the powder room on my way out, but she said, "Can you believe this?"

Assuming that she meant the misery that was Hebrew, I said, "I know."

She said, "Do you have any candy or gum?"

"Sorry."

She took out a pack of cigarettes and asked if I wanted one.

I hesitated, but when she handed the cigarette to me I took it, and when she lit the match I leaned forward. I imitated my mother accepting a light from my father and exhaled as she did, ceiling-ward.

Margie held her own cigarette between her teeth like a killer; she was imitating someone, too—maybe the Penguin from *Batman.*

It was fascinating to see myself smoke, but I forced myself to turn away from the mirror in case Margie was observing me. I kept my eyes on the wallpaper, maroon-and-silver ladies with swirls for hair, such as you would see in a Peter Max print. Then, looking at the swirly wallpaper, I felt seasick. I pretended I'd dropped an earring in the shag rug so I could put my head between my legs.

"Did you lose something?" she said.

I couldn't speak.

When I felt better, I fidgeted with my earring and sat up.

I held the Marlboro until it had burned down low enough to be considered smoked and went to throw it in the toilet.

I stood there a moment, relieved to the point of elation: I hadn't gotten caught smoking and hadn't done anything Margie could make fun of or report to the Foxes.

In the powder room, she held out her hand in what I realized was an offer or challenge to thumb wrestle. I sat down again. We clasped fingers. Our thumbs tapped out the requisite side-to-side one-two-three.

Her nimble thumb danced while mine lumbered—hers was a swashbuckler, mine a polar bear. She pinned my thumb down hard.

"Best of three," she said.

I tried to copy her fancy thumb work, but again she won.

After best of seven, I said I was going back to class, and she didn't stop me.

She herself returned at the very end, when Moreh Pinkus was writing our assignment from *Hebrew I* on the blackboard. He faced us and asked if we had any questions.

Without raising her hand, Margie said, "Is this homework?"

He said, "Pardon?"

"We get homework from regular school," she said. "We're not supposed to get any from you." I wondered if this was true—I hoped it was—but it seemed more likely that it was just another coughing fit.

"If you wish to learn Hebrew," he said, in his interminably slow voice, "you will need to study."

He dismissed us with a formal, "Shalom," and a few of us mumbled shy shaloms back.

Margie walked outside with me, where all our mothers waited in station wagons. When she found hers, she turned to me and said, "See you 'round, basset hound."

. . . . .

At dinner, my father said, "Well? Was it the torture you thought it would be?"

I said, "Worse," and was ready to elaborate. I was hoping that if I told the truth, he would say that he was glad I'd given Hebrew school a try, which was what he'd finally said about tennis.

I could tell that he was both let down and a little angry; his eyes got tired, as they did when he looked over my report cards.

Robert rescued me by describing his first day of tutoring Doug Sloane, who'd been held back two grades; Robert imagined out loud how hard that would be.

It would be impossible, I thought, *because you are a genius and Doug Sloane is mentally retarded.*

Jack said that Doug's older brother, who'd also been held back, was on the football team. This led to a description of a catch that Jack himself had made off of what he called "a long bomb" in practice. He drew a diagram of the play on a napkin we passed around.

My father turned back to Robert. "So you think it was wrong for Doug to be held back?"

Robert said, "I feel sorry for him."

"I can understand that," my father said. "But didn't what you learned in fourth grade prepare you for fifth?"

For a while, they debated how the educational system might best serve Doug, and then Robert turned to me. "You know Doug Sloane, right?" Robert knew I did; he was just trying to include me in the conversation.

My mother jumped in: "Does anyone have any idea how high the adult illiteracy rate in this country is?" I doubted she herself knew. Like me, my mother didn't learn facts or acquire knowledge; instead, she had feelings—insecurity about not being knowledgeable, for example.

She looked around the table; none of us knew how high the adult illiteracy rate in this country was.

She said, "Seventeen percent."

I thought, *Eighty-five percent of statistics are made up on the spot.*

. . . . .

I hardly saw Margie in regular school. Flynn Junior High was huge compared to Surrey Elementary, and we didn't have any classes together. The first time I ran into her in the hall, she said a solemn, "Shalom," and I could tell by the way her Fox friends laughed that they thought she was imitating me instead of Moreh Pinkus.

Once, during her lunch and my math period, I looked out the window and saw her sitting on the high wall in the courtyard; the rest of the Foxes were stretched out single file, sunbathing, their shirts pulled up to get their tan stomachs tanner. Margie stood and said something that sounded like, "Good-bye, cruel world," and jumped down and landed hard. None of the Foxes even sat up.

. . . . .

Unlike the other Hebrew-school teachers, Moreh Pinkus did not give us a break halfway through class; when Margie suggested it, he misunderstood and said, "Please use the restroom whenever you need to." She left class immediately, and returned only to leave again.

Moreh Pinkus went through the Hebrew alphabet, but now the class called out each letter's name and pronunciation without his assistance. I seemed to be the only one who hadn't memorized the alphabet, the only one who'd forgotten to do the homework, the only one who hadn't learned the vocabulary words. It was just the second week, and I was already the Doug Sloane of the class.

When Margie came back to the room, I left.

In the hall, I heard my name and turned around. It was my first-grade teacher, Miss Bell.

I was thrilled that she remembered me.

She told me that she didn't teach anymore; she assisted the rabbi now. She was on her way to his study, and I walked with her.

I said, "Do you like your new job?"

She said, "I miss students like you."

When she asked who my teacher was and how I liked Hebrew, I remembered my father's disappointment in the truth. I told Miss Bell that Hebrew and Moreh Pinkus were great.

Then she took a left through the temple and I took a right to the powder room. I was washing my hands when the door banged open, and Margie said, "Get a paper towel."

On it, she drew the blanks and noose for hangman.

I didn't mind playing; what I minded was not having a choice. I was better at hangman than thumb wrestling. Margie hung herself again and again. Still, she kept saying, "One more." When I got up to go, she offered me the rest of her cigarettes if I played one more game.

I did, but I wouldn't take the cigarettes.

"Come on," she said. She told me that she had an endless supply; her parents bought their cigarettes by the carton. She said, "They don't care," which I assumed was her bravado way of saying they wouldn't notice. She pulled a cigarette out for herself and then threw the pack at me.

I caught it almost by accident. "Okay," I said, "thanks," and got up to leave.

"Sophie?"

It was a shock to hear Margie say my real name. It took me back to a time when I hadn't been afraid of her at all—fourth grade, Girl Scouts. I remembered waking up in a tent, and that the clothes I put on were warm because her mother, the troop leader, had told us to put them at the bottom of our sleeping bags.

When I turned around, Margie had a cigarette dangling from each nostril.

. . . . .

We had a string of Indian-summer days, and everyone hung out in the courtyard. During math, I saw a group of boys, possibly eighth- or even ninth-graders, talking to the Foxes who sunbathed on the wall.

Margie sat at the very end. She was making faces—mimicking the boys—for her own amusement.

The next time I checked the courtyard, I didn't see Margie. Instead I saw Eric Green—or, that is, I caught a glimpse of his blond head. Through breaks in the crowd, I saw that he was walking his bicycle—a white ten-speed Peugeot—but I couldn't see much else until he got to the archway. Then I had a clear sight of him from behind; he had his arm around the narrow back of a girl I didn't know, and one finger through a belt loop of her jeans.

I was almost grateful when the math teacher, Mr. Faye, pulled the shade down and closed the window.

. . . . .

In Hebrew school, Moreh Pinkus called Margie's name twice, as he had that first day, and then marked her absent.

It seemed possible that he hadn't learned any of our names, except those of his star pupils: Mitchell Cohen, a shy genius who reminded me of Robert; and Leslie Liebman, whose hand remained perpetually in the air, the Hebrew word—or, as the class progressed, sentence—pursed in her prissy lips.

When anyone else raised a hand, Moreh Pinkus said a reluctant, "Yes?" But he preferred calling on "Mr. Cohen" or "Miss Liebman," whose answers were guaranteed to be correct.

Those of us who never raised our hands seemed invisible to him. He didn't even look up when I left the room.

I went down the hall to the lobby and browsed at the display case ambitiously called the gift shop, never open. There was nothing in that case I wanted—not the menorahs or the Jewish-themed jewelry, not the illustrated children's books about Jewish holidays or history—but I scanned the case as though it might contain a Bob Dylan album I didn't have or the cross-stitched peasant blouses I liked.

Then into the powder room. I was slouched down in one of the cushy chairs when I heard pounding coming from the bathroom.

I pushed the door open. Margie was trying to get dimes out of the Kotex machine.

"I didn't think you were here," I said.

She said, "I'm not here."

I was impressed that Margie was unwilling to go to class even for the one second it took to say, *Here.* It made her cutting seem more fearless and forthright than mine.

"Do you have anything to eat?" she asked.

I didn't.

When she lit a cigarette for me, I noticed that she still wore her baby bracelets. She was the only one who did. The bracelet of choice now, worn by both girls and boys, was a stainless-steel cuff engraved with the name and serial number of a soldier missing in Vietnam. It was called an MIA bracelet, and my impression was that you had to order it, but from whom? I asked Margie if she knew.

She said, "I don't know what you're talking about," and got up and tried the door to the supply closet. It was locked, but a few minutes later, she got up and checked it again, as though with time and patience the door might open. I didn't understand her fascination with the closet, which I said was probably just where extra paper towels and toilet paper were stored.

"Really?" she said. "Then why do they lock it?"

I said that I was going back to class, and she said, "What for?"

I said, "I am learning the Hebrew language."

On the spot, she invented an excellent nonsense language that sounded as much like Hebrew as Hebrew did.

I answered in kind, mixing in the few real Hebrew words I knew with sound-alikes. At first we were animated and theatrical, but then I got serious. I found myself telling her about seeing Eric Green with his new girlfriend. In made-up Hebrew, I found the words to describe exactly how I felt. It was a relief just to say them.

Margie responded with a jokey, hand-waving argument, and I thought, *Did you not understand the importance of what I just told you?* I reminded myself that I hadn't spoken in English. Still, I had trouble forgiving her.

I stood and said, *"Mishpoka,"* meaning, *See ya,* and she said, *"Mishpoka,"* back.

Then I was out in the hall. I couldn't bring myself to go back to class yet, so I stopped at the gift shop to browse again through all the items I wouldn't want even if they were free.

I started at the sound of Miss Bell's voice: "Aren't you supposed to be in class?"

I turned around and waited for her to recognize me, a student who made her miss teaching.

She just blinked.

All I could do was nod, *I'm going,* and go.

I walked up the long hallway back to class. Right before I opened the door, I turned around and saw that Miss Bell was still standing there in the lobby, watching me, her arms folded below her chest.

. . . . .

When I got home from Hebrew school, Jack was sitting on the kitchen floor reading his favorite novel, *The Stranger*, Albert at his side.

I got down on the floor, too. I said, "I hate Hebrew school."

Jack said, "Everybody does."

I realized that he was home early. "Don't you have practice?"

He acted like he hadn't heard my question, but I'd learned from my father that if you waited long enough, Jack would answer.

Finally, he said, "We had an away game."

I said, "Why aren't you away?"

When he answered, his voice was so quiet I didn't think he wanted me to hear him: "I wasn't going to get to play."

"Why not?"

He raised his voice to normal volume, but it sounded louder because of how quiet it had been. " 'Why?' " he said. "Because I'm not good enough."

I was about to say, *That's not true,* but I realized that it was true; he wouldn't have said it otherwise. I waited a minute, and then I said, "That sucks."

He laughed, which was a relief. Then he said, "Want to watch cartoons?"

"Cartoons?"

He said, "I was just thinking how we never watch cartoons anymore."

I thought, *Did we ever watch cartoons?*

We took glasses of milk and a plate of oatmeal cookies upstairs to the guest room where the television was.

Jack turned the channel to the cartoon *Spider-Man* and said, "It's Spidey."

I said, "We should get a big color television."

He said, "Mom and Dad don't want one," as if I didn't know.

We'd been watching *Spider-Man* for about three minutes when he said, "The problem is that I don't really like cartoons anymore."

"I never liked them." I got up and changed the channel to a *Brady Bunch* rerun. "Why is that a problem?"

His voice got serious. "I guess I'm afraid I'm running out of things I like."

"You like new things," I said. "Like football."

As soon as the words were out I was sorry. I was trying to take them back when I said, "I don't get why you went out for it in the first place."

I waited a long, long time for him to answer. Finally, I put my hand on his bicep, and without a word he flexed it for me.

I asked if he had any ideas about how I could get out of Hebrew school.

He said, "Talk to Dad."

"What should I say?"

"Say it's interfering with regular school."

I'd hardly done any homework since school had begun. "I don't think I can say that."

He studied me for a second. "You should do your homework, Sophie." He turned off the television and went to his room.

I snapped the TV back on, but I was too angry to watch.

At the stairs to his bedroom, formerly our attic, I knocked on the wall.

"Don't come up," he called down.

I said, "I want to talk to you."

He didn't answer.

"Don't tell me to do my homework," I called up. "You're not my father."

He came down the stairs in his sweatpants.

I said, "Did you hear me?"

"I'm not your father," he said.

"Right," I said, following him down to the kitchen.

He said, "Okay," in the tone my father used when he said, *Point taken.*

I stood by while he put on his socks and tied his sneakers.

He was almost out the door when I said the line from *The Sound of Music* I'd repeated each time he'd left to go running that summer: "You can't run away from your problems, Liesl; you've got to face them."

He'd smiled whenever I'd said this before—he appreciated repeating jokes as much as I did, but I could see he didn't appreciate this one anymore; he opened the door and ran down the driveway.

I was helping my mom with dinner when he came back, sweaty and red-faced. He was stretching against the station wagon. I opened the door and, without thinking, made the joke I'd always made upon his return: "I knew you'd come back!"

This time he smiled, so I kept going. I pretended that he'd been gone for years, and he let me hug him. "I told you he'd come home," I said to my mother. "This calls for a celebration!"

. . . . .

I decided I would talk to my father after dinner; I planned to tell him that I had no Hebrew aptitude and also to convey the message of Bob Dylan's song "It Ain't Me, Babe." Though obviously written about a girlfriend, this song contained the overall message I needed to deliver to my parents: Unfortunately, we all had to face that I was not the person they wanted me to be.

The door to my father's study was open but, as usual, Jack was in there. I decided to wait in the hall. I'd just sat down when I heard Jack say, "It's interfering with my applications."

My dad said, "I don't see any evidence of that."

There was a silence, and I knew he was waiting for Jack to tell the truth.

"I want to spend time with Robert and Sophie," he said, "before I go away."

"That's a nice thought."

"I'm worried about Sophie," Jack said.

"That's not your department, Buddy."

Jack said, "She seems sort of lost."

I thought, *Lost how? How am I lost?* Suddenly I felt lost.

My father said, "You want to quit football to take care of Sophie?" He had a gift for rewording a point so you could hear how idiotic it was. "I thought you liked football."

"I don't know," Jack said. "I don't know what I like." Then he was talking about *The Stranger* and meaninglessness, which was meaningless to me; I considered going upstairs to worry about myself.

My father's voice was gentle, but I could tell he was getting impatient when he said, "Let's save existentialism for another night." Then he asked exactly what I had—why Jack had wanted to go out for the team in the first place—and I thought, *Score one for Sophie,* and maybe I wasn't so lost after all.

Jack waited a long time to answer. "I guess I wanted to be the kind of guy who plays football."

"What kind is that?" my dad said, which was exactly what I wanted to know.

Jack said, "Or I didn't want to be the kind who *can't* play football."

My father said, "What's wrong with being a nerdy Jewish intellectual?" meaning himself.

It was funny just hearing my father use a word like *nerdy,* and I expected Jack to laugh, but he said, "I tried so hard," and the pain I heard in his voice made my stomach hurt.

My father said things like, "You never played before," and, "You made the goddamned varsity," and then they were talking about backup schools, Penn versus Cornell.

I lay down on the rug and studied its repeating rams. It was fraying, and one long string looked very much like it wanted to be pulled. I told myself that if I didn't pull it, my father would let me quit Hebrew school.

I woke to my father saying, "Sweetheart?" and the rough rug on my cheek.

I sat up.

He said, "Did you want to talk to me?"

I nodded, and yawned.

He yawned, too, and asked if it could wait until tomorrow, and I said it could.

But tomorrow was Thursday, his night to play indoor tennis, and Friday he decided to go to services. Robert went with him, acting like it was a big treat. From my window, I watched the two of them walk down our street, my father's hand on Robert's shoulder.

. . . . .

In math, I could feel how cold and dreary the afternoon was, the drizzle and the gray sky, though I couldn't see it; since our week of Indian summer, Mr. Faye had kept the shades down.

It was the sound of a ball booming against the side of the building that made him go over to the window and lift the shade.

We all turned to look: Margie was out in the courtyard by herself. She was holding a brown-red ball and was about to drop it for another kick when Mr. Faye got the window open.

Before he could speak, she called out, "Sorry."

After Mr. Faye closed the window and pulled the shade down, I remembered Margie playing kickball at Surrey. When she was up, everyone in the outfield would automatically move way out. I'd seen her kick it over the fence for a home run. I remembered her running the bases. Afterward, she'd looked miserable—flushed, sweaty, squinting, winded—but now it occurred to me that she'd been happy.

Hardly anyone played kickball at Flynn, and no girls. I felt sorry for her then, but I doubt she felt sorry for herself. Mr. Faye had just returned to the board when another kick boomed against the wall.

. . . . .

That Wednesday, I brought a Baggie of gingersnaps to Hebrew school. I knew Margie wouldn't be in class, but I thought she might be in the powder room, and she was.

She was sitting upside down on the velveteen chair, her head on the rug, high-tops in the air. She held our sixth-grade graduation booklet from Surrey, entitled "Memories: The Way We Were."

She asked me to fish her cigarette out of the waste can, and I did, making sure it hadn't started a fire that would burn the synagogue down.

When she thanked me for the cookies, her voice had no expression in it at all, but I assumed this was from the strain of being upside down.

I wished I could've brought milk, which made gingersnaps taste better, especially if these were as stale as I suspected. She sat up and ate them slowly, thoughtfully, softening each bite in her mouth before chewing.

I sat in the chair next to hers, and she shared the graduation booklet with me. She had it opened to a page on which one of the Foxes had written, "Don't ever change!" and another, "Foxes forever."

On the opposite page, I caught a glimpse of my own picture and signature. What I'd written sounded sarcastic now: "Good luck in Jr. High!"

She said, "I'm glad I kept this," as though the booklet were a crucial piece of evidence that would prove her innocence and the Foxes' guilt in an upcoming friendship tribunal.

Then she said, "I'm not the one who changed."

I was suddenly enraged. I remembered the Foxes ganging up on anyone who was alone during recess. I thought of their regular victims: Richie, who was pale and thin, they called "Queer"; Sheralynn, who was shy, "Weird"; and Charles, who was retarded, "Retarded."

"Sofa" was mild by comparison, and at first I hadn't really minded their singing, "Sofa and Eric sitting in a tree, K-I-S-S-I-N-G . . ." I'd even hoped that it would remind Eric of his feelings for me and bring them back. But when it didn't, the song was torture, as were their smooching sounds.

I'd known my mother couldn't help; she pronounced *clique* the French way, CLEEK, and would just tell me that the Foxes were jealous and to ignore them.

I'd gone to my dad. As usual, he'd wanted to know the full story; he'd wanted to know my part in it. "What do they tease you about?"

I told him they called me weird.

"Oh, sweetheart," he'd said. "The meek shall inherit the Earth."

At the time, I'd heard only the implication that I was meek, which felt even worse than being called *lovesick* and *Sofa*. But now I remembered how gentle his tone had been, and I wondered if he'd just meant meek as the opposite of bossy, and if his unspoken message was that one day the bossy shall fall.

This day seemed to have come for Margie. It had become important to be pretty, and she wasn't; important to have boys like you, and none liked her. Everyone I knew had dropped out of Girl Scouts. I was sure all the Foxes had; I doubted the Foxes even thought of themselves as Foxes anymore, except as it meant "sexy ladies."

Margie's thumbs were pushed up against her eyelids—she was crying—and I was surprised to find myself feeling sorry for her. I tried to think of something to say. I remembered how happy she'd seemed in Girl Scouts, wearing her pale green uniform and her dark green sash with all the badges sewn on it. To earn them, you had to perform impossible tasks, such as visiting an elderly person for a year; at the end of my stint in Girl Scouts, I'd safety-pinned exactly three badges to my sash. Now I marveled aloud at how many she'd earned.

She said, "My sister Joy helped me." Both of her sisters were away at Penn State now, she said, and hardly ever came home "except for vacations."

I told her that my brother was going away next year and had already changed.

She said, "Joy got engaged," as though this was the culminating betrayal. A moment later, she added, "His name's *Ted.*"

She seemed more forlorn than ever, so I tried to bring the topic back to Girl Scouts. "You know what I liked about the camping trips?"

She handed me another cigarette. "What?"

I didn't have an answer ready; I tried to think of what I had liked. "The outdoors."

She told me that there was a camping trip in a couple of weeks. "You want to come?"

"Can I go if I'm not a Girl Scout anymore?"

"Lee goes." When she saw that I didn't know who Lee was, she said, "Miss King."

Miss King—or Miss K, as some of the girls called her—had played guitar and sung folk songs on our camping trips. She'd always worn the same outfit, jeans and a jean shirt, a suede coat, and old leather boots you'd expect a folksinger to own. She was husky, and her face resembled Arlo Guthrie's and her hair fluffed up like Bob Dylan's. I'd wanted to like her but hadn't; once, after we'd all sung "Blowin' in the Wind," Miss K had told me that I'd been flat.

I said, "But she gets to go because she plays the guitar, right?"

"She goes because she's best friends with my mother," Margie said. "She practically lives at our house."

Later, I would hear that Miss King was in love with Mrs. Muchnick.

Now Margie said, "My dad doesn't like her."

I couldn't picture any friend of my mother's, even Aunt Nora, living with us, and especially one my father didn't like.

"Anyway," she said, "you can come if you want."

"I'll ask," I said, though I knew I wouldn't.

The bell rang then, so I couldn't even go back to class to get my *Hebrew I,* which made me feel like a criminal.

. . . . .

At dinner, my father said that he had been meaning to ask how Hebrew school was going.

I swallowed. "The same."

He said, "Are you giving it a fair chance?"

I'd forgotten that I was supposed to do more than show up, and, picturing my *Hebrew I* on my desk in the dark classroom, I could hardly get my head to nod.

After dinner, when I was sent to get the cigarettes in the basement, I was glad to be by myself for a minute. I stood in my cardboard kitchen. It had belonged to Rebecca first, and by the time Aunt Nora had given it to me, as a birthday present, it appeared to have undergone years of industrial food preparation. I'd been bitterly disappointed, especially by the stove; it was white with three red concentric circles for burners, and what should have been the fourth was ripped down to its brown corrugated cardboard. I'd stared at the stove incredulously and thought, *I can't cook with this!*

My mother had said, "Did you want to thank Aunt Nora?"

"Thanks."

Right in front of me, Aunt Nora had said, "You're not strict enough with her."

Later my mother had scolded me about my manners. I'd said, "Isn't it bad manners to give a used present?"

She'd said, "Sometimes that can make a present even more special."

. . . . .

Moreh Pinkus held up my *Hebrew I*, and I took it from him. I didn't know whether to thank him or apologize. I wound up saying nothing.

After attendance, he announced that we would not have class next week, "in observance of Yom Kippur, the Day of Atonement," and though his voice was heavy with the importance of the holiday, I still felt the joy of an unexpected reprieve. I would have clapped if anyone else had, but instead I hid my hands inside the desk, and my fingers performed a merry folk dance.

It seemed possible that the whole class was as thrilled as I was; whenever Moreh Pinkus asked a question, almost everybody raised their hands. It was as though they'd all suddenly turned into Leslie Liebmans, and, as though they had, Moreh Pinkus was calling on all of them.

Then he said, "Please put your books on the floor and take out a pencil."

I thought, *You can't give a test without warning.* But no one else seemed surprised, and I realized that he'd probably announced the test at the end of last week's class, when I'd been in the powder room; he could've announced the test a hundred times and I wouldn't have known, I'd been in class so little.

The first half of the test was Hebrew and the second half English, sixteen sentences in all, each with a blank line underneath for the translation.

I thought, *Did you ever hear of multiple choice?*

When I looked up, he was watching me. He said, "Just do the best you can."

I stared at the test for a long time, and particularly at the sentence "The teacher brought the book to school," and prayed for a divine force to fly the Hebrew translation into my brain.

None came and there was no point in guessing. Finally I decided to write a note:

> DEAR MOREH PINKUS,
>
> I DID NOT HAVE MY BOOK, AND THEREFORE COULD NOT STUDY FOR THIS TEST.
>
> SORRY,
> SOPHIE APPLEBAUM.

I handed in my test and left the room, even though I could feel Moreh Pinkus staring at me. I went down the hall to the powder room.

Margie was standing at the closet door. Her cheeks were as flushed as they'd gotten after her home runs, and I noticed her hair was back in a barrette instead of up front in two bunches.

She stepped aside and ceremoniously opened the door to the closet; like a lovely assistant in a game show, she gestured at the shelves lined with plastic-wrapped merchandise from the gift shop.

"It was unlocked?" I said.

She set her woolly hair free and demonstrated inserting the barrette in the lock.

She'd already made a pile on the floor of what she wanted to take—mostly jewelry, but also boxes of multicolored Hanukkah candles and net satchels of gold-foiled chocolate coins. "Check it out," she said, handing me a big plastic bag of jewelry, each piece in its own little bag. I dumped the bag and spread its contents on the counter.

She brought her own stash over to try on next to me.

I found a silver cuff that looked a lot like an MIA bracelet, except it had Hebrew writing where the soldier's name and number belonged.

I looked at my wrist in the mirror, and then I saw all of me and then both of us, and what I saw was the enormity of this crime through my father's eyes: If there was a God, this was about as close as you could get to stealing from Him in the modern world; this seemed so obviously wrong, so symbolically wrong, we might as well have melted the jewelry down and created a golden calf to worship.

But it wasn't God or religion or my father that made me take the bracelet off. It had nothing to do with getting caught or getting in trouble with anyone but me.

I thought, *What am I doing?* and I surprised myself by saying it aloud. As soon as I did, I got this great feeling; it was like I'd been holding my stomach in for a long time—only what I'd been holding in was my personality—and I let it out now.

All Margie said was, "What's your problem?" but she spoke as though she was once again the boss of the world, addressing the Sofa of yesteryear.

She looked at me in the mirror; she was fastening the catch on a Star of David necklace. She was going to wear it.

I said the thought as it occurred to me: "You want to get caught."

"I don't care," she said. "I think my parents are getting a divorce."

I wasn't sure what her parents' divorce had to do with her theft, but I knew it did. Maybe she was getting back at them, or she felt she deserved these stolen goods in return for what was being taken from her.

"I'm sorry," I said, and meant it.

She shrugged. "You don't want anything?"

"No."

She didn't even look up when I left.

Miss Bell was coming down the hall.

Instead of saying hello, she asked if I knew that there was a bathroom right by the classrooms.

"Yes."

"So why don't you use it?"

I said, "This one's nicer."

Her eyes didn't register that I'd answered her question.

It was scary to walk away from her, just as it had been to walk out on Margie, but I was determined: I would be a slave to no person.

In class, a few students were still struggling with their tests. Leslie Liebman was reading her answers with obvious pleasure—she just couldn't get over how correct they all were.

Moreh Pinkus was saying, "Finish up," when Miss Bell appeared at our door. "Pardon me," he said to us, and joined her out in the hall. Everyone turned around to look; Margie was out there, too.

Miss Bell appeared as agitated and angry as Margie appeared calm and bored.

I kept trying to convince myself that I hadn't gotten caught and wasn't in trouble, but I felt I had and was.

When Moreh Pinkus came back in, I was ready for him to lean down and tell me to collect my things. But he walked right past me and only once he was back at his desk caught my eye. He sighed, and asked everyone to pass their tests forward.

. . . . .

That night, my parents announced that they'd smoked their last cigarettes. I got their pack from my cardboard refrigerator, and they made a ritual of running the leftover cigarettes under the kitchen faucet, as they had in the past.

For the next few days, Robert described the triumphant march of my parents' bodies back to health, their blood vessels expanding, their cilia waking up. During dinner, he'd say, "Doesn't everything taste better?" And afterward, "Why don't we all take a brisk walk?"

My father ground his teeth; my mother wrung her hands.

. . . . .

On Yom Kippur, my father wanted to walk to the synagogue, but my mother took too long getting dressed, and it was all worse because they weren't smoking.

Even though we drove, we were late.

The only seats left in the synagogue were in the last row, right behind where Moreh Pinkus sat with his family. My mother sat directly behind him, and I behind his youngest son.

There were four sons, all wearing pin-striped suits like the one Moreh wore each Wednesday. He himself was in a black suit. Mrs. Pinkus wore a silky flowered dress and a purple hat, and her hair hung in a glossy pageboy my mother would later tell me was a wig.

In front of me, the littlest Pinkus was bending his thumb back as far as it could go; he released it, and then bent it back again. Himself his only toy, he did the same with each of his fingers, and then began to experiment with the mobility of his ear.

Pretty soon the novelty of observing the Pinkuses wore off, and the service became like every other one I'd ever gone to. The rabbi, whose black robes reminded me of the ones my father wore in court, did what seemed to be an imitation of God; when he raised his arms to motion for us to sit or stand, his sleeves hung down a little like bat wings. He droned on, and when the word *congregation* appeared in the prayer book it was our turn to drone.

I looked around to see if anyone was atoning. I knew that Leslie Liebman's face probably had atonement written all over it, in fluent Hebrew, but I just saw her from behind, standing with her family.

Jack whispered in my ear, "My kingdom for a Life Saver; pass it down."

I said it to my mother, who opened her pocketbook. She took out the sugar-free mints that she carried around whenever she was trying to quit smoking. They hardly had any taste, but I took one. The slight entertainment it offered my mouth was more than my eyes and ears were getting.

It was then that Moreh Pinkus began mumbling and rocking back and forth in his seat. I must have seen my grandfather do this when I was little because I knew it was how religious men prayed.

My mother appeared almost girlishly embarrassed.

Jack put his mouth to my ear and whispered, "Rock and roll."

I said a very quiet, "Shh."

It occurred to me that Moreh Pinkus might be the only truly religious person in the whole synagogue, the only one who believed and understood everything he was saying. He wasn't even reading from the book.

It was out of respect for Moreh Pinkus that I stopped saying the congregation parts aloud with everyone else. I read them silently. But what did "Hear, O Israel" mean? And "The Lord is one"—how many would He be? This might have moved Israelites in the desert thousands of years ago, but it did not move me here in the suburbs now.

I decided to try atoning. It wasn't hard to think of things I'd done wrong, with Moreh Pinkus rocking right in front of me, or to feel bad, with my father sitting just down the row.

But I couldn't think of how to fix anything, until everyone was saying the mourner's prayer for people who had died. It was in Hebrew, and though I'd heard it many times—it was said in every service—I'd never learned it. The prayer was spelled out phonetically in English, and I read it quietly at first, and then louder. I said it as clearly as I could, remembering my grandfather, and I hoped that my father could hear me.

After the service, Moreh Pinkus stood in the aisle at the end of our row.

"Hi," I said, the only word I had ever spoken to him, except "Here."

He shook my hand with both of his and said, "Gut Yomtov, Sophie."

I wasn't sure whether it was *Yomtov* or *Yuntov,* so I just said, "Thanks," and, "you, too."

My parents were standing there, and though I was afraid of what he might say about me, I said, "This is Moreh Pinkus; these are my parents."

My father said, "Gut Yomtov," exactly as Moreh Pinkus had; my mother's enunciation was so precise and clipped that her "Good *Yuntov*" sounded more like the King's English than Hebrew.

They shook hands, and then Moreh Pinkus rejoined his family.

On the way to the car, my mother said, "That's your teacher?"

"Yes," I said.

"He's Orthodox," she said to my father.

He didn't answer her. To me, he said, "What kind of a teacher is Moreh Pinkus?"

I tried to think of a word that described him. "Meek?" I said.

. . . . .

I was looking for my *Hebrew I* when I heard my mother blow her nose in the kitchen. When I walked in, she was sitting at the table crying. Albert had one paw in her lap.

"What is it?" I said.

She said, "I just love cigarettes so much," and I took her hand, and didn't let go even once she stopped crying.

"You've been a good sport about Hebrew school," she said.

"Mom," I said. "I haven't."

"You went," she said, in my defense. "And you didn't complain about it."

I noticed her use of the past tense and adopted it. "But I wasn't really there."

She said, "You did the best you could," and she seemed to believe I had.

I said, "I've just been going through the motions," using the expression my father had after he'd watched my first tennis lesson.

"Sweetie," she said, "that's what a lot of life is."

In my meaner days, I would've said, *That's what* your *life is,* but I kept quiet.

The next moment, my mother said, "You don't have to go, if you don't want to." I could tell that it pleased her to say this; relieving me of my misery seemed momentarily to relieve her of hers.

I hadn't thought of her as having the authority to make this decision. "Really?"

She nodded.

I said, "I will go one last time."

She said, "You don't have to."

"I know."

. . . . .

I got there before Moreh Pinkus arrived. Leslie Liebman was telling everyone that Margie had robbed the gift shop and had been expelled. Then she noticed me and said, "How's Margie doing?"

I didn't know; I hadn't seen Margie in school. All I could think to say was, "She hated Hebrew school."

Moreh Pinkus arrived, and after a few minutes, he found our tests in his briefcase. He handed them back slowly. He turned my test facedown so no one could see that it was blank except for my note to him and his note back: "Makeup test."

I thought, *Makeup test?* and imagined Moreh Pinkus asking me to take out an eye pencil and lip gloss; it wasn't that funny, but I still wished there was someone in the class I could tell.

At the board, Moreh Pinkus wrote out the correct translations, and I copied them onto my blank test in the manner of a devoted Hebrew scholar.

Afterward, he opened *Hebrew I* to Section II.

I was determined to stay in class for the entire period. It was an act of atonement and a belated attempt to honor the agreement I'd made with my father. It was for my mother, too; if she could endure the torment of withdrawal, I could endure the torment of Hebrew school.

My torment, however, was unexpectedly great. After what seemed like hours, I gave myself permission to take a short break.

When I opened the door to the powder room, I heard, "What took you so long?" As ever, Margie was sitting sideways in the velveteen chair, smoking.

I knew she could get in trouble just for being here, and I was about to ask why she'd come, but I stopped myself. I knew that she was here to say good-bye to me.

She repeated what I'd just heard from Leslie Liebman, adding that Miss Bell had been "a real asshole. She thought you were guilty."

This hurt.

"But Moron Pink-Ass said you weren't a thief."

"He did?"

She said, "Do you have any food?"

I shook my head.

She lit a cigarette for me, and I took it, though I was aware of the trouble I could still get into. She told me that she'd transferred to an alternative school called Susquehanna; her parents had decided the kids at Surrey Junior High were a bad influence.

I asked if her parents were still getting divorced.

She said, "They're going to counseling."

"That's good."

We were quiet, as we'd been for so many minutes and hours in this room. Margie went to the supply closet and turned the knob—for old times' sake, I guess—and it reminded me that Miss Bell could walk in. I got up and threw my cigarette in the toilet. It made a sizzle sound.

I checked to make sure no one was in the hall, and then Margie and I walked out of the powder room together. We said good-bye at the lobby. I wished her luck at Susquehanna, and I walked up the hall, back to class.

She waited until I had opened the classroom door before she shouted, "See ya soon, you big baboon."

Everyone turned to look at me as I took my seat.

I'd heard that the best way to learn a foreign language was just by being in that foreign country, and I told myself that this could happen to me here and now. I listened to the Hebrew spoken all around me and waited for the miracle of comprehension until the bell sounded.

Moreh Pinkus said his standard, "Shalom."

Everyone said it back to him, pretty much in unison.

I looked at Moreh Pinkus for a long moment, and with my face I thanked him for knowing that I was not a thief. Then I was out of class and down the hall, out the door, and in the driveway.

To myself, I said, *Free at last, free at last, thank God Almighty, we are free at last.*

I found our station wagon in the line of cars. Robert had already gotten in the backseat with Albert so I could have the front.

As we pulled out, I watched the other kids finding their cars, and I thought, *Shalom, suckers.*

Robert resumed the conversation he'd been having with my mother. He was saying that no matter how hard he tried, he couldn't help Doug Sloane understand fractions. "I think he just wants me to do his homework."

Then, abruptly, Robert stopped talking.

My mother didn't seem to notice; she was driving even more slowly than usual, looking in the windows of a house, which she said gave her ideas about decorating.

When I turned around, Robert was staring at me.

"What?" I said.

He shook his head.

At home, he went upstairs without taking his jacket off. He was waiting for me in my room when I got there, and he closed the door after me.

"I know," he said.

When I breathed in, my chest was icy. I said, "Know what?"

"I know you've been smoking," he said. "I smelled it in the car."

I tasted the cigarette on my breath. "I was just trying it."

"Don't lie to me," he said. "This is a matter of life and—" I thought he was going to say "breath," like the TV commercial against smoking, but he said "death." His face was as grave as it had been at our grandfather's funeral.

He asked how much I smoked and with whom and where, and I told him.

When I said Margie's name, he nodded, and to himself he added, "From Girl Scouts," and, "one of the Foxes." Robert remembered everything I ever told him.

After I answered his questions, I told him about Margie robbing the gift shop and getting expelled; I repeated what she'd said about her parents getting divorced and Miss King living at their house. It was a relief to tell him, even though he was just my little brother.

"Well," he said, sounding like the sheriff in a Western, "I don't think you'll be spending much time with Margie Muchnick anymore." Then he said, "Where do you keep your cigarettes?"

I opened the bottom drawer of my desk, and Robert took the pack of Marlboros Margie had given to me.

I said, "Are you going to tell Mom and Dad?"

He said, "I will if I have to." He said he would do anything to get me to stop smoking. "I will make your life miserable," he said, and I knew that he would.

THE TOY BAR

VENICE LAMBOURNE was famous the way a beautiful girl can be in a small circle of places and parties, but hardly anyone knew her. *Knockout* was the word people used to describe Venice, and *bombshell,* and she did seem to stir violence; men could seem almost angry at her for being so pretty.

I met Venice when we were both eighteen. She was my roommate. This was at Rogers, the not-very-good school in Klondike, New York—according to *Barron's Profiles of American Colleges,* median SAT: 1100, average GPA: 2.9. Venice said the reason she was there was that her SATs had somehow not arrived at the better schools she'd applied to; she said that her application to Rogers consisted of one phone call her uncle placed to the admissions committee. I doubted the story, as I did almost every story Venice told, but it turned out to be true—or true enough.

Venice didn't arrive until the night before classes started, hours after the last parents had kissed their freshman sons and daughters good-bye and gotten into station wagons headed homeward for Darien, Connecticut, or Katonah, New York, or, in my parents' case, Surrey, Pennsylvania. Venice pulled up in a cab and carried her sole suitcase inside.

She knocked on what at that moment became our door and walked into what still felt to me like my room.

She was very thin and very tall—five foot ten in flat shoes. She almost always wore flats, one pair until they wore out, and then she'd get another. She didn't have many things—not many clothes or many possessions, either; she believed in owning only perfect things, or, as she said, "one perfect thing."

Her hair was blond and straight, and she tucked it behind her ears; she had blue eyes that you noticed partly because her brows were so dark and thick.

She said, "I'm Venice Lambourne," and when she shook my hand her formality unnerved me so much that I answered as I'd been instructed to as a child: "How do you do?" Then I said, "I'm Sophie. Applebaum."

She told me that she'd been traveling and was exhausted; she'd come all the way from Antibes.

I hadn't heard of Antibes but vaguely remembered a movie called *Raid on Entebbe*, and was it in Israel or somewhere in Africa? Was Israel in Africa?

"Wow," I said, and then suggested that maybe she wanted to check in with our resident adviser, a button-nosed teddy bear named Betsy, who'd been worried.

This Venice seemed not to hear. "I need a drink," she said.

When I told her about the soda machine in the basement, she turned and looked at me as though I was the last and possibly the longest leg of her trip.

She'd passed a bar that she said was close and open. "Those might be its only virtues," she said, "but they are the only virtues I care about at the moment."

I hesitated; with the lack of self-knowledge I'd exhibit for years to come, I'd signed up for an eight o'clock class.

I told her that the bar was called the Pines, and it was the college bar, basically the only bar, but fine; I was hoping that if I talked long enough she'd realize how tired she was.

She raised her thick eyebrows, asking why I was talking about a bar we should be walking to, and I said, "I have an eight o'clock class."

She said, "I don't even know what I'm taking," and won.

It took her about thirty seconds to get ready. She didn't change her clothes—a robin's-egg-blue boatneck, white capris, and black flats, each a perfect thing—and didn't wear makeup, herself a perfect thing. All she did was wash her face.

As we were leaving the room, she noticed my fiddle in its case. "Do you play the violin?"

"I fiddle," I said, and I felt the way I sometimes had when I was little and needed to defend my younger brother from someone older than both of us and hoped I could.

Sort of jokey, she said, "Will you fiddle for me some time?"

"Probably not," I said.

. . . . .

The Pines was packed. We worked our way up to the bar, where we stood drinkless, waiting for one of the busy bartenders. Standing there, I said aloud what I'd been noticing all weekend: "Does everyone seem unusually good-looking to you?"

She looked around. "No."

I thought maybe her *no* was retaliation for my *probably not.* I said, "The reason I said I wouldn't play my fiddle for you . . . I don't really play for anyone."

"Why not?"

I didn't want to tell her that I wasn't good enough to play for anyone, so I made my face look like I was pondering the question until one of the bartenders came over to us. He was an older guy who turned out to be the owner. "What can I get you girls?"

"Hello," Venice said.

The man's expression didn't change.

"I've been traveling all day," she told him, "so I need something really, really good."

All around us other student drinkers were waiting to order.

She said, "What kind of red wine do you have?" But right away, she said, "No," and again, "No." "Cassis?" she said to herself. "Campari?" As far as I knew, she was naming towns that surrounded Entebbe.

She brightened: Something fruity might revive her—a piña colada, maybe, or a daiquiri. Did he use fresh fruit? He didn't.

"Maybe bourbon," she said. Could he make a mint julep?

He knew his customer now and said, "I don't have mint."

"No mint," she repeated, but she agreed to it, with a sigh, as though she was to face many deprivations here that had been previously unknown to her.

I asked for a White Russian, the drink I'd ordered at bars on the New Jersey shore, where I'd bused tables that summer.

She looked at me like we'd been disagreeing and now she suddenly saw my point. "Two," she said, and the bartender spilled out the bourbon he'd already poured into a glass.

I paid for our drinks—she said she'd used up her dollars on the cab and had only francs and lira—and while I was waiting for my change, I noticed one guy looking in our direction. He said something to the guys he was with, and they looked over, too.

We'd barely sat down when one of them came over to us.

"Hi," he said. He was cute and, like so many students at Rogers, blond; only Scandinavia could claim a higher blond-to-brunette ratio.

"Hi," I said.

He asked if we were freshmen, and I said we were, and I might as well have said, *You can kiss me if you want to.*

Then Venice jumped in, introducing both of us, and I understood that she was being efficient rather than friendly, and he did, too; introducing himself, he seemed slightly crestfallen.

Once she'd learned his name, she used it: "Tad," she said and told him how tired she was and that she'd been traveling all day and would he please forgive her?—she was incapable of conversation.

"Sure," he said. "Absolutely."

But he didn't go, maybe because his crowd of friends was watching. He said, "Where are you coming from?"

She looked at him for a long moment, a reprimand, before saying, "Antibes."

His "wow" had more bravado in it than mine, but I could tell he was a fellow untraveler when he immediately turned the conversation back to the world he knew: "Where are you living?"

Venice had given him a chance to exit gracefully, and he was not taking it; now she answered in the perfunctory manner of filling out a form: "Bancroft."

"Nice," he said. "Bancroft is nice."

She looked away from him to me, a signal to resume our conversation. He was looking at me, too, now, for help. It was hard for me not to give it to him, but I could see that this was between them, and my role was auxiliary—I was the nurse and she was the doctor; I was the nanny and she the mother.

"Well," he said.

She said, "It was nice to meet you, Tad."

"Likewise," he said.

I felt bad for him when he walked away and said, "He seemed kind of nice."

Venice didn't respond. She closed her eyes, and I thought that she really must be tired, and that Tad had made her even more tired, and that soon we would go home, and I would have a chance of waking up for my eight o'clock class and becoming the good student I'd always meant to be.

But when she opened her eyes, her face was dreamy instead of sleepy. Almost to herself, she said, "This morning I was in Antibes," and I thought, *I'm going to be here all night.*

. . . . .

It was after one when we got back to Bancroft. We undressed with our backs to each other, and I noticed that hers was evenly brown from her shoulders to her underpants—no hint of where a bathing suit top might've been, and I wondered if she'd just pulled the straps down and unhooked the back or if she'd gone without.

We were in our beds when I looked over and saw that all that separated her from the mattress was a beach towel. She was using shirts for a blanket. I said, "You want a sheet or something?"

"I'm fine," she said. "Thanks." She explained that she'd mailed her bedclothes from Italy a month before, and they were probably waiting for her at the post office. "But," she added, "you know how slow the mail from Italy is."

No, I didn't, and it kept me from offering her my top sheet and bedspread.

We said good night, and I turned off my light.

In the dark, though, it occurred to me that she was probably the only freshman whose parents hadn't brought her to school. I wondered if that bothered her. I wondered if her parents were having too much fun in Antibes to leave and help her get ready for school and buy her sheets and connect her speakers and meet the other parents. I found myself feeling sorry for her.

I turned the light back on, and we made her bed. I had only one pillow but two cases, and I offered to stuff the spare with socks.

Her voice was smaller than it had been and apologetic when she said, "Do you mind if I sleep with your husband?"

I stared at her. It took me a minute to realize that she meant my reading pillow—it was corduroy with arms—and as I handed it to her, I said, "Did you make that up?"

She said, "That's what it's called."

It would be another year before I told her that at that moment I'd thought she was a split-personalitied nymphomaniac. After that, out of nowhere, she'd sometimes put on a twisted, sexed-up voice and say, "Do you mind if I sleep with your husband?"

I turned off the light again, and we said good night, but then she was saying my name—not addressing me, but musing. "Sophie. It's a pretty name," she said.

"I was named after my great-grandmother," I said.

She said, "It's old-fashioned," which was what I hated about my name. "You don't hear it too often."

"What about yours?" I said, though I wasn't sure what I meant.

She said, "I was named for the place of my conception," and it sounded like she was claiming that the city had been named for her.

But then she said, "I'm lucky they didn't name me Gondola. Or Canal," and I went all the way from hating to liking her, and the distance made me feel like I loved her.

. . . . .

Those first weeks, Venice caused a big stir. I'd go to parties with her—we traveled in packs of at least five or six to fraternities—and once we got there she was always surrounded.

But there were nights when she'd say, "Let's not go," and she'd act like we were cutting a class.

Usually we stayed in to watch a movie on television, a movie she said I absolutely needed to see—*12 Angry Men, The Shop Around the Corner, The Best Years of Our Lives.* We'd go down to the basement TV lounge and turn off all the lights. It would be dark except for the TV and the red of the soda machine and its everlasting NO CHANGE light.

I loved all of the movies she did, and *The Heiress* so much that I forgot all about Venice until the commercials, when she'd repeat the lines she liked best.

Her favorite came at the end of the movie: Years after standing Catherine up on the night they're supposed to elope, Morris comes back, and he's knocking and then pounding on her door, and she says to her servant, "Bar the door, Maria."

" 'Bar the door, Maria,' " Venice said. "The rallying cry of jilted women everywhere."

. . . . .

In her closet, Venice kept a bottle of Shooting Sherry, just a regular medium-dry sherry, but its name made me think of hounds and horses, plaid blankets, and roaring fires. Some nights after studying we'd drink it out of glasses she'd taken from the dining hall. We'd lie on our beds and talk. I'd smoke cigarettes.

She'd talk to me about a book she'd read for a class—she kept up with her reading, as I never could—or she'd mention an article from the *New York Times,* which she read every day, as no one else did. Or she'd read aloud from a novel she was crazy about; that fall it was *Lolita,* and in the winter *Anna Karenina.*

. . . . .

Venice didn't confide in me for a long time, and even when she did, it sounded less like a confidence than just a story she wanted to tell because it was interesting.

The first one she told me was about Georges. Their families had rented the villa together in Antibes; he'd come for the last week. As she spoke, I realized it was Georges she'd been thinking of that first night in the Pines when her voice got dreamy and she'd said, "This morning I was in Antibes."

"He's incredibly smart," she said. "But sweet, too. That's rare, I think."

I thought of Doug, the busboy I'd made out with on my last night of work, and it occurred to me that he was not particularly smart and not that sweet, either. "Yeah," I said.

Georges had beautiful manners. "He always stands when a woman enters the room," she said. "I love that kind of thing."

"Me, too," I said, because suddenly I did love that kind of thing, though I wasn't sure I'd ever seen a guy my age stand for a woman unless he happened by coincidence to be leaving at that moment.

Venice told me that Georges spoke six languages fluently, and though English was one of them, the lovers spoke French.

She said that they didn't sleep together until the last night, and she closed her eyes, remembering.

"What?" I said.

She repeated something he'd said to her in French.

I told her that it sounded romantic but I spoke zero foreign languages.

She said, "He kept saying, 'Please don't sleep,' and every time I'd doze off, I'd wake up to him saying, 'Don't sleep, my love. Don't leave me before you have to.' "

"Wow," I said.

She said, "I know."

Maybe she could tell I doubted the story because she got his powder-blue aerograms out, and line by line she read and translated his romantic French.

"Wait," I said. "*Ma puce* means 'darling'?"

She told me that, literally translated, *ma puce* meant "my flea," but, "It's like our 'honey'—no one thinks of actual honey."

I got her to give me the literal translation for every "darling" or "sweetheart": *Mon chou* meant "my cabbage," *mon lapin,* "my rabbit."

After she told me about losing her virginity to a Swiss ski instructor, she looked over at me. I knew she was waiting for me to tell her my story, and it occurred to me to make one up. Instead, I admitted that I'd never skied.

. . . . .

Our resident adviser invited Venice and me into her homey room, saying, "I just want to have a little chat." She asked if we wanted tea or coffee, and she also had hot chocolate and chicken noodle soup.

I was sort of excited at the idea of chicken noodle soup. "I'll have some soup," I said. "Thanks."

Venice gave me a look: *Let's not make this any longer than it has to be.* She said, "Nothing for me, thanks."

Betsy plugged in her hot pot. She asked how we were liking Rogers, and who our favorite professors were. She was a nice girl from Syracuse, and you could tell that she took her job as resident adviser seriously.

She handed me the mug of soup; it was hot, and I blew on it.

She said, "You guys are spending an awful lot of time together." She was struggling. "You know, this is the time for making new friends," she said. "Meeting everybody."

We both said we'd made other friends, which was a little truer for me than for Venice.

Betsy said, "I just want to make sure you're open to other relationships."

I said, "I'm open."

Venice couldn't make herself say words like these, but she nodded and widened her eyes to convey openness.

Betsy said, "College is when you make the friendships that will last for the rest of your life." She looked miserable saying this.

She went from cliché to cliché, as though stepping from one flat stone to the next across a roiling river, until finally Venice said, "I think I understand what you're trying to say," though neither of us did.

A few days later we found out: There was a rumor that Venice and I were lesbians.

It didn't bother Venice at all, and I tried to act nonchalant, too. I asked if she wasn't afraid the rumor would prevent some hypothetical man from hypothetically falling in love with her.

She said the rumor wasn't going to prevent anyone from anything, just the opposite: According to Georges, ninety percent of men had lesbian fantasies.

I said, "But what if he's in the other ten percent?"

She said, "The other ten percent are gay."

Then Venice met Hugh, and that was that.

. . . . .

Technically, Hugh wasn't as handsome as Venice was beautiful. He had dark hair and always a few days' worth of dark beard. His skin was bad—red and rough and maybe damaged from acne; there were scars. Yet this seemed to make him more attractive, as it never would a woman. Like Venice, though, Hugh was admired from afar, and he affected women as strongly as she did men, and maybe more deeply—not that he had any idea.

He lived off campus, in a dingy apartment with worn-out upholstered chairs and an olive vinyl sofa, but leaning against the walls were his own beautiful landscape paintings. The apartment had an unheated sunporch facing the lake, and Venice said he'd bundle up and paint out there, wearing his winter coat and gloves he'd cut the fingers off of.

The two of them were always inviting people over to his apartment before and after parties. He always offered Pimm's—he'd been to London the year before and had brought back cases of it. If you wanted to drink something else, you brought it.

It was Venice who kept these evenings going. Hugh was no good at parties, even in his own home. He seemed older—much older—than his guests, almost grandfatherly. He reminded me of someone deaf, or nearly so; he had trouble keeping up with conversations, and contributed the non-est of non sequiturs. I once heard him interrupt a joke about Reagan to say that Millard Fillmore's birthplace was in nearby Locke, New York. He didn't seem to know how awkward he was, or if he did, didn't care; I don't think he cared what anyone except Venice thought of him. He trusted her opinions and sought them out; when she didn't like something he said, he wanted to know why—he was really eager to hear.

They didn't call each other Honey or Babe, let alone Flea or Cabbage; to each other they were Venice and Hugh. They hardly touched each other in front of other people. Their kisses hello or good-bye didn't say, *Sex.* But there was something private between them, enviably private. They were a couple in a way that didn't exclude anyone but seemed superior to every other relationship in the room.

. . . . .

I never saw Venice get upset. Even after her worst fight with Hugh—he'd read an aerogram from Georges—Venice just said, "Hugh's being idiotic." So it was shocking and terrible one afternoon to find her crying in our room.

I didn't know what was wrong, and for a long time she was crying too hard to tell me. Finally, she got out enough words to let me know she'd gotten into Brown.

She hadn't told me she'd applied to transfer, and I wondered if she'd told Hugh. Not that it would matter; Hugh was graduating, anyway, and Brown was closer than Rogers to Manhattan, where he was looking for a job.

"You don't have to go," I said.

She gave me a look that reminded me of the first night when she'd wanted a drink and I'd told her about the soda machine.

Then more tears.

I told her I'd do anything if she would just stop crying, and right away she said, "Play your fiddle for me."

"Shit," I said, but I got it out of its case and looked through my records for one to play along with. The only songs I knew were the cowboy and miner ballads of the variety called High Lonesome, but I put on the happiest one I could think of—one about a cowboy's love for his horse.

I hadn't played for anyone in a long time, and I wasn't sure I could do it now. I had to stand with my back to her, which in itself was embarrassing.

When I stopped playing, Venice smiled—a huge relief, even though I wasn't sure if she was smiling with me or at me.

. . . . .

That summer, Venice sent me a postcard a week from Europe. She'd seen Georges in Tuscany and described it in six languages, including pig Latin: *"Elt-fay othing-nay."*

In late August, she called from Capri to invite me to spend Labor Day weekend on Long Island, where Hugh's family had a house. I'd never gotten a call from Europe and wasn't sure how expensive it was, and I found myself saying yes because it was faster than saying no, which would have required an explanation.

Hugh and Venice picked me up at the train, in his grandparents' old station wagon. Venice gave me the front seat, and I looked out at the bushes of blue hydrangeas, the huge shade trees, and the houses with their silvered cedar shingles.

Hugh's was on the bay side, across Dune Road from the beach. The house was big but shabby; his family had managed to hold on to the house but had no money to keep it up. You'd open a drawer and the pull would come off in your hand.

I was worried that I'd feel awkward as the guest of Venice, as a guest of a guest, a guest once-removed. But Hugh introduced me to his mother and grandparents and sister as his "great friend," and that was how I felt.

. . . . .

My favorite time of day was the late, late afternoon with the sun golding up the ocean and sand and sea grass and dunes. Venice said it was called "magic hour" in the movies. She knew because she'd read a few scripts by then, given to her by a director she'd met that summer.

One magic hour, after swimming, we got dressed on the beach in jeans and sweaters. We unpacked a dinner picnic of leftovers—cold crabs and cold corn on the cob and tomatoes Venice had flecked with fresh basil. Hugh made a fire, and we drank wine and stayed out there on the beach late into the night.

When we got back everyone was asleep, and Venice went off to Hugh's bedroom, as she did every night. She'd come back to ours just as the sky was getting light, and sometimes I'd wake up and remember where I was and I'd feel as happy then as I ever had.

. . . . .

The three of us were happy as quahogs until Labor Day. It was overcast, and I thought that was what made the morning seem slow and thick.

Without much enthusiasm, Hugh suggested sailing.

Venice looked dubious; she noted the lack of wind. Then she said, "Our train leaves at four."

Hugh said, "I know what time your train leaves."

Venice seemed oblivious to his tone, and maybe she was at first. However upset she'd been when she'd gotten into Brown, I knew she was excited now about going. She wasn't talking about it, but she radiated the exuberance you can feel about going to a new place or starting a new thing.

Hugh wasn't going anywhere or starting anything; he hadn't found a job yet.

Finally we went sailing, without any of us really wanting to. It was a little boat, not much bigger than a Sunfish, and it looked old. As I got in, I asked Hugh when it had last been used.

Hugh seemed to wonder himself for a minute, and I thought, *Three drown in boating accident.*

Both Venice and Hugh knew how to sail, and all I really did was watch them and the bay, lower my head when the boom crossed over, and look forward to going back to the house and taking one last outdoor shower before getting on the train.

The sky clouded over, and there was no sun at all anymore, and no wind, either. Finally Venice said, "We should head back." Hugh didn't answer, just turned the boat around.

They had to tack—zigzag—the whole way back across the bay. Hugh kept sighing, and he seemed annoyed. He was giving Venice orders, like, "Just get over there," and she was obeying them. She didn't seem angry or upset or embarrassed, as I would have been. I thought maybe the windlessness was more dire than I realized, and the two of them were following emergency sailing procedures, which included the captain acting like a jerk and his mate ignoring him.

But neither changed, even once we got close to shore and out of danger; again, I wondered if Venice was thinking less about where she was now than where she'd be later.

We were pulling the boat up onto the sand when I saw how wrong I was. Behind Hugh's back, her face was full of sympathy. Venice knew exactly what he was feeling: The life he'd known was about to end; it would end as soon as she got on the train. She knew that he was scared of losing her and scared of not finding a job, and this was her way of telling him he didn't have to be.

On the beach she did a cartwheel, and he did one, too, a failure, but she laughed and got him laughing.

Back at the house, Venice took the first shower. I was packing when Hugh came and stood in the doorway and said, "Why don't you stay another night?"

I told him that my older brother expected me to spend the night with him in Manhattan.

"Stay with me," he said, and his look let me know I would be doing him a favor.

. . . . .

At a restaurant on Main Street, Hugh and I sat outside, drinking scotch for dinner. We weren't talking at all. I felt awkward and tried to think up topics other than the girlfriend who'd left and the job he didn't have.

When he recognized someone he knew and called him to the table, I was overjoyed.

Hugh rose and said, "Have a drink with us."

The guy tipped his head bar-ward and said, "I'm in the middle of something," and his tone said, *In the middle of some girl.* Then he said hi to me, and, "I'm Michael Whitmore," and I told him my name, and we shook hands. To Hugh, he said, "Call me at the office on Tuesday," and was gone.

Another year of silence passed before Hugh said, "I should've majored in economics."

It reminded me of how I'd felt applying to college. Night after night, I sat with my father in his study while he read aloud from *Barron's*. He'd read the name of the college, the number of men and the number of women, and a description in guidebook prose; then he'd say, "How does that sound?" and I'd think, *Sounds just like the last one.*

It took me a few nights to realize that my father was reading only the colleges that I had some chance of getting into—not Brown but Bowling Green; not Wesleyan but Ohio Wesleyan; not Williams or Smith, but William Smith. Until that moment, it hadn't occurred to me that my grades and test scores over the years were anything more than individual humiliations; I hadn't realized that one day all of them would add up and count against me.

My father was waiting to hear my reaction to whatever college he'd just read me the description of. He looked over at me. "What is it?"

"I wish someone had told me," I said.

"Told you what?"

I hadn't answered. I'd already figured out that not understanding my failings was another of my failings.

Now I wanted to convince Hugh that whatever prevented him from finding a job was not a failing but a strength. "You're a painter," I told him. "I don't even know why you're looking for a job in investment banking."

He said, "I need to make a living, Sophie."

"Maybe you could do something with art, though," I said.

He asked if I had any idea how much private-school tuition was.

"No." I waited for him to make his point. Then I realized he already had. He was talking about the cost of educating the children he planned to have with Venice.

I told Hugh that I didn't think Venice cared too much about money, but as I said it I realized I didn't know.

"She doesn't care about it," he said, "because she doesn't have to."

. . . . .

I worried about Hugh, but there was no need: He got a job in Michael's bank, and ended up moving into Michael's apartment.

Venice didn't like Michael, and I was there the night Hugh asked her why. "Just tell me," he said. "I want to know."

She shrugged.

"Because I sleep in the living room?" Hugh said. "Is that it?"

"No."

He said, "It's his apartment."

Venice reminded Hugh that he paid half the rent.

He asked her once more what she had against Michael. When she wouldn't answer, he said, "Michael's a good friend of mine." His voice was serious, even stern.

She gazed at him—loving him, I think, for his loyalty to his friend—and then she said, "Okay."

. . . . .

Venice spent almost every weekend in Manhattan, and the weekends I came in the three of us stayed at her parents' apartment, their pied-à-terre, on Seventy-ninth Street off Park. Friday afternoon, I'd take the bus down from Klondike, and Venice would take a train from Providence.

We'd meet near the apartment, at the Toy Bar. It was small and cozy, and you could ask the bartender for dominoes or checkers or practically any board game—Risk, Life, Operation, Parcheesi, Monopoly, even the Barbie Dating Game. There was a model train set, too, and a few times a night the bartender would press a switch and the train would clack and whistle around the track above our heads. The engine had a light on it.

We'd spend an hour or two there—Venice always made time for us to talk by ourselves—and then Hugh would join us. Sometimes she mentioned a party she knew of, though we rarely went; Hugh's awkwardness at parties had begun to bother Venice.

Hugh was obviously relieved to have a job, but I don't think he liked the actual work—selling bonds, I think; at least he never talked about it. When I asked him about his job, he'd say, "It's fine, fine," and his double fine made me think it was totally unfine. He was working hard, though. There were nights when he couldn't meet us until very late.

. . . . .

Thanksgiving break was the first time Venice mentioned Anthony. He was from England, and she pronounced his name not with a *th* but a *T* and a breath, as in *Antony and Cleopatra.*

We'd decided to walk all the way from her parents' apartment to Penn Station, where I would get the train home to Philadelphia and she'd meet Hugh for the one to Long Island.

Anthony was "incredibly smart," she said, and "incredibly charming," and "incredibly fun."

I said, "He sounds incredible."

She didn't compare him to Hugh directly, but she let me know that it was nice to be with someone who could hold his own at a cocktail party.

"Are you seeing him?" I said.

"God, no!" she said. "We just go to parties together."

I gave her a look: *Are you sure?*

She said, "He's a total lothario," and by then I felt comfortable enough with her to ask what a lothario was. "A seducer," she said. "A womanizer."

I had a bad feeling about him, but I didn't want to say so. What I said was, "Would I like him?"

"I think he'd intrigue you," she said. "But I'm not sure you'd like him."

We were in the Thirties on Fifth Avenue when someone handed us flyers for a sample sale, and Venice looked at hers. She said she'd heard of the designer and the showroom was on our way and, "Let's go."

Venice hated shopping, and I thought maybe she wanted to go to the sale to avoid more questions about Anthony.

On the elevator up, I said, "Does Hugh know?"

She said, "There's nothing to know."

Then we were in the frenzy of the sale, and Venice asked me to keep an eye out for a floor-length gown she needed for a formal party Anthony had invited her to—"a ball," she called it.

She found one, in cobalt silk, with a low, drapey back.

There were no dressing rooms—we had to try on our dresses in an aisle between racks—and no mirrors, either, so we had to rely on each other's judgment.

Venice said, "Don't be kind."

The cobalt dress looked fantastic on her, but I said so hesitantly; it occurred to me that if I could talk her out of the dress, maybe she wouldn't go to the ball with Anthony.

She didn't seem to hear me. She was staring at me and what I was wearing—a strapless black taffeta cocktail dress with a tight, boned bodice and a skirt that flounced and swirled to my knees.

Her voice was almost awed when she said, "Sophie." Then: "Take your bra off."

I looked at her, *Really?*

Her look said, *Obviously.*

I did as I was told, and she nodded.

I looked at the tag. "It's four hundred dollars."

She said, "These dresses go for thousands," and asked if I had enough in my checking account to cover it.

I said, "Are you kidding?"

She said, "Do you have a credit card?"

I did, but my father had given the card to me with specific instructions for its use—emergencies, and once a week I was to take myself and a friend out for a good dinner. I had, but never Venice; I'd been afraid she'd order a lot of drinks or an expensive bottle of wine, and then the big bill would go to my father, and he'd know I was turning out wrong.

I said, "I'm just supposed to use it for emergencies."

"This is an emergency."

I unzipped the dress.

She said, "Have I ever told you to buy anything before?"

We'd only shopped together once, at the Salvation Army thrift shop in Klondike, where she'd tried to talk me out of a sweater. "Of course it's not perfect," I'd said. "It's a dollar."

Now I said, "Name one place I could wear it."

She said, "I'm going to buy it for you if you won't."

I said, "Name one place."

She said that maybe I could go with her and Anthony to the ball. She thought for a minute. "You can wear it anywhere as long as you show up late. People will think you're coming from somewhere else, a gala or whatever."

I reminded her that I wasn't the kind of gal who went to galas.

"You don't understand," she said. "This is your one perfect thing."

When I told her it was just too expensive, she said that hers cost twice as much.

We were in line for the cashier before I thought of the ball she was going to with Anthony. For Hugh's sake, I said a doubtful, "Is yours a perfect thing, do you think?"

She said, "Perfect enough."

. . . . .

That night, at home in Surrey, in my childhood bedroom, I tried on the dress and looked in the mirror.

What I saw was so foreign to me that I couldn't take it in at first. In the dress, I was glamorous. I was elegant. I was a movie star, there in my bedroom with its canopy bed and Bob Dylan posters.

Venice was right: The dress was perfect, and it was perfect on me. The low-cut bodice accentuated my large breasts and made my waist appear tiny and my hips merely full. I wasn't used to seeing my bare shoulders, and especially not the flesh above my breasts, which even at a standstill called to mind the word *heaving*.

I looked at myself for a long while, and I remember it as one of the only times in my life when I saw myself as beautiful.

When my father knocked on my door, I told him that I was undressed, not a complete lie.

"Come say good night," he said.

I put on my nightgown and bathrobe and went into my parents' bedroom. I sat at the foot of their bed. My mother put down the old *New Yorker* she'd been reading.

"I have something to tell you," I said.

My mother looked worried, but my father, a judge, appeared as imperturbable as ever.

"I bought a dress," I said. "It was expensive."

"How expensive?" my mother said.

I couldn't make myself say the price out loud. I told my father that I would skip taking friends out to dinner for the rest of the year.

My father said, "You don't have to do that."

"Yes," I said, "I do."

My mother said, "How much was it, Sophie?"

I said, "It was on sale."

She kept her eyes on me. I said that it was by a famous designer, but then I couldn't remember who, and the label had been cut out of the dress.

Finally I told them the price.

Neither of my parents spoke.

I said what Venice had: The dress was worth thousands of dollars.

My father said, "And you feel you need a dress that's worth thousands of dollars?"

I didn't answer.

My parents took turns talking about my values. We all agreed that it was not appropriate or reasonable for me to buy a dress this expensive. We all agreed that I would return the dress. Then I remembered that my receipt was stamped FINAL SALE.

I said, "I'll pay you back."

My father nodded.

Then my mother said, "Do you love it?" which was what she said whenever we were shopping and I wanted to buy something expensive.

She'd say, "Do you really love it?" If I said yes, she'd go on to say that I could wear that expensive garment forever, for years and years, and all year round; whatever the fabric—sheerest cotton, heaviest wool—she'd proclaim it seasonless. She'd name places I could wear it, events in the near and distant future: I could wear it to a cousin's bar mitzvah, my brother's graduation, my own wedding, and I could be buried in it.

On the rare occasions when I could sustain the enthusiasm required for the purchase—there was always one final "Do you really love it?" at the register—at home the garment would hang in my closet like a cinder block around my neck.

Now my mother got in the spirit: "Try it on for us."

I said, "Tomorrow."

. . . . .

That winter, whenever I met Venice at the Toy Bar, she talked about Anthony; she seemed to need to—it was urgent. She talked fast so she could tell me everything before Hugh showed up.

She now admitted that Anthony was pursuing her. For her birthday, he'd taken her to Block Island, and driving to the ferry they'd passed a huge billboard that read HAPPY BIRTHDAY, ZSA ZSA.

She said, "He calls me Zsa Zsa."

"I got that," I said.

She heard the disapproval in my tone and said, "I've never even kissed him, Sophie."

. . . . .

One night, she told me that Anthony wanted to charter a plane to fly her to Maryland for soft-shell crabs.

I said, "Can't you get crabs in Providence?"

She looked at me.

"Are you falling in love with this guy?" I wanted to call him a lothario.

"No."

"So, what are you doing with him?"

I didn't like her at that moment, and I could tell that she didn't like me, either. I wondered, not for the first time, why we were friends.

She said, "We're not sleeping together, if that's what you're asking," and I heard the distance between that and "I've never even kissed him."

Hugh walked in then.

He seemed unsure of himself that night, and maybe that was why he'd brought Michael, a surprise to Venice, though she didn't show it, even when Michael kissed her cheek.

He sat down next to me and said, "We met in Quogue this summer."

I couldn't really talk because of what had just happened between Venice and me—and then because of what was happening between Venice and Hugh.

He was holding her hand, which I'd never seen him do before, and she seemed to be just barely allowing it. Once, she sort of snatched it away—she pretended it was to sip her drink—but the gesture stayed there in the air, and no one spoke for a long moment.

Michael said, "We need to play a game," and by "we" he meant he and I.

I assumed that he was just giving Venice and Hugh time alone. At the bar, though, he said, "What do you want to play?" and I heard something in there that had nothing to do with his friend or my friend or friendship.

"Checkers?" I said.

It was dark at the bar, but that wasn't the only reason I found it hard to see what Michael looked like. For one thing, his eyes were so deep-set there was a shadow across them. And he kept looking at me, and when I'd look over, he'd look away. I noticed his hair, though. It was straight and dark and longish, and I liked it.

I found myself drawn to him in a way I wasn't used to, and it was distracting. I kept losing at checkers. Every time he said, "King me," I stopped breathing.

He said, "Tell me your life story, Sophie Applebaum."

"You first," I said.

He made one up. He was a circus brat, he said. He told me that his father was a trapeze artist, and his mother, wearing a headdress and a spangled costume cut like a bathing suit, rode the tiger around the ring. After school, he fed the elephants, Floozy and Poco.

"Then the circus disbanded," he said. He shook his head. "It was really pretty sad."

His father couldn't find work and his mother became a chorus girl. He said her kicks had put him through Williams.

Another vodka tonic, and my knee touched his. When I moved it away, he said, "No," and I moved it back.

He was looking at me now, and not talking; neither of us was talking. I sent him an ESP message: *Touch me.* But he didn't, and I shocked and thrilled myself by reaching under the bar for his hand.

He was looking at me more intently than I'd ever been looked at, and I saw in his eyes that he needed me and wanted me, and I felt that I'd never needed and wanted anyone so much, and probably never would again.

What I thought was: *We are falling in love.*

"I'm a little tired, Sophie Applebaum," he said. He looked at me. "I think I'm going to head home."

I knew what he was asking, and it reminded me of a scene Venice had read to me from *Anna Karenina*, when Kitty and Levin are playing a parlor game of initials and they telepathically know the words the initials stand for. I thought, *We are telepathic; we are Kitty and Levin.*

Just then the model train went around the track, and we both looked up.

We walked over to where Venice and Hugh sat.

"I'm going to head out," Michael said, and I said, "Me, too."

Venice looked up at me, and I saw an expression I hadn't seen before—concern, I thought, or even worry. I assumed it was because of our bad crab moment, so I leaned down and, with all the affection I had for her, said, "I'll talk to you tomorrow."

"Are you sure?" she asked.

"Yes," I said.

Michael said, "See you Monday," to Hugh.

Then we were outside, on the curb.

Michael said, "Are you sure you want to do this?"

I said, "I'm sure."

"I'll want to see you anyway," he said, "whether you come with me now or not."

To be fair, it was the only real lie he told.

I cringe even now, remembering my response: "I know that."

. . . . .

For weeks, every time the hall phone rang it wasn't Michael; every letter in my mailbox wasn't from him.

Venice never brought him up. When I'd ask if she'd seen him, she'd sigh and say she had. I knew it was wrong to blame her, but I did a little. When I tried to name how she was responsible or what she'd done wrong, all I could come up with was that it wouldn't have happened to her.

I thought about *The Heiress*, and what I'd do if Michael did finally knock on my door. I knew what Venice would say; if you thought about it, though, "Bar the door, Maria" was what Catherine says on her way upstairs to spend the rest of her life alone.

I didn't know what I'd say. I hoped that Michael's excuse would be so good, his apology so enormous, his gesture of reconciliation so *Happy Birthday, Zsa Zsa* that I wouldn't need to say anything.

. . . . .

I still met Venice at the Toy Bar, and she still talked about Anthony, though not as much. She tried to act like he was slowing down and possibly giving up and that she didn't care either way. She spoke in the calm, even voice people use in an accelerating emergency.

It was harder for me to see Hugh now because of what I knew about Anthony. I felt like I was lying, even when I was just saying hello. Hugh must have sensed what was going on, though—he seemed less and less sure of himself.

. . . . .

"I have to tell you something," Venice said to me one night at the Toy Bar. "Before Hugh gets here."

I already knew that she was sleeping with Anthony, but I didn't want to hear it. Once she said the words out loud, everything would change. I shook my head: *Please don't tell me.*

I could see that she didn't want to. She steeled herself. Then she forced the words out: "Michael won't stop calling me." Her voice was a little shaky as she told me; she knew the risk she was taking.

She was trying to be a good friend, and I appreciated that, in theory.

"Don't tell Hugh, please," she said. "He has few enough friends as it is."

. . . . .

Hugh had more friends than Venice did, though—or fewer enemies.

We never found out who'd seen her with Anthony that weekend in Manhattan, the weekend she'd told Hugh she needed to stay in Providence to write a paper.

She kept going over every public moment of that weekend, trying to identify the one that had cost her Hugh. She'd helped Anthony choose a tie at Barneys; they'd spiraled up and down the Guggenheim; they'd gone to the Carlyle to hear Bobby Short. She said she hadn't seen anyone see her, not anyone she knew, and it occurred to me that she wouldn't have noticed anyone's gaze, she was so used to being looked at.

. . . . .

I avoided meeting Anthony until the following winter.

Venice didn't hear the dread in my voice. She told me to bring my perfect dress and she'd bring her cobalt—Anthony would figure out somewhere good for us to go—and I carried the dress in a garbage bag on the bus down.

I stowed it with my duffel bag under the table at the Toy Bar and waited for Venice.

She was late and walked in apologizing. She said that Anthony would be here any minute; they'd fought, she said, and he needed to cool off. She couldn't talk about their argument because he might walk in, and she couldn't talk about anything else.

She looked as beautiful as I'd ever seen her, but different. I saw that she was wearing makeup, and I was so surprised that I said it out loud.

She said, "Anthony likes to make me up."

"He puts makeup on you?"

She nodded.

"He's good," I said.

She said, "He's sort of an artist."

I said, "Maybe he could make me up sometime."

She either didn't like the joke or didn't hear it; she was nervous. She kept looking at her watch and taking her bangle bracelet off and putting it back on.

When some guy came over to the table, she surprised me by inviting him to sit down. He was no more captivating than any of the men I'd seen her dismiss over the years, but she kept talking to him, and she let him buy our drinks. He was still there when Anthony walked in, and it occurred to me that she'd staged this.

Anthony was very tall and conventionally handsome, and there was something flashy about him, or flashing—his eyes flashed; he flashed a smile. Later, whenever Venice talked about him, I pictured him in a Dracula cape.

He didn't sit down. He looked around the Toy Bar, and he didn't like it. He said, "I thought we might go to the Algonquin," and Venice stood, though we hadn't finished our drinks.

I got my bags from under the table, and Anthony took them from me.

"Nice luggage," he said, giving my garbage bag a twist. "I have the same set at home." I thought I might like him.

In the cab, he and Venice talked about the Algonquin Round Table and repeated the witty remarks they knew. When we got out of the cab, he held his garbage-bag arm out for her and said, "Mrs. Parker," and she took it and said, "Thank you, Mr. Benchley."

Inside, though, it was just a hotel bar, and it felt like no one had said anything witty there in a long time.

"Maybe we should get a round table," Venice said, but Anthony said we were better off where we were. Venice moved a stool aside and stood, and Anthony sat between us. He alternated between holding her waist and his drink.

"So," he said, "you're the famous Sophie from Roger."

"Rogers," I said.

He said, "Sorry?" using the word but not the intonation of apology.

"It's called Rogers."

"Right." He said a sorrier, "Sorry."

Anthony seemed restless. The whole time we were there he talked about where else we could go: He'd been invited to a party uptown, or maybe we should go to Studio 54; there was a great after-hours club he knew of, but, he said, it might be early for that.

"You know what?" I said. "I'm tired."

Venice looked worried. When I said that I was going to stay at my brother's, she didn't argue.

We were saying good-bye when she smiled at me, and I knew what she was about to do; in a sexed-up voice, she said, "Do you mind if I sleep with your husband?"

Maybe she wanted to restore something between us, but it seemed more like a performance for Anthony—*My Funny Friendship with Sophie*—and it didn't come off. She was still explaining the joke to him when I left.

. . . . .

"I'm sorry Anthony was so rude," she said on the phone the next morning.

Anthony had seemed cold, arrogant, bored, and capable of cruelty, but not rude. What I'd mainly noticed was how nervous she'd been.

"He felt threatened," she said.

I thought maybe I'd misheard her, and I said what Anthony would have: "Sorry?"

"Because of Hugh," she said. "Because you're a friend of Hugh's."

I didn't know what to say; I hadn't talked to Hugh since before they'd broken up. He hadn't returned my calls.

Venice was saying, "He's insanely jealous of Hugh," and I thought I heard a trace of an English accent in her voice. "Anyway," she said, "we'll go out tonight, and you can wear the dress."

Suddenly, I missed Hugh.

"Anthony wants to take us to some party in SoHo," she said. "We'll go really late."

I didn't answer right away. It occurred to me to make up an excuse, but then I said, "I don't want to."

She was quiet, and I was, too.

I couldn't really believe that she'd decided to be with Anthony, whom I would never choose over Hugh, or choose over anyone, or choose over no one. That made it hard for me to believe that Venice and I were the same person underneath everything, which was what I thought love required.

. . . . .

I wore the perfect dress three times.

In my senior year at Rogers, I wore the dress to a fraternity formal, and it was thrilling to be approached by men who'd never noticed me, and thrilling to be swarmed. I thought, *This is what it's like to be Venice,* and at first I liked it; I loved it. But it was tiring, too, and also I didn't like my date as much as he liked me, and it seemed wrong to wear a dress that might make him like me more.

The second time was to a Halloween party at my brother's girlfriend's apartment. I wore the dress with a deer mask. On the elevator up to the party, a tiny pirate said, "Who is she, Mommy?" and when Mommy asked me, I told her I was Bambi, Rudolph's mistress.

She looked down at her son and said, "She's Bambi, Rudolph's sister."

The last time I wore the dress was to a party Venice asked me to. It was one of those parties people gave then, men mostly; they'd rent a restaurant and invite people off of lists. You had to pay to get in. Her idea was that we go very late, and wear our dresses.

I'd been working in New York for a year by then, and Venice had, too. She had a small part in a soap opera. We'd hardly seen each other. When I'd ask her about Anthony, she wouldn't say much. She wanted to know when she was going to meet my new boyfriend. I said that Josh was pretty busy writing poetry.

The party was on East Sixth Street, at an Indian restaurant decorated with magenta velvet ottomans and gold drapes. Everyone else was wearing work clothes; the men who approached me asked where

I'd just come from. I stayed there for about an hour, waiting for Venice to show.

. . . . .

Maybe because she felt bad about standing me up, Venice told me about Anthony as she never had before. They'd had a horrible fight, she said, maybe their worst, though she added that the competition for this title was stiff. She told me how insane Anthony was and that he called her horrible names and was always accusing her of sleeping with other men, or wanting to.

When she said that she knew she had to leave him, I said, "You absolutely do."

She said, "I know," but there was no resolve in her voice.

She did finally leave him, though; she found out he'd been pursuing another woman all along.

. . . . .

I wasn't sorry that I went to the party.

Michael looked pretty much the same, though it had been dark outside the restaurant in Quogue and in the Toy Bar, and especially dark in his bedroom. The Indian restaurant was brightly lit.

I saw him out of the corner of my eye, and for the first time that night I was glad to be wearing my perfect dress.

I'd envisioned this moment many times: I'd pictured turning my back to him or slapping his face or pretending that I couldn't quite place him, I'd had so many lovers since him, my first, and all of them so much more memorable.

But when our eyes met and his look asked if I remembered him, my look answered that I did.

He came up to me as I was leaving. He asked if I wanted to go somewhere else for a drink, and I said that I couldn't.

How was Hugh? I asked. He was fine. Was he painting? He did paint sometimes.

Michael walked me outside, and we stood talking on the sidewalk—or he talked. I was pretty sure I wouldn't fall under his spell again, but to be safe I kept my eyes on his nose.

He was talking fast—he had a girlfriend but she was in Prague—

and anyway they were breaking up—they'd practically already broken up—and I nodded while he talked, the way you do when you're waiting for someone to finish.

"Well," I said, "I have to go."

He said, "Can I call you?"

I waited a long time before answering, though not, of course, as long as he'd made me wait. I let him stand there with the question in the air while I took a good long look at him, let him stand there while I stepped to the street and raised my arm for a cab. At exactly that moment, as though dispatched by some god I didn't really believe in anymore—the god of drama or god of perfect things—or maybe by my own fairy god god, a cab came. I got in, and closed the door.

20TH-CENTURY TYPING

1.

New York gave me a feeling of possibility I'd never gotten in the suburbs, driving home from Lord & Taylor with my mother, say. There, when I'd see people in other cars, I'd know they were on their way home, where their choices would be the same as mine: They could watch TV or read. In New York that summer, especially at dusk, in the Village or in midtown or on the Upper West Side, walking in a crowd of people or looking up at all the lit windows of an office or apartment building, I could feel like there were a thousand ways my life could go.

I'd just graduated from college and was teaching myself how to type at my brother Robert's apartment, a prewar dust factory on 119th Street and Broadway, just a few steps from a bank of pay phones that served as an alfresco urinal.

"Pissoir," my older brother called it, when he came for dinner; Jack lived by himself in a beautiful one-bedroom in the historic West Village.

Robert had three roommates, including his girlfriend, Naomi, who was quiet and serious. She was an unusually slow speaker, and I thought this might have something to do with her being Orthodox. I wondered if this strictest form of Judaism also dictated her sometimes wearing a bandanna over her long, wavy hair, which made her look like a girl from the shtetl in *Fiddler on the Roof.*

That summer, Naomi was applying to doctoral programs in psychology and Robert was studying for his MCAT; they lived in the library at Columbia and slept in her bedroom. It was the brightest room, but it faced the street and could be loud. Salsa music came in and fought the Mozart on her stereo. I lived in Robert's room, where I attended my own private secretarial school.

The apartment was big but dingy and full of cockroaches no one but me seemed to notice. It was especially depressing during the day when the sun shone through the dirty windows and let you know just how dirty everything was and always had been and always would be.

I was told that there were separate dishes for meat and milk, but I kept forgetting which was for which. One morning, when I was eating breakfast, Naomi came in and her mouth opened in what looked like a shriek. Instead, one of her ultra-white hands went up to her black hair, as though to calm her crazy self down.

"What?" I said.

I'd been eating my cereal out of a meat bowl.

When I offered to wash it out, she just stared at me.

I said, "What about if I use really, really hot water?"

She said the bowl would have to be thrown away, which seemed a little extreme, but as the criminal I wasn't in a position to choose the bowl's punishment.

. . . . .

She got Robert to talk to me about what I'd done, which I didn't think boded well for her future as a psychologist.

That evening the two of them came through the front door together, but Naomi took a left to her bedroom and Robert a right to the living room, where I sat with his roommate Leah.

He said hello to both of us and went to the kitchen and mixed his evening cocktail, a cranberry juice and seltzer.

He leaned in the doorway, sipping it, while Leah told me about the teaching fellowship she'd start in the fall in Tel Aviv. Her words were boring to me, but her voice, a soft monotone, was so soothing I kept asking her questions so she'd go on: "What does Tel Aviv look like?" "How do Israeli universities differ from the ones here?"

Robert stood there, waiting for Leah to finish, and when it looked to him like that might never happen, he motioned with his head for me to join him in his room.

I did, and he closed the door. I sat on the bed he never slept in, and I wondered about that: It seemed unlikely that the Orthodox leaders who shook their long curls at the cereal in my meat bowl would say, "Fine, fine," to premarital sex.

I tried to pay attention while Robert explained that Naomi's strict observance of rituals stemmed from deep religious beliefs. I came to life when he started talking about our family. In Naomi's eyes we were about as Jewish as Episcopalians. She'd been horrified that we'd had Christmas trees when we were growing up, and, as he told me, I remembered Robert as a little boy, dumping out his stocking of chocolate coins and matchbox cars, and his glee, in contrast to his current gloom.

I tried to cheer him up with a joke about the meatlike cockroaches illicitly lounging on milk plates in the cabinet, but he looked hurt, and when he said, "Sophie," a reprimand, I got a sick feeling. He'd been going with Naomi to synagogue some Friday nights and Saturday mornings; I'd assumed Robert was just being Robert, i.e., a good egg, but now I worried that maybe he was on the way to becoming a Torah-thumper himself.

He said, "We opened our home to you," which I knew was a direct quote from Naomi.

I said, "Did you just say, 'We opened our home to you'?"

His face registered that I'd busted him, and for a second his face belonged to the Robert I knew. Then we heard Naomi go down the hall for her shower, and he fixed his face back to dead seriousness.

I told him I'd apologize to her.

He said, "I think that's a good idea."

I asked if I needed to apologize to the other roommates, Leah and Seth, and he said no, Naomi was the only one who kept kosher. He seemed to think it was normal for one person to dictate the dietary laws for five.

In the kitchen, he pointed out which dishes were for what. As it turned out, there was a separate set of milk silverware I hadn't even known about, as well as separate pots and pans. He found a Magic

Marker and wrote out labels on masking tape and stuck them on the shelves and drawers. We both acted like, *Problem solved.*

. . . . .

After Robert left to go back to the library, I went down the hall to Naomi's room. The door was open; she was sitting at her desk writing a paper that might have been on conflict avoidance. Her hair hung thick and wet on a towel she'd draped over her bathrobe. It occurred to me that her hair would take all night to dry and that she'd sleep with a towel on her pillow, as I had when I was little. This made me think of her as young and clean instead of strict, which was the word that stuck in my mind from Robert's speech about her religious observance.

Strict came back, though, in her expression, when I knocked on the door frame and she turned around. She seemed to know that she was not only right in this specific instance, but generally right, righteously right, and I pictured her acting like this with Robert.

I was standing up for him and for my entire assimilated family and even the Christmas trees of my childhood, which I myself found strange, when I said, "Sorry about the cereal," as in, *Let's not forget we're talking about Cheerios here.*

. . . . .

I was just starting to go out with Robert's MCAT tutor, whom my genius brother called a genius.

Josh was gentle and polite, a poet and a lover of classic novels and foreign movies. He didn't drink and had never tried a single drug, and even during the Hades days of July, as he called them, he gave the impression of having just showered; he smelled faintly of baby powder.

He had long hair, which he pulled back in a ponytail, and he was lanky without actually being tall. Robert told me Josh was a great tennis player, and one night I went to the courts to see the two of them play. I loved watching Josh—especially his huge, powerful serve; he had beautiful form.

Afterward, walking home, I said, "You should see me type sometime."

. . . . .

Along with my father's huge IBM Selectric II, I'd brought a book called *20th-Century Typewriting* that I'd checked out from the library during my brief stint of postgraduation paralysis at home in the suburbs. A faded olive hardback, bound at the top like a pad, this was the book I'd used in junior-high typing class. I'd hoped some of the lessons would come back, but they hadn't.

On breaks from typing, I studied the résumé book I'd bought, *Advertisements for Yourself*, though even its encouragement discouraged me. These job-seekers had spent their entire lives preparing for the jobs I only now realized I might want. Tim J. Sullivan had been a journalism major, the editor of the campus newspaper, and a summer intern at a Detroit metropolitan daily with a circulation of twenty thousand. Laura Johnson, whose goal it was to assist a photographer, had already assisted one, worked in a gallery, and received an honorable mention in a juried exhibit at the Minnesota State Fair.

Only Lisa Michele Butler was of any use to me. Though I hadn't written a prizewinning thesis entitled "Regionalism in the Short Stories of Sarah Orne Jewett" or spearheaded a volunteer-based literacy initiative, I had been an English major. Therefore, like Lisa Michele, I sought an entry-level position in book publishing, preferably as an editorial assistant.

. . . . .

Following the book's advice, I had my résumé typeset and was stunned by the effect: In plain, beautiful type, my lack of experience, accomplishments, and honors came across as understatement and modesty. I loved how my résumé looked so much that I forgot my fear about its content and showed it to Josh.

He said, "I don't know what you've been so worried about."

I said that he should see the résumés in *Advertisements for Yourself.*

"Honey," he said, "those aren't real people."

I said, "I know that. Now."

. . . . .

I called the first person on Jack's list of people he knew in publishing, but either Jack got the name wrong or his friend had left the company; I was transferred to personnel.

I explained that I was looking for a friend of my brother's. "I'm sorry," I said.

The woman said, "Take your time."

I managed to say that I was looking for a job as an editorial assistant, and the woman, apparently a saint, asked if I could come into the office that afternoon.

I put on my seersucker suit and panty hose and pumps, which blistered my feet after only a few blocks.

The personnel saint was even nicer in person. She nodded at my résumé and smiled even when she told me that she'd never heard of the college I'd graduated from.

I told her not to worry: No one had heard of Rogers. "My brother calls it Hammerstein," I said.

"Fine," she said. "Can you type?"

I heard this as, *Are you willing?* and I said, "Absolutely."

Then she gave me the test.

After calculating my score, she said, "I'm sorry," and explained that I needed at least forty-five words per minute to be considered for any entry-level position in publishing.

I said, "How did I do?"

"Nine," she said.

. . . . .

That night, instead of seeing Josh, I typed. I was restless, though, and kept going into the kitchen for a diet Coke or another coffee. Each time, Naomi appeared. She'd get herself a glass of water or look in the refrigerator, but I knew she was just in there to make sure I used the right dishes and silverware. I smiled at her: *But you don't know which I use when you're not around, do you?*

. . . . .

Josh liked to stay in New York on weekends. He liked how the city emptied out, and you could go to museums or eat in restaurants that were usually crowded. I understood that, but my parents had a house on the New Jersey shore, and I wanted to go there sometimes. I wanted to swim in the ocean.

I said this to Josh one Friday night in August, when the humidity made me feel desperate and shrill.

Josh said, "We've already been there twice." He said, as he had before, that he wanted us to have new experiences together.

We began to have one right then, when he suggested we go to Coney Island to visit his Russian grandmother, Bubbe, who, on our first meeting, asked why I hadn't come to see her sooner.

I kept my voice even. "We've already been there," I said.

"Oh," he said. "Right."

Irrelevantly, I added that I hadn't seen my own grandmother even once.

Josh said, "Didn't I just meet her?"

He'd met my mother's mother, Steeny, at the shore. "I'm talking about my father's mother, Grandma Mamie," I said. "She lives in the Bronx."

"Well," he said, as though we had a wonderful solution right in front of us, "let's visit her."

I said that the last thing I wanted do on a summer day was see anybody's grandmother. "Don't you understand?" I felt like I must not be speaking clearly, and I tried to find the right words. "I need to get out," I said, and even to myself I sounded like a child throwing a tantrum over something like a drop of coleslaw touching my hamburger.

"You want to take a walk?" he said.

I shook my head. My frustration was escalating, a headache coming on.

He said, "Why don't you stand by the fan?"

Josh became eerily calm; he was the eye of the storm, and I became its mouth. Finally, I took my ranting self out of there and walked up Broadway to Robert's.

When I got there, I couldn't find my keys. I buzzed the intercom and waited; I buzzed again. When I stood back and looked up, I saw a light on in Naomi's bedroom—or rather, candles lit, and I remembered that it was the Sabbath.

I called from one of the pissoir phones. The answering machine picked up, and Leah's recorded "shalom" calmed me down. After the beep, I said, "It's Sophie," and, "I'm locked out."

I waited, and the voice-activated machine hung up on me.

I was pretty sure the library closed at ten o'clock on Friday nights. It was 10:10 now. I figured that Robert would come home soon. I sat on the stoop and waited.

But then a terrible thought occurred to me: What if Robert was upstairs? I couldn't picture him refusing to let me in, no matter what Naomi said. But she ruled the kitchen, and the front door was just down the hall.

Finally, a delivery man was buzzed into the building, and I followed him inside. Upstairs I knocked on the door, and a few minutes later Naomi answered in her bathrobe. She said, "I was asleep," which came out as a statement of fact, but if it listed anywhere it was closer to reprimand than apology.

I got into bed and lay there, listening for Robert. A few minutes later he unlocked the front door. He went down the hallway to Naomi's room without turning on a single light.

. . . . .

When I woke up, Robert and Naomi had already gone, probably to her synagogue.

There were two messages from Josh on the answering machine. The first—"It's Josh . . . I have Sophie's keys"—was so cold and matter-of-fact it made me feel we'd already broken up. The second—"Please call me"—was so sad and intimate he might have been whispering in my ear.

He was sorry; I was sorry; we were sorry. We spent all Saturday making up in his apartment.

. . . . .

On Sunday, Robert said, "I'm sorry about Friday night."

I said, "It's not your fault."

Without mentioning Naomi, he defended her: He explained what couldn't be done on the Sabbath and why.

I waited until he'd finished. Then I said, "Are you Orthodox now, Robert?"

He shook his head but told me he liked observing the Sabbath—"It's nice and quiet"—and reminded me that he'd always liked going to synagogue. "What's not to like?" he said. "It's a roomful of Jews."

Later, Naomi knocked on my door, and when I turned around, I realized that she was standing just as I had when I'd gone to her room to apologize.

She said, "Sorry about the buzzer."

. . . . .

She went off to the library, and Robert and I had dinner with his roommates. Leah was leaving for Tel Aviv in just a few weeks, and Seth said that they had to start looking for another roommate now. "What about you, Soph?" Seth said. "Don't you need an apartment?"

Leah's eyes widened, and I realized that Naomi had talked to her about me.

Robert had stopped eating. He was looking down at his plate, and when he looked up at me, his face was helpless. On it, I could see that a yes to me would mean a no to Naomi. I didn't want him to feel that it was Girlfriend vs. Sister, but I knew he would no matter what.

I made my face say, *It's okay.*

I told the table that I needed to find a job before I rented an apartment.

. . . . .

I could see that Robert was relieved when I told him that I was going to stay with Jack for a while.

It was awkward when I moved out. I stood with Naomi and Robert by the door for a few minutes, saying good-bye. Josh had carried my stuff downstairs, where Jack was waiting for me in his convertible. I had all my clothes on hangers draped over my arm when Robert tried to hug me.

"Well," I said, and then, accidentally: "Thank you for opening your home to me."

2.

Jack called Naomi "Gnomie" and "The Gnomester," and he laughed at my cockroach joke. When I repeated Robert's "We opened our home" remark, Jack shook his head and said, "Robby, Robby, Robby."

It was my first night in Jack's apartment, and we had just finished a great dinner that his girlfriend, Cynthia, had cooked. She'd put tulips on the table, and the kitchen was dark except for candles. It was a nice atmosphere, and I was glad to be there, but I also felt bad about the way the conversation was going.

Jack said, "There's a word for what our little brother has become."

I said, "I don't know about that."

He said, "Oh, I think you do."

He was talking to me, but he was also teasing Cynthia, who was from Alabama and probably didn't cotton to words like *pussy-whipped.*

"Jack," I said, "I think he's going to marry her," and I realized it was true. Now that I thought about it, they acted like they were already married.

I wondered how Jack would feel about his little brother getting married before him. Maybe Cynthia wondered, too; she was looking at him.

He was quiet, and I could tell he was picturing the talk he might have with Robert; he even moved his lips a little. Whatever he imagined, I was pretty sure Robert wouldn't listen. Jack knew how to make women fall in love with him, but that didn't exactly qualify him as a guidance counselor.

When Jack came out of his reverie, he asked how my job hunt was going and whether I'd met any of the editors whose numbers he'd given me. He didn't mention their names in front of Cynthia, and it occurred to me that they were all women he'd gone out with.

I said that I was waiting until I could type forty-five words per minute.

Cynthia gave me a big, encouraging smile: *You'll get there, Sugar Bear.*

She was tall with very long arms and a big, red-lipsticked mouth. She was a clothing designer and had one of those personalities that drapes itself all over you at first. She'd hugged me when we'd met, for example, and talk-talk-talked all through dinner, not that I minded. She had a pretty voice and in it you could hear the song of the South at the end of a sentence.

We stayed up a long time talking, and I did the dishes. Afterward, when I went out to the living room, Cynthia was tucking sheets and a blanket into the futon sofa I'd sleep on.

Jack opened his bedroom door just enough for his head, so I knew he was in his underwear or nothing; he said, "Good night, Tinkerbell."

Cynthia gave me a little squeeze. "I'm glad you're here," she said, which made me love her.

. . . . .

I'd never heard anyone having sex before, and it took a few minutes for me to realize that's what it was. Faintly, I heard Cynthia whimpering. Jack sounded the way he had lifting weights in our basement, sort of a growl that got louder and in the past had ended with the crash of barbells. Then they were both laughing, and I kind of laughed, too.

Josh and I were silent when we had sex, and I thought the next time I would make some noise.

I didn't, though. The next night at dinner, Josh told me that he needed to spend more time writing poetry.

We were at Szechwan West—Szech West, we called it—around the corner from his apartment; we'd just ordered.

Before meeting me, he explained, he'd spent every night writing in the library; now, he said, he was just going to his day job and seeing me at night. He said, "My poetry is really suffering."

I smiled when I said, "I don't want your poetry to suffer."

I tried to keep the conversation on poetry, instead of asking, say, whether he'd fallen out of love with me. But "What are your poems like?" dead-ended into him saying that he'd show them to me; "Who are your favorite poets?" resulted in a list.

When he asked who mine were, I sighed, as though musing among many, and tried to think of one. Finally, I recited my favorite poem:

> Shake and shake
> the ketchup bottle
> none'll come and
> then a lot'll.

Our dishes arrived, and he warned me about the hot peppers in mine. He said, "I ate one of those once, and it made me want to blow my head off."

At his apartment, in his bedroom, it was harder to pretend that everything was okay. I told him I was going to smoke a cigarette, which meant going outside the apartment. One of his roommates smoked, but just in her bedroom; Josh complained about the fumes that came out when she opened her door.

I felt better as soon as I was out in the stairwell. I sat on the dusty black steps and lit a cigarette. I sat there and tried to get my personality back.

Back inside, I opened the door to Josh's bedroom. He'd already turned out the light. I inched forward in the dark. My knee found the bed, and I got in. I lay very still. Then Josh put his arms around me, and it was safe to love him again.

. . . . .

Every time I called home, my mother told me she'd received another overdue notice for *20th-Century Typewriting.*

Its main author was D. D. Lessenberry, and those Ds might have stood for Deadly, Dull, Dread, or Doom. All day, D. D. bored me with exercises and drills called "Know Your Typewriter" and "Reach Stroke Review," for which I typed such paragraphs as

> Do you think you can learn to type well? It is up to you, you know. You build the right kind of skill through the way you work

and the way you think; so think right and type right and you will have this prize of fine skill.

Around 6:30, Cynthia came through the door, with groceries for dinner and clothes in dry cleaner's plastic; she had her own apartment and supposedly wasn't living with Jack. She carried her groceries in a string bag that bulged with big and little brown bags. Instead of shopping at the supermarket around the corner on Bleecker Street, she went to the fish store or the butcher, to the cheese shop and bakery and the farmers' market. She said this was how people shopped in Paris, where she'd lived after art school.

She'd ask how my day was, and I'd say, "Okay," or, "All right." I wanted to say more, but a day of typing did not produce fascinating anecdotes. What could I say? *Well, Cynthia, I'm finally settling into the home keys.*

When Jack came through the door, I turned off the typewriter and carried it from the kitchen into the living room; I stowed it under the coffee table.

He'd say, "What's the score?" meaning how many words per minute, and I'd tell him the miserable number. Sometimes he called me Katie, which I didn't get; Katie, one of my best friends from college, had been a diligent student, but did he know that? When I finally asked him, he explained that Katie was short for Katharine Gibbs, the secretarial school.

Cynthia called Jack "Big Old Bear," which she pronounced *bar* and said in the voice of a little girl with a cold. It was apt: Jack was big and meaty and covered with fur everywhere but his head. She said it with great affection, and usually he'd take her in his big beary arms and maybe kiss her.

The living room was small, just the futon sofa and a few chairs that you were supposed to look at rather than sit in. But the kitchen was big and airy and looked out on leafy trees turning yellow and red, and that's where we all hung out.

While Cynthia cooked, Jack read the newspaper, and I'd read a section, too, even though I was dying to talk and be talked to. I'd make myself be quiet, though, and that felt nice after a while.

Sitting down for dinner, I could feel that we were a small, happy family.

After I'd done the dishes, I'd meet a friend for a drink or go up to Josh's. If I didn't have plans, I'd take a walk around the neighborhood to give Cynthia and Jack privacy. I'd walk up Christopher Street, which was still the center of gay life then. When I saw men kiss I didn't believe it at first.

. . . . .

Finally, I reached twenty-five words per minute, where I peaked and plateaued.

I told Jack this when he came through the door. "I'll be an old lady and typing twenty-five," I said, and I made my voice creaky and said, "Still twenty-five."

He laughed, but the next night when he came home, and I said my creaky, "Still twenty-five," he said, "Fabulous," a word I'd never heard him use, and he said it like he was imitating someone.

As usual, I carried my typewriter into the living room and returned to the kitchen.

He was reading the paper. Cynthia bent down and kissed his head. I saw him flinch.

. . . . .

Jack was talented at every art form. On the living-room wall, he'd painted a mural of the street outside—the trees and sidewalk, a boy on a skateboard, and a woman carrying a string bag full of groceries; it took me a week before I realized she was Cynthia. In his bedroom were dozens of framed black-and-white photographs he'd taken of his bed, rumpled and made.

Jack had gone to graduate school for architecture at Yale and to Harvard for art history, a year apiece; he'd written for a famous magazine and rocked in a band. Now he wanted to direct movies—or, as he called them, pictures.

He was working for a production company, but I kept realizing that I didn't know what he did, and every time he explained it to me,

I knew even less. All I'd remember were the names of famous actors he said were "attached" to movies his company would produce.

"Tell me what you do again," I said one night when he'd folded up the newspaper and Cynthia was putting a big bowl of pasta on the table. I said it because the kitchen felt quiet, and not in the nice way it had in the past; it was loud with quiet.

He said, "I'm a P.A.," and I could tell from his tone that was all he wanted to say.

I knew he was in a bad mood, but I was hoping to talk him out of it. I said, "Riddle me this, Batman: What does P.A. stand for?"

"Production assistant."

With all the surprise I felt, I said, "You're an assistant?"

He said, "Yup."

. . . . .

I always looked forward to the moment when Jack came home, and not just because it signaled the end of my typing day. Hearing him on the stairs, I'd think, *Let the fun begin!* But when he actually did walk in, the apartment itself seemed to tense up and go gloomy.

Now when Cynthia said, "Big Old Bear," she seemed to be trying to remind him of how he felt about her; she was asking him to be the *bar* of yesteryear.

I noticed that he didn't always answer her questions. He'd be reading the paper, and she'd say something ordinary, like, "What's the news of the day?" and silence would follow.

I knew she didn't care about the actual answer to her actual question; it was her way of saying, *Hello,* or even, *I love you.* When he didn't respond, she'd go back to washing her lettuce or sautéing onions, like she hadn't asked anything in the first place.

I told Josh about it, and his answer, a long blink followed by a blank expression, made me wonder if one day soon he'd stop answering my questions. So I said, "Don't you think that's rude?"

He sort of shrugged.

I was defending myself when I said, "It just seems wrong."

He said, "It's between them, though."

. . . . .

In a way, I hadn't really seen Jack up close before. He'd lived in the attic bedroom, which was like a separate house on top of ours. Then he went away to college, and he didn't always come home for vacations. He'd visit a girlfriend somewhere or go on a trip. Sometimes he'd promise to come home and then change his mind.

Once, when I'd been really disappointed, my father had tried to explain that I couldn't count on Jack the way I wanted to; I had to learn to appreciate him for what he could do and not be too crestfallen about what he couldn't.

I knew what my father meant. One year Jack drove a thousand miles to have dinner with our mother on her birthday; the next he didn't even call.

He loved doing huge favors and surprising people with his generosity. He liked going above and beyond the call of duty, but he didn't like duty itself.

It occurred to me that he might think I expected him to ask my typing score; anyway, he stopped asking.

This was a relief, since my score wasn't improving. How could I type all day, every day and not get better? The answer: I wasn't typing all day, every day. I'd started taking long breaks in the afternoon. I'd pack a sandwich and go to Washington Square Park, intending just to stay an hour. I'd linger awhile by the dog run, especially if there was a puppy. I'd sit by the dry fountain, where a comedian tried out jokes on the NYU students. I pretended to be one of them. Sometimes a mime performed. A voice in my head would nag me to get back to my typing, but another one would say, *Just a little longer.*

I might walk over to St. Marks Place and try on sunglasses that were displayed on tables. Or I'd get lost, looking at clothes in a boutique. I stayed out later and later until my goal was to get back to the apartment before Cynthia got home.

. . . . .

Josh and I went out to inexpensive restaurants—to La Rosita on Broadway for Cuban breakfasts, to V&T up by Columbia for pizza, to any place on East Sixth Street for Indian food, or to the Corner

Bistro on West Fourth for burgers. Every once in a while, though, he'd ask me to meet him at a nicer restaurant, and I came to realize that we went when he'd finished a poem. He'd read it to me during dessert, and I'd applaud and kiss him.

It was after one of those dinners that I finally worked up the courage to whimper in bed.

It felt like acting at first, but then it wasn't. It was great. At the end, I let out a big yell, which made me laugh afterward and say as a joke, "I came."

Josh was quiet. "Honey," he said, "I have roommates."

. . . . .

One night before dinner, when Jack didn't answer Cynthia I glared at him, and he said, "What?"

I said, "Cynthia asked you a question."

He looked at me for a long moment, like he was trying to remember liking me. Then he turned around to Cynthia. With more affection than I'd heard in weeks, he said, "What was that, sugar pie?"

. . . . .

She didn't come over the next night.

When Jack walked in and said, "What's the score?" I knew he was trying to make me feel that everything was all right, so I knew it wasn't.

"I didn't take a test today," I said. For the first time he was the one who carried my typewriter to the living room and stowed it under the coffee table.

"Chinese?" he said, and handed me a menu.

We agreed on a few dishes. He called and ordered. Then he sat down with his newspaper in the kitchen.

I went to the living room and opened the book on Edward Hopper.

He called out: "You're not going to keep my company?"

"I'll be there in a second," I said, but I didn't join him until our dinner was delivered. We unpacked the cartons and sat down at the table.

"Sophie," he said, once we were eating.

I kept my eyes on his hands as though absorbed in learning how to hold my chopsticks by watching him hold his. I said, "Uh-huh?"

He spoke slowly. "What happens between Cynthia and me is between Cynthia and me."

I knew he was right, and I felt embarrassed—and embarrassed to be embarrassed in front of him.

After a moment, I said, "Maybe I should stay somewhere else for a while."

He didn't answer right away. Then he said, "Where could you stay?"

I had a terrible feeling—*I don't have anywhere to stay.*

I'd gone to Robert's for dinner a couple of times, but I'd noticed that he only invited me when Naomi wasn't going to be there. I thought of my friends from college and pictured their apartments. No one had enough room for me or my clothes, and especially not for my huge typewriter.

I thought of Josh. Usually just the idea of him cheered me up. Right then, though, I experienced the sensation of being in love for the uncertainty that being in love is.

The only other possible host was Grandma Mamie. I still hadn't visited her. It was hard even to make myself call her every few weeks.

I said, "I could stay at Grandma Mamie's," hoping against hope that Jack would say, *Don't be ridiculous.*

. . . . .

"Don't be ridiculous," he said during our farewell dinner, when I said the dress Cynthia gave me was too big a present for me to accept. It was a sample from her showroom, a dress made of blue-black wool jersey, which she said I could wear on job interviews.

I went to the bathroom to try it on. In the mirror, I saw that the dress was a little longer on one side. I didn't want to embarrass Cynthia, so I hunched my right shoulder and lowered my left to make the dress hang evenly.

Cynthia understood; she said, "It's cut on the bias," which meant that its unevenness was deliberate.

"It's great," Jack said.

. . . . .

Jack surprised me by offering to drive me up to my grandmother's. This was just the kind of favor Jack liked doing most. He was going to make a difficult thing fun. It was cold, but he put the top down on his convertible and turned the heat on. We drove along the river. The sky was a cold blue.

Grandma Mamie lived in the Riverdale section of the Bronx, one exit past the first toll on the Henry Hudson Parkway. When we got to her apartment house, Jack tipped the doorman so we could park in the circular drive, between NO PARKING ANYTIME signs.

Jack carried my big typewriter in the elevator. He hid while I rang my grandmother's doorbell.

When she opened the door, he showed her his handsome face.

She was thrilled to see it.

He was flirty with her, calling her Mamie instead of Grandma and telling her how fantastic she looked. He sat down and ate a pastry she'd made, a yellow briquette he proclaimed "delicious."

When it was time for him to go, I walked out with him. We stood by his car. I wanted to make a joke so that everything would be okay between us. I considered saying, "Thank you for opening your home to me," but it seemed like a joke at Robert's expense, and maybe bitter.

Instead, Jack spoke. He took both my hands in his and said, "I'm for you, and you're for me." This was something my uncle had said to me when I was little, and I hadn't heard it since and understood it only now.

Jack hugged me good-bye. He had a way of hugging that could pull you all the way in, and make you feel safer and more loved than you ever thought possible.

Then he got in his little car and was gone.

3.

My grandmother's apartment looked out on the Harlem River, which is no Hudson; our cut of the Harlem wasn't mighty or mythic, not blue or green or gray, but varying shades of brown that evoked no metaphor save human waste.

The apartment had two rooms and could feel spacious if you were the only one in it, which I never was except when my grandmother went downstairs for the mail or out to Gristedes for groceries.

She was on a perpetual diet and didn't eat dinner with me. Mostly she stood nearby, at the ready to refill my water glass or serve the seconds I never asked for.

I couldn't. Everything she made had been sautéed or boiled or baked too long. I could eat the salad—iceberg lettuce, mealy tomatoes, and carrot pennies smothered in lo-cal dressing—but the chicken was a dried-up dishrag and the baked potato a shiny sack of mush.

She kept calling me "Sophilla," her pet name for me, and the sound of it made me feel like a sack of mush myself.

She asked how Robert was, but it was Naomi she wanted to talk about. "She's a nice girl, Naomi," my grandmother said, her tone implying there was something more important that Naomi wasn't. "You can't blame her for wanting to get married."

I said, "I don't think Naomi's so interested in getting married," though I didn't know.

My grandmother turned her head to the side.

"Really," I said. "She's pretty busy with school."

She sat down with me and sighed. She sighed again and then said, "It's hard after college, Sophilla?"

I thought she was talking about finding a job, starting a new life, joining what we recent college graduates called "The Real World," and I agreed: It was hard.

"Not that it isn't hard in college," she said. "The boys want the younger girls."

I said, "Um."

"It gets harder, Sophie," she said, squinting at me, as though seeing despair and loneliness in my future. "Harder and harder."

"You know what?" I said. "I should practice my typing."

She told me that I'd practiced all day, and I had. But I cleared the dishes and wiped off the green place mat we'd agreed I'd use underneath the typewriter to protect the finish of her dining-room table. She wouldn't let me do the dishes.

Once I was sitting in front of the typewriter, she said, "I'm just trying to tell you how life is, Sophilla."

I didn't know what to say, so I said, "Thank you."

She said, "Maybe Jack or Robby could introduce you to someone."

I made my face say, *Hm,* and began to type.

. . . . .

I planned to call Josh once my grandmother went to bed, but she stayed where she was on the sofa, knitting an unwearable sweater of Orlon.

Josh was a maniac about sleep and I had to call him before eleven. At 10:55, I went into the bedroom and dialed. I only had time to say, "Hi," before she came in.

"Excuse me," she said and went to her closet.

Josh said, "How's it going?"

I said, "I'm here at my grandmother's," in a voice meant to convey both the hardship of this and her presence in the room.

He said, "How is she?"

. . . . .

Without comedians, mimes, or puppies to distract me, I broke through to thirty-two words the next day. I made a few calls and set up appointments. At dinner I was exultant. I ate the strings of what must once have aspired to be pot roast, and I was considering a second helping when my grandmother said, "You have to let people know you're looking, Sophilla."

Thinking she meant for a job, I was about to say, *I have,* but then I realized she was talking about men again. I said no to seconds and cleared the table, though she fought me on this and blocked the sink so I couldn't wash the dishes.

I was about to start an exercise on numbers, my nemesis, when she said, "Jack doesn't have any friends you could meet?"

Even as I said the words, "I did meet somebody," I regretted them and began typing up a storm of nonsense.

"Oh!" she said, pulling up a chair. "What's his name?"

"Josh," I said.

"Josh what, if you don't mind me asking?"

"Rudman."

"Jewish?" she said.

I said, "He is Jewish," though her pleasure in it rankled me. "I have to type."

"Excuse me," she said. "I didn't mean to bother you."

She returned an exercise later. "What does Josh do, if you don't mind me asking?"

"He's a poet," I said.

She didn't say anything.

"He writes poetry." I said, "He's really good," though I hadn't understood any of the poems he'd read to me.

She said, "This is his living?"

I told her that he programmed computers for a research group at Columbia Presbyterian.

"The hospital?" she said.

"Uh-huh."

She thought for a second. "Maybe he'll decide to go to medical school."

"He already went and didn't like it."

He'd said, "I realized I was too creative to be a doctor," which had bothered me; Robert was going to be a doctor. Remembering how I'd felt, I frowned.

To make me feel better my grandmother said, "He could change his mind."

"I don't think so."

She said, "You could talk to him."

I said, "I'm having dinner with him tomorrow," even though we hadn't made plans.

A little later, I went into the bedroom to call him. I told him that I would be in Manhattan for interviews the next day.

My grandmother walked into the bedroom and, seeing that I was on the phone, said, "Excuse me," and left.

She closed the door, but not all the way, and it occurred to me that she was standing on the other side.

I lowered my voice. "Maybe we could have dinner."

"I can't tomorrow," he said, and he named the ex-girlfriend he'd made plans with. One of his principles was that he maintained contact, as he called it, with his ex-girlfriends; another was that he did not cancel plans.

The phone sat on a stack of paperbacks, the entirety of my grandmother's library, and I chose this moment to read the titles. My eyes were on *Love's Urgent Flame* when Josh said, "What about Thursday?"—three nights away.

I had to force myself to return to the typewriter, and was almost grateful for my grandmother's interruption— "You know, Sophilla . . ."

I looked up.

"Grandpa wasn't interested in me at first," she said. "He had a lot of girls."

I'd heard this story maybe 250,000 times before. As she spoke, I mentally mouthed the details: My grandfather, whom for the purpose of the story she called Abie, was friendly with her brother and would come over to play cards Friday nights.

"When Abie walked in, I walked out," she said. "He thought I had a date. I was a very popular girl. I took myself to the movies," she said.

I said, "I think I understand what you're trying to say." I flipped to a new exercise.

"You've got to be a little smart, Sophie," she said.

"Got it," I said.

She was quiet after that, and when I glanced over at her, she looked worried.

At the end of the evening, I took a timed test. I'd typed thirty-six. I got into bed, thinking, *You typed thirty-six words per minute.* I closed my eyes, thinking, *Thirty-six, thirty-six, thirty-six.*

I was almost asleep when my grandmother said, "Sophie?"

"Yes?"

She said, "Maybe you should let Josh call *you* once in a while."

. . . . .

I couldn't wear my interview suit, as seersucker said "summer" as clearly as did corn on the cob and flip-flops; I was grateful for the dress Cynthia had given me, though in the mirror it looked more uneven than cut on the bias. I put on my trench coat. Remembering the blisters from my first interview, I placed my pumps in the cardboard accordion file with my envelope of résumés and wore sneakers.

My grandmother said, "You look like a little doll," which was not exactly the look I was striving for. Still, it was one of her highest compliments, along with, *You're a modern girl in every way.*

I tried to tell her that I wasn't having dinner with Josh until Thursday, but it seemed like proof that I should be faking dates and letting him call me.

All I could manage was, "I won't be too late."

. . . . .

I stood outside waiting for the express bus to Manhattan, and even in the morning sun I was cold. I had three interviews—on Fifty-third and Lexington, Sixteenth and Union Square West, and Sixth Avenue and Forty-eighth. Before and after each appointment, I changed my shoes on the sidewalk. I'd face the building and try not to notice people noticing me.

I thought the last interview of the day, with a Rogers alum, might be easier than the rest because he'd at least have heard of our alma mater, but Clay White seemed bored and annoyed from the start. All through the interview, he was occupied with a paper clip he was unbending into uselessness. After a half hour, holding the straightened paper clip he'd achieved between his thumb and index finger, he said, "Tell me again what you've been doing since graduation."

I said that I'd been learning how to type, and I tried to make this sound hilarious. I'd just begun to tell him about the patron saint of lost job-seekers when his phone rang.

I thought this interruption might be one of those serendipitous opportunities to discontinue a failing anecdote, but after he hung up he said, "You were saying?"

I told him that I'd heard her, "Can you type?" as, *Are you willing?* and delivered what I hoped would be an acceptable end of the story, if not the punch line: "Then she gave me the test."

"How'd you do?"

The effect of his question was to turn my anecdote back into a real experience: Once again, I saw the pencil counting up the words I'd typed and subtracting the errors I'd made; I knew that I hadn't done well but I was hoping, which struck me now as the basic emotion of my entire life.

I told Clay that I'd typed nine words a minute.

He said, "Call me when you get to forty."

I almost said that I was up to thirty-six now, but I liked not saying it better. Not saying it made me feel I would do fine without the help of Clay White.

Then I was outside on the sidewalk, changing from my pumps into sneakers.

. . . . .

I turned off Sixth Avenue onto Forty-seventh Street and found myself in the diamond district as it was closing: Necklaces were removed from velvet necks and rings from velvet fingers; metal curtains and iron gates were pulled shut and locked. The people rushing by me looked cold and seemed more desperate to get away from where they were than eager to get to wherever they were going. I was cold myself, and my feet hurt from their brief imprisonment in pumps. My accordion file was weighed down with the publishers' catalogs I'd amassed. I'd been given at least one at the close of each interview, like a consolation prize—*I can't give you a job, but here is a catalog. Oh, thank you for this catalog.*

I'd already flipped through the catalogs, but I didn't know what to look for. What was I supposed to do with them? Throwing them out seemed like giving up.

Walking down Fifth Avenue, I couldn't work up any excitement about being in New York. It was hard to feel that anything was possible in a dress and sneakers. In a dress and sneakers, I was just me, pretending to be on a date while my boyfriend was having dinner with an ex-girlfriend. In a dress and sneakers, I was just me, killing time before going back to my grandmother's.

It began to rain, and I ducked into a phone booth. I told myself I was not going to call home, but I pictured it: My father would have pulled up the driveway a few minutes earlier, and now I knew he was standing in the kitchen having two fingers of gin with ice and hors d'oeuvres my mother had prepared for him, and they would be talking about the day. The kitchen would be warm, and there would be the smell of a well-cooked dinner almost finished.

My mother was the one who answered, and she accepted the charges. She must have heard the despair in my, "Hi"; she said, "I'll put your father on."

"Mom?" I asked her to send me a coat, and she said, "Of course."

I told my father everything, and I felt better just having him on the other end. He was quiet. My father listened more closely than anyone, so he didn't have to make the sounds of listening; he didn't say, "Uh-huh," or make comments, or ask questions.

When I finished, he told me what I already knew: Soon I would find a job and get an apartment of my own.

In the background, I heard my mother ask him to tell me that another overdue notice had come for *20th-Century Typewriting,* but he said, "Why don't you come home this weekend?" He made his voice light, like it might just be a good idea.

I thought how nice it would be to go home, but then it occurred to me how hard it might be to leave again.

"Think about it," he said. "We're here."

. . . . .

I typed furiously. I typed as though my life depended on it. I typed like a madwoman. Even with all of my errors to subtract, that afternoon I counted up forty-five words per minute.

I called the saint with my typing news, and she congratulated me and promised to keep me in mind. I called everyone I'd put off calling; I set up appointments with anyone who would see me.

Before dinner, I was lifting the typewriter off the table when my grandmother said that maybe I would have some news for her soon. I assumed that she meant about a job, and I said, "I hope so."

It was her smile that made me ask what she'd meant. "Maybe you'll get engaged," she said.

"Grandma," I said, and I turned full around to look at her. "I'm not ready to get married yet."

She said, "Why, if I may ask?"

"I'm just, you know, twenty-two."

She turned her head to the side.

I didn't know what to say. "I'm just starting my career."

She said, "Let me ask you a question."

"Okay."

"You like this Josh."

"Yes," I said.

"So?"

"So . . . ?" I said.

"You don't want to marry him?"

"Not now."

She nodded. "Let me ask you a question," she said again. "If a twenty-two-year-old girl met a nice Jewish guy who made a good living, she would be crazy not to marry him."

"I'm sorry," I said. "What was the question?"

"Does he want to marry you?"

"I don't know," I said, and I tried to make my tone say, *I don't care,* but just then I did.

. . . . .

I had three personnel interviews and aced each typing test, which filled me with pride.

In the late afternoon, I had an appointment with one of the editors from Jack's list. She said, "How's Jack?" like she didn't care, so I knew she did.

Her name was Honey Zipkin, and I thought of my grandmother saying, *You look like a little doll,* because Honey really did look like one. She was very pretty, but she had a bigger head than you'd expect on her little frame, plus long blond hair.

It wasn't until close to the end of the interview that she told me she needed an assistant. She gave me a manuscript, pages in a box, to critique over the weekend.

I had an hour before I had to meet Josh, and I walked up Park Avenue. Catching sight of Grand Central, and the big clock and the statue on the roof, I got this huge feeling: *This is your life, Sophie Applebaum.*

Soon I would be working as an editorial assistant in a major publishing house. I would be leaving the dull brown Bronx for sparkling, silvery Manhattan. I would be moving into my own apartment.

And, I thought, *I am about to have dinner with the man I love.*

Outside Szech West, I changed from sneakers into pumps.

Josh sat at a corner table, studying a page of the yellow legal pad he wrote poems on. He stood up and gave me a kiss that was more suited to a cheek than lips; his embrace seemed to be holding me off instead of pulling me in.

I reminded myself that this was Josh: He was reserved; I couldn't take his personality personally.

He picked up his menu and, handing me mine, said, "I need food." He seemed to think of being hungry or tired as an early stage of illness.

After we'd ordered, he reached for my hand and held it. "How's your grandmother?"

"Hard," I said.

He nodded, which was how he told me to go on.

"I don't know." I said, "She's always talking to me about getting married," and I looked at his face to see if there was anything on it for me to know.

"You should ask her about her life," he said. "Where she came from. That's what I talk to Bubbe about."

Up until that moment, I'd been at the earliest stage of love, when you feel it will turn you into the person you want to be. Now, his gentle voice and sage advice took me to a later stage: I felt I needed to pretend to be a better person than I was so he'd keep loving me. This was hard because it made me hate him.

I couldn't look into his eyes, so I looked down at his hand. I'd never said anything about the turquoise ring he wore; usually, I tried not to notice it. "Where'd you get the ring?" I asked.

He said, "I bought it myself in Santa Fe."

I nodded. It was good that the ring had not been given to him by one of the ex-girlfriends he maintained contact with. But, like Josh, I had principles, and one of mine was that, except for a watch and a plain gold wedding band, a man ought not to wear jewelry. A ring, even this small and un-diamond, put him in a country that a man in a fur coat ruled.

"You don't like it?" he said.

"No," I said. "I like turquoise."

. . . . .

I spent all day reading the manuscript I would have to report on. It was a novel called *The Wives of Armonk*, about women with a lot of money and how they liked to spend it plus have affairs with young men who had big penises. The main character, Jacqueline, fell in love with the pool man. He was skimming the pool for leaves, and she dived in naked. Then they were in the pool house, and she was saying, "Yes . . . yes . . . oh, Lord . . . yes."

At dinner, my grandmother said, "So," and I could tell she was about to bring up Josh.

"You know what I was just thinking?" I said. "I don't know too much about your childhood."

"I was a little girl," she said, and I realized I'd asked her this question before. She sometimes said she grew up in Austria, other times Germany, and once Poland, and she'd left when she was twelve, fourteen, and sixteen. Her family was always very poor, but sometimes her father was a shoemaker and other times a farmer.

"What was your father like?" I asked.

"Sick," she said.

"What was wrong with him?"

Tapping her chest, she said, "Weak lungs."

Finally I asked why she didn't like talking to me about her past. "Is it painful?"

"To tell you the truth," she said, "I don't remember."

. . . . .

I was a slow reader, and I didn't start writing my report until midnight on Sunday. I stayed up all night and at sunrise saw the Harlem River turn unscenically from black to brown.

I proofread my report twice and was especially proud of the last line: "This is dreck."

I didn't have time to take a shower, change my clothes, or put in my contact lenses. I took the express bus down to Manhattan and got to Steinhardt Publishers just before five.

The receptionist asked for my name, and I told her.

As she picked up the phone, I said, "I'm just supposed to drop this off."

She said, "I'll tell Honey you're here," and a moment later, out came Honey.

"Come on back," she said, taking the manuscript and my reader's report from me.

Incoherent with sleeplessness, I tried to apologize for wearing jeans.

She shook her head like I was a little crazy.

I sat in her office while she read my report. She tipped herself back in her chair and her eyes widened as she read. Then she laughed.

I hadn't made any jokes in my report.

She laughed and laughed, and when she could speak, she told me Steinhardt was publishing *The Wives of Armonk.*

"Oh," I said. "Sorry."

She said, "No." Then she asked me when I could start.

. . . . .

When I gave my grandmother the news, she said, "How much are they paying you, if you don't mind me asking?"

The salary was very low, and I didn't want to say the number out loud. Instead, I told her what my father had told me: I was an apprentice, learning a craft.

She turned her head to one side.

I was too tired and too happy to let this bother me. I said, "Maybe I'll cook you dinner one night before I go."

She said, "That's nice," but I could see she didn't care for the idea.

She sat down with me on the sofa, where I was splayed out in my exhausted bliss.

She said, "I bet you'll be happy to leave your old grandma."

"No," I said. "No." *Yes, yes,* I thought in the cadence of an Armonk wife, *oh, Lord . . . yes.*

When she began to ask me about Josh, I said, "Listen, Mamie." I looked at her, old lady to old lady, and said, "I don't want to talk about my romantic life." It occurred to me that *romantic life* was the phrase you'd use if you didn't have one; for a moment, I went back to the night when I'd faked a date with Josh and wandered around midtown in the rain.

"Why," she said, "if you don't mind me asking?"

"I don't know," I said. "It makes me feel bad."

She took one of my cigarettes and lit it. She puffed but didn't inhale. It reminded me of a picture she had of herself with my grandfather in a nightclub. They were sitting at a big round table, and she was wearing a shiny dress and lipstick.

"I'm trying to tell you how life is," she said.

I said, "Things have changed, though." I tried to make my voice sound certain. "Things are different."

"How?" she said.

I thought of the professor who taught Introduction to Women's Studies at Rogers and tried to think of some sure, smart thing she would say. Instead, I remembered that she'd broken her foot and even once the cast came off she walked with a cane. For some reason, this seemed to weaken my case. "Women have careers now," I said. "We don't care as much about, you know, men."

"Is that so?"

I wanted to give her a specific example of my new modern relationship with Josh, but all I could think of was that we split the check. It was his idea, an offshoot of the principle that everything should be equal between us. When the check came, Josh divided it, calculating how much more my soda and coffee were. He himself drank only water.

"Anyway," I said, "I don't want to talk about it."

She got up from the sofa and went to the kitchen. In a few minutes my dinner was set out.

I said, "Thank you."

"You're welcome."

For the first time, she didn't sit down with me or hover nearby. She turned on the television and pretended to watch it.

The chicken was undercooked; it was pink inside. I considered putting it back in the oven, but I didn't. I got up from the table and hid the chicken underneath other garbage in the pail. I cleared my dishes and washed them, without any protest from her.

"I'm going to take a walk," I said.

She said, "Have a good time."

I went across the street to the pizza place and ordered a slice. I sat there eating it under fluorescent lights. The only other diners were an old man and a young couple with a child who whined. They didn't seem unhappy or happy. It was impossible to learn anything from looking at them.

Sitting there, I thought of my grandmother saying, *I only want what's best for you,* and I knew that if I could get myself to believe this

I'd feel better about her and myself. But like everything else I was supposed to think, it didn't feel true.

. . . . .

Robert called to congratulate me on my job and asked if I'd have dinner with him and Naomi. Jack was coming, too. "Bring Josh if you want to," Robert said.

When I mentioned the invitation to Josh, he said that he was at a critical stage with a poem, but if the dinner was important to me he'd go.

He seemed to be stating a principle of his, though I wasn't sure exactly what it was and didn't ask. Lately, his principles had begun to feel like bars on a cage I was supposed to fit inside.

I said, "It's not important."

. . . . .

At Robert's, Naomi gave me a hug, and I thought, *Is all forgiven?* In the kitchen, I saw that Robert's MEAT and MILK labels were still on the drawers and cabinets.

There were only four places set at the table, so I knew Cynthia wasn't coming, and Jack himself came late. He walked in tired and full of jokes about what he called "the shoot."

I asked him what the movie was about, and he said that the shoot was for a commercial.

"I thought you made movies," I said.

He said that commercials were the company's bread and butter.

Robert and Naomi had cooked a big dinner, a lamb stew and some mushy starch that was supposedly Middle Eastern and made me think the two of them and my grandmother could benefit from a cooking lesson from Cynthia.

Robert kept smiling at me in what felt like the private way of our pre-Naomi past. I thought maybe he was proud of me for finally getting a job.

I mentioned that my new boss was an old girlfriend of Jack's.

Jack said, "How did you know that?"

I said, "She wouldn't stop talking about you."

Robert sounded like a little boy when he said, "Were you nice to her?"

Jack said, "I satisfied her needs"—I think to mortify Naomi.

But Naomi stood up to him; she said, "How do you mean, Jack?"

At dessert, Robert came out with a bottle of champagne.

I thought it was sweet of him to celebrate my job, and I was about to say so when he held up his glass and announced his engagement to Naomi.

I made my mouth smile, say, "Wow," and kiss them both.

It was hard not to feel happy for Robert, though, since he seemed so happy for himself. It reminded me of the way he'd looked in the mirror when I'd helped him get ready for his prom.

Seeing himself in his tuxedo, he'd said, "Good, right?"

. . . . .

Jack and I walked out together and down Broadway.

I had keys to Josh's apartment; I was supposed to meet him there after dinner. I knew he was probably already home from the library, but when Jack asked if I needed to rush off to Ovid I said that I didn't.

We went to a bar on Broadway, and Jack ordered scotch for both of us. I pulled out a cigarette, and Jack took my matches and struck one for me. We sat there with our drinks and didn't talk at first, which felt nice.

"Well," he said, "there goes our little boy."

I remembered Jack saying, *What happens between me and Cynthia is between me and Cynthia,* so I hesitated before saying, "What's wrong with Cynthia?"

He said, "There's not a thing wrong with that woman."

"I mean, why didn't she come?"

He thought for a moment. Then he told me that he'd suspected Robert's announcement. "I think Cynthia wants to get married."

"Oh," I said. "Do you want to marry her?"

He said, "I am giving it some very serious thought," but the way he said it made me think he wasn't.

I remembered my father's speech about what Jack was capable of and wasn't; he'd said, *It has nothing to do with how much Jack loves you.* I thought about all the girls he'd stopped loving; it was like he had a timer, and at a certain point it just buzzed.

I said, "Does she say she wants to get married?"

"She's from Alabama," he said. "She doesn't talk like that."

"So, how do you know?"

"She's thirty-two," he said.

"That sounds like something Grandma would say."

"Which one?" he said.

I knew he was just dodging the topic, but I answered anyway. "Mamie. Obviously."

We'd finished our scotches and he raised his hand to the bartender; I thought he was going to signal for the check, but he pointed to our glasses: *Another round.*

Then he laughed, and his mood got about a hundred pounds lighter. "I can't believe you're going to work for Honey Zipkin."

I said, "What happened with you two?"

"Not what she wanted to happen."

"Meaning?"

He said, "I didn't fall in love with her."

. . . . .

I let myself into Josh's apartment. I was a little drunk. I stood in the hall waiting for the bathroom for a long time before I figured out that the door was just closed and no one was inside.

When I got into bed beside Josh, I put my arms through his and kissed the back of his neck.

"You smell like a bar," he said.

I thought, *You smell like a library.* But I wanted to have sex right then, so I said, "You smell like a poem."

. . . . .

"I'm trying to think of Naomi as Robert's first wife," I said to Josh. We were having breakfast at La Rosita.

He looked at me with something like disapproval, and I was surprised to feel disapproval right back at him.

"That was a joke," I said.

"But you don't like her."

"I don't like her yet," I said. "But maybe I will."

"I think you should at least pretend to like her," he said. "She's going to be a member of your family."

I was getting that caged feeling again. But right then I saw my key. When the check came, I said, "This is on me."

. . . . .

Jack told me about the apartment, a walk-up above a cigar store on Thirty-third Street. Maura Edwards had made documentaries all over the world; now she was going to New Jersey to have a baby and needed to sublet her apartment.

When I met her at the apartment, she was eight months' pregnant, and her skin was waxy and pale. She said, "You're on time," but her intonation said, *You're late.*

She said the apartment was her refuge and spoke of it with more affection than she did either the boyfriend she was moving in with or the baby she was about to have. Her voice was almost loving when she said that the apartment had no bugs. A gecko she'd brought back from Brazil ate them. He lived in the walls.

Even by New York standards the apartment was tiny, and the few pieces of furniture were child-sized, which made the apartment feel like a dollhouse—or doll cell—though the intention was obviously to make the apartment seem bigger. What made the apartment seem smaller was that everywhere, on every surface, were vases and sculptures, tchotchkes galore.

She seemed deflated when I agreed to the terms of the sublet: It might last a month or a year, she said; she might want to use the apartment herself sometimes, and if she did she'd give me twenty-four hours' notice and a rent reduction.

Since it was an illegal sublet, I was to make myself as invisible as possible. If anyone asked, I was her sister. I couldn't receive mail here, and I would have to forward hers.

I said, "No problem," and explained that I could easily send it from my office, which was just a few blocks away.

She wasn't listening. She was resigned now, showing me how to work the answering machine, though a moment later she asked me never to touch it. She played the outgoing message she'd recorded, which was in English first and Spanish second and gave her phone number in New Jersey. She seemed to be concentrating as she listened to her own voice, as though it might have something important to tell her.

She was more sure of herself than anyone I'd ever met, except maybe my father. You could tell that she'd gotten camera crews on overbooked flights all over the world and knew when to stand up to a customs official and when to offer a bribe. Her voice was full of certainty, even when she said, after good-bye, "I have no idea what I'm doing."

. . . . .

I put my typewriter way in the back of my grandmother's closet. It took up a lot of room, but she didn't have many shoes. I promised that I'd come back for it soon. "I'll borrow Jack's car," I said, even though he'd never lent it to me and I doubted that he would.

I was putting my bags by the door when my grandmother said, "You're a modern girl in every way."

I wasn't too sure about that, but I thanked her. "Well, roomie," I said.

She looked upset, and I thought that maybe she'd heard my "roomie" as *roomy,* as in big and fat, so I said, "Roomie as in roommate."

Her face didn't change.

I was happy, and maybe it made her see how unhappy I'd been living with her. Or, knowing that her life lectures hadn't stuck, maybe she was envisioning my impending spinsterhood.

She double-sighed, and in a voice that sounded as sad as she looked, she said, "The world is your oyster."

I'd heard the expression, of course, and I knew it was supposed to refer to pearls to come. But it made me think of an actual oyster, and picturing the hard gray shell and the slimy animal inside, I thought, *My world* was *like an oyster, but not anymore.*

4.

At 375 Madison Avenue, Steinhardt Publishers occupied three floors of a building that had once been grand. Like a faded beauty trying to conceal her age, the lobby was lit dimly; your eyes acknowledged the gold-domed ceiling and marble walls without really seeing them. The red exit sign glowed like a night-light.

I worked on the floor the elevators called 14, though it came right after 12. My desk was one of five in a makeshift secretarial pool we called the Cave, short for Bat Cave. Floor-to-ceiling file cabinets blocked all sunlight; the shredding carpet was variegated with the splash patterns of spilled coffee.

I shared the Cave with three girls and one Boy Wonder, Adam, whom I adored. He was the kind of man who might've fished Zelda Fitzgerald out of the fountain at the Plaza, draped his cashmere coat around her shoulders, never asked for it back, and never told anyone the story. He was slight, with a hairline well into recession even at twenty-two, but his character was so impeccable, his manner so graceful, that even then, when I saw him every day, I thought of him as tall and strikingly handsome.

With endless patience, he answered all my questions, even those I was too embarrassed to ask. This was lucky, as I was scared of Bettina, who'd already acquired a novel; once a week or so she'd shush us and announce, "I'm calling my author." Sue, a broad-backed workhorse from Minnesota, was perpetually on the phone with her boyfriend, a sophomore at what she called "the U." When they argued, as they often did, she didn't talk at all; she was a silent fumer. The phone wedged between her ear and shoulder, she typed letters and logged manuscripts, waiting for her boyfriend to grow up.

I sat across from Francine Lawlor—our desks touched—but whole days went by without our eyes even meeting. She was pale and thin, with pale, thin hair and pale, thin lips she pursed. A dozen years earlier, she'd arrived at Steinhardt to learn that the editor she'd been hired to assist had been fired. During what should have been a brief bossless interim, a position had been created for her. Now she was thirty-three, and Floating Assistant was still her title.

. . . . .

My apartment was only seven minutes from Steinhardt, which gave me a fighting chance of being on time, though I usually wasn't. If Honey noticed, she didn't complain. She herself got to work practically at dawn, but her office, at the end of the Hall of Grown-ups, was the farthest from the Cave. If she wanted me, she called rather than walked down.

I opened her mail; I answered her phone; I typed her letters. Instead of asking me to read manuscripts, she said, "Take a look." Sent by lesser agents and friends of friends, these were the manuscripts she herself didn't want to read; early on, I understood that my job was to tell her that she didn't have to. A few weeks after she gave a manuscript to me, I'd return it to her with a typed rejection letter for her to sign. I used the language she herself used: "This story isn't quite compelling enough"; "The characters don't quite come alive"; or the ever-popular "This isn't quite right for our list," whatever that meant.

. . . . .

Those first weeks I worried about how to dress for work. I looked to my fellow Cave-dwellers for guidance.

Invariably, Adam wore a starched button-down Oxford-cloth shirt, khakis, and a black—not blue—blazer, his urbane twist on the classic ensemble.

Bettina had mastered the look of a bad girl from a good girls' school—a cashmere twinset with a miniskirt or a crisp little blouse slyly unbuttoned just enough to whisper, *Lacy bra.*

Sue favored fuzzy angora sweaters in Easter's palette.

Francine Lawlor alternated between two suits—one gray, the other a startling red-orange—and with them, she wore fluffy once-white blouses, the worst of which had a Louis XIV flap she decorated with a Phi Beta Kappa pin. She wore coffee-colored panty hose and navy blue pumps, low of heel, round of toe.

. . . . .

As floating assistant, Francine was supposed to help us when we were busy, but we never asked and she never offered.

Mostly, she devoted herself to slush, the unending supply of unsolicited manuscripts sent by authors. No one cared about slush except as carton upon carton of it narrowed the hall where the copier lived; no one appreciated Francine's work except as it widened the path.

. . . . .

One rainy lunch, Bettina decided we should take turns reading slush aloud. She opened a fresh carton and handed out a manuscript apiece to Adam, Sue, herself, and me.

It seemed rude to leave Francine out, so I asked if she wanted to read one.

She barely shook her head, so anathema was the idea to her.

Bettina laughed as she flipped through her manuscript and said, "I'll start." She read a sex scene from a wild Western, making her voice twangy for the cowboy, who hollers, "Ride me, baby bitch."

Adam read: " 'The witty journalists walked down Madison Avenue, where cabs swarmed like fireflies.' " He stood and raised his hand in imitation of hailing a taxi and called, "Firefly!"

Sue was about to read when her phone rang.

I got a dull thriller; every other paragraph began, "And then suddenly." Before reading, I happened to look over at Francine. Her face was stricken.

"Is this mean?" I said.

Bettina said, "Oh, shut up."

On principle, I returned the manuscript to the carton; the principle was I couldn't stand being told to shut up.

Adam backed me up, though: "She's right."

. . . . .

Bettina said that Francine lived in the Cave and went through our desks at night.

Adam said, "What makes you say that?"

"She's always the first in," Bettina said, "and always the last to leave."

"That's your proof?" he said.

Bettina didn't answer.

"Take it back," he said, and he kept saying it until she did.

But Francine did seem guilty of something, even if it was just hating the rest of us.

5.

AFTER ABOUT A MONTH, Honey came alive to my many failings, namely that I was slow—slow at reading, slow at typing, slow at understanding her directions—and her noticing how slow I was only made me slower.

A letter that would have previously taken me a morning to type now took an entire day, and looking over that letter, Honey remarked not only on how long it had taken me to do but how badly it was done; suddenly, she was anti-Wite-Out.

When she gave me a stack of manuscripts, she now told me when they were to be read by, and each "Monday" or "Wednesday" or "Friday" seemed to be a reprimand for how long I'd taken in the past.

One afternoon when I returned a manuscript to Honey, she read my rejection letter and looked up at me. "Why?" she said.

"Why . . . ?"

"Why isn't *Temple of Gossamer* right for our list?"

By then Adam had explained that "our list" meant the books Steinhardt published, though I had no idea what unified them, except that they were books I wouldn't want to read. By that criterion, *Temple of Gossamer* fit our list perfectly.

Usually impatient, Honey now seemed to have all of eternity to wait for my answer.

I said the only thing I could think of: "It's bad."

Honey turned the cover of the manuscript over and took a look for herself. I stood there while she read, not sure whether I was supposed to stay or go. Finally, she stopped reading and said, "Okay."

She told me that if I was having trouble keeping up with my reading or typing I could always ask Clarisse for help—Clarisse was what Honey called Francine.

I nodded, as though I was on my way to ask Clarisse for help right now.

. . . . .

One morning I opened Honey's mail to find a letter from a Jenny Ling, who said how nice it had been to talk to Honey; she'd enclosed her résumé, "as promised."

I felt like I'd caught my boyfriend flirting with another girl and reflexively threw the letter and résumé in the garbage.

Right away I was horrified at myself and fished them out.

I went down the hall, past the restrooms, supply closet, and mystery doors, and opened the one that led to the tiny balcony where Adam and I smoked cigarettes.

I smoothed out Jenny Ling's résumé. An editorial assistant only since June, Jenny had managed to acquire one novel and line edit two others she mentioned by name. She'd been the editor of a literary magazine at Yale, from which she'd graduated magna cum laude. Here, the résumé got a little repetitive—honors, honors, honors.

Her résumé put Lisa Michele Butler's to shame, but it was Jenny's cover letter that got to me: The girl claimed she could type sixty-five words per minute. I stared at that sixty-five until I finished smoking my cigarette, and went back to the Cave.

Adam must've seen how sick I felt; he looked at me for a long moment before turning to the crumpled papers I'd handed him.

He skimmed the résumé and letter and said, "I think Miss Ling will be fine without our help."

"I am going to Hell," I said.

"You're Jewish," he said. "You can't go to Hell."

I said, "You can if you're really assimilated."

I didn't throw the letter and résumé away; I couldn't. I filed them in my TO FILE file, where I put everything that I would figure out later; it was huge.

All that day I was so intent on avoiding Honey that I didn't realize she'd been avoiding me until she called. It was just after five. She said, "Can you come see me for a minute?"

I said, "Sure," which was what I always answered when I wanted to answer no.

After I hung up, I didn't move. It seemed possible that in a few minutes my life was going to change, and I wanted to stay on this side of it for as long as I could.

Adam was on the phone, going over copyediting changes with an author. In the tone of repeating what had just been said to him, he said: "Page one-forty-three, the penultimate paragraph, third line from the top, delete the comma."

As ever, Sue was on the phone, and I could tell by her posture—she was half lying on the desk—that she was crying. I knew this was not distress but joy: She always cried when her boyfriend admitted that he was a complete idiot.

It took me a second to register that Francine was looking at me. There might've been concern in her face, or maybe it was curiosity; she looked away too fast for me to tell.

Honey was on the phone, and I stood just outside her door, acknowledging myself as second fiddle to the fiddle she was talking to.

She said a Sweet 'n Low, "Have a good weekend," into the phone and a pesticidal, "Close the door, please," to me.

"Hi," I said.

She swiveled her chair sideways so she was facing the wall instead of me. I got her profile: *Honey in thought.*

"Sophie," she said, her eyes on the wall.

I waited. When she didn't say anything, I said, "Yes?"

"Sophie," she said again.

She swiveled face-front now and looked at me.

I nodded, *I'm ready.*

"I don't expect you to come in when I do," she said, and for the first time it occurred to me that she did. "But you come in later than anyone else," she said. "You're the last one in every day."

I did not nod.

She said, "Do you know what that says?"

I didn't; I didn't even know if it was a rhetorical question.

"You're telling Bettina and Sue and Adam and Clarisse that you're special."

I thought, *I'm not telling anyone anything unless I'm talking in my sleep.*

"You're telling Wolfe that you don't care about your job."

His full name was Bernard Wolfe, but no one called him Bernard or Bernie. Wolfe was quiet and humble and seemed less like an editorial director than a clerk in a used-record store. The prospect of him noticing me—even because I was late—was exciting, but I kept it off of my face, as I waited for Honey to tell me what my lateness told her.

She was rubbing her thumb and fingers together the way people usually do when they're miming money; she'd told me that handling books all day made her hands feel dirty, even if they looked clean. She was taking a good long look at me. "Why *are* you late every day?"

I panicked. I didn't really know why I was late. The only reason I could give was that I had trouble deciding what to wear. I tried to think of a reason that would make Honey say, *Well, why didn't you tell me before?* But what would that reason be? *I'm taking care of my aging parents? I have three small children? I'm blind?*

I said, "I'm sorry," and when it didn't seem to have any effect, I said it again.

Honey nodded, still waiting for an explanation. After another minute, though, she seemed to give up. She smiled at me then, and I had no idea why; it wasn't a genuine smile, or a happy one. I guessed that it meant, *Don't be afraid,* and I made myself smile back, *Okay.*

But my smile made hers disappear. "This is serious, Sophie."

I let my face become as grave as I felt. I said, "I will come in earlier."

. . . . .

I'd believed my vow in Honey's office, but reporting back to my sympathizers in the Cave, I knew I couldn't change for Honey.

"You'll just come in earlier," Sue said. In her face I could see both the weariness of her daylong phone fight and relief at its resolution.

"What difference does it make what time you come in?" Bettina said, picking up the phone to make a call. "She is such a bitch."

Francine had stopped typing, and Adam and I noticed at the same moment. She immediately started up again, probably typing, *zzuuwwxxyy.*

Adam said one word to me and that was: "Cocktail."

. . . . .

He took me to a hotel bar with murals painted by Ludwig Bemelmans, the author and illustrator of the *Madeline* books I'd grown up with.

Adam ordered a martini for himself and one for me, the first of my life. While I sipped, he came up with lines in the cadence of the *Madeline* books:

In the middle of the night,
Honey Zipkin turns on the light,
It's time for work, and sneakers on,
she braves the day and Wolfe and dawn.

I felt better; then I remembered Honey saying, *Why* are *you late?*

Adam saw the change in my face and told me to try not to take Honey's behavior personally; he'd seen her pull this with another assistant. "She found fault with everything the poor girl did," he said. "Sheila."

"Was she fired?"

"Not exactly," Adam said. "She didn't come back from lunch."

"Then what?"

"Then nothing," he said. "Sheila was . . . troubled."

I said, "I am troubled."

He smiled and shook his head.

I wanted to be like Adam, and yet after a few sips of my second martini, I said a sloppy, "I suck at being an editorial assistant."

"You lack artifice," he said. "You lack the instinct to be a good slave."

This wasn't a bad way to think about it, but it didn't take me off Honey's hit list. I asked if he'd ever had trouble with his boss.

"Lord, no," he said. "But Wolfe is Wolfe and Honey is Honey."

Adam insisted on paying the check. Outside he said, "Shall I put you in a firefly?"

. . . . .

I met Josh at the Paris Theater. I was late, but no matter: The movies Josh wanted to see were the ones no one else did; we had the theater almost to ourselves.

I could tell by the quick kiss he gave me and the way he drew back that he was annoyed—either at my lateness or at the martini on my breath. He was quiet, which was his way of saying I'd done him wrong.

Afterward, we walked toward the subway, not holding hands.

It was January, and Josh and I were pale and cold, and it seemed to me just then that our lives were smaller than they had to be. We were a check split down the middle.

He was unlocking the door to his apartment when he said, "I wish you'd be on time."

I thought, *Who doesn't?*

I knew I was supposed to say I was sorry, but I'd already used up my *I'm sorry* allowance for the day.

In bed, he switched off the light and turned to the wall, away from me. Once my eyes adjusted to the dark, I saw that he'd put his second pillow on top of his head, like a sandwich, to drown out the sounds of the city so he could sleep.

I lay there thinking that I did not deserve this punishment. I'd only been a few minutes late, and early enough to see all the previews of the movies I didn't want to see and, with the way things were going, never would.

Then I thought of him waiting outside the Paris. He'd probably looked at his watch about a hundred times. Maybe he'd worried about me. As he waited, he might've wondered if I cared about him.

When I looked over at him, he'd taken the pillow off his head and was lying open-faced.

I said, "I'm sorry," and hearing myself say these words made me feel better.

. . . . .

I worried all weekend about being late on Monday. I didn't stay over at Josh's Sunday night because I was afraid I wouldn't be able to sleep, which was what happened at my own apartment.

I was awake at two A.M. and then three and then four, thinking how much slower and dumber I'd be the next day.

I woke up at eleven.

I knew everyone was still in the editorial meeting, where I should've been, but I called Honey's line and then Adam's, and each time the call was bounced to Irene at reception; when she answered, "Steinhardt," I hung up.

I took a shower; I made coffee; I hyperventilated.

Just before noon, Adam answered: "Editorial."

"I overslept," I said.

"I am going to hang up now," he said, "and walk down the hall to tell Honey that your grandmother died."

. . . . .

I got to work early on Tuesday; only Francine beat me. So I knew that she was the one who'd turned on my tensor lamp, simulating my early arrival, as she would every day from then on. She was eating a butter sandwich that she'd brought from home, and when she looked up I thanked her with my face, and she nodded.

Honey came down to the Cave a little while later.

She half sat on the edge of my desk and said, "This was the grandmother you stayed with?"

I couldn't lie into her eyes, so I lowered my head, as though in grief. "Uh-huh."

It seemed possible that my lie would bring on my grandmother's death. For a moment I felt like she had died, and I wished I'd been nicer to her in her lifetime. I thought, *She only wanted what was best for you.*

Honey said, "I'm so sorry, Sophie."

I said, "Thank you."

When I looked up, Francine was trying to conceal a smile, the first I'd ever seen.

. . . . .

By Thursday, Honey and I were back to normal.

She handed me a paper-clipped wad of receipts so I could compile her expense report to send to our business office in New Jersey; she said, "I want this to go out in the noon pouch."

I said, "I will do it right away." Everything I said to her now sounded like a written pledge.

I did do it right away and as fast as I could. I put all the slips in chronological order, hailing taxi receipts for every lunch and dinner and drink date and copying them all onto the request-for-reimbursement form. Bettina was away from her desk, so I couldn't ask to borrow her calculator; I did my own math.

When I returned to Honey's office, she was on the phone but, seeing the form in my hand, motioned me in and signed it.

I took the form down to Wolfe's office for his signature.

His door was open, but all I could see were his long, long legs, stretched way, way out onto the coffee table. Wolf was about nine feet tall and one inch thick; basically, he was flat.

I knocked on the door, and he told me to come in. He had a manuscript on his lap.

I said, "Hey."

He said, "Hey, Sophie," with warmth I'd never heard from him before.

He reminded me of someone Jack might've been friends with in high school. I could picture teenaged Wolfe walking past my childhood bedroom and saying, *Hey, Sophie,* like I might be someone he'd want to talk to if he didn't have a gig playing air guitar to a Jimi Hendrix record upstairs with my brother.

I stood there while he looked over Honey's expenses.

He had music playing on his stereo, and I recognized *Kind of Blue,* which Jack had given me for my birthday.

I said, "That's my favorite jazz tape," though as soon as I said, *jazz tape,* I worried that I'd given myself away as someone who owned only one.

He said, "Want to listen to it at lunch?"

"Okay," I said, cool as a jazz aficionado.

He signed the form, handed it back to me, and said he'd order sandwiches in for us, and what kind did I want?

I said, "What're you having?"

He thought a minute, in imitation of making a large decision, and said he would order turkey on pumpernickel with tomato and onion and Russian dressing.

"Two," I said.

"Pickles?"

I said, "Obviously."

I went back to my desk and sat there, feeling better than I had in weeks. I'd been waiting for something good to happen to me, and here it was. After Wolfe called to tell me that our turkeys had arrived, I didn't hurry to his office; I took a minute to appreciate the full pleasure and anticipation of what I was about to do. Walking down the hall, I thought, *You are walking down the hall to Wolfe's office for lunch.*

He was taking our sandwiches out of the bag.

He said, "Come on in," at the same time he picked up the phone and dialed, which was what Honey did; *Come in and sit here while I talk on the phone.*

But Wolfe was calling Irene; he told her that he was going into a meeting and to hold his calls, please.

After he hung up, he said, "You have something to read?"

"Right," I said.

When I returned with a manuscript, Wolfe was sitting on the sofa, his sandwich set out on the coffee table; mine was on the desk. Was I supposed to sit on the sofa beside him or in one of the chairs opposite his desk? *Sofa or chair, sofa or chair?*

I sat down on the chair.

He put on the record, and went back to the sofa and put his feet up on the coffee table. "Put your feet up, if you want to." That was the last thing he said. When I turned around, he was reading.

I did the same. I stopped only to lift my head as though appreciating the nuances of the music.

When the first side of the record finished, he walked over to the stereo, saying, "You know, Miles recorded this in a single session."

I said, "You're kidding," though it hadn't occurred to me that any record took more than one session.

I was noticing the picture on his desk. It was a girl who looked like him, just as skinny, with his bulging eyes and kindling for arms, except she wore her hair in braids. She had only one boot on and was reaching for the other and laughing. There were mountains in the background, and she was sitting by a campfire.

Before he picked up his manuscript again, I said, "Who's the happy camper?"

He didn't answer right away, and I worried that I'd made a mistake. It was wrong to talk while the music was playing or wrong to ask personal questions.

"That's my sister." He hesitated. "Juliet."

I didn't know what to say, and I considered saying nothing, and later wished I had. "Where does she live?"

He seemed to think for a minute; I thought maybe he was trying to remember her address. Then he shook his head.

I was about to say, "I'm sorry"; the words were forming in my mouth at the exact moment that I heard them come out of his.

He said, "I'm sorry about your grandmother, Sophie."

. . . . .

I took Friday off for the funeral.

I slept late, and spent the day reading two manuscripts I'd brought home with me. Honey had marked them "Wednesday," and I wondered if when I turned them in on Monday she'd think I was two days early or realize that I was five late.

All that afternoon I worried about work and Honey, and it spread over to Josh. I hadn't told him how much trouble I was in, which made me feel that I was lying to him, which made me feel that he loved me under false pretenses, which made me feel that he did not really love me.

It was because I felt so tenuously loved that I arrived at the restaurant almost a half an hour early. It was a beautiful French bistro, tiny and charming, with big windows, a piano, and a thousand candles; the candlelight seemed to dapple to the music. This restaurant was about ten times nicer than any of the others we'd gone to, and it occurred to me that Josh must be very proud of a new poem.

He was so surprised that I was early that he lifted me off the ground to kiss me—or rather, I felt lifted off.

All through dinner, I could see how happy Josh was. We'd be talking, and then satisfaction would appear on his face and stay there: I imagined him thinking, *This steak is delicious, and also I think this is my best poem.*

He seemed so excited that I thought he might not wait until dessert to read his poem. But he did wait. We ate everything and sopped up the sauces with bread, so that our plates were shiny when we'd finished.

When the waitress cleared them, Josh asked her to wrap up our leftovers, and she smiled.

He held my hand and leaned over the table and kissed me. When he said, "You're so beautiful," I heard, *My poem is so beautiful.*

I was a little nervous, as I always was, that I wouldn't like his new poem—or rather, that I wouldn't be able to pretend to love it.

"Well," I said, "are you going to read it to me?"

"Read what?" he said.

It was our six-month anniversary.

. . . . .

I went to bed happy, but I woke up in the middle of the night. "What's the matter?" Josh said.

"I'm worried about my job," I said.

"Don't worry," he said.

I got up. I wandered around the dark, cavernous apartment and then went outside to the stairwell.

I smoked one cigarette, and then another.

I tried to pinpoint the problem. To myself, in the stairwell, I said, "Honey doesn't like me."

This brought back third grade, when I'd handed my father my report card and said, "Miss Snell doesn't like me." He'd said that my excuse disappointed him more than my grades.

Even though I knew that my father might be disappointed in me now, I also felt that he was the only one who could tell me what to do. But even wanting to call my father made me feel younger than I was supposed to be.

I tried to think of what he would say. It would be along the lines of, *Soon you'll find a job and get your own apartment.* What he said would be simple and even obvious, so I tried to think what the simple, obvious thing was.

I got it almost right away, along with the sensation that always came with my father's advice: *How could I not have known?*

I would have to work harder.

. . . . .

In the morning, when Josh asked if I wanted to go to the Met, I told him I needed to go in to the office. He went to the library for a bonus session of poetry writing.

At 375 Madison, I signed in with the guard in the lobby, and I saw that Francine Lawlor had signed in, too, at nine A.M.

She was sitting at her desk when I walked in, and, except for saying hello to me, she acted like it was a regular workday. From her waist up, it was: She had on a fluffy blouse and her orange-red jacket. When she stood, I saw that she was wearing jeans and sneakers—Wranglers cuffed over Keds.

I worked all day Saturday and went in again on Sunday. I made copies of a manuscript Honey wanted to hand out in Monday's editorial meeting; I typed all the letters she'd left for me on Friday. I made a neat pile of them, along with letters for the manuscripts to be rejected. I figured out what to do with everything in my TO FILE file; I recrumpled Jenny Ling's résumé and letter and threw them away.

I removed every piece of paper from my desk, and now I saw what was underneath: *20th-Century Typewriting.* I put it in a padded envelope and addressed it to the Surrey Free Library and left it in my OUT box.

Then I turned off my tensor lamp and said a fond farewell to Francine.

In the lobby, I signed out. The guard was doing a find-the-word puzzle in the newspaper. He was drawing what looked like a long worm around a word when I told him my name and asked for his. It was Warren. We shook hands.

It was dark outside, and cold. But the air felt good. I had worked hard and now it was over. I was tired and happy, a friend to guards and a worker in the workforce, and in the morning my boss would discover that even though I hadn't been the editor of the Yale literary magazine or received honors, honors, honors, even though I hadn't acquired a novel or edited two, I was the best editorial assistant in New York, and possibly the world.

6.

IT TOOK HONEY a few weeks to believe that my vast improvement was not a joke I was playing on her.

I went into the office every Saturday. At first, Francine and I hardly talked, except for hello and good-bye, and when I was going out I'd tell her what I was getting—a sandwich, a soda, a bagel—and ask if she wanted anything from the outside world; she never did.

Then, one Saturday, I asked her if she wanted coffee, and she said, "I just made a fresh pot."

I heard this as both an offer and a test; I said, "Do you mind if I have some?"

She said, "Of course not."

Our coffeemaker was just outside the conference room. During the week a pot was always on the burner, but only the truly desperate drank it. I poured myself a cupful and spooned in some nondairy powdered creamer.

Back at the Cave, I took a sip and tasted thousands of pots of coffee that had burned themselves into black bitterness; I tasted the burner itself.

After that first sip I sipped only for show, not letting the coffee enter my mouth; I smoked the peace pipe without inhaling.

It gave me the courage to ask Francine a question: "Where are you from?"

"Pennsylvania."

I said, "I'm from Pennsylvania," though usually I said that I was from Philadelphia, since Surrey was only a half-hour away.

"You're not from where I'm from," she said.

"Where are you from?"

She said, "You've never heard of it."

I waited.

"Lesher," she said.

I said, "I think I've heard of Lesher," though I hadn't. "Do your parents still live there?"

She seemed to be considering whether to answer me. "They're old."

"Oh." I didn't know what to say. "That's a drag."

. . . . .

For a while that's how it was: I'd ask Francine questions, and she'd grudgingly answer them. Where did she live? Carteret, New Jersey. Who was her favorite writer? Theodore Dreiser. Where had she gone to college? Ursinus.

It wasn't until the weekend after Bettina's promotion was announced that Francine talked. I came in late that Saturday afternoon, and she said, "I was wondering when you'd show up," the closest she had come to any familiarity. Was it a joke? In case it was, I smiled.

Once I was settled in, she said, "I can't believe Bettina got promoted."

"Yeah," I said. "Why?"

"Well, for one thing," she said, "her knowledge of punctuation begins and ends with her own beauty mark."

I laughed, and she did, too. I'd never heard her laugh before; it was a *k-k-k-k* sound, dry, like tiny twigs snapping.

. . . . .

"It's interesting to consider why an editor hires or promotes an assistant," she said one Saturday, handing me a cup of coffee from the pot she'd made.

"I know," I said, as though this was a thought I'd had myself.

"Mostly, it's narcissism," she said.

Then she was quiet, and I worried she was thinking about herself and why no editor had chosen her as a mirror. In case she was, I wanted to distract her. I said, "Why do you think Honey hired me?"

"I was just wondering about that," she said.

I hesitated before saying, "Honey used to go out with my brother."

Francine nodded. "That's perverse."

. . . . .

Francine rewrote the form letter that Steinhardt sent out with rejected slush manuscripts and asked me to proofread it for her.

"Is there anything you would change?"

I told her that signing "The Editors" above the typed "The Editors" looked a little strange to me.

"Strange?" she said, hating me for my word choice.

I tried to explain. "I mean 'the editors' is so anonymous I'm not sure you want to sign it."

She nodded, but her lips were still pursed from my *strange.*

I said, "Why don't you just sign your name?"

I could see she'd agonized over this question; it worried me how much thought she devoted to slush. "Then I'd have to use my title," she said.

"I think that's okay."

She said, "If I'd spent a decade writing a novel, I don't think I'd want to have it rejected by a floating assistant."

"Well," I said, "then the author could say, 'Yeah, well, what the fuck does she know? She's just a fucking floating assistant.' "

I was afraid I'd offended her with my *fuck* and *fucking,* but when I turned around she was smiling to herself. Maybe she liked the idea that her low status could serve a noble purpose.

. . . . .

I noticed that she was deep into a manuscript, and I asked her if it was good.

She said, "It is frightfully bad."

She appeared to be about four hundred pages in, so I said, "Why do you keep reading it?"

She said, "Every author deserves a chance."

. . . . .

I helped Francine push another carton of slush from the copier to her desk. As she pulled out the first manuscript, I saw her face: It was full of hope.

It hadn't occurred to me until that moment that Francine wanted anything more than what I wanted—not to get fired. But I'd been wrong: Francine was ambitious. She was looking for her promotion in those cartons.

She was no Honey and she knew it; she wasn't going to get a great manuscript messengered to her after a fancy lunch with a big-deal agent. No, Francine would have to read page after page, manuscript after manuscript, carton after carton to find the novel that would make her promotion indisputable.

It seemed impossible to me. I didn't think there was a publishable novel in any of those cartons, much less a great one. Even if there was, how could Francine ever find it, reading, as she did, all the pages of all those manuscripts?

I kept thinking that as her friend I should tell her so. In my head, I practiced speeches I would give her; they were gentle, full of praise but also reality.

. . . . .

Francine and I never talked in front of the other Cave-dwellers. The few times I tried, she just shook her head. I thought she was trying to protect me—maybe from Bettina—but it wasn't that. I think she wanted to distinguish herself from the rest of the assistants; I think she was trying to see herself as an editor whose paperwork had just been held up.

So I was surprised one Friday afternoon when I looked up from my typewriter, and she was standing above me.

"Would you read something for me?" she said. "For the editorial meeting on Monday?"

"Sure," I said, and I realized that she thought she'd found the slush novel that would transform her career. I told her that she should probably give the manuscript to some editors to read, too.

Francine hesitated.

I said, "Their support is going to mean a lot more than mine."

She didn't answer.

"That's what I'd do," I said.

Then I figured out what her hesitation was, and I said, "I can ask Honey if you want."

She said, "I'll make another copy."

. . . . .

I caught Honey right before she left for the weekend. She was going to the country and had dressed for it. She wore a beautiful suede jacket and a full skirt and dark brown boots.

"I need a favor," I said.

She tilted her chin up at me.

I noticed that the novel was entitled *We* and its author named I. Tittlebaum, neither of which sounded too promising. I noticed, too, how heavy the manuscript was—i.e., long—and I realized what a big favor it was to ask Honey to read it over her weekend in the country.

When I repeated what I'd told Francine about Honey's opinion meaning more than mine, her expression said, *Obviously*, so I said, "Obviously."

"Sure," she said, "that's just how I want to spend my weekend." But she took it.

. . . . .

We was about the principal of a high school in New Jersey the year his French-teacher wife leaves him and their children, and it was so great

I forgot that I was reading the novel as a favor. I read *We* all weekend and I was still reading it at 3 A.M. Sunday night.

Sometimes the editorial meeting started late or was postponed until the afternoon, and this was what I prayed for when I woke up at 9:45. I left the apartment without even brushing my teeth.

Not everyone looked up at me when I walked into the conference room; Honey didn't. Francine was sitting beside her at the table. I sat with the other assistants along the wall.

There was a huge stack of copies of *We* in front of Honey, and her Post-it note was still on top of the original. Without reading the note I knew it asked me to make however many copies were now beneath it.

The editors went clockwise around the table, talking about the novels and nonfiction they'd read and wanted to buy or pass on. Everyone tried to be fast, except one editor who liked to talk about all of her impressions.

Finally, it was Honey's turn. She began by just looking around the table until everyone was looking back at her. Then she said, "Francine Lawlor found this novel in the slush pile." I was relieved that she didn't call Francine "Clarisse."

Francine opened her mouth, and I thought she was going to take over but Honey went on.

Honey was a good saleswoman; she'd prepared an eloquent speech but made it sound like she was just talking to us. I noticed that while she compared I. Tittlebaum to the classic writers everyone admired, she compared *We* to books that had sold millions of copies.

She'd taken the liberty of calling I. Tittlebaum over the weekend to make sure that he hadn't sold the book to another publisher—he hadn't—and she went on to say what a wonderful man he was, and also that he was happy to change the book's title.

I was so captivated by her speech—everyone was—that at first I didn't notice the change in Francine's smile. It had been twitchy with excitement, but now it was frozen solid, and I understood why: Honey had made *We* her acquisition.

Honey apologized for the length of the novel; she said that she'd edit it down by a third.

This was the only shift I saw in Francine's expression; her eyes came to life for a second.

When Honey finished, she turned to Francine and said, "Is there anything you want to add?"

I admired the way Francine recovered. She tried to make her smile warm and said, "I hope you will all read this extraordinary novel."

I'd never spoken in an editorial meeting before, and it felt hard to now, especially without having brushed my teeth. But I wanted to do something to make *We* Francine's again.

I heard myself say, "Um," and saw heads at the table turn toward me.

Honey's look almost stopped me; it didn't show anything more than surprise, but it made me realize that she hadn't sanctioned my speaking in the meeting, which made whatever I said subversive.

Everyone was looking at me, waiting.

I thought of saying that Francine had read a thousand manuscripts to find this one, and that she'd read them with care and respect and all the way through. But I wasn't sure this was the speech I should give, and it was more than my mouth was capable of, anyway. "Francine asked me to read *We* over the weekend," I said. "And I loved it."

I could tell how slowly I'd said these words by how fast Honey cut me off: "Good," she said.

Then Francine passed out the manuscripts.

Back in the Cave, Bettina dropped hers on her desk and said, "Shit," at its heft.

Sue said, "Congratulations," to Francine, who said, "Thank you very much."

I went over to Francine and said, "I am so sorry."

Francine closed her eyes, and she kept them closed, and I knew suddenly that "I'm sorry" was the worst thing I could've said; she was trying to pretend that nothing bad had happened.

As fast as I could, I said, "I'm sorry you had to copy all those manuscripts instead of me."

She waited another minute to open her eyes and another to speak. "That's okay," she said. "I got the mail room to do it."

I wanted to ask if she'd seen Honey drop the manuscript off before the meeting, and if Honey had seemed mad that I hadn't been there. But it seemed wrong to worry about myself after what had happened to Francine, and I thought I'd find out soon, anyway.

I didn't, though. I didn't find out until Wednesday morning when I came in, and there was a message from Honey taped to the base of my tensor lamp.

The note said to call her, and I did.

She said, "Can you meet me in Wolfe's office?"

I said, "Sure."

. . . . .

Wolfe was sitting at his desk, and Honey stood at the window, too agitated to sit.

"Come on in," Wolfe said to me. "Have a seat."

I took the chair I'd sat in during my lunch with Wolfe.

He called Irene and asked her to hold his calls.

When Honey sat down next to me, I wanted to stand up and go to the sofa. But I stayed where I was.

She faced me, her hands clasped like Act One of the hand play *This Is the Church.*

As it turned out, Honey had gone to the Cave for the last three mornings and found my tensor lamp on, though I hadn't yet arrived. "It's the deception I mind," she said, and her voice was so angry that it trembled a little; for the first time it occurred to me that some of what she felt for me might belong to Jack.

I said, "I never asked anyone to turn my lamp on."

I worried that Francine would get in trouble because of me, but Honey moved on. Apparently it was not only the deception she minded. She went on about my lateness and the warning she'd given me and my promise to come in earlier.

She was building her case.

I looked at Wolfe: *Save me.*

But he was looking at Honey. In his face I saw that this meeting was distasteful to him.

He got up and went to the stereo. He spent a minute looking through his records, and I saw Honey roll her eyes. I realized that she didn't like Wolfe.

I wondered if he liked her. I hoped he didn't, but I knew it didn't matter. He was fair, like my father; even if Wolfe liked me more than he liked Honey, he would be on the side of the argument that was right, no matter whose it was. This was the way you were supposed to be at work, and it probably deepened my respect for him, though I couldn't feel that yet. What I felt was that he was not going to protect or defend me.

He put on *Kind of Blue*. I took this as a message from him to me, though I wasn't sure what it meant.

When he sat down again, he nodded at me.

"I *am* late almost every day," I said. "But I stay late to make up for it."

Wolfe's expression relaxed a little.

"I come in every weekend," I said.

No one spoke or moved for a minute.

Then Honey plopped down on the sofa as an adolescent might. This seemed to strengthen my case.

"Okay," Wolfe said to me, my signal to go. "Thanks."

I felt I'd won for the moment, if only in the impartial court of Judge Wolfe. For the first time in my life, I'd done my homework, and it made me feel strong and hardworking and virtuous, as I never had before; I felt impervious.

This lasted about thirty seconds, until I got back to the Cave and realized what I'd done. Even if I'd won with Wolfe, I'd lost and lost big with Honey. I'd made my own boss look bad in front of hers, and it occurred to me that I was now in roughly double the trouble of lateness and deception, and I didn't know what punishment might come next.

Still, I didn't feel scared. I felt calm. I felt like I was beginning to understand something.

Across from me, Francine was reading a manuscript. She was more virtuous than I would ever be, she had done more homework than I would ever do, and here she was, buried in slush.

Adam, the embodiment of discretion, called me on the phone.

"Are you okay?" he said.

I told him that I was alive and unfired.

. . . . .

I. Tittlebaum drove in from New Jersey later that week.

Honey called and asked me to come down to her office to meet him. "Bring Clarisse," she said.

I said, "Francine."

Francine looked up at me.

I. Tittlebaum was taller than his name seemed to suggest, and much younger than the character in his novel. He couldn't possibly have teenaged children, and if his wife had left him, she'd come back or he'd found somebody else; he wore a wedding band.

Wolfe nodded at Francine and me, but he let Honey make the introductions. She said, "Irv, I want you to meet the assistant who found your book in the slush pile: Francine Lawlor."

For some reason, he reached out to shake my hand.

"No," I said, and my voice was louder than it should've been, because his thinking I was Francine, or wanting me to be, added insult to the injury of her not getting her due.

Honey's expression didn't change, though I was pretty sure she thought my faux pas had ruined her faux tribute.

"This is Francine," I said, though she was already shaking hands with the author.

She said, "It's a wonderful book, Mr. Tittlebaum."

He said, "Thank you," and in it you could hear that he was thanking her for everything, thanking her for more than Honey would've liked.

He stood there gazing at Francine until Honey nabbed the attention back. "And this is my assistant, Sophie Applebaum," she said, pronouncing my name like it was an important one for him to know.

I said, "Hi."

Wolfe said, "Francine, will you join us for lunch?"

"Thank you," she said, "but I have work to do."

. . . . .

Francine and I walked down the hall back to the Cave without talking. She stopped at her desk, but I knew that if I were in her place, I would need to cry—I felt like crying in my own place—so I said, "Come on," and led her out the back door and past the restrooms. Her eyes widened a little when I opened the door to the smoking balcony.

"I'm surprised it isn't locked," she said.

I said, "I know."

The sky was cloudy, with a pale sun. It was almost spring. I'd never seen Francine in natural light, and in the sun I saw now that her hair was more white than blond.

We were both looking out at the buildings, though there wasn't really anything to see. I was trying to think of something reassuring to say to her; I was trying to think of what I'd want someone to say to me.

But when I looked over, her face wasn't sad. If anything, she looked serene. Maybe she was remembering the grateful look I. Tittlebaum had given her. She might have just felt glad that she'd done her job well and found a good book for Steinhardt to publish. Or maybe she knew that in a few weeks Wolfe would promote her.

Whatever it was, I was relieved that she wasn't upset. It made me feel less guilty about giving *We* to Honey.

I took my pack of cigarettes out and offered one to her almost as a joke, but she took it. I lit it for her.

I thought she'd just hold it and take non-inhaling puffs like my grandmother, but she smoked like a smoker.

"You smoke?" I said.

"Yes," she said.

This cheered me up a little. It made me think that there might be other things I didn't know about this talented editor, Dreiser lover, Ursinus alumna, and citizen of Carteret, New Jersey. I hoped there were.

RUN RUN RUN RUN RUN RUN RUN RUN AWAY

WHEN MY BROTHER tells me he's been seeing a psychiatrist, I say, "That's great, Jack."

He says, "What—you think I'm fucked up?"

I say, "How'd you find him?"

He says, "What makes you think my psychiatrist is a man?"

Her name is Mary Pat Delmar, and Jack tells me she is brilliant. He says, "She blows me away," and I think they must be talking a lot about junior high.

"Wow," I say.

He smiles. "I told her you'd say that."

When he tells me how beautiful she is, I say, "But not so beautiful that you have trouble concentrating?"

"She's pretty beautiful," he says. Plus impressive: She won a scholarship to college, for example, and put herself through medical school; she grew up in rural Tennessee, where her parents still run a luncheonette.

I say, "She told you all that?"

"Yeah," he says. "Why?"

"I don't think of psychiatrists talking that much."

It's not until he tells me that they're not in Freudian analysis and breaks out laughing that I realize he's not in analysis at all. Mary Pat is his new girlfriend.

He laughs like a madman, and I say, "Very funny," though it is, in fact, very funny just to hear Jack laugh, as well as a huge relief: Our father died not even two months ago.

My eggs and Jack's pancakes are set before us, and we stop talking to eat; we're at Homer's, the diner around the corner from his apartment in the Village.

I ask how he met Mary Pat.

He tells me, "Pete referred her."

For a moment he gets waylaid talking about the fishing shack he helped Pete restore this summer. Pete lives year-round on Martha's Vineyard with his Newfoundland, Lila, who expresses her heartache by howling to Billie Holiday records: *Dog, you don't know the trouble I seen.*

Jack says Pete called when M.P. moved to town. "I think he's always been a little in love with her."

I say nothing; I have always been a little in love with Pete.

. . . . .

Though Jack didn't say he'd bring Mary Pat, I'm a little disappointed when he arrives at Homer's without her. "Just coffee," he says to the waiter.

He tells me that M.P. was mugged on her way home from work, and he was up half the night trying to calm her down.

"Jesus," I say, and ask where and when, and was there a weapon?

A knife; ten P.M.; a block from her apartment on Avenue D.

I say, "She lives on Avenue D?" D is for Drugs, D is for Danger, D is for Don't live on Avenue D unless you have to.

Jack says, "It's what she can afford."

"I thought psychiatrists cleaned up."

"Maybe in private practice," he says.

As Dr. Delmar, Mary Pat treats survivors of torture in a program at NYU Hospital.

From spending weeks at my father's bedside I have become alive to a level of pain I'd never known: Now I feel it on every street of Manhattan, in every column in the newspaper, and just the idea of someone who works to ease suffering eases mine.

I say, "When can I meet her?"

"Soon."

Sounding like a worried mother, I say, "She should take a cab when she works late."

"She says walking is her only exercise."

. . . . .

When I arrive at the White Horse, Jack says, "Want to sit outside?"

It's November. "Why would I want to sit outside?"

He tells me that M.P. will; after spending all day in the hospital, she craves fresh air. He takes off his leather jacket and hands it to me, an act of chivalry in the name of Mary Pat.

I give in. "You love this girl."

He howls a mock-forlorn, "I do," imitating a country singer or Newfoundland.

We maneuver our legs under a picnic table; we are the sole outsiders, and Jack has to go inside to get the waitress.

We both order scotch for warmth.

Jack yawns and tells me that he and Mary Pat were up most of the night, discussing his new screenplay. He tells me that her notes are incredibly smart, unbelievably smart—smarter than his actual screenplay.

It occurs to me that I have never heard him more sure of any woman and less sure of himself.

He catches sight of his dramaturge across the street, and I turn to look.

She is tall and skinny in high heels. She has long, wavy hair. Her cheeks are flushed, and when she sees Jack she smiles, activating dimples.

Her hand is limp in mine, her voice shivery as she says, "Pleased to meet you."

She kisses Jack full on the mouth and then says she thinks she's coming down with something; do we mind sitting inside?

Once we're seated, I pretend, as I always do with Jack's girlfriends, that I already like her: I tell her that I can hardly sit in high heels, let alone walk in them, and how does she do it?

"I don't know," she says.

Jack puts his hand across her forehead, and his eyebrows slant up in worry. "You have a fever."

"If you're sick," I say, "we can have dinner another night."

"No, no," she says. "I like a fever." Her smile is wan, her skin shiny. "You know, through the glass darkly."

I do not know; I'm not even sure I've heard her correctly. Her voice is so quiet I strain just for fragments.

We pick up our menus.

"I'm going to have a cheeseburger and fries," I say.

Jack says, "Same here."

Mary Pat says, "I don't think I can eat a whole one myself."

"You can share mine," he says.

"You don't mind?"

My brother, who usually slaps my hand if I take one of his fries, does not mind.

When our burgers arrive, Mary Pat ignores the extra plate brought for sharing and eats right off Jack's. Instead of cutting the cheeseburger in half, she takes a bite, and then he does. She even uses his napkin to wipe her mouth. I am reminded of the aid organization Doctors Without Borders.

"Jack told me that you met through Pete," I say.

"Oh, yes." She says, "He warned your brother about me," and the two of them seem to think this is funny.

I play along—ha, ha, ha: "What did he say?"

Jack asks Mary Pat, "What did he say?"

She says, "I'm trouble?" her voice so lush with sex, I think, *Hey, M.P., I'm right here, Jack's little sister, across the table.*

Her body reacts to the smallest shift in his; they are in constant bodily contact. She doesn't touch Jack directly, but rubs herself against him almost incidentally, like a cat. The one time he reaches for her hand, she lets him hold it for less than a minute; then she takes it back and hides it in the dark under the table.

Maybe because of her whispery voice or her ethereal skinniness or her glass-darkly fever, Mary Pat gives the impression of not quite being here at the table, here at the White Horse, here on Earth. To assure myself of my own existence, I counter her quiet voice by raising mine, counter her little bites by taking big ones.

I try to talk to her, but it is just me asking questions and her answering them. My questions get longer, her answers shorter. Still I don't quit. I'm like a gambler who keeps thinking, *Maybe the next hand.*

The name of her parents' luncheonette? Delmar's.

The division of labor? Her father cooks; her mother serves.

If we were at Delmar's now, we'd order . . . ? "Meat 'n' Two."

I say, "Meat and two?"

"One meat and two sides."

I love sides; I ask which are best.

"Butter beans," she says. "Grits, if you like grits."

I nod the nod of a grits liker, though not a single grit has ever entered my mouth. I say, "Did you hang out at the luncheonette a lot growing up?"

"Yes."

I say, "Was it fun?"

"No," she says, making clear that she doesn't want to talk about this or to talk to me or to talk. She says, "Excuse me," and goes to the ladies' room.

"What?" I say to Jack.

He says, "She can't talk about her father."

"Were we talking about her father?"

When she returns, Jack puts his arm around her.

I say, "I didn't mean to pry."

Mary Pat says a wounded, "Don't worry about it."

. . . . .

Jack does not call to ask what I think of Mary Pat, as he has with every other girlfriend he has ever introduced to me. He doesn't call at all.

When I call him, he is in bed with a fever of 103.

I offer to bring him soup, and he says that he has soup and juice and everything he needs—left over from when he took care of Mary Pat.

. . . . .

A week later, when I call to ask if we're meeting at Homer's, he's still in bed.

He says that his fever is down; he just doesn't feel good.

I say, "What's the matter, Buddy?" our father's nickname for Jack.

"She hated my revision."

"What?"

"I told you she gave me notes on my script," he says. "She said I didn't understand anything."

I say, "You want me to come over?"

"Yeah," he says, and I go.

His night table is a mess of drugs—NyQuil, DayQuil, Sudafed, Theraflu—a sticky dose cup, a mug, and a tea bag that looks like a mouse in rigor mortis. His bed is covered with screenplay pages and used Kleenexes, which, he says, are of equal value to Mary Pat.

"Does she know that your father died nine weeks ago?"

He says, "I asked her to be honest."

It takes me a minute to understand that he is defending her against me.

I clean up, I take his temperature, I make tea. I am stirring soup when Mary Pat calls, apparently contrite.

"She's coming over," Jack says, which means I'm supposed to go.

. . . . .

Jack arrives at Homer's, blurry with exhaustion and hobbling. He tells me that he's been working out. "I just overdid it." He says something indecipherable through a yawn, and, ". . . up really late."

I ask if he was working on his screenplay.

"No." He yawns. "No."

I yawn.

"We stayed up late, talking," he says.

"Do you babies ever sleep through the night?"

He says, "She was upset."

I think of the work that Mary Pat does and the stories she must hear every day.

"I woke up," Jack says, "and she was crying."

I nod in sympathy.

His voice is cloudy with sleep. "She kept telling me how sorry she was."

I say, "Why was she sorry?"

He seems suddenly to focus, and to realize that he might not want to tell me this story. He hesitates before going on, but he does go on, too tired to obey his instincts. "She's still in love with her old boyfriend."

The words seem to spell out *The End,* and yet I don't hear *The End* in his voice or see *The End* in his face.

I say, "If she loves him so much, how come she broke up with him?"

I watch Jack try to remember. "She didn't feel she deserved to be happy back then."

What comes to mind is Jack's rendition of the Talking Heads' song he changed from "Psycho Killer" to "Psycho Babble," and the refrain, "Run run run run run run run away."

I say, "When didn't she deserve to be happy?"

"Her freshman year," he says. "He was a senior. Physics major. He played squash."

I'm confused. "So, she's been seeing him since her freshman year?"

"No," he says.

"She ran into him?"

"No."

"But she wants to get back together with him?"

"No," he says. "He's married with two kids. She doesn't even know where he lives."

It occurs to me that I might understand this story better if I were really, really tired.

My poor brother's eyes are tiny and his skin clam-colored; his hand trembles as he returns his coffee cup to the puddle in his saucer. He says, "The good thing is . . ." and drifts off.

I say, "The good thing is . . ."

"She finally feels like she deserves to be happy."

. . . . .

Jack calls and says that he wishes he hadn't told me about M.P.'s old boyfriend.

I say, "I understand," and I do. There are things that two people say in the middle of the night that don't make sense to a third at breakfast.

. . . . .

The next few times I ask, Jack tells me that Mary Pat is great, and then she is good, and then she is fine, and then she is okay.

Saturday night, at four A.M., he calls me from her apartment. I know without asking that he is sitting in the dark; I can hear it in his voice.

"I blew it," he says.

I say, "I'm sure you didn't."

"I did," he says. "I blew it."

"How?"

"I just blew it," he says. "I blew it."

"Try to remember that we're having a conversation," I say, "and your goal is to impart information."

He says, "I should've proposed to her at the Boathouse."

When I don't answer, he says, "In Central Park," as though to clarify. "That was the perfect moment."

I force myself to say the consoling words: "I'm sure you'll have another perfect moment."

"No," he says. "She said that was the perfect moment, and we can never get it back."

"Hold on there," I say. "You've known each other for, like, twenty minutes."

He doesn't answer, and I hear how irrelevant these words are to him. I'm worried that he's going to hang up and propose now. "Just bear with me," I say. "Forget about perfect moments for a minute. Do you really want *Mary Pat* to be your *wife*? You want *Mary Pat* to be the *mother of your children*?"

"Yes," he says.

I do not ask him if he thinks he would be happy with Mary Pat. Happiness, I realize, is beside the point. I realize, too, that he doesn't want to figure anything out or to feel better. He wants me to help him win Mary Pat.

"Okay," I say. "Here's what I think you should do. Don't ask her to marry you. Give her room. Try not to need anything from her for a little while."

How can I tell that I have said something he wants to hear? The silence is just the same, but I know.

I imitate our father's calm authority: "We'll figure the rest out in the morning."

. . . . .

I've only called Pete a few times in my life, and as soon as I hear his hello, I remember why. He has settled in for the night, his feet by the fire, Dostoyevsky in hand, Lila's head on his lap; a phone call is breaking and entering.

We talk, but only about one percent of Pete comes to the phone. You get close to Pete by swimming or clamming or fishing, by weeding his garden or singing while he plays guitar.

Every exchange is more strained than the last until I get to the emergency of my brother's love. When I finish, Pete says, "I don't think there's anything you can do, Soph." He is sympathetic but resolute; I imagine this is the voice he uses to tell clients a house is beyond restoration.

"You don't understand," I say. "I think he's going to propose to her."

"They all propose," he says.

For myself, I say, "Did you propose?"

He laughs. "No." It occurs to me that I have never known Pete to have a girlfriend.

I say, "How are you?"

"You know," he says. "Okay."

"How's Lila?"

He says, "How are you, Lila?"

What I hear in the moment of quiet that follows is Martha's Vineyard in winter—the clouds in the sky, the wind on the beach, and the cold that stays on your clothes even inside.

. . . . .

Jack does not return my calls. I ask my mother if she's heard from him. She has. She says, "I can't wait to meet Mary Pat."

. . . . .

I know how hard my little brother is working, and I am reluctant to worry him. But when he asks me what I think of Mary Pat, I tell him everything. "He's losing weight," I say. "He doesn't sleep anymore." It occurs to me that this is how cults weaken the will of initiates.

Robert says, "It sounds like he's in love," and adds that the world's most coveted state is characterized by unrelieved insecurity and almost constant pain.

The effect of his words is to remind me that it has been a long time since I have been in love.

"What about you?" Robert says. "Have you met anyone?"

He always asks, and I always have to say no, and I say no now. For the first time, he says he wants to introduce me to someone he knows, a pediatric heart surgeon.

"That's good," I say. "I have a pediatric heart."

He says, "Don't talk about my sister that way."

Before we hang up, I say, "Are you in love?"

"No," he says.

I ask if his wife knows.

"Of course," he says. "Naomi's the one who told me."

. . . . .

When Jack finally calls me, at work, he says, "Can you meet me?" instead of *Hello.*

I say, "When?"

He says, "Now."

Before I can ask where, he hangs up.

Even though it's six P.M. on a weekday, I assume Homer's, and I'm right. Jack's at the counter, his head bowed.

His face looks haggard, but his body is surprisingly buff.

He says that he can't sleep or eat or think or write.

"Apparently you can work out, though," I say.

"She won't call me back," he says.

"I know how that feels."

He misses the jibe. "We had a fight," he says.

"About what?"

"It wasn't really a fight." He tells the waiter, "Just coffee."

"He'll have pancakes and bacon with that." To Jack, I say, "Or do you want eggs?"

"I don't want anything," he says.

I tell the waiter, "He'll have the pancakes."

Jack doesn't even seem to hear.

"You seem like you're in a coma," I say, and as soon as I say it, I feel sick. Our father was in a coma for days, and I have said *coma* the way people who don't know anything about it do, which is like calling out, *Can we get another coma over here?*

I say, "I meant stupor," but Jack is in such a stupor, he didn't even notice my *coma.*

When his pancakes come, he pushes the plate aside. He sighs, and sighs again. His voice is so quiet, it's as though he's talking to himself when he says, "I can't hit her."

"Sorry?"

"I can't hit her," he says, and I realize how tired and desperate he must be to say these words to me.

"And you want to hit her?"

He shrugs. "She wants me to."

"In bed," I say.

"Of course in bed," he says. "Where else?"

"Oh, I'm sorry," I say. "Of course, she wants you to hit her in bed. And you can't. Go on."

"She thinks it means I don't love her."

I say, "Can I hit her?"

"Sophie." His voice is a reprimand. "Her father used to beat her."

I think, *She probably deserved it,* but then I turn back into a human being.

My brother's face is so tired and so sad it makes my face tired and sad. "Buddy." But even as I say, "If I were you, I'd try to get out of this thing," I know that nothing I say, no matter how wise or well put, will separate him from this woman.

"It's not like I have a choice," he says.

I say, "Of course you do."

"She's been seeing someone else," he says. "Some guy she works with."

I am about to say, *A victim?* but I correct myself in time: "A survivor?"

He defends Mary Pat even now: "She would never go out with a patient."

There are so many things I could say about Mary Pat. I could call her the one word you save for occasions such as this, the only sacred profanity. But my brother loves this woman, whoever she is, and deriding her would only deride him for loving her.

What else is there to say? I tell him that I've been editing a celebrity diet book at work. I say, "News flash: Eat less, exercise more."

When I slide the plate of pancakes in front of him, he says, "I'm not hungry."

"Do you think I care if you're hungry?" I say. "This has nothing to do with hunger. Hunger is beside the point. Hunger is a luxury you can't afford."

I pour syrup over the pancakes. When I cut into the stack, he says, drily, "Leggo my Eggo," repeating a commercial circa our childhood.

"You need a nap," I say.

He eats one bite, and then another.

While he finishes his pancakes, I plan the future. I will walk him home, and up the stairs to his apartment. He'll lie down. I'll shop for groceries. I will take him to a movie and out to dinner. In case my father is listening, I think, *We will look after each other.*

DENA BLUMENTHAL + BOBBY ORR FORREVER

My mother is at her bereavement group, and I am on the phone with a distant relative I don't know, an ancient guiltress, who says she's sorry about my father but turns out to be a lot sorrier that no one bothered to let her know at the time, so she could've come to his funeral. She keeps saying things like, "Is it so hard to pick up the phone and dial?"

I am saved by the beep of Call Waiting and ask her to hold on a minute, please. She says, "This is long distance."

A second beep. "Well, nice talking to you," I say, and, "I'll give my mother your message," though I don't think I will. "Good-bye."

The other call is Dena, and I launch into an instant replay of the guilt festival I've just attended, which fascinates me now that it's over, but not Dena. I hear indulgence in her, "Uh-huh."

I say, "She didn't even know my name. It was like the guilt equivalent of anonymous sex—"

Dena says, "How are you?"

She is asking big, but I answer little: "Fine," I say. "How are you?"

This she treats as a digression, as though I am a patient inquiring after my doctor's health. She allows only a few questions about her life before switching back to mine. "Have you talked to Demetri?"

I haven't.

"Good," she says. "When are you coming back to New York?"

I make my voice casual: "I don't know."

I expect her to laugh when I tell her that I have an interview at *Shalom*, the newsletter we grew up not reading.

She doesn't say anything.

I wait and then say, "I should get ready," even though my interview isn't for another three hours.

She says, "Bob," her nickname for me and mine for her since high school, "you're living in Surrey," and she says these words with the sympathetic authority of one familiar with Surrey's social opportunities—the kids smoking cigarettes outside the skating rink; the housewife returning a nylon nightie at Strawbridge & Clothier; the mustached neighbor walking a miniature schnauzer named Pepper.

I say, "The good thing about being nowhere in your career is that you can do it anywhere."

She says, "Bob."

"Yeah?"

She hesitates. "Good luck."

. . . . .

I'd only been with Demetri for a few months when he asked me to go to Los Angeles with him.

"Come with me," he said, and my heart stopped hurting for the first time since my father's death.

I was thrilled quitting my job, thrilled giving up my apartment. It seemed like the first real risk I'd ever taken. I felt like I was kissing life right on the lips.

I started to panic the week before we were supposed to leave. Suddenly I heard everything everybody had been saying and not saying about Demetri: Dena had called him a pathological narcissist; my older brother had said, "There's no there there"; my younger brother had sighed.

But it was the idea of my father that I couldn't shake. I knew what he would've thought of Demetri—not that he would've said so. He would've said, *What are you going to do in Los Angeles?*

"What am I going to do in Los Angeles?" I said to Demetri.

He didn't know I was saying the *Dear* of Dear John. He told me I would spend my days fantasizing about the sex we'd have that night, and then that night we'd have it.

. . . . .

All my life, I've seen *Shalom* on our mail table, and now that I want to read it, it's gone. My mother threw it away, and the garbage men have come and gone. Everyone she calls has thrown theirs out, too. She's sure she saved the issues announcing my brothers' bar mitzvahs: We spend the hour before my interview fruitlessly rummaging through drawers stuffed with the memorabilia of childhood—sponge paintings of snowmen, compositions with sentences like, "The bird hops across the lawn."

My mother feels terrible about throwing out *Shalom* and insists on driving me to my interview. Lately, she's been giving me career pep talks, though she herself has not held a job since before my thirty-three-year-old brother was born. If I'm interested in journalism, she says now, *Shalom* is as good a place as any to start. "It's all about networking," she says. "And expanding your skill set."

"Well," I say, "you would know."

She starts to apologize, and I stop her. I tell her that I know she's trying to help, though her advice seems to be cutting off the air supply in the car and that's giving me brain damage.

I change the topic: Does she know Elaine Brodsky, the publisher I'm about to meet?

When she says, "I've known Elaine forever," her voice boards the *Mayflower*, a bad sign.

"Are you friends?" I say.

She says, "We're not close," her way of saying she dislikes a person. I hope it's one-way; my first boss was a disgruntled ex-girlfriend of my older brother.

We park in the lot for the Professional Offices at Manor, a concrete box with windows tinted brown like sunglasses. My mother says she'll wait for me; she's brought an old *New Yorker* to read, as she did during my violin lessons in high school.

As I get out of the car, she wishes me good luck and says, "You'll be fabulous."

The walkway is encrusted with ice; even in low heels I'm slow and unsteady, a toddler learning to walk, an old woman afraid of breaking a hip.

A moment after the receptionist announces my arrival, out comes Elaine Brodsky in an inexplicably familiar kilt with an oversized gold-tone safety pin.

In her office, she says, "How's Mother?" Her voice isn't as cold as my mother's, but it isn't warm. She says, "I was so sorry to hear about Dad," like we're all one big unhappy family.

She's somber for a respectful moment before launching into the exciting happenings at *Shalom*.

I try to mirror her enthusiasm for their new volunteer staff—a cub reporter from the Hebrew school and a secretary from the Jewish Home for the Aged: "Wow."

She says, "We're helping each other." Then she turns the topic to me: She just loves my publishing background! Do I like to write? That'll certainly come in handy, as I'll be doing most of the reporting myself.

It is possibly the best interview I've ever had. I can tell she's going to offer me the job. In a few minutes I will again be one with the working world.

She wants me to meet *Shalom*'s current editor. After she dials his extension, she hands me the most recent issue of "The Weekly Newsletter Serving the Jewish Community of Greater Philadelphia" and she says, "Hot off the press."

I read the headline of the lead story: MRS. JACOBY'S FIFTH-GRADE CLASS LIGHTS THE HANUKKAH MENORAH.

The fifth grader in me knows that however desperate I am to get a job I am more desperate not to have this one, and once Elaine is off the phone, out of my mouth these words come: "I don't know anything about Judaism—is that a big part of the job?"

I'm as stunned as she is. The man who would have been my predecessor walks in and we shake hands, and then Elaine Brodsky is saying, "Give my best to Mother."

Mother and I drive home.

I'm lying on my bed when I spot Elaine Brodsky's kilt on Molly, the doll my grandmother Steeny brought back from Scotland for me. Molly sits on a shelf along with Gigi from France, Frieda from Germany, and Erin from Ireland, each dressed in her country's native costume. I haven't noticed the dolls for a long time, and now that I do, they seem to sing, "It's a small world after all," about mine.

When my mother calls, "It's Dena," I pick up the phone.

She says, "How was it?"

"Great," I say. "Amazing." Then I tell her.

She laughs, and tries to make me see how hilarious the interview was. I do for about one second. Then I remember I am living at home with my mother in Surrey, and I will be living here forever. Lying on my canopy bed, looking at my costumed dollies, talking on my Princess phone, I can feel myself aging at an accelerated rate. Soon people will mistake my mother and me for sisters.

Dena says, "You need to get out of the house."

"Where should I go," I say, "the drugstore?"

"Go downtown and see a movie," she says. "Go to my house." She likes this idea so much she repeats it, and now it's an order: "Go to my house." She tells me she's calling her mother as soon as we hang up.

Recently Dena started liking her mother, or at least seeing why someone else might.

"I'm calling her right now," she says.

. . . . .

The Blumenthals live in the only real mansion in Surrey, the house all other houses aspire to. It's old and vine-covered, with a pool hidden in back. There's a big formal living room no one uses, and the dining room ditto, but there are also rooms that seem private and warm—a little alcove with a window seat, Mrs. Blumenthal's dressing room with its deco vanity, and the library with its fireplace.

Growing up I envied their kitchen most, which had anything and everything you could want—white-papered packages of cold cuts, fresh rye bread, and bagels from the delicatessen, Coke and Tab and Sprite, Doritos and Fritos, Mallomars and Oreos, ice-cream cones covered with a helmet of chocolate and nuts, and at least two flavors of Häagen-Dazs, usually chocolate chocolate chip and butter pecan; if what you wanted wasn't in the kitchen, it was in the butler's pantry. I'd go home comparing their staples to ours—leftover chicken, celery, and vanilla ice milk.

The Blumenthals' housekeeper did the shopping, cleaning, and what little cooking there was. Her name was Flossie, and everyone seemed to like her better than they liked each other.

Dena's sisters, Tracy and Ellen, identical twins were both gymnasts and both cheerleaders. Dena called Ellen shallow and Tracy witchy, but they were indistinguishably fascinating to me. When the three sisters found themselves together, always by accident—to watch television or sit by the pool—the mood was reluctant forbearance.

Their father occasionally announced that he wanted them to behave like a real family, and he would suddenly decide that they were all going to Florida to play tennis or to Utah to ski; he'd insist that they were going to sit down as a family for dinner, though he himself would be the one missing the next evening.

In a pearl-gray cashmere sweater large enough to fit over his belly, Dr. Blumenthal gave the impression of being expert at his own comfort. I don't think I ever saw him without a drink in his hand—a beer after tennis, a gin and tonic by the pool, a martini in the evening, a Bloody Mary on Sunday, and so on. He could be convivial or blustery—often convivial then blustery.

Mrs. Blumenthal seemed immune to both. Taller than her husband and lithe, she carried herself like the great tennis player she was. Her hair was long for a mother, frosted a color Dena called "Surrey blond," and with her regal demeanor made her look a lot like her Russian wolfhounds before they got old.

She was always reading in a big armchair by the fire or on the white divan in her pristine bedroom, with a cup of tea or a glass of wine and an ashtray on the table beside her. She'd ask me if I was reading anything I loved, and if I was, she'd write down the title.

This afternoon when she opens the door, she's holding her place in *Madame Bovary*. She kisses me on both cheeks and says, "Sophie"; she has a throaty, smoker's voice.

"Hi," I say. She's asked me to call her Stevie—short for Stephanie—but I can't bring myself to call her anything but Mrs. Blumenthal, so I avoid calling her anything.

As I follow her into the library, she says, "What can I get you to drink?"

I ask what she's having.

"I haven't started yet."

I say, "What would you drink if . . ." I try to think of a crisis that would make her feel as bad as I feel now. "If Dr. Blumenthal said he was leaving you?"

"Champagne," she says, deadpan. Then: "I think we're in a brown mood—scotch, bourbon . . ."

"Bourbon," I say, though I can't tell the difference.

We sit in the big armchairs by the fire, and she lights a cigarette for herself and one for me. "Let's talk about money," she says.

"Okay."

She says, "Are you in debt, Sophie?"

"No."

"Good." Then: "I'm assuming your father left you something."

"He did."

She asks how much, and I tell her. I can't tell whether she thinks it's a little or a lot. "And how much would it cost you to move back to New York?"

"I don't know."

"Well," she says, "think about it."

I tell her that my father specifically asked me not to use the inheritance for living expenses; he wanted me to use it toward a down payment on a house or for a trip—something momentous.

"That's a nice idea." She pauses. "But you could always pay it back, once you're working."

I want to be closer to the fire, and I slide off my chair to the rug, where the wolfhounds once lounged. I wonder if Mrs. Blumenthal misses them.

She says, "Maybe we should talk about why you're in Surrey."

I try to think of the dogs' names: *Masha and Ivan*?

"I don't know whether you're trying to go back to a time before your father died," she says, "or whether you can't bring yourself to move on."

It's both—though I realize it only now.

"You just don't have the energy it takes?" she says.

I nod.

She says, "I've felt that way."

I'm amazed that she's speaking so honestly about her life. No one my mother's age ever does, or at least not to me.

I'm warm by the fire, but it's gotten dark outside; looking at the black windowpanes, I can feel the cold. The house seems quiet and still. I wonder if Dr. Blumenthal is home more or less now that all the girls are gone. I wonder if he is on his way home now, and if Mrs. Blumenthal herself knows. My father always called before leaving the courthouse to ask if my mother needed him to pick up anything, even though in all those years she never did.

It occurs to me that maybe Mrs. Blumenthal wasn't kidding about the champagne.

She says, "What about this boyfriend of yours in Los Angeles?"

I wonder what Dena has said. "Ex-boyfriend," I say. "Demetri."

"What does he do?"

I say that he writes for a sitcom now, but he's a comic. For some reason I think she may think he's a clown, so I say, "You know, he does stand-up—"

"Thanks," she says. "I know what a comic is. Is he funny?"

I say that he is. Onstage he does shticks, like the one about his role on a soap opera: "I'm not an actor, but I play one on TV." But alone with me he could be hilarious. I consider imitating his imitation of what his pets would say if they could talk. But thinking of Demetri at his funniest makes me miss him.

I hear myself say, "I keep expecting him to call." I haven't admitted this to anyone, and it's a relief to say it out loud. Still, I don't say the whole truth: I've been hoping he'll call and say how much he misses me and how much he loves me and how much he still wants me to move out to Los Angeles with him. Meanwhile, he hasn't even called to say hello.

She gets up to refill our glasses. "Why don't you call him?"

"Mrs. Blumenthal." I wait for her to say, *Stevie,* but she doesn't. "He never told me he loved me."

"Some men don't," she says. "Some men say it all the time and don't mean it."

I recognize myself in the latter category, not with Demetri but with one of his predecessors. I sometimes said "I love you" to Josh because I was afraid I didn't; toward the end, I hardly said it at all, and when I did I meant, *I wish I loved you.*

Now Mrs. Blumenthal says, "What a man does is more important than what he says."

She tells me that I know what I need to know about Demetri, and I appreciate how she says it, like she doesn't have the answer herself, or any stake in what I decide.

I ask if she thinks I should go back to New York.

"I don't see any reason not to," she says. "You could stay with Dena at first." She considers this. "I think it would be good for her."

I wonder what she means, but while her remark doesn't seem disloyal, my asking about it would be.

Suddenly I feel tired. I say that I think I'll stay until my mother is a little stronger.

She says, "You'll move when you're ready."

It takes another month. I worry about telling my mother, but when I do, she looks about seventeen years younger.

. . . . .

I've known Dena since seventh grade. We were in homeroom together; I learned her name from the blue-cloth loose-leaf binder on which she'd written, "Dena Blumenthal + Bobby Orr Forrever." This was the year the Philadelphia Flyers won the Stanley Cup, and it was a mark of Dena's social preeminence that she could get away with pledging eternal love to Mr. Orr, the star of the archrival Boston Bruins.

I myself loved Bob Dylan; I didn't care about the Flyers or ice hockey or skating. But everyone I wanted to be friends with went to the rink on Friday nights, and one Friday night I decided I'd go. I was getting a ride with some girls I didn't know too well. This seemed better than arriving alone.

My mother insisted I wear my green parka, an end-of-season sale item she'd bought without my consent the previous winter. It looked like a rolled-up sleeping bag with a belt and seemed impossible to make friends in. "You'll be as warm as toast," she said.

In my unzipped coat, I sat waiting for my ride while my family finished dessert. After a few minutes, I took off my coat and held it with my mittens and hat on my lap.

It was almost 7:30 when my father said, "What time are they coming for you?"

"Seven," I said.

My older brother said, "I'll take you over."

I said, "Thanks, anyway."

Finally, a honk came from the street.

Whenever anyone honked for my brothers or me, my mother usually made the face of a person driven insane, but tonight she just said, "Have a good time."

My little brother, who liked to skate, called out, "Fall forward."

At the rink, the girl whose father had driven us didn't even go in; she was meeting a boy from ninth grade in the parking lot. The other two had brought their own skates and were out on the ice before I'd even reached the clubhouse to rent mine.

The man at the window told me he was out of white in my size and gave me a pair of black skates, which reminded me of old-fashioned shoes an orphan would wear. After lacing them up, I lingered a moment on the carpeted bench; it was warmer in the clubhouse, and you could buy hot chocolate. But I walked out, my blades chop, chop, chopping on the vinyl mat.

I'd never skated before, but it didn't look hard. The boys seemed just to be running on ice; the girls seemed to be doing ballet to the scratchy waltz that played over the PA system.

I couldn't find an entrance onto the ice and considered going back to the clubhouse for hot chocolate. Then someone brushed by me and opened a door that was part of the wall, and I followed. I slid onto the ice and kept sliding until I was in what seemed like the fast lane of a circular speedway. The boys on the hockey team were chasing each other and, despite the NO ROUGHHOUSING sign, were roughhousing. I was afraid they'd knock me down.

I fell all by myself, onto my back.

The parka padded my fall but made it hard for me even to sit up. Finally, I was able to kneel and then stand. I lurched across the super-highway to the shoulder, where I stood gripping the wall. My two friends skated by and waved, and I waved back, an orphan in a sleeping bag.

A skating rink was unlike a pool, I realized; you couldn't stand still without standing out. But I couldn't make myself move. I felt sure that everyone was looking at me and then realized that no one was, and I experienced the distinct shame of each.

Dena was in the center of the rink, in a white fur hat with pom-pom ties and a short red skirt, practicing a twirling jump that might have qualified her for the Olympics. She was small and thin, with large breasts her posture didn't acknowledge—and wouldn't, even once she'd grown up. She had dark hair, blue eyes, and a long nose—both of her sisters would have theirs fixed, but not Dena—which made her more striking than pretty.

She skated backwards. She pirouetted so fast she became a blur. Then she was whipping around the rink, her arms linked to a chain of similarly skirted champions.

As she skated by, I saw her notice me. I was afraid that she'd point me out to her friends, but she broke off from her chain and skated toward me.

She said, "Hi, Sophie," and I was surprised she knew my name.

I didn't say hers; I wasn't sure if she was making fun of me.

She said, "You want to skate?"

She took my arm, and slowly we went around the rink. She told me what she was doing, pushing off and gliding.

I kept hearing jingling, and I looked down and saw the tiny bells attached to Dena's skates.

She said, "Try not to look at your feet."

"Okay," I said, and nearly fell.

She said, "Just hold on to me."

. . . . .

Most of my friends live in studios, or in larger apartments with serious flaws—a roommate in the living room or a methadone clinic across the street. Dena's apartment is perfect, a big one-bedroom with a view of Gramercy Park. She doesn't say what her rent is, but I assume she lives as frugally as she does because it is high—though I also know she enjoys frugality for frugality's sake.

Over Christmas, she took a trip to India, and now she's in love with what she calls the simple life. She gets serene talking about it; her speech slows and her eyes glisten when she describes an Indian boy who amused himself for hours with a piece of string.

I nod, but I think, *You watched somebody play with a piece of string for hours?*

The first night, she shows me where she keeps the coffee beans, grinder, and what looks like a watercolor brush for getting every coffee speck into the reusable cotton sock she uses as a filter. Her cupboards are virtually bare and make me pine for the Blumenthals' larder of yesteryear.

Dena shows me the big pot of soup and bowl of salad she prepares each Sunday to last the week so she won't be tempted to eat out or order in.

The salad bowl contains nothing but brown-edged lettuce. "Yum," I say.

Dena laughs and says, "Richard calls it *'Salade Fatiguee.'* "

. . . . .

Richard was her professor in graduate school at MIT, and though she doesn't say she's seeing him, she's seeing him.

One night I say, "How's it going with Richard?"

She's ladling soup into bowls for our dinner, and the only sign that she's heard my question is that she pauses mid-ladle. When she hands my bowl to me, she says, "You ask a lot of questions. The whole Q-and-A thing is so . . ." She moves her hands in a gesture of, *How you say?* "American."

I think, *We are Americans.*

It reminds me of her sweet-sixteen party, when she forbade the singing of "Happy Birthday."

Her speech becomes slow and serene. "There are a million ways to find things out."

I think, *Name a thousand.*

. . . . .

I keep telling Dena that I want to pay rent, and finally I insist. That's when she admits that her father bought the apartment for her.

I'm surprised. Her father is always trying to give her things, and she always refuses. I say, "It's still your apartment." I tell her I'd feel more comfortable paying rent.

She says no, but she lets me buy the groceries, and I fill the refrigerator, Flossie-style.

"We don't need this much food," Dena says. "It's wasteful."

I tell her I don't want to emulate the diet of a boy who has only string to play with.

She says, "Are you making fun of me?"

I say, "I am."

. . . . .

The previous summer, I watched Dena's father try to persuade her to give up her old Saab and take the new Mercedes convertible he was trading in for a newer one.

We were in the den; a baseball game was on the huge television, and Dr. Blumenthal glanced at it while he made our martinis. He'd showered and shaved and was wearing a silk robe over trousers. Mrs.

Blumenthal was still getting ready for the party they were going to; faintly I could hear the sound of a blow-dryer.

I didn't know if he was serious about the Mercedes; he seemed to be trying to bait Dena. If he was, it was working.

Her arms were crossed in front of her. I knew that her reason for turning down the Mercedes was that she didn't want to be a princess, but that's what she sounded like turning it down. She acted more like a princess around the king.

As Dena got angrier, I kept thinking that maybe I'd casually get up and go to her mother's dressing room and watch her dry her hair, which I'd wanted to do for years.

Dr. Blumenthal was enumerating the virtues of the Mercedes. He was on to safety now, and it occurred to me that maybe he wasn't baiting her after all. He seemed genuinely concerned about her welfare, and it made me miss my own father and his concern for mine.

Dr. Blumenthal described the extensive plastic surgery he'd had to perform on a patient who'd been in a horrible car accident. He was saying, "An air bag would have—" when Dena interrupted.

Her voice was loud, her words drawn out: "No, Dad."

I turned to her. "Bob." My tone said, *Don't be hasty:* "We're talking about a convertible here."

She said, "Shut up."

I think she felt she could talk to me this way because we'd known each other so long that we were like sisters. But her saying *shut up* proved that we weren't; in my family, we were taught that *shut up* was the meanest thing you could say.

"Okay, okay," I told Dr. Blumenthal, as though giving in. "*I'll* take the Mercedes."

. . . . .

To compensate for the rent I'm not paying Dena, I try to be extra helpful. I clean the bathroom and the kitchen. When I do my laundry, I do Dena's. I move her Saab from one side of the street to the other, as mandated by street-sweeping law.

I'm surprised every morning to find her stereo still in the dashboard. But I notice that even nice new cars are parked on the street now, and I don't see the signs I used to in car windows—NO STEREO; NOTHING IN TRUNK OR GLOVE COMPARTMENT; and EVERYTHING ALREADY STOLEN.

When I mention it to Dena, she tells me that New York is safer now than it was in the mid-eighties, and I marvel at her ability to generalize.

. . . . .

Dena keeps promising to make a set of keys to the apartment for me. I remind her twice to no avail. It doesn't matter in the morning—we leave the apartment together, she to work and I to temp—but it means we have to coordinate our return each night. When she's going out and I'm not, she gives me the keys, but it doesn't feel right for me to copy them.

. . . . .

She seems annoyed letting me in, even though it's not late.

I worry that I'm getting on her nerves. If I don't have an interview or an apartment to see or plans after work, I go to a diner in Union Square for a hamburger and drink diet Cokes while I read.

I realize my mistake one Sunday, when she's making the week's soup and salad; she acts like she just needs to know how much to prepare, but I hear the edge in her voice when she says, "Are you going to be out every night again this week?"

. . . . .

I tell everyone that I'm looking for an apartment; I check the listings in all the newspapers; I go to see every apartment I can afford, all of them unlivable.

At the Laundromat I see the sign for a sublet on Washington Square. Only one fringe with a phone number remains, but I call anyway.

The tenant, a graduate student named Dewitt, says the apartment is still available; I can see it if I come over right away.

I've just put the laundry in the dryers. I weigh how glad Dena will be if I get my own apartment against how mad she'll be if I lose her laundry. But maybe New York is so safe now that no one steals laundry anymore.

I hail a cab.

The address is 19 Washington Square North—right on the square!—and I picture a town house like the one the judge from *Oliver!* lived in. I imagine myself as Oliver looking out the window at the glorious street scene below, and singing as he did, "Who will buy this wonderful morning?"

The sublet is a basement studio with bars on the windows, duct-taped pipes, a cement floor, and a urine-and-kitty-litter odor that makes me woozy.

Dewitt is going to Scotland to research Celtic folk songs in two weeks and desperate; he's willing to lower the rent.

I tell him I'll think about it, though I don't have to. It's the worst apartment I've seen or smelled, and even though it's cheap I'd still have to use some of my father's money because Dewitt needs all the rent up front.

Back at Dena's, I've only begun to regale her about the horribleness of the apartment when Richard calls.

She talks to him for just a few minutes and comes back to the kitchen, where I'm washing the dishes. I say, "How's Richard?"

"Fine," she says, drying the silverware. Then: "His wife is back from Italy."

I assume I've misheard her, and I turn off the water. "Sorry?"

She doesn't answer, just sorts the silverware in the drawer.

Before I can stop myself, I say, "Richard is *married*?" and, "You're seeing a *married* guy?" in the intonation of, *Richard is* dead? *You're seeing a* dead *guy?*

She says a bland, "I told you."

"No," I say.

I wash and she dries the dishes in silence. We don't look at each other. Afterward, she goes into her bedroom and closes the door.

It's then that I remember the laundry. I rush downstairs and run all the way to Third Avenue. The Laundromat is closed. The woman who tends it is mopping the floor. I knock. She shakes her head. I knock again.

"My laundry's in there," I say when she comes to the door.

She tells me to come back for it in the morning.

Suddenly it seems criminal for me not to bring Dena's laundry back—this on top of what I said about Richard. "Please."

Maybe the woman sees how upset I am; she lets me in.

It's close to midnight when I get back to Dena's.

We fold the laundry together on the dining-room table.

I say, "I'm sorry I sounded so harsh before."

Her face is blank, neither admitting that I've done something wrong nor forgiving me for it.

I want to feel closer to her, but I don't know how. "Are you in love with him, Bob?"

She says, "God, no."

"That's good, I guess. Right?"

She says, "It doesn't really matter."

I have no idea what she means.

. . . . .

In ninth grade, Dena told me that my boyfriend was cheating on me.

It was the beginning of June, early evening.

While I cried, she patted my back, which was totally un-Dena-like. She suggested I get in the pool. "You can scream underwater," she said. "That's what I do."

It was hard to imagine Dena screaming. The most emotional I'd ever seen her get was annoyed. "What do you scream about?"

"My father, mostly," she said.

I changed into a tank suit of hers, which was too big for me; she tightened the straps with a shoelace, racer-back style. I walked into the pool. Underwater, I cried and screamed.

When I got out, Dena said, "How was it?"

I nodded and tried not to cry. I knew I was letting her down.

When I could talk, I said, "I don't know what I did wrong."

Dena sighed. "You care too much."

. . . . .

Dena helps me move into the basement on Washington Square, which she's named the Heiress. I expect her to revise the name once she sees the apartment—the Airless seems more fitting—but she only has compliments for its raw, industrial feel. When I bring up the kitty-litter odor, she suggests scented candles.

Afterward we go to Caffe Reggio on MacDougal Street. We order cappuccinos, and she takes a few drags of my cigarette, which reminds me of when we were younger. I feel easier with her than I have in weeks, and she seems to feel easier, too, until we're leaving the cafe.

She holds the door for me. "I keep forgetting to tell you," she says. "Demetri called."

"When?"

She admits that it was a while ago.

"When?"

"I don't know," she says. "Six weeks?"

"You just forgot?"

"I'm sure subconsciously I didn't want you to talk to him," she says. "You seemed so much better."

I say, "Is that your subconscious speaking?"

"Sorry," she says.

"Don't do that again," I say, and hope it encompasses the larger issue that I can't quite name.

As we cross the park, she tries to make everything okay; she says that our apartments are probably the same distance from each other as our houses in Surrey.

In front of my apartment, she says, "Sorry about Demetri," and I say, "It's all right," even though it isn't yet.

As soon as I get back to the Heiress, I call him.

He says, "I didn't think you'd ever call me back."

"Sorry," I say.

He says, "No worries." He's called just to talk.

. . . . .

By late August, I'm on my second sublet, and I've been working as a copywriter long enough to know I'm not good at it. I seem to be reliving the life I had when I was twenty-two, but I'm about to turn twenty-eight, which feels like the opposite of twenty-two.

When Dena calls to ask what I'm doing the weekend before my birthday, I tell her, "I thought I'd lie in bed and drink bourbon."

She says, "That sounds good."

A few days later, she invites me to an all-expense-paid weekend with her in the Berkshires, where she's been renting a house for years with a bunch of friends I've never met.

The invitation comes in the form of a postcard she's addressed to "Mrs. Robert Dylan" c/o me: "Mrs. Robert Orr requests the pleasure of your company at seven-thirty o'clock on the twenty-seventh day of August in the year of our Lord nineteen-hundred and eighty-eight . . ." On the other side, she's done a pen-and-ink drawing of the house with its garden and surrounding hills, by which she's written, "Ticks not pictured."

On the appointed Friday evening, at seven-thirty o'clock, she buzzes my apartment, a walk-up in Hell's Kitchen she's named the Hot Plate. I'm not quite ready and ask if she wants to come up. She does; she wants to see my sublet.

I look around to see what she will see. I took a few tips from a *House & Garden* article on sprucing up your summer rental; red geraniums sit in front of the windows, and white sheets cover the sofa and armchair. In the magazine, the red and white brought out the blue of the ocean view.

Now I see that my red and white brings out the gray of the airshaft view. The sheets over the furniture make my studio look like it's waiting to be painted and emphasize that it needs to be; the bright geraniums accentuate its overall gloom. Neither address the apartment's central flaw: It seems dirty. There's nothing you can point to and clean, but you sense the dirt, as you do the presence of cockroaches.

Dena says, "Hey," and walks in.

She's wearing dungaree cutoffs that go all the way down to her knees; I call her Huck and tell her I have a polka-dotted satchel on a pole she can borrow.

She doesn't answer; she's looking around. "It's not as bad as the Heiress," she says.

I say, "It's a different kind of bad," but I don't want to dwell on its particular badness, since I'll be dwelling in it through November.

She says, "It'll look better once it's painted."

I ask if there's anything I need to bring to the country.

She says, "A bathing suit and water shoes."

"Water shoes?"

"You know, those black slipper things."

I say, "I don't have black slipper things."

She tells me to bring sneakers I can swim in. "I like the tin ceiling," she says. Then she remembers that she's double-parked, and says she'd better go down.

Once she's gone, I say, "You do that." Her appreciating the ceiling, appreciating anything about the Hot Plate except the sheets or geraniums, bothers me, though I can't pinpoint why.

I put my tennis sneakers in my duffel bag and zip it up. I say, "See ya later, suckers," to the cockroaches I can't see.

When I get downstairs, Dena is standing on the sidewalk, her arms at her sides. Her Saab is gone.

. . . . .

A phone call to the police reveals that the car hasn't been stolen but towed. Since the tow pound is on the river, out of reach of public transportation, we have to take a cab, and this seems to annoy Dena almost as much as getting towed. Dena is anti-cab; it doesn't matter that I pay the fare.

We follow signs up a ramp and into a trailer. There's a line, and we get in it. No one's talking—too angry. We're all waiting for one woman, the clerk, who sits bank-teller-like behind glass I hope is bulletproof.

When it's our turn, she tells us that we owe $165 for the tow and $55 for the parking violation.

Dena's eyes widen, and I think of the watercolor brush she uses so as not to waste any coffee dust.

I say, "I'm paying."

"You are not," she says. "It's my stupid car."

"I'm the one who was late."

We argue—*Yes I am; No you're not*—until the guy behind us in line says, "I'll pay."

I turn around and there he is, the nicest, funniest man in the world, and one of the shortest.

I ask him if he wants to come with us to the country.

He says, "Sure," and asks where we're going, and my eyes ask him to ask me for my phone number—though I'm not sure I'd be able to give it to him in front of Dena.

. . . . .

On the West Side Highway, I say, "I liked him." We're in traffic and barely moving; Dena maneuvers from the left lane to the middle and back, basically trading parking spaces.

She makes her thumb and index finger into a *C* for *Context.*

"The guy who offered to pay our fine," I say. "He reminded me of that skit."

"What skit?"

When I open the glove compartment to look for a tissue, she says, "What are you doing in there?"

"Going through your private stuff." I find my prop, a hanky that serves as the ribbon for the damsel who can't pay the rent, the mustache for the villain who says she must, and the bow tie for the hero who says he will.

My favorite line is the villain's, "Curses! Foiled again!"

"Where'd you learn that?"

I say, "My father," so she can't make fun of me; I learned the skit at camp.

. . . . .

Once we get past the traffic for the George Washington Bridge, we speed along. The cloth ceiling of the Saab is coming down and luffs like a sail in the breeze.

I say, "Think how nice it would be to have your dad's convertible now."

She shakes her head, but she's smiling, and I am glad just to be leaving New York, glad that it's the beginning of a weekend, glad the windows are down and the radio's on.

My joyride lasts only until the exit for Riverdale, dale of my grandmother, whom I cannot bring myself to visit.

Dena says, "I'll go with you, if you want."

I appreciate the offer, but her mind-reading gives me a sick feeling: She expects me to do the same, and I can't.

. . . . .

On the Taconic Parkway, we begin eating the picnic Dena packed—hunks of bread and slivers of cheese, almonds and raisins, water for her and beer for me.

She holds her hand out for the water bottle, and as I pass it to her I ask who's going to be at the house this weekend.

She says, "Just Matthew."

I want to ask about him, but she says: "Do you ever hear from Demetri?"

I tell her that he sent me a postcard with his new jokes on it.

"God," she says.

"They were pretty funny."

When she says, "Do you still think about him?" I wonder why she can ask me questions I can't ask her.

I say, "I feel like I broke up with him partly to please my father."

"Or maybe it was because the guy has a packing peanut where his heart's supposed to be." Then, in a softer voice, she says, "You don't think you made a mistake?"

"No."

"Good," she says. "I know it was hard." She praises my strength.

"Bob," I say, "I chickened out."

"Is that what you think?"

"That's what happened." Then I say, "How's Richard?"

"He's fine." She takes a deep breath, and I hope that she's going to say more. "I went to a lecture he gave at Columbia last week."

I say, "Does he have kids?" and instantly worry that I've gone too far.

"In college." She reaches behind her and hands me a bag. "Happy birthday."

It's a tape of one of my favorite novels, *Washington Square.* She puts it in the cassette deck and presses Play.

After a minute, she says, "I'm sorry."

I turn to her. I think maybe she's going to talk to me about herself or about Richard or about why she can't talk to me about herself or Richard.

She says, "It's abridged," meaning the tape.

. . . . .

We get to the house after midnight. I grab my bag out of the back and walk barefoot on moss and then pebbles across the driveway. When we pass a very old Jeep Wagoneer with wood on its sides, I tell Dena that it's my favorite car or truck or whatever of all time.

Dena says, "It's Matthew's."

The house has low ceilings and wide-beamed floors that slant. The only light comes from candles, which make everything look soft but also haunted.

Maybe because of the candles, we whisper.

"No lights?" I say.

She says, "We're experimenting."

"What's your hypothesis?"

She says something about lowering the electricity bill, and then she turns on a light.

The kitchen is painted a fifties' yellow or was last painted in the fifties, and there are tomato-print curtains and a cat clock—its eyes and tail go back and forth on *tick* and *tock.* The room manages to be nostalgic without being cute, maybe because its charm borders Rattytown.

Dena calls out, "Margaret, Margaret," and an ancient yellow Lab lumbers in. Dena pets the dog and says, "Hello, old girl," which was what she called the female wolfhound, whose name I can't remember.

I get down on the linoleum, and Margaret is licking my face when I feel the presence of another human, standing above us.

I look up and see a tall and rangy stranger, rumpled, with blond, brillowy hair parted on the side, warm-looking pink skin, and blue eyes behind wire-rimmed spectacles—handsome, though I get the feeling that's the last thing he wants you to notice about him, which makes him more handsome.

"Hey," Dena says. "Sophie: Matthew."

He says, "Hi, Sophie," and his voice seems quiet, without actually being quiet, and for a second he and I seem to be alone in the kitchen, and then the kitchen itself fuzzes out, and he and I are alone in a moment of placelessness.

Dena breaks the spell. "Is the shower fixed?"

From the floor, nuzzling Margaret, I study Matthew while he and Dena talk house. He's reserved, I think, and opaque. There's something about him that seems inaccessible—or, at the very least, hard to know—and I don't know why: He's friendly; he's warm; he answers the questions Dena asks.

She pulls out three wineglasses, but Matthew says he has work to do yet. He puts a kettle on for tea.

I hear myself say, "I think I'll have tea, too," even though I want wine, even though I hate tea.

Dena tells him about getting towed.

I tell him how furious everyone at the tow pound was and that I think the clerk has the hardest job in New York, worse even than sanitation or advertising.

Matthew smiles at me, which makes me want to talk more. I think of telling him about the man who offered to pay our fines and then acting out my damsel-villain-hero skit, but I can't do it again in front of Dena, no matter who taught it to me.

He asks how I take my tea.

I say, "Milk and sugar," hoping they'll cut the tea taste.

To Dena, he says, "How'd the meeting go?"

She didn't tell me about any meeting, and it occurs to me, as it has many times before, that Dena is more forthcoming with her other friends.

"It was stressful," she says. "But I liked the guy you told me I'd like."

"Anders," he says.

"He was nice."

Dena works in the urban-planning office at Roosevelt Island, but beyond her taking the tram to work, I have no idea what she does. I feel that I should know, too, because she's been doing it for a long time.

I say, "What was your meeting about?"

"It was with some people from Swatch," she says. "I want them to do a tram watch."

I nod as though I understand what a watch has to do with urban planning.

She goes back to telling Matthew how stressed out everyone in her office has been since hearing the rumor about layoffs.

Matthew says, "The worst part about stress is that it makes us all so shallow."

Once he's gone upstairs, I say to Dena, "He's smart."

She says, "Since when do you drink tea?"

"I have for a while." I add another spoonful of sugar to help the medicine go down and drink as much of it as I can.

While she gets towels and sheets from the linen closet, I try to decide which of my many questions to ask about Matthew. I decide on, *Does he have a girlfriend?* and say, "Bob?"

When she looks at me, her face is pinched, and I say, "What were the names of your Russian wolfhounds?"

"Ivor and Magda."

"That's right."

As I get undressed, I worry that my description of the tow pound annoyed Dena; she paid a lot of money and I turned it into a joke. I tell myself that I'll find a way to pay her back. But maybe she's annoyed that I asked about Richard's children; maybe it reminded her of how I spoke the night I'd found out he was married, and I can't undo that.

Lying in the dark, though, I forget about Dena. I'm thinking about Matthew, and the thought of him makes me both excited and calm.

I realize that he reminds me of my father, though I'm not sure why. He seems smart; he seems strong; he seems self-contained. My father could seem inaccessible, too—with everyone but my mother. There was something just between the two of them. And that's what I want with Matthew.

. . . . .

In the morning, Matthew's in the kitchen, washing dishes.

He says, "Good morning," and I love his quiet-sounding voice and his loose-fitting jeans and his bare feet.

I say, "Morning."

Dena's at the grocery store, he says. Do I want pancakes with fresh-picked blueberries? He holds up a bowl of blueberried batter.

I say, "Maybe when I wake up."

He pours me a cup of coffee from an old-fashioned percolator. He's awkward as he says, "You work in advertising?"

"Sort of," I say. "I'm between careers." Then I remember that I have an assignment due on Monday, and I tell him I'll pay him a dollar if he'll help me with it. "We have to name a club for people who stay in Comfort Inns a lot."

He says, "What do you have so far?"

I say, "The Comfort Inn Club," and ask him what he does.

"I'm an architect," he says, and I think, *Of course you are. Like Henry Fonda in* 12 Angry Men, *you are a man who fights for justice and builds tall buildings. You are a man who will change the skyline of my life.*

I ask what he's working on now.

He says, "A kitchen."

I get up to refill my coffee cup and stand beside Matthew at the counter. I look out the window at the backyard and the hills in the distance.

He asks if I want to see the vegetable garden, and I say that I do.

Outside, he points out Boston and red lettuces, tomatoes, carrots, basil, mint, and cilantro. He picks two sprigs of rosemary, and we're chewing on them when we walk into the house.

Dena's putting away groceries, and after Matthew goes upstairs, she says, "What were you guys doing out there?"

It reminds me of the time she came home late from the rink, and I waited for her in her sister's room. Ellen was getting ready to go out, and she let me look through her closet with her. "Wear this," I said, about a beautiful navy blue sweater with tiny red flowers embroidered at the neck.

"It's too small for me," Ellen said. "You want it?"

That was when Dena came home; she appeared in the doorway.

I mouthed, *Thank you,* to Ellen about the sweater I folded over my arm and followed Dena to her room. She shut her door and said, "What were you doing in Ellen's room?"

The true answer was, *Having the time of my life.* But I said, "I thought it was Tracy's."

. . . . .

Dena wants to give me a tour of the nearest town. In her car, I taste the rosemary in my mouth, and I think of Matthew tasting it in his.

She points out the farmers' market, the eclectic bookstore, the restaurant she likes, and the thrift shop where she bought the long madras shorts she's wearing. We pass an antique store that she says is great and cheap, and I ask if she wants to take a look inside.

She says, "It's too nice out to shop," which sounds like a reprimand, one suburban girl scolding another for being suburban.

. . . . .

Dena and I are packing a picnic when Matthew appears and asks if we're going to the lake.

Apparently we are.

"Would you mind bringing Margaret?" he asks. "You can take my car."

I say, "Sure," at the same time Dena does, and it occurrs to me that it is not for me to say.

"If I get enough work done," he says, "I'll ride the bike over."

"You always say that," she says. "And you never come."

He says, "I will if I can."

. . . . .

I love the old-fashioned bulk of the Wagoneer. As Dena drives it up and down a long, hilly dirt road, I picture Matthew and me driving as boyfriend and girlfriend. Then I imagine us older, as husband and wife, my stepdog, Margaret, in the back.

"What are you thinking about?" Dena asks.

"I was thinking I'd like to take a road trip."

The beach around the lake is just a rim of muddy sand, and the widest stretch is occupied by other lake- and sunbathers. No matter: Dena has a grassy spot staked out, a clearing by a glade of low-slung shade trees.

Margaret goes and sits in the water.

After lunch, Dena closes her eyes, and I think she's about to take a nap.

I lie beside her. In a sleepy-time voice, I say, "Did anything ever happen between you and Matthew?"

"No," she says. "Why?"

Her *why* comes so fast and sharp that I say, "I just wondered."

She sits up and pulls out a big fat book called *The Power Broker: Robert Moses and the Fall of New York.* She's wide awake now.

I'm between books, so I've brought three, plus the newspaper, which I can't read because the wind has picked up. I take out my notebook and decide to start my advertising homework. After a while, I have two names—"Comfort Innsiders" and "The Red-Carpet Club," both of which seem awful, but can a name for a Comfort Inn club be great?

I say that I'm going for a swim.

Dena reminds me to wear sneakers. "It's mushy," she says. "And there are snapping turtles."

I hesitate; I think of Matthew joining us and how I'll look in my bikini and sneakers.

Dena looks up from her book. "You need them."

I decide to put off swimming until she takes her nap. I pick up my notebook and try to think of a third name; in advertising, you always need three of everything.

"You're not going in?" she says.

"Not yet."

Dena lies down. She's asleep when I see Matthew riding a mountain bike toward us. I remember Dena telling him, "You never come," and I think, *He came for me.*

I watch him set his bike down on the grass. He's wearing a rumpled shirt over seersucker bathing trunks.

I point to Dena and mouth, *Sleeping.*

He looks at Margaret sitting in the water and asks if she's gone swimming at all. I shake my head.

He tells me that she needs to swim—it's good for her hips—and that he's going in.

When he takes off his shirt, I see that his shoulders are narrow and his chest almost hairless and almost concave. For a second I'm disappointed but right away I think, *Grow up; this is the chest of a husband.*

He puts his spectacles in their case and tells me that he's blind now and depending on me to get him to the lake. I tell him that when I don't have my contacts in I'm blind, too; without them, I say, the world becomes an abstract painting, and he smiles without looking at anything, the way blind people do.

We're halfway to the lake when I say, "We don't need sneakers?"

He says, "Dena thinks we do," and laughs.

He runs into the water—it's cold—and dives under. Margaret swims beside him, and, like a good father, he encourages her.

I squish into the lake up to my waist. Standing in the pale brown water, I realize that I haven't actually swum in a long time. I'm used to the ocean—ducking under waves and floating and getting pulled around in the surf. I try to remember the swimming lessons I took at camp, but all that comes back is the odor of chlorine and wet Band-Aids.

Matthew says, "You want to swim across?"

For a moment, I act like I'm too absorbed in the majesty of the scenery to swim. Then I decide to be truthful with him; I say, "I don't really know how to swim anymore."

"Want me to teach you?"

"Teach me," I say.

He moves his arms to demonstrate the crawl, and then, standing behind me, moves mine. His touch is light but sure.

He says, "And just do a flutter kick."

I ask the question that has been nagging me for years: "Do you keep your legs straight?"

"Slightly bent," he says.

I look toward shore, and I see Dena: She's using her hand as a visor and watching us.

. . . . .

The three of us make dinner together. We have corn on the cob and a salad with tomatoes and lettuce from the garden. When I start to tell Matthew about Dena's *Salade Fatiguee,* she says, "Shut up."

As ever, I want to say, *You shut up.* Instead, I walk out of the kitchen as though remembering an appointment upstairs.

Matthew grills fish, an unfavorite of mine, but it tastes better than I thought fish could, and I think, *He even makes fish taste good,* and this seems to be a metaphor for the hard things we will face together.

We sit on the screened-in porch. There's the sound of crickets. I talk about my dad, and Matthew tells me about his—a priest, still alive, in Kansas.

Dena insists on clearing the dishes herself, and a few minutes later she comes back carrying a chocolate cake with candles and singing "Happy Birthday."

Matthew joins in: he has a deep, deep voice, which makes me think, *Swing low, sweet chariot, coming for to carry me home.*

I make a wish and blow out the candles.

When Dena goes into the kitchen for plates, Matthew says, "I didn't know it was your birthday."

I tell him it isn't until Wednesday, and that my brother's having a party for me. "You should come," I say. "Dena's coming."

We only eat a few bites of cake before Dena looks at her watch and says, "We have to go."

"Where are we going?" I ask.

She says it's a birthday surprise.

Matthew pours scotch into a silver flask and tells me to get a sweater. "You don't think you'll need it," he says, "but you will."

. . . . .

The amphitheater is crowded, and just as we find seats in the bleachers, six black women in pastel dresses walk onto the stage. In a perfectly synchronized move, they turn their backs to the audience and place their white pocketbooks on the floor, which seems funny, and Matthew thinks so, too; he catches my eye.

They sing gospel and sound like The Staples Singers, especially on "I'll Take You There," one of my favorite songs of all time.

After a while, practically the whole audience is standing, and Matthew and Dena and I are, too. Everyone is clapping along, and if I do not believe in Jesus exactly, I believe in whoever or whatever it is that makes these singers sing the way they do and this night breezy and Matthew's fingers touch mine a little longer than necessary when we pass the flask back and forth.

Toward the end of the concert, Dena sits down. I ask if she's okay, and she says, "I'm tired."

Now it is just Matthew and me and the flask of scotch and our lingering fingers.

Everyone sings the encore, "Amazing Grace." I close my eyes at "I once was lost, but now am found." Matthew's voice is loud and clear for me to love. I myself am tone-deaf, but I mouth the words with all my heart.

. . . . .

"What does *gospel* mean?" I ask in the car.

"The message of the Lord," Matthew says.

"The truth," Dena says.

"So when people say 'That's the gospel truth,' are they saying 'the truth truth'?"

Matthew shrugs twice.

At home, I announce that I'm going to have another scotch scotch on the porch porch.

The chill in Dena's "Good night" makes me wonder if I thanked her for the cake and the concert. Maybe I haven't been helpful enough in the kitchen. I wash the rest of the dishes.

Then I get a glass of scotch with ice cubes and go out to the porch. I stroke Margaret's back and look out at the moon lighting up the hills. *Another minute,* I think, *and Matthew will come downstairs and out to the porch and he will kiss me, and our life together will start.*

An hour passes before the porch door opens.

It's Dena.

I try to make my face look happy to see her, and I notice that hers is grim.

She sets her own glass of scotch on the table and sits across from me. "You asked me if anything ever happened between Matthew and me."

She takes a deep breath. "The first year that we rented the house."

I can see how hard it is for her to talk, and that she doesn't want to; I say, "You don't have to tell me."

I think maybe she's decided not to; she is studying her glass, turning it around, as if to figure out how the factory made it. She keeps her eyes on the glass while she speaks. "We both had a lot to drink one night. Or I did. I went into his room," she says, "and got into bed with him."

I can tell that she's remembering that night, and she is with him in his bed more than she is with me on the porch. Maybe she's putting her arms through his or kissing him.

Then her face sort of freezes into a smile, and I see the humiliation in it. "He said, 'No.' He kicked me out."

I realize I've been holding my breath only when I hear myself exhale, and I hope Dena didn't hear.

She says, "The next day he told me that he didn't feel that way about me, and he said he never would. I would have to know that if we were going to be friends." She looks at me. "We never even kissed."

I want to put my arm around her, but I can tell she does not want consolation.

She asks if I have any cigarettes, and I get them. I light one, my first since arriving; I haven't wanted Matthew to know I smoke. I hand the cigarette to her, and she holds on to it, so I light another.

"How many years ago?" I ask.

"Four?" she says. "Five?"

"Isn't it hard to share a house with him?"

"No," she says, and her voice is adamant. "We're friends. We're great, great friends."

. . . . .

After she goes to bed, I drink another scotch on the porch. Dena has finally talked to me the way I've always wanted her to, but I don't feel any closer to her. Maybe it's because her story seemed pointed—not that I know what the point is.

On the stairs, I realize I'm a little drunk. I go into the bathroom and wash my face and brush my teeth until I don't taste scotch or cigarettes anymore.

Matthew's door is open a crack; his light is on. I stand here, trying to decide whether to go in. I think of what Dena told me and wonder if it was a warning.

I knock.

After what seems like a long time, Matthew says, "Come in."

He's sitting at his desk, marking up a big piece of honey-colored tracing paper. He waits a moment before turning around to me.

"I just wanted to say good night," I say.

He says, "Good night."

. . . . .

In bed, I try to think what gave me the idea that Matthew felt as I do. He came to the lake—but maybe he just got enough work done; he stood behind me and moved my arms—but maybe he just wanted to teach me to swim; his fingers lingered on mine when I passed the flask but maybe he was just being careful.

I tell myself I will know in the morning, and in the morning I do know.

The house feels deserted, though both the Saab and the Wagoneer are in the driveway. There's coffee in the percolator, and I pour myself a cup. The only movement in the house is the cat clock's shifting eyes and switching tail.

Matthew comes in through the screen door, saying, "Morning. Dena's taking a bike ride."

He offers a section of the newspaper to me. Our eyes meet, but his look at mine like I'm anybody, any weekend guest or any friend of Dena's; he looks at me like I am nobody to him.

I say, "I'll take whatever you're not reading," because I need the paper between us.

There's no need, however; he goes out to the porch to read.

. . . . .

The pain is sharp at first, and then without easing exactly, it becomes steady and deeper, more ache than pang.

At the lake, I imitate how I'd act if I didn't care about Matthew.

When he asks me what Dena was like at fourteen, I say that she was pretty much the same as now.

He says, "Tell the truth truth."

She says, "Don't tell him anything."

I don't; I know that they are just talking to each other through me.

Everything this afternoon calls forth my faults and flaws, all the reasons why this man I want doesn't want me, and those reasons call forth more reasons.

When Matthew and Dena go swimming in the lake, I ask myself why I've never learned to swim or skate or draw or sing or play the piano. I'm lazy; I lack discipline; I have no patience. I can't think of a single skill I've mastered or a single talent I have. I barely have a job, let alone a career.

When Dena walks along the shore in her black slippers, seeming not to care how she looks, I think I care too much, and I'm not pretty enough.

When she lies down and picks up her book on Robert Moses and New York, I realize that I don't know anything about the history of New York or the history of the United States or the history of anywhere, modern or ancient; I have no grasp of geography; I don't even really know what physics is. All this contributes to my overall lack of substance.

I think of my father then. It occurs to me that in striving to please him I hoped to become the kind of woman a man of his stature would love.

Matthew swims to the other side of the lake. He looks very small now and far away.

Dena stands. "I want to show you the nature trail."

I can't think of anything I want to see less than the nature trail, but I go because it means that I won't have to look at Matthew.

I follow her into the woods. It's cool and dark; there's only the occasional flicker of sunlight through the trees. We don't talk. Every few yards she stoops to examine a leaf or flower, none of which seem worthy of examination.

We walk a long time, and I think, *I hate nature.*

"Isn't it amazing here?" she says.

I say, "It's okay."

"You want to turn back?"

I say that I do.

She decides we should take a different path back and chooses a less-traveled one; it's skinny and overgrown. I walk at her musing pace, which makes me feel like I'm in a harness.

She stops to pick some purple flowers that look like weeds you'd see by a trash can at a highway rest stop.

To her back, I say, "Dena."

She doesn't turn around. "Uh-huh?"

I say, "I hate it when you say 'shut up' to me."

"Okay," she says, straightening up. "I won't say it anymore."

I remember that I asked her not to say "shut up" once before, in tenth grade, and she answered, "Shut up," as a joke.

She starts walking faster. I follow a few feet back so I won't bump into her if she stops to revel in more wonders of nature, but she doesn't stop. She keeps picking up speed, and it becomes hard to keep up with her. After a while I don't try. I lose sight of her.

She is waiting for me where our path rejoins the main trail. She's kneeling in ferns.

When I reach her, she stands up. "I want to ask a favor."

"Sure," I say.

She doesn't answer right away. It occurs to me that she is choosing her words. "Don't go out with Matthew."

"What?"

She's holding the rest-stop flowers at her side like the weeds they are.

I say, "Nothing's going to happen with Matthew," and it hurts to say.

She hears that this is not a promise; she raises her head in only half a nod.

I look at her. "You said you were just friends."

"I hate that expression," she says. "What's bigger or deeper or more important than friends?"

I translate this to mean that whatever is between her and Matthew is bigger or deeper or more important than her and me; or him and me; or me.

She says, "I don't want to lose you, Bob."

I say, "You're not going to lose anyone."

She is waiting for my answer.

It would be easy for me to promise; there doesn't seem to be any chance that I will ever go out with Matthew. But it seems wrong for her to ask—wrong to ask me to forgo the possibility of my happiness for hers, which may not even be happiness but less misery.

I say, "No."

She stares at me. Then she says, "After all I've done for you."

. . . . .

My only consolation as I pack to go back to New York is that I will never have to see Matthew again. I will never have to be in his company and think of all the things I am not and never will be.

He leaves just before we do. He comes to my room and says, "It was nice to finally meet you."

"Same here." I think, *Please get out of here.*

"Well," he says, "see you Wednesday."

I don't know what he's talking about. Then I remember: I invited him to my birthday party.

. . . . .

On the drive back to New York, Dena and I are silent. We listen to the public-radio program *Weekend All Things Considered.*

When she drops me off at the Hot Plate, she says, "Good-bye," and I'm surprised to hear in her voice what I myself have been trying to conceal: Whatever affection we have for each other is from a long time ago.

. . . . .

I think of all the reasons Dena was wrong to ask me not to go out with Matthew, and all the reasons I was right to refuse.

I escape feeling sympathy for her by reminding myself that she's chosen to spend weekend after weekend, summer after summer, with a man who reminds her of all the things she isn't, a man who doesn't want her and never will; meanwhile she's chosen to sleep with a man who's married. I tell myself that these are choices I would never make.

. . . . .

My brother throws the party at his girlfriend's loft in TriBeCa. They've only been going out for a few months, and it seems like too much to ask. But Jack says Kim wants to do it.

It's a big, fun party. They've invited their friends, too, and everyone I know in New York comes—everyone except Dena.

It isn't until after Jack's toast that Matthew shows up. I see him walk in and notice that he's empty-handed; he is the only guest who hasn't brought flowers or wine or a card.

I wave to him, but I don't go over. It's easy to avoid him, there are so many people here. I see him talking to my brothers, Jack first and then Robert; later, a pretty girl who works for Kim goes up to him, but they don't talk long.

I'm surprised by how late Matthew stays.

He waits near the door while I say good-bye to a series of departing guests, and then he comes up to me and says, "Happy birthday."

I say, "Thank you." I'm not looking at him exactly. I'm waiting for him to go. But he doesn't.

Finally, when I do look at him, he holds my gaze.

He says, "I want to see you."

Everything I felt rushes back. I give him my number at the Hot Plate.

He gives me a kiss that barely touches my lips—it means nothing or everything.

After he's gone, I think, *Happy birthday to me.*

Jack says, "That was the guy?"

"That was him."

Jack shakes his head.

"What?"

"He's not for you," he says.

I say, "How do you know?" but what I mean is, *How do* you *know?*

"He's like Ashley Wilkes," he says. "Any one of these guys is Rhett-ier than he is."

Again, I ask my benignly inflected, "How do you know?"

"How do I know?" he says, tackling me into a bear hug. "How do I know? I know, that's how I know."

. . . . .

When Matthew doesn't call, I feel bad but don't drown myself in it. I let Jack's *He's not for you* comfort me. I know I have to watch that, though.

Not that I regret breaking up with Demetri. I see now that everything everyone said about him was true: He was selfish, self-absorbed, self-aggrandizing, et al. He was also fun. Fun might not have mattered to my father, but it matters to me. That's one problem with going by his lights, or anyone's, instead of mine.

. . . . .

In late September, my brothers and I go home to Surrey. In the car, Jack asks if I ever heard from Ashley, and I say I didn't.

He says, "I thought he was gay."

"That's so funny," I say. "I think Kim's a lesbian."

It's the first time the four of us have been together in a while, and my mother makes a good dinner. As ever, *Shalom* is on the mail table, and I tell my brothers about my job interview, and they laugh, and my mother can laugh now, too. Then I remember aloud how distraught I was that afternoon and how Mrs. Blumenthal came to my aid.

My mother says, "I wish I could've helped you."

I say, "I think the important thing is that somebody did."

I imitate Mrs. Blumenthal's throaty, "You need a drink." I tell them I asked what she'd have if Dr. Blumenthal left her and do her deadpan, "Champagne."

I don't feel I'm betraying her; I don't say what she told me about not having the energy to move on.

My mother sighs.

I say, "What?"

She hesitates, and once she speaks, I realize that she's been going over in her mind whether the story is appropriate. "One night when Dena was here for dinner, in high school, she mentioned that her father spent the night at the hospital a lot. Whenever he had an emergency."

I don't get it.

"He's a plastic surgeon," my mother says.

I still don't get it.

Robert says, "There aren't a lot of emergencies in plastic surgery."

. . . . .

Later, lying in bed, I wonder if Dena knows about her father. I decide that she probably does, and I imagine how I would feel if I knew that my father was unfaithful to my mother.

Then I remember Richard, and I think that marriage might not mean much to Dena. I can't really blame her: She learned about marriage from her parents, just as I did from mine. For all I know, sleeping with Richard is just Dena's way of trying not to be her mother.

. . . . .

Sunday afternoon, when I get back to the Hot Plate, the phone is ringing. I think it may be Dena, and am relieved when I hear a man's voice.

He says, "This is Matthew Stevens," to identify himself, even though I never learned his last name.

I say, "Hello, Matthew Stevens."

He says, "I wondered if you'd meet me for a drink."

. . . . .

We meet at a restaurant in the West Village.

It's not quite warm enough to sit outside, but we do. Maybe we're both trying to pretend that it's warmer so we can act like less time has passed than has.

We both order scotch.

Matthew isn't wearing his glasses. He's probably more handsome without them—you can see his blue eyes and long eyelashes better—but he looks to me like he's missing something. I remember how blind he said he was, and I wonder if my face is just a flesh-colored oval to him; he does seem to be looking at me indistinctly.

When our drinks come, he says he's sorry he didn't call me sooner.

I wait for him to explain.

Instead, he tells me he took a trip to Paris, and how pretty it is in September, prettier even than in April. He describes the light on the Seine. It was golden, he says; it had the effect of making you feel nostalgic for a moment you were still in.

I described that exact feeling to Dena once about the light in Venice and say so.

He asks if I've heard from her and doesn't seem surprised when I tell him that I haven't.

I say, "Have you?"

"Oh, yes." He hesitates before going on; I think he's aware of betraying her, but he does anyway. He says that Dena still calls him, asking him not to go out with me.

Suddenly I know that she talked to him about me after the gospel concert. When I say, "She said you two were just friends," I remember her saying how much she disliked the expression *just friends.*

He nods.

"I don't really understand," I say.

"What part?"

" 'What part?' " I say. "Um, if you're just friends, why would she care if you went out with somebody else?"

"Not somebody else," he says. "You."

It seems obvious now, though it didn't occur to me before. The way I phrased it in my own mind was that she didn't want anyone to be with Matthew, *not even me.*

I realize I will never hear from Dena again, and I will never call her. It gives me a chill. It is a strange thing to end a friendship, even if you know it's what you want. It's like a death; all of a sudden your experience of a person becomes finite.

I take a long sip of scotch. I say, "And you give your friends the right to decide who you go out with?"

When he says, "She was upset," I hear that he's defending himself. I see Matthew now as my brother did. I think of how little help Ashley was to Scarlett after the war.

He puts his glasses on. He tells me that Dena has gotten even worse lately—he mentions crying—and though there is concern in his voice, my impression is that he's talking less about her than himself; he is trying to convince me that it isn't strange for him to obey her wishes.

He says that he's always been clear with Dena. "I told her I didn't feel that way about her, and I never would." I remember the look on her face as she told me the story.

"It doesn't matter what you say. The way you act with Dena gives her hope." I look right at him. "The way you acted with me gave me hope."

He nods, and I see that he's admitting something—guilt? weakness? failure? At the very least, he is admitting that he's gone through this before, and more than once.

I want him to tell me why, but he doesn't say anything. It seems possible that Matthew is gay and possible that he isn't; possible that he is just a little more afraid than the rest of us and possible that he is much more; it even seems possible that what he has with Dena is bigger or deeper or more important than anything else to him.

I don't know. But I no longer believe, as I did that last afternoon at the lake, that my many, many flaws are what prevented Matthew from wanting a life with me. It seems more likely that it is his flaw that he can't or won't love anyone—and that he is indiscriminate in his unlove.

When the waiter comes to the table and asks if we want another drink, I say, "That's it for me."

Matthew says, "Just the check, please."

I say, "Let's split it," but Matthew shakes his head, and I don't argue; it is just a drink.

He puts some bills on the little tray.

The waiter says, "Do you want change?"

He doesn't.

Before getting up, Matthew says that he's sorry for the problems he's caused between Dena and me. "I feel responsible," he says.

I say, "Don't," and I mean it. After all, he barely did anything.

TEEN ROMANCE

Even before I really saw Bobby, I sensed him, as a sheep does a wolf. I could feel him maneuvering around the easels and stools toward me. This was in Mixed Media I, Wednesday evenings, 6:00–9:00, at the New School. The only other man in the class was a retired principal.

Bobby was good-looking enough—boyish and a little scruffy, with meaty shoulders, dark eyes, and a square jaw—but that didn't explain his magnetism. When he sat beside me, my shell gave way to feathers.

"Bobby Guest," he said in a hoarse voice.

I said, "Sophie Applebaum."

Then our teacher stood up. She was wiry with muscles and had long, thick, auburn hair. Her name was Maureen and she was the kind of fifty that made getting older seem like a reward instead of a punishment for living. She spoke with a Midwestern accent and said "you guys," like a camp counselor; meanwhile, you could tell how smart she was.

Her teaching style, she confessed, was loosey-goosey and had become even more so since she'd adopted a three-year-old insomniac from Vietnam. If we wanted serious instruction, she said, she'd give us the name of another instructor.

After telling us her hands-off theory of teaching, she asked us to go around the room and introduce ourselves.

First up was the woman on my right, whose face and neck were beiged with foundation. She was younger than Maureen but seemed older; she reminded me of a hotel lobby with overstuffed chairs, thick rugs, and no natural light or air. "Margo," she said. "I'm in PR."

I said, "Sophie," and hoped that was enough. Maureen, friend to all the Earth's awkward, nodded that it was.

Bobby was the only one in the class who provided both first and last names. Then he coughed, changing his voice from rough to smooth, so that when he said, "I'm a waiter," I was reminded of Mel Tormé's nickname, the Velvet Fog.

We had a cancer survivor, an accountant, and a sexy squirrel who was an actress and told us her name was "Cheryl with a *C*." The oldest member of the class was a great-grandmother, the youngest a twelfth grader who didn't turn down the volume on her Walkman when she introduced herself. She practically shouted, "I want to design CD covers," and Bobby said, "For the deaf," just loud enough for me to hear.

Maureen said, "Talk amongst yourselves," and from a grocery bag, she produced the objects we were to draw—an old boot, bottles, a chiffon scarf, apples, grapes, an umbrella.

Bobby opened an old tackle box of art supplies, and I opened my brand-new one. He squeezed paint onto his palette like he'd done it a thousand times before. I was sharpening a pencil when my neighbor Margo sighed in my direction.

She said, "Can you believe this?"

"What?"

She said, "I only took this class to meet men."

Bobby reached his hand out to her and, for the third time in less than an hour, said, "Bobby Guest."

Margo said, "Age-appropriate men," but you could tell she was flattered.

She turned back to me and said, "It's crazy, right?" and I realized that she saw herself and me as one and the same, two lovelorn peas in a manless pod.

She started sketching. He started painting. I stared at the boot and bottles.

Without looking up, Bobby said, "Get to work."

I dug in. Soon I forgot myself and him; it was just the boot and my drawing, the boot and my drawing.

I started at the sound of Bobby's voice: "You want to smoke a cigarette?"

. . . . .

The brisk evening was turning into a cold night, and Bobby took off his black leather jacket and said, "Here."

I said, "Thanks, I'm okay," even though I was cold.

"Come on," he said, and I put it on.

He offered me a cigarette, a Camel non-filter, but I took out one of my own Benson & Hedges.

"I've never known anyone who smokes Camels," I said. "I think of it as a cigarette you'd smoke in the desert."

He said, "Whereas you'd smoke a Benson and Hedges at your babysitting job."

"So," I said, "what do you do besides wait tables?"

He said, "You know, not every waiter in New York aspires to something else."

"So you're a career waiter?"

He said, "I do this and that."

"Like name one thing."

He said, "I smoke cigarettes."

I wasn't sure why I was uncomfortable, but I thought facts might help. "How old are you?"

He said, "How old do you think I am?" and I thought, *Actor.*

I said my age: "Thirty-three?"

He picked a piece of tobacco off his tongue. "Why do you want to know?" he said. "You want to pin me down? You want to say, 'Bobby Guest is a thirty-three-year-old waiter'?"

"No."

He said, "What do you really want to know, Applebaum?" and his calling me by my last name made me feel like we were ninth graders. I liked that. He said, "You want to know if I'm seeing anyone? I'm not. Are you seeing anyone? Sorry. Don't answer that."

"Okay."

"You can ask me one question," he said. "One question, and I'll answer truthfully."

"Okay," I said. "What are you trying to do now?"

He gave me a wolfy smile. "This minute? With you?"

I said, "What's your goal in life?" and winced at how corny and earnest I sounded.

He looked away. He thought. "I guess I'm trying to become a better man than the one I'm hardwired to be."

He seemed surprised to hear himself say something he meant. Then he put the cigarette out with his boot and kicked it into the gutter. "I'm thirty-seven," he said.

. . . . .

Upstairs, Cheryl was standing in front of Bobby's painting. He said an elementary school, "Beep, beep."

She turned around so that when she went by him her breasts skimmed his chest. She said, "Your painting is excellent."

It was. It reminded me of Hopper's lonely landscapes of Cape Cod. I said, "What are you doing in Mixed Media I?"

He said, "Same thing you're doing here."

"Really," I said. "Why aren't you in Advanced Painting?"

He said, "Wouldn't be the best in there."

. . . . .

On our second cigarette break, he offered me his jacket, and I took it without a word. He said, "So, what line of work are you in, Applebaum?"

When I told him I wrote advertising copy, he asked if he'd seen any of my ads.

"Live live live girls girls girls?" I said. "That's mine."

He seemed to know that I'd made this joke before; he went right by it. He asked if I enjoyed my work.

I said, "The important thing is that at the moment I don't hate it."

"Ah," he said. "Aiming high."

"Excuse me," I said, "you were saying how much you enjoyed waiting tables."

"Waiting tables is a day job," he said.

"Until you make it big as a smoker?"

He moved closer to me, as though for warmth. He was looking into my eyes, but I got the feeling that he wasn't trying to see who I was as much as gauge his effect on me. I said, "You're an actor, aren't you?"

"What kind of thing is that to say?"

I said, "I didn't mean it as an insult."

"Yes you did."

. . . . .

Upstairs, Maureen walked around the room, looking at everyone's work. Her face was as impassive regarding my muddy sketch as it was Bobby's masterpiece. When he and I walked out of class, though, I saw her gazing at his canvas.

The elevators were crowded and slow, so Bobby and I took the stairs. He was carrying a helmet, and I said, "You ride a motorcycle?"

"I do," he said.

"Isn't it really dangerous?"

He shrugged.

Outside, he asked where I lived, and I told him the Upper West Side. He lived in the Village.

He was looking indistinctly down Twelfth Street. "You want to get something to eat?"

I did. "Are we talking about a date here?"

He laughed.

He made me feel both younger and older than I was, both inexperienced and past experience. I said, "I try not to go out with guys like you," a line for a junior-high or a nursing-home cafeteria.

He said, "What do you mean 'Guys like me'? Waiters? Actors? Writers?"

"Satyrs," I said.

I noticed his eyebrows then—they slanted upward—and I realized they said what he couldn't or wouldn't; I'd hurt his feelings. He nodded, as people do when they get a joke and don't think it's funny. "I was just hungry," he said.

I was pretty sure we were headed toward a restaurant, but I didn't know. We weren't talking. We walked down Fifth Avenue like two pedestrians who happened to be moving at the same pace.

Almost to myself, I said, "I knew you were an actor."

He shook his head.

At his motorcycle, I said, "What do you write?"

"This is my stop," he said. "Good night, Applebaum."

. . . . .

I thought about him during the week. I didn't want to, but I did.

I called my friends. I said, "I mean, what kind of thirty-seven-year-old calls himself Bobby?"

One said, "Hockey player?"

Another said, "Bobby Kennedy?"

I repeated the question to my older brother, who said, "Can we get to the point of this conversation?"

Just a minute into my description of Bobby, my younger brother imitated a robot in a television program from our childhood: "Danger, Will Robinson."

. . . . .

I got to the New School early and sat in last week's seat, across from Cheryl with a *C*, whose jeans were so tight her crotch was a rounded *W*.

I pretended not to see Margo walk in, though I sent her an ESP message: *Please don't sit next to me.*

She sat next to me.

"Hi," I said. "I sort of thought you were dropping the class."

"Why?"

"You said you wanted to meet men."

"Well," she said, "art for art's sake, I guess." She opened her tackle box. "I might meet somebody who knows someone."

I was trying not to watch the door; when Bobby came in, I hunted for nothing in my tackle box.

I heard the scratchy metal static of a Walkman and looked up to see the twelfth-grade CD designer sitting on the stool I'd thought of as Bobby's.

Bobby was sitting next to Cheryl.

I told the twelfth grader I'd forgotten her name, and she said, "Michele."

I wanted to ask if she'd mind turning her Walkman down; instead I heard myself say a friendly, "What are you listening to, Michele?"

She said, "Zeppelin." She was wearing the outfit she'd worn last week—an oversized sweater with holes, a long black skirt, and army boots.

I said, "I didn't know anyone still listened to Zep."

"My dad does," she said. "He's a DJ."

"What station?"

She said, "Parties," and let her wavy black hair fall in front of her face.

I wished I had hair I could disappear under.

A fainting couch on a platform had replaced our still life, and Maureen announced that we had a model. In the hallway I heard whistling—I have always been partial to whistlers—and in walked a portly man in a plaid flannel bathrobe and yellow flip-flops. His thinning hair was dyed an unfortunate maroonish brown, though not, as I would soon see, everywhere. He held his clothes in a bundle.

"This is Bert," Maureen said. "He's a painter himself."

We all watched as she opened a locker for him, and we all saw his big white underpants fall to the floor. I felt like my own underpants were suddenly on display, or worse, my father's. But Bert just stooped and grabbed them and threw them in the locker, whistling.

He untied his bathrobe and flip-flopped over to the couch, where he settled his big belly and small penis into a pose.

"Is that comfortable, Bert?" Maureen said. "Can you hold that?"

It was; he could.

Instead of a pencil, I took out brushes and paints, which allowed me to portray the subject more impressionistically. I started with Bert's head and left a big blank space for his body. I concentrated on his eyes and nose.

I needed a cigarette as badly as I ever had, and when Bert stood up to stretch, I grabbed my jacket and headed out.

As I passed Bobby, he leaned back and said, "Hey."

I said a flirtless, "Hi," and kept going.

A few minutes later, he joined me outside. He lit his cigarette, cupping it against the wind.

When he held out his jacket to me I said, "I have a jacket."

He said, "Why are you mad?"

"I'm not mad."

He said, "I'm the one who should be mad."

"Why should you be mad?"

He said, "If you don't know, I can't tell you."

We stood, smoking, and the quiet made me uneasy. "Just out of curiosity," I said, "why do you call yourself Bobby?"

"What do you mean?"

"I mean, instead of Bob or Rob or Robert." I tried to soften my tone by adding, "My brother's name is Robert."

"He's probably a Robert, then."

I said, "He is a Robert."

Bobby said, "You know the poet Billy Collins?"

"No."

"You should," he said. "You'd like him."

I nodded, as though I often read poetry and always understood it and would seek out the poems of Poet Collins at my earliest opportunity.

Acquaintance to acquaintance, he said, "How're you liking the class?"

"I like it."

He said, "What about Maureen?"

I was relieved to talk about her, and I went on and on; talking about her made me feel stronger and also looser, like Maureen herself. At the end of my appreciation, I said, "I hope I'm like her when I'm fifty."

He said, "You don't look that good now."

When I could talk, I raised my hand and called out, "Medic! Medic!"

"I'm teasing you," he said.

"You're an asshole," I said. "You'll never get beyond your hard-wiring."

"You can't do that," he said.

"What?"

"You can't take something I trusted you with and use it against me."

"Why?" I said. "You just did it to me."

. . . . .

Maureen was standing at my easel, her fingers at her mouth.

She said, "Sophie," and I liked how she said my name; it was thoughtful, even affectionate. She suggested using the whole canvas, and, for the sake of composition, getting my subject down completely before focusing on any one detail.

Out of the corner of my eye, I focused on the detail of Cheryl's lip-glossed lips smiling at something Bobby was saying.

I pretended not to notice them. I pretended to be lost in my art. I pretended to be a painter painting.

When I felt Bobby staring at me, I looked up. Our eyes met, and he held my gaze; he held my gaze like he was holding me, and I held his as though holding him. Then he looked away, he was gone and it was over—a one-minute stand.

Before the end of class, Bert put on his bathrobe and walked around the room, pausing before each easel to regard the painting or drawing or collage of himself. He said nothing to the principal, who sat with his hands folded in his lap, and nothing to Great-grandmother, who beamed at her own sketch. Who knew what Bert saw or hoped to see? His face was expressionless, but I worried about how we all must have wounded his vanity.

I took a few steps back from my painting and saw it now as I hadn't before. It had many failings, but I stared at the most glaring of them: I'd made Bert's belly even bigger and his penis even smaller than life had made them.

It would be harder to shrink his belly than to enlarge his penis. The problem was, I'd avoided looking at his penis while I'd had the chance, and now I couldn't remember its specifics. I tried to call forth penises I'd known. I'd stared at some of them, but even in front of me they'd seemed unknowable, and not a single one came to my aid now.

I mixed more skin color. Blindly, I added length and girth to the tiny stem. I painted frantically, while monitoring Bert's progress around the horseshoe.

When he was only two easels away, I stepped back to see what he would see: His penis was now porn-long and log-wide, and even worse, waved up and sloped down like the trunk of an elephant.

I had just enough time to reshape it and stopped mid-stroke as Bert approached; I wasn't about to paint his penis while he watched. Instead, I touched up his earlobe.

I held my breath. But Bert sauntered right by my easel and on to Margo's, where he stood, watching her sketch.

"Well?" she said to him. "Say something."

He said, "I like my chin."

Margo laughed—it was a good, loud laugh—and Bert laughed with her.

In case they wanted to be alone, I got up to wash my brushes. En route, I glanced at Michele's painting, a fantastical forest in which Bert, medievally clothed and pierced by an arrow, was bleeding to death.

Through her headphones I heard: "If there's a bustle in your hedgerow . . ."

As I waited for the sink, I saw that Cheryl was reading a script with one line highlighted. Faintly, I heard her trying out various intonations under her breath—a cheerful, "Awesome pudding," a blasé, "Awesome pudding."

When I got back to my easel, Bobby was sitting on my stool and smiling at my painting.

"Get away from there," I said.

He said, "I'd like you to paint me sometime, Applebaum."

. . . . .

That week, I worked with Sam on a pitch for L'Institute, a new line of antiaging skin-care products.

At fifty-two, or roughly 3,100 in advertising years, Sam knew about aging as no one else in the agency did. He'd once been a creative director and now was a freelancer; he'd once produced award-winning TV campaigns and now was designing a mail package containing a moisturizer sample.

I asked Sam what I'd been wondering ever since I'd started in advertising: "Where are all the older people?" Deadpan, he said, "Dead." Then he said that maturity was valued almost as much in advertising as it was in cheerleading.

He was the only art director who still used a marker and pad instead of a computer. I kept the products on the windowsill for him to draw and me to try—facial cleanser and body scrub, toners, masks, and moisturizers for day and for night. I taped a sign that read L'INSTITUTE to my door, and Sam added MENTAL. I hung a poster warning of the dangers of sun and cigarettes and extolling the benefits of eight glasses of water a day.

When Sam and I ran out of ideas, I'd say, "Water," and get us each a bottle. Or I'd hand him the moisturizer and say, "You look a little dry."

We showed our work on Monday and again on Tuesday, and everyone loved it until late Wednesday when we met with Bruce, the highest of the higher-ups.

We took the elevator from 9 down to the lobby and switched elevator banks to go up to 23. We shuffled into Bruce's big office with the teams from 18 and 20. At six o'clock, when everyone was still getting sodas from the fridge and joking around, I pictured Bobby walking into Mixed Media I.

It was after seven by the time Bruce said, "Good work," to the other teams as they left to make negligible changes to their TV and print campaigns.

His face changed from pleased to disconcerted as Sam presented our concept of mailing the package from Switzerland, where le nonexistent institute supposedly was; he shook his head while I read the fictional director's letter aloud in a Swiss-ish accent.

As though Sam and I were children living in a fairy tale, Bruce reminded us that there was no real institute, and these products had been developed in Trenton.

Time was suddenly short; Bruce didn't even want to see the rest of our concepts. "It's more important to show synergy," he said, and asked us to execute mail packages off of the TV spots "A More Beautiful You" and "About Face."

As ever, Sam showed nothing but his own equanimity. He took off his glasses and let them hang on their string around his neck. "What's the time frame?"

Bruce wanted to see our work the next morning.

Sam and I didn't talk on the elevator down, down, down to 1, or on the one up to 9. We ordered dinner. He called his wife. At eight, when we sat down to work, I pictured Cheryl standing outside with Bobby while he smoked.

"Why so sad?" Sam said. "You got a date, pal?"

I said, "No," and felt especially dateless and lifeless and hopeless realizing how much I'd wanted to see Bobby.

Sam said, "You need water," and got us each a bottle.

We put on night moisturizer.

I suggested the line "Trenton makes, The world takes."

"Shh," Sam said. "Hand me a bindi." I passed him one of the Indian cigarettes he'd smoked since quitting smoking.

About three minutes later, he held up his pad and showed me designs for brochures based on the TV spots.

"How did you do that?"

Sam said, "When someone asks me to eat shit, I don't nibble."

. . . . .

Before the next class, I watched the door for Bobby, but he didn't show up.

Maureen announced, "Bobby was in a motorcycle accident."

I heard a gasp, and realized it belonged to me.

Cheryl and I spoke in unison: "Is he okay?"

"He hurt his leg," Maureen said. "He'll be here next week."

When I opened my tackle box, inside was a paperback of Billy Collins poems. It was inscribed:

FOR APPLEBAUM,
GRUDGINGLY,
BOBBY GUEST

I assumed that Bobby had given me the poems to show that he was smart or deep or poetic himself; I assumed it was just Bobby saying his name out loud again.

Still, I took the book to bed with me. I thought I'd read one poem, roll my eyes, and go to sleep. I stayed up half the night reading.

. . . . .

"Listen to this," I told Sam, and while he drew, I read the first stanza of "Another Reason Why I Don't Keep a Gun in the House":

> The neighbors' dog will not stop barking.
> He is barking the same high, rhythmic bark
> that he barks every time they leave the house.
> They must switch him on on their way out.

"Go on," Sam said. "What're you stopping for?"

I read the poems at my desk during lunch and in line for the ATM; I read the poems waiting for the subway and waiting for a friend to meet me for dinner, and then I read them to her.

She said, "You act like Bobby wrote them."

. . . . .

When Bobby walked into class everyone applauded.

He bowed and leaned his crutches against the wall. He hoisted himself up on the stool next to Cheryl.

Maureen looked exhausted and yawned before resuming class. She asked if anyone would mind if Bert changed his pose.

Only the retired principal raised his hand. He kept it in the air.

Maureen seemed to be lost, and Bobby, our wounded hero, rescued her: "I'm afraid you're out of luck, Mr. Marshall."

Tight-lipped, the principal lowered his hand. "Fine," he said, "if I'm the only one." His tone was punishing, though, and it occurred to me that he probably missed the authority he'd once had to suspend and expel.

I went over to Bobby and asked if he was okay.

He was, he said, and he thanked me for asking.

"I really like the poems."

He said, "Good."

"I love them," I said. "Thank you."

He said, "Anytime," and Cheryl nodded as though the gift were from both of them.

Bert struck an excellent new pose in which his thigh obscured his penis from my view, and I found myself doing exactly as Maureen had instructed; I got all of him down, and he filled the entire canvas.

When Bert got up to take his break, Bobby said, "Psst, Applebaum." He motioned to the door.

"Did you just say 'Psst'? No one says 'Psst' anymore." I followed him onto the elevator. "So, what happened?"

He didn't answer until we were outside and I'd lit our cigarettes. "I got clipped on the West Side Highway," he said. "Had a little too much bourbon."

"You were drinking bourbon on the West Side Highway?"

"Not *on* the highway, Applebaum."

"That is the stupidest thing I ever heard," I said. "Are you just a fucking idiot, or what?"

That's when he leaned forward on his crutches and kissed me. He kissed me, and I kissed him. Then he pulled back and said, "Yes, I am a fucking idiot."

. . . . .

Upstairs, I painted sloppy and free; I painted like an artist on Quaaludes. Previously, I'd been desperate to make a painting that Maureen, or anyone, might think was good, but I forgot all about that now. I was painting what I saw and felt. I was painting large.

Maureen took a look, and her face said, *What's up, Pussycat?*

At the end of class, I closed my tackle box and leaned my painting against the wall to dry. I stood there, waiting for Bobby to finish talking to Cheryl. Meanwhile, I studied the artwork of my classmates.

Margo passed me on her way out with Bert, and her "Good-bye" was the unified kick of a hundred Rockettes.

Bobby was still talking or listening to Cheryl, who saw me and pretended not to. I headed toward him, losing heart at about two hundred beats per minute. I thought all I could manage was a good night to both of them; instead, I heard myself say, "You want to get something to eat or something?"

Bobby said, "Let's go."

. . . . .

We went to Cafe Loup on Thirteenth Street and sat at one of the front tables so we could smoke. We ordered red wine and salads and rare steaks with fries.

"So," he said, "where you from, sailor?"

"Outside of Philadelphia," I said. "A town called Surrey."

"Never heard of it."

"No one has," I said.

Bobby told me he'd grown up in Manhattan and gone to Collegiate, a private school for boys on Seventy-eighth Street, and then to Yale. I thought I heard pride in his voice when he said he was one paper shy of graduation.

"That seems stupid," I said.

"Obviously," he said, deadpan, "it hasn't held me back."

"Didn't it make your parents crazy?"

"They were already crazy." He said they'd briefly acted in B movies—no, I wouldn't have heard of them—and they hadn't done anything but dress for dinner since.

I said, "Like what do they wear?"

"They dress," he repeated. He described his mother in chiffon, his father in a dinner jacket.

"It sounds so elegant," I said.

"It would be more elegant if cocktail hour didn't start at noon."

Answering my unasked question, he said the money came from his grandfather, who'd made a killing in the demolition business. He'd leveled Penn Station.

Bobby admitted then that he himself had done some acting—one soap opera, a few commercials, an off-Broadway play; he was good at it, he said, but it was bad for him. He wrote stories now. He half-read, half-sang them, accompanying himself on guitar, at a club in the East Village. A few months ago, a literary agent had seen him there and asked him to type the stories up and send them to her. But he hadn't.

"Why not?"

He said, "What if she rejects them?"

"You'll send them to someone else."

He shook his head. "This way, I can always say an agent asked me to send my stories." He said, "I get to be the one who stands in the way of my success."

We noticed at the same time that we were the last table in the restaurant, and Bobby looked at the check. I said, "I'll split it with you."

He was adding it up. "You can pay . . ."; he paused, and instead of *next time,* said, ". . . never."

At the coat check, I saw that the restaurant sold T-shirts and baseball caps with its logo, fingers making a shadow wolf.

Outside, Bobby asked me if I wanted to take a walk to Union Square.

"You're crippled," I said.

He said, "I'm fine," and he was. He moved easily on crutches, and when I said so, he told me that he'd become an expert after his last motorcycle accident, when he'd also learned to write with his left hand.

I said, "Do you have some kind of death wish?"

I'd just lit a cigarette, and he said, "What about you, Smokey?"

At Union Square, he leaned me up against a wall and kissed and kissed me. He unzipped his jacket and pulled me inside it. I was fifteen just then, there in the park, at night, under the trees.

We could hear barking from the dog run, and he asked if I'd read the poem "Another Reason Why I Don't Keep a Gun in the House."

"I read them all."

He asked if I had a favorite, and I said, "The revenge fantasy."

Bobby said, " 'The Rival Poet.' "

I said, "I love: 'You are the one below / fidgeting in your rented tux / with some local Cheryl hanging all over you.' "

" 'Some local *Cindy* hanging all over you,' " Bobby said.

"Isn't that what I said?"

"You said 'Cheryl.' "

"*C* names," I said. "Are you sleeping with her?"

"No," he said. "I've been living like a monk."

"That's funny," I said. "I've been living like a monkey." I waited a second. "Why do you sit with her?"

"So I can watch you," he said, "from a safe distance."

We kissed, and then he pulled back. "Hear that?" he said.

It was the wind, and we stood there listening.

I lit a cigarette and said, "Really, why do you sit with Cheryl?"

He pulled my hand over to light his cigarette off of mine. He said, "She reminds me of myself."

"You're kidding," I said. "How?"

He thought a minute. He said, "When they were making *Marathon Man* Dustin Hoffman asked Sir Laurence Olivier why he acted—what drove him. You know what he said? 'Look at me, look at me, look at me, look at me.' "

The barking was making Bobby feel guilty, he said; he needed to get home to walk his dog, Arlo.

I started to hum the chorus of Arlo Guthrie's song "Alice's Restaurant," and Bobby joined in.

I was stunned by how beautiful his voice was.

He was lifting his crutch to hail a cab for me when I said, "You make me nervous."

He said, "You make me nervous."

"Good," I said. Then I gave him all of my numbers.

. . . . .

I was in bed and had just turned off the light when the phone rang.

Instead of *hello,* Bobby said, "Why do I make you nervous?"

I said, "You seem like a lothario," a word I hadn't used since college, and didn't like the sound of now.

He didn't answer right away, and it occurred to me that I'd made him angry. But it wasn't that. "I have been," he admitted.

I didn't say anything.

He said, "I don't want to be like that with you."

"Don't," I said.

I asked what made him nervous about me.

He said, "I'm not going to tell you everything." Then he asked if he could take me out to dinner and a movie on Saturday night.

. . . . .

At work, I told Sam, "I think I really, really like this boy."

I didn't even realize that I'd said *boy* until Sam said, "Did you kiss him on the Ferris wheel?" Then, a moment later: "Can he sing?"

"He's a great singer," I said. "Why?"

"It's nice to be around someone who can sing," he said. "Gloria's voice probably saved our marriage."

. . . . .

That evening Bobby called to tell me how the sky looked over the river. Later he called from the restaurant in the Village where he waited tables between motorcycle accidents. He said, "What would it take to get you down here to smoke a cigarette with me?"

I was wearing sweatpants and glasses and needed to wash my hair. I told him I'd come if he promised never to ride his motorcycle drunk again.

He said, "Done."

I said, "Give me an hour."

The Lion's Head was known as a writer's bar, and the covers of books written by its patrons hung on the walls. The man Bobby introduced as a writer objected: In an Irish accent, he said to me, "I'm a schoolteacher—"

Bobby interrupted: "Whose book is coming out anytime now," and the writer-teacher allowed this much.

Bobby was drinking bourbon with shots of beer. He said, "What would you say if I asked you to spend the night with me?"

"I'd say it was too soon."

"You're right," he said.

. . . . .

After work, I walked over to Saks and bought a dress I couldn't afford. It was a turtleneck but sleeveless, short but not a minidress. In it I was a woman who was soon to leave advertising for a new, thrilling career as yet undecided; in it, I was a painter at my first opening in a SoHo gallery.

When I got home, the phone was ringing. I picked it up and heard, "I miss you."

I said, "I miss you, too," and then worried that I'd said too much, and kept worrying while we talked.

I told him about my brothers, and he told me he wished he was as close to his. His were much older, and both lived in Los Angeles, where one had a small part on a sitcom and the other, a producer, worked for "the Mouse," which was what the worker mice apparently called Disney.

He asked me about my childhood, and I asked him about his. He told me a story about falling off the Hans Christian Andersen statue in Central Park; he'd cried, and his nanny had said, "Don't be such a baby," right before he'd blacked out.

"Was she fired?"

"No." He moved right along: "I think you should know that in sixth grade I won the Faversham Cup for Best Athlete."

"Not the Faversham!" I said. "Jesus!"

He said, "How long before you move in with me, do you think?"

I told him I thought we should wait until after our first date.

He said, "You know, we're going to have to start making babies right away. Don't drag your feet on this, Applebaum. You're not young."

. . . . .

Saturday, I went to the gym. I lifted weights for my impending sleevelessness. I ran on the treadmill and walked up the StairMaster; with every step I was closer to Bobby.

At home, my answering machine was overloaded with messages,

among them Jack ordering me not to drink too much and Robert asking me to take a quarter for a phone call in case my date got fresh. There wasn't a message from Bobby.

I was sure he would call while I was in the shower.

I was sure he would call while I blow-dried my hair.

I picked up the phone to make sure it was working. I listened to the dial tone.

At 7:30, I put on my new dress. I mascaraed my lashes, I blushed my cheeks, I glossed my lips.

At 8:00, I poured myself a glass of wine. I tried to read. I tried to do the crossword puzzle, but it was Saturday and too hard.

At 8:30, I called Bobby and got his answering machine. "What's going on?" I said. "Call me back."

At 9:30, I unzipped my dress, put my bathrobe on, and ordered Chinese food.

At 10:00, the phone rang, and I said an icy, "Hello?" It was the doorman: "Food delivery."

At 11:30, I called my friend Laurie.

"What do we know about this guy?" she said. "Tell me everything."

I told her he'd grown up in Manhattan.

She said, "I probably know him."

When I told her his last name, she said, "I know Bobby Guest," and for a second she was excited by the coincidence.

I was afraid she'd gone out with him. "You know him?"

"I know who he is," she said. She told me that he was one of a few boys who were famous for being handsome and cool in high school. A friend of hers from Spence had gone out with a friend of his at Collegiate. "I'm going to do a little research."

When the phone rang at 1:00, I was still hoping it would be Bobby.

"He's a bad guy," Laurie said. He wasn't just a womanizer; he'd betrayed friends, he'd mistreated acquaintances, he'd offended strangers. She said, "Everybody has a Bobby Guest story."

While she enumerated his crimes, I remembered kissing him in Union Square, and I thought, *I will never feel like I'm fifteen again.*

"Eventually, Bobby Guest lets everyone down," Laurie said. "That's who he is."

Even knowing this, I lay in bed that night going over everything I had said and done, trying to place the moment when I'd lost him.

· · · · ·

On Sunday, I left another message for Bobby.

Whenever the phone rang, I ran for it.

Both my brothers offered to kill Bobby, and I thought what fine men they'd grown up to be.

· · · · ·

At work, Sam said, "Well?"

I said, "His voice didn't save our marriage."

I felt sick all Monday and Tuesday. *Satyr,* I remembered saying; and, *You'll never get beyond your hardwiring;* and, most of all, *I miss you, too.*

Late Tuesday night I finally told myself, *Enough.* Even if I had said something wrong, it probably wasn't what I would guess.

Replaying everything was just like what I did when I got a shot: I'd pinch myself so I could feel like I was in charge of the pain.

· · · · ·

Wednesday, I still hadn't decided whether I was going to the last class.

"Are you nuts?" Laurie said. "What else do you need to know?"

"Go," Sam said. "See what the guy has to say."

On the subway down to the New School, I was disgusted with myself. I'd once read that Ronald Reagan always followed the advice of the last person he'd talked to. I thought, *You're like Ronald Reagan.*

· · · · ·

Bobby wasn't in class.

I found my painting from the week before and placed it on my easel. It was so wild it was hard to believe it was mine.

Bert reclined into last week's pose.

Margo moved her stool closer to mine. In a low voice she said, "I went out with Bert."

"You're kidding," I said. "How was it?"

"Fun," she said. "He drives a cab. Did you know that? I drove around with him."

She acted like we were good friends, and just then we were.

For over an hour I looked from Bert to my painting and back. When Maureen came up and stood looking at it with me, I said, "I don't know what to do with this."

She said, "Maybe it's finished," and I decided it was.

I didn't have time to start a new painting before our end-of-class party, so I went outside to smoke a cigarette.

. . . . .

Bobby was leaning against a car and stood when he saw me; he'd traded his crutches for a cane. "Be nice to me," he said. "I'm a cripple."

He lit a cigarette for himself and one for me. He said, "I'm sorry about Saturday," in a tone that was polite and detached; he might've said, *I'm sorry about your cold.*

What I'd loved about him in Union Square was what I hated about him now: He made me feel fifteen. Polite and detached, I said, "What happened?"

"I was watching an old movie of my mother's on TV. I mean, she just had a small part." She was a nightclub singer, he went on to say; he struggled to remember the title of the movie, as though this was the information I wanted from him. "Anyway," he said, "I passed out."

"No," I said. For a moment, I was as Maureen-strong as I wanted to be. "What I meant was, *What happened?*"

I saw now that his hand was trembling. "I don't know."

"Is that it?" I said. "You don't know?"

He said, "We were moving so fast."

I said, "We *were* moving fast."

He sighed and said, "Thank you," and the gratitude I heard was the only acknowledgment that he'd done anything wrong.

"You should've called me back," I said.

"I know," he said. "I wish I had."

What I thought of then was that he had managed to write stories and sing them in front of people, but he couldn't type them up and put them in an envelope.

Still, I waited for him to give me something—a sincere apology, a thorough explanation, a promise for the future—anything at all.

Instead, he reached for my hand. "What about Saturday?"

"What *about* Saturday?"

"Dinner and a movie," he said.

"No."

"No you have plans," he said, "or no you won't give me another chance?"

I shook my head.

"Wait," he said. "This is all because I didn't call you *once*?"

I stared at him, and the best-looking senior at Collegiate looked back at me.

"Jesus," he said. "You're tough."

"No," I said.

"One time I didn't call you," he said. "One strike and I'm out?"

It was hard to believe that the Bobby Guest who stood in front of me was the Bobby Guest I'd wanted so badly.

"Well," he said finally. He walked with me to the door. "At least we talked. Just talking about this with you is a big step for me."

I was about to say good-bye when he opened the door for me and himself. He'd come for the party, I realized; he'd wanted to talk to me first so I wouldn't embarrass him in front of everyone.

"You know the problem?" he said on the elevator. "You expected me to change all at once."

. . . . .

What made it a party was that Maureen had brought in bottles of soda, a huge bag of pretzels, and a boom box. A babysitter had brought Maureen's daughter, who clung to Bobby. I marveled at the power he had even over three-year-old women. She was playing with his hair and ears; she was slapping his hands, as I wished I had.

As though nothing had happened between us or as though something still might, he winked at me.

Bert and Margo were sitting together on the fainting couch up on its platform; they looked like King and Queen of the May.

Only Michele stood at an easel. She was painting shocked letters that would soon spell, *"Jimi Hendrix, Electric Ladyland."*

I didn't hear any music coming from her headphones, and I said, "What're you listening to?"

"Nothing," she said. She smiled like she was letting me in on a secret.

I wondered what it was—maybe wearing the Walkman helped her feel less awkward or self-conscious; maybe it helped her to be alone. I kept my eyes on her, hoping she would tell me, and she did: "It's a good hair band."

She seemed to remember something and said, "Oh," and handed me her dad's business card. "If you need a DJ."

I thanked her.

The cancer survivor had to leave early, and she came over to me to say good-bye. She held my hands and looked me in the eyes and said, "Be well," and I said, "You, too." She smiled at me and squeezed my hands; she seemed to know what I'd been through with Bobby.

Then I heard her say the same thing to the principal and the accountant, who were having a good-natured disagreement about what art was, refereed by Great-Grandmother.

Before I left, I caught a glimpse of Cheryl, and I saw now what Bobby had meant; they were alike. Even though she stood by herself, she was performing. She touched her neck and filled her eyes with soul, practicing for the moment when she would be discovered.

THE ONE AFTER YOU

1.

I NEVER EXPECTED anyone in my family to change, and especially not my father, who changed first and most profoundly: He died. For a long time afterward, my mother was not herself. She lost weight. She had trouble sleeping. She caught every virus, cold, and flu. Once when I visited her, she scuffed around the house in pink pile-lined slippers you'd wear only while waiting for the police to discover you many days dead.

This was grief, though, and not change; what changed my mother was love.

The slippers were a present from her mother, with whom she had dinner every Friday. I said, "And they're not returnable?"

My mother didn't answer, and I didn't press her. It was her birthday. To celebrate, we were reading the condolence letters that my mother separated from the rest—the Weepers, we called them. She kept the letters in an antique basket on her night table, and we had them spread out across her bed.

I liked reading them; a good Weeper could bring my father back to life for a few seconds. But there were letters in there that made the cut for reasons mysterious to me. I'd kept quiet about these—it was her basket—but more than seven years had passed since my father's death, and now seemed like a good time to go back to normal.

In a voice trembling with false emotion, I read what was essentially a form letter from the office of the deputy mayor of Philadelphia: " '. . . It was a privilege and an honor to have known Judge Applebaum.' "

She said, "I thought it was sort of a proclamation."

"Hm," I said.

"Well," she said, "it is an honor."

"And a privilege."

She said, "Hush."

For my next mystery missive, a card with nothing but a preprinted message and a signature, I said, "God, this one always gets to me."

"Which?" my mother said.

" 'In deepest sympathy.' " I paused before taking a stab at the illegible signature—"Len Rollhoff."

She looked over my shoulder. "It's Lev," she said, "Polikoff," and I heard something in her voice that I'd only ever seen—dozens of tiny silver fish jumping out of the bay in Martha's Vineyard—and it was as surprising and beautiful a sound as it had been a sight.

She took the card from me as though I'd intercepted a private note, and as though I had I said, "I already read it."

I could hear her attempt at calm in, "I just thought it was . . . thoughtful of him to write."

I said, "It is a thoughtful signature."

The look she gave me said, *Don't take something nice away from me,* and of course she was right.

"So who is he?" I said.

"He's just somebody I used to know," she said—and again the flash of silver fish.

I said, "Who?"

"Never mind," she said.

She got up and scuffed over to her closet, where I hoped she would change into the ballet slippers she usually wore around the house, but she was just hiding there. She said, "I was thinking I'd come to New York for a weekend."

She said this all the time. It wasn't a memory problem; she liked to repeat herself. Saying the same things over and over seemed to have the calming effect of repeat-motion hobbies like knitting or needlepoint, while for me the effect was more like the repeat motion of knitting or needlepoint needles puncturing my eardrums.

As I hadn't answered, she turned around and again said, "I was thinking I'd come to New York for a weekend."

"You should," I said. "And bring Lev Polikoff."

She turned back to her closet, where she said that my apartment, a studio without a sofa bed, would be tight for the two of us. As ever, she added, "I hope that doesn't offend you," and, as ever, I said, "Not at all."

Then she moved on: "I don't think it's a good time for me to stay with Robert."

She waited for me to ask why, and because it was her birthday I did.

Then she got to say, "He's just got so much on his plate." It was true that my younger brother's plate runneth over, with his adorable children and busy medical practice, but the real reason that it wasn't a good time for my mother to stay with Robert was that he was married to Naomi.

I said, "They want you to stay with them," which was at least half true; Robert did. My younger brother was so dutiful he didn't even think of duty as duty; he'd been born with his duty gene lodged in the pleasure center of his brain.

My mother said, "I can always stay with Jack." A dozen times I'd heard her ask, and a dozen times heard him answer, "Fine." Thus, the arrangements were all set for the weekend that would never take place.

Her hypothetical host called a few minutes later. I could tell it was Jack by the relief in her voice, and I was relieved, too; my older brother was the wild card among us. She spoke with him for a few minutes, thanked him for his birthday wishes, and passed the phone to me.

He said, "What are you guys doing?"

When Jack visited, he made an effort to take my mother to see art and hear music—to do things she hadn't done enough while my father was alive.

"We're reading the Weepers," I said.

"Great," he said. "Where're you taking Mom for dinner—the cemetery?"

I told him I wasn't taking her anywhere because the birthday girl wanted to cook.

"So you're in all night?"

"Unless I can get her to the movies," I said.

"It's already seven."

I said, "We're in all night."

An operator cut in and asked my brother to deposit another seventy-five cents, and I said, "Where are you calling from?"

"Titty bar."

"Seriously," I said.

"Damn." He told me that he'd tucked his last quarter into the stripper's G-string. "Let's just talk until we get cut off."

When I said that the threat of being disconnected made it hard for me to talk, he said, "There's something I have to tell you."

"What?"

"It's hard for me to say," he said.

"Just tell me."

"I've never told anyone."

Then we were cut off, and I realized he'd been teasing me.

My mother gathered the Weepers and put them back in their basket. "Should we have a glass of wine?" she said.

"Sure."

"I thought we could have wine in front of the fire," she said, but instead she got back into bed.

I picked up the newspaper and looked at the listings for a movie my father wouldn't have wanted to see, one with subtitles or without a plot.

She picked up *The House of Mirth*, which had now taken her longer to read than it took Edith Wharton to write.

. . . . .

While my mother started dinner, I built a fire, taking fake logs from the hall closet and real ones from the porch.

"Tell me about your job," she said, nuzzling into me a little on the sofa. She'd become more affectionate since my father had died, and I tried not to mind.

I said, "I'm trying to get out of advertising."

"Really?" she said. "I've always thought of advertising as glamorous and exciting."

I said, "I'm not in that kind of advertising."

"Isn't advertising advertising?"

"Sure," I said. "Like driving a bus and driving a race car are both driving."

She said, "What kind of advertising are you in?"

She'd asked before, and I'd told her, but each time it was hard: "I write junk mail, Mom."

"Oh." Then she said, "A lot of people say that commercials on television are more interesting than the programs."

We both looked at the fire. She said, "I meant to tell you, Dena's grandmother moved into Grandmom's building." Then: "Do you ever see Dena?"

"No," I said, though I had recently, at the farmers' market at Union Square, buying apples with an older guy in loafers; her arm had been linked through his, which seemed if not exactly sexual not completely platonic either, and I wondered if he was Richard, the boyfriend she'd refused to call her boyfriend; he was married.

I'd never told my mother about Dena's married un-boyfriend. It would shock her even more than it had me—it would horrify her, and permanently change the way my mother saw Dena, which seemed wrong, even if she was an ex-friend.

"She's kind of standoffish," my mother said. "Dena's grandmother."

"Mom," I said.

She stiffened. "Yes?"

"Your slippers are depressing me."

She said, "They were a present from Grandmom."

"I know," I said. "I think they might be a gag gift, though."

She said, "They're very comfortable."

My mother was double-jointed, or something, and was sitting with her long, pretty legs snaked around each other, like a contortionist in repose. She looked down at her slippered feet; she studied them for a moment.

She took the slippers off, stood, and tossed them into the fireplace; unfortunately, like me, she lacked eye-hand coordination, and the slippers landed too far from the fire to catch. She used tongs to place the slippers on top of the logs, where the action was.

They caught right away, as pure synthetic fibers will. We watched them burn. It was fast but satisfying.

"I'm sorry," I said, when she'd returned to the sofa and resnaked her legs. "You were telling me about Lev Polikoff."

"It was a long time ago." She smiled privately and seemed almost expansive, maybe as a result of the ceremonial slipper fire.

"When?"

She said, "I met him when I was working at the museum," meaning the Philadelphia Museum of Art, where she'd been a tour guide after college. "He was an artist."

I tried to speed things up: I said, "He was a beau," using her terminology.

She allowed this.

I said, "And?"

"Grandmom didn't like him."

"Why?" I asked.

"I'm not sure she ever said why."

I said, "And you just stopped seeing him?"

She said, "My generation was more obedient than yours."

"Why do you think Grandmom didn't like him?"

"He wasn't marriageable, I guess."

I looked at her: *Marriageable?*

"He didn't make a good living," she said. "Grandmom didn't want me to waste time." Then she remembered: "And she didn't like his beard."

I said, "Too Jewish?"

"She used to say, 'It would be one thing if he kept it neat.' "

"She just wanted what was best for you," I said, my mother's standard defense of both my grandmothers. Then, seriously, I said, "Thanks for never talking to me about wasting my time."

"You're welcome," she said. "I was just afraid."

It was a nice surprise to hear her say the truth. But right away the public-relations part of her brain rushed in with a revised press release: "I trust you to make the decisions that are best for you."

I got up for wine refills, and when I placed our glasses on the coffee table, I asked if she'd written back to Lev Polikoff.

"No."

I said, "So there was just the one note?"

She said, "He called me."

"Joyce," I said.

"I've talked to him quite a few times," she said. "He's very nice."

I said, "That's great," and it did seem great.

She put on a tape Lev Polikoff had sent her; it was Cuban music, and listening to it she became not so much listless as relaxed, less wan than Juanita. Her dark eyes had something new in them—I couldn't say what, just that they seemed to see more than what was in front of them.

I would have asked more questions about Lev Polikoff, but we heard the back door open and Jack call out: "Surprise," like the one-man birthday party he was.

. . . . .

My brother brought excitement and direction to the evening; he got our show on the road. *Lights, Camera, Action:* My mother tossed the salad; I set the table; Jack got himself a beer.

Jack always managed to arrive home with news, and at dinner he delivered tonight's lead story: JACK HAS MEETING IN LOS ANGELES ABOUT TURNING SCREENPLAY INTO SCRIPT FOR TV PILOT; PRODUCERS PAY FOR FLIGHT AND HOTEL.

My mother beamed; she seemed to see Jack's meeting as an award or prize she'd never doubted he'd win.

I was a little more skeptical: So far, the many meetings he'd told me about had led only to more meetings. Once, when he'd gotten discouraged, he'd said that he was less a screenwriter than a professional meeter; but then he'd reminded himself and me that only one in a zillion scripts were ever produced, a statistic he seemed to forget now. "I'm setting the show in New York," he said, "so I won't have to move to L.A."

Everyone I knew called Los Angeles "L.A.," and yet when Jack did, I remembered the father of one of my college roommates telling us that abbreviations were slick and lazy and indicative of bad character.

I said, "I didn't know you wanted to write for TV."

"It's a lot of money," he said. "If the pilot gets picked up, I'll be the executive producer."

My mother said, "The executive producer!"

I got up to clear the table and bring in the birthday cake. I lit candles. We sang. She made a wish and blew.

I gave my mother her present, an old photograph I'd had restored and framed of her as a little girl on the lap of the grandmother she'd adored.

Jack himself hadn't brought a present; as my mother told him and might have cross-stitched: "Your presence is my present."

. . . . .

On Sunday, after brunch, Jack looked at the weekend section of *The Philadelphia Inquirer*. "What about the Rodin?"

My mother looked over his shoulder and pointed to another listing.

They didn't ask my opinion. They knew that I didn't want to look at art; I'd go wherever they went and endure whatever exhibit they chose. In this way, I was the new Dad.

"I was thinking about 'Intimates,' " she said.

I said, "Lingerie?"

"They're portraits."

Portraits were my mother's big interest. She'd commissioned the portraits of several judges, including my father, and curated the exhibit in the lobby of the criminal courts building.

She told my brother that "Intimates" was around the corner from a building she thought he'd want to see. We'd go after we visited her mother, she said.

Jack shook his head. " 'Intimates' closes at five," he said. "Grandmom's is always open."

. . . . .

My mother and Jack hardly talked while they looked at the paintings in the gallery, which made them seem closer to each other than I was to either of them.

I lingered over each picture as they did, but I didn't see what they saw. The paintings were just people posed, which seemed like the opposite of intimacy.

I went up to my mother, who'd been standing at one picture for a long time. "What makes these intimate?" I asked.

She explained that the painters were called Intimists because they painted their models in context. I nodded to keep her talking; I liked hearing the authority in her voice.

"Thanks," I said, once she'd finished. "I'll be in Sleepwear."

As we were walking out, I said, "I think galleries should have gift shops."

Jack said, "Galleries are gift shops."

The building we went to see was designed by an architect Jack had worked for. He walked around the building, looking up.

I thought the building was ugly, and said so.

My mother, ever the diplomat, half agreed: "It is radical."

. . . . .

When we got to my grandmother's block, I pictured what it would be like up in her apartment. I told Jack and my mother that I needed to stop at the deli.

She said, "We're already late."

"Come on," Jack said.

"Oh, now you're in a hurry," I said. "I went to *your* art gallery and *your* building; now here's something *I'm* interested in."

I tried not to let them rush me. I studied the sandwiches listed on the board, and the per-pound price of lunch meats. I looked at the potato salad and coleslaw in the case.

My mother said, "Grandmom can give you something to eat upstairs."

I told her I was just admiring the composition in the deli case. "I like the way the cellophane catches the light."

I would never bring food to my grandmother's—it would be bad manners—but I was already getting that deprived feeling that would come on full strength as soon as we got to her apartment, where nothing tasted good.

I went over to the flowers. All together they looked colorful and pretty, but if I looked at any one bunch, I noticed brown or missing petals. If I could spot a flaw, I knew my grandmother would spot a hundred; she had a gift for flaw-finding.

I picked the most robust bunch, big yellow mums.

Sounding dubious, my mother said, "That's a nice idea."

. . . . .

As we walked into my grandmother's building, I said, "I think this is going to be a really good visit."

The guard called my grandmother on the house phone. "Mrs. Parker?" he said, and announced our arrival.

On the elevator, I said, "I think we're going to get really close this time."

I watched my mother steel herself.

I said, "I just have this feeling."

. . . . .

My grandmother was annoyed that we'd gone to the exhibit first and annoyed that we'd arrived late; my grandmother was annoyed because annoyed was her resting state.

She was in great shape, very thin but not haggard, and she wore a red cashmere sweater with a red-and-white silk scarf tied at her neck and white pants you'd call slacks; she looked better than we did, and you could tell she thought so, too.

She ushered Jack in first, like he was the guest and my mother and I the help.

My brother said, "Hello, Steeny," which was short for Bernstein, her maiden name, and what her friends still called her.

When I handed her the bouquet her eyes widened, which made me feel bad for not giving her flowers more often.

She asked my mother what they were called.

"Chrysanthemums," my mother said. "Mums."

"That's right," my grandmother said. "I've never liked mums." She stuffed the paper into the garbage, complaining about how much waste there was in the world today.

The bad feeling was coming on, so I said, "I was going to get roses, but Jack thought you'd like mums better."

My mother and Jack turned to me, but I kept my eyes on my grandmother.

"Roses are too expensive," she said, cutting the stems.

"What flowers do you like?" I asked.

She said that all flowers were too expensive.

"Let's say all flowers cost a penny," I said. "Then what would your favorites be?"

"A penny?" she said.

"Okay," I said. "Fifty cents."

"I do like roses," she said.

"I told you!" I said to Jack. "What color?"

"Yellow," she said.

"I knew it!"

"Little ones," she said. "Sweetheart roses."

"Good," I said. "Next time we'll bring little yellow roses."

"No," she said. "They're too expensive." Then she asked what she could give us; she never offered a specific beverage or food, which seemed like inviting someone to your house without mentioning a specific date.

To me, she said, "You look like you've put on weight."

I hadn't, but my grandmother had the ability to fatten me up just by looking at me. "Thank you," I said. "You know, I think maybe I'd like a scotch."

She glared at me.

I toned myself down. "Or sherry," I said. "Mom, would you like a glass of sherry?"

"That sounds wonderful," my mother said.

I'd gained ten pounds since our arrival, and my mother had aged at least as many years; her roots were suddenly visible, an unbroken white line dividing her brown-hair highway.

I saw my grandmother notice and whisper to my mother, who aged another year or two.

"Sherry?" I asked Jack, a little louder than necessary.

"I'll have a pink squirrel," he said, for his own amusement.

"You'll have to fix that one yourself," my grandmother said.

Instead, he helped himself to an already-open family-size bottle of diet Coke, long since fizzless.

My grandmother headed to the den for sherry. I followed her as far as the living room. It was a room you'd call grand, with floor-length curtains and velvet armchairs, everything big and matching, chintz and mahogany and brass. The only difference—and it took me a second to see it because it was such a surprise—was a teddy bear on the pristine yellow sofa I hadn't sat on since I'd been forbidden to as a child. My grandmother had said, "The grease in your hair will stain the fabric," and I'd thought, *I have grease in my hair?*

My mother looked at the bear only for a second and then seemed to decide it wasn't there after all. Her eyes moved to the painting above its head, a gold-framed portrait of a woman in an ivory satin evening gown, one strap off her shoulder. My mother told me that the painter had been a student of John Singer Sargent. She said, "This is a great portrait."

"What makes it great?"

"See the flesh tones?" my mother said. "And the way the hands are painted?" One criterion for a portrait, she told me, was whether the artist could paint hands or had to hide them.

I'd taken an art class a few years ago, and the hands I'd painted had looked like birds. I said, "Hands are hard."

My mother was still describing the portrait's greatness when my grandmother returned with three tiny glasses of sherry on a silver tray.

As my mother and I took ours, my grandmother said, "Pay attention," and, "Be careful," as though we'd already spilled a first glass of sherry and giving us a second was against her better judgment.

It was then that I decided to sit on the forbidden yellow sofa. "Scoot over," I said to the bear.

I asked if there was a story behind the portrait, and my grandmother said, "It was in the attic on Welland Road."

It was nice to have some new information. "Finders keepers?"

"No, no," she said. "I called the people we'd bought the house from—the Biddles—and it was too much trouble for them to pick it up."

Of greater interest to her was whether we'd run into traffic on the expressway.

Somehow, I couldn't bear the answer. "Do you have a cracker, by any chance?" I only half stood because even if my grandmother was entertaining stuffed animals I knew she'd never allow me to go into her kitchen alone; she didn't like anyone going through anything of hers, even her saltines. This made me want to go through everything, from her impressive paper-bag collection to the jewelry boxes she triple-bound with rubber bands.

"I'll see what I have," she said.

My grandmother returned with a plate of saltines and Ritz crackers. She placed them on the coffee table. Now everyone wanted crackers; my mother, Jack, and even my grandmother took one.

We all crunched, and that was the only sound until my grandmother said that we'd just missed a call from my mother's brother.

My grandmother said, "I told Dan that you'd be here," as though his call from Chicago had required special planning and hard-to-find equipment, as though his call was a special favor that we hadn't been gracious enough to receive.

I had a brainstorm: "We could call him back."

My grandmother seemed not to hear; her point was not that we talk to my uncle but that we'd missed talking to him.

My mother said, "I spoke to him yesterday."

I turned to my grandmother and said, "You know what I'd like to hear about?"

Her eyes widened; she still saw me as a child, as in, *Children are to be seen and not heard,* and, *Children are to speak only when spoken to.*

Still, I went on: "I'd like to hear what my mom was like when she was younger. Before she met my dad."

My mother gave me a warning look, and I realized that she thought I was going to ask about Lev Polikoff. This hadn't occurred to me, but I was often the last to know my own mind.

My grandmother said, "There isn't much to tell."

My mother said, "Thanks."

I laughed—it was a thrill to hear my mother make a joke—and Jack laughed, too.

"What about you, Granny?" I said. "What were you like when you were younger?"

She said, "What's this about, Sophie?"

I wasn't sure myself. "Well," I said. "I was thinking that we could get to know each other better."

No one said anything.

I turned to my grandmother. "So," I said weakly, "do you want to tell me anything . . . or no?"

Her eyes narrowed, possibly with the strain of trying to think of something to tell me.

"You know what I'd like to hear about?" Jack said, teasing me and entertaining himself. "I'd like to hear about how Grandpop got you to marry him."

She began as she always did, with her parents saying he was too old for her and she was too young to get married.

"How old were you?" my brother asked, looking at me.

I mouthed, *Seventeen?*

"Seventeen," she said. "I already had lots of suitors."

On cue, my mother said, "Your grandmother was a very beautiful young woman."

"Grandpop was very jealous," she said. "He even followed me on a date once. He sat in the row behind us at the movies. Can you imagine?"

"He was in love with you," my mother said.

"He said he couldn't stand to see me with other boys."

My mother said, "How many years did you make Daddy wait?"

Five? I mouthed to my mother.

"Five," my grandmother said. "By then, he really was desperate. I felt sorry for him," she said. "I really did."

My mother asked, "What did you do?"

"I told him to write my parents a letter. And that won them over."

"What did the letter say?" my brother asked.

"Mostly it was about what a good husband he would be."

I waited a moment before I said, "Do you still have the letter?"

"Of course I do."

I said, "Can I read it?"

"I have no idea where it is," she said.

I asked my mother if she'd ever read the letter.

"I don't think I ever did," she said. "I love that story."

"Now I'd like to ask you something," my grandmother said to Jack.

"Lay it on me."

"How's . . . what's her name . . . Nora's child?"

Nora was my mother's oldest friend, but when she said, "Rebecca," my grandmother seemed not to hear.

"Rebecca," my brother said.

"That's right," my grandmother said.

"She's great," Jack said. "She has a new boyfriend."

According to Jack, all of Rebecca's boyfriends were black, which seemed, if not racist, race-ish, and I wondered, *Why the black guys,*

Becky? just as I wondered in the case of my friend Alex, *Why the Asian women?* Or in my own case, *Why the pirates?*

My grandmother said, "Oh, that's a shame."

Jack laughed. "I think she really likes him."

"I meant for you."

My mother said, "Jack has a girlfriend."

"You met Mindy," he said. "Blond. Bossy."

My grandmother said, "She's no Rebecca."

Jack said, "Rebecca's my cousin," a rerun retort.

My grandmother said, "By marriage," a rerun rebuttal.

"They're friends, Mother," my mother said.

"Plus," I said, "she's into black guys," thereby changing the topic forever.

"Well," my grandmother said. "I didn't know that."

My mother glared at me and shook her head.

It was for her that I tried to repair the hole in the atmosphere, but when I said, "Granny, would you tell me about this bear?" my mother shook her head again.

Her mother described finding the bear in the closet and restitching his nose and paws. "Isn't he adorable?" she said. "I just thought he was so adorable."

I said, "Does he have a name?"

"Of course not," my grandmother said.

Jack said, "He's pretty cute."

"Well," she said. "You should probably go now. I don't want you to run into traffic."

Traffic was the great looming fear of her life.

2.

I GOT A RIDE back to New York with Jack in his old Karmann Ghia convertible. It started to rain, and the roof leaked; every now and then I wiped the dashboard with a rag that I recognized as a former guest towel of my mother's, green with embroidered daisies, and I thought about the hard trip that towel had taken from the riches of the powder room to the rag of the dashboard.

On the Pennsylvania Turnpike, I asked Jack which screenplay he was turning into a pilot.

"The Judge," he said.

"The one about Dad."

"It's not about Dad," he said.

"Okay." I asked what he would have to change, and how. I asked about the meeting and about the producers, and what he thought of Los Angeles. Then I said, "I was just noticing how you never ask me any questions."

"Sorry," he said. "What time is it?" He waited another exit before asking a real question: "How's work?"

"Sucky," I said. "Suckeroo."

He said, "Well, back to my life then."

"I need a new job," I said.

"Didn't you say a headhunter called you?"

"About writing advertorials." I reminded him that I was trying to get out of advertising.

He was quiet. I hoped he was thinking of how to help me find a new career, but then he smiled, and I knew he wasn't.

I said, "What do you think I should do?"

"Maybe you should try publishing again," he said. "You love to read."

"I like to eat," I said. "It doesn't mean I should work in a restaurant."

He thought for a couple of minutes. "You'd be a good teacher."

When I reminded him that I'd been a terrible student, he said, "You could teach retarded kids," and laughed his head off.

"Seriously."

He said, "What about real estate?"

I was about to say, *What about dogcatcher?* when I remembered that his girlfriend worked in real estate.

I said, "How is Mindy?" though what I really needed to ask was, *Who is Mindy?* I'd only met her a few times and hadn't paid much attention; as Robert said, in the romantic world of our older brother, all good things must end, as well as all bad things, usually inside of a year.

"I haven't seen her," he said.

"No?"

He was quiet. "She gave me an ultimatum," he said finally. " 'Shit or get off the pot.' "

"That's what she said?"

He didn't answer, which meant yes.

"Very romantic," I said.

He explained that she was ready to have a family, and a girl couldn't put off having babies indefinitely.

"How old is she?" I said. "I thought she was my age."

"She is your age."

A few exits later, I said, "Did she give you a deadline?"

"She won't see me until I decide," he said. "I might actually have to shit."

. . . . .

After I repeated what Jack had said about Mindy, Robert nodded in what appeared to be appreciation. When I said, "Don't you think that's sort of coarse?" he shrugged, as in, *Never mind about that;* unlike me, Robert never failed to distinguish between what was important and what wasn't.

"Did he sound serious?" he asked. "How did he say it?"

I tried to imitate Jack: " 'I might actually have to shit.' "

Robert and I were having lunch around the corner from his office at a new Chinese restaurant. GRAND OPENING flags adorned the awning, and it seemed possible that the Jade Garden would close with those very flags waving good-bye: My mixed vegetables in brown sauce looked like a diorama of a swamp; Robert's lobster sauce reminded him of a placenta. We had just finished, or given up, when Robert said, "Hey, Neil," to another hapless diner who'd wandered in.

He was tall and gangly in his white lab coat, boyish, with black-rimmed glasses that gave the impression that he was looking inward instead of at us.

"This is my sister, Sophie," Robert said. "Neil Resnick."

"Hi," I said.

"Have a seat," my brother said.

For all of Neil's height and angular skinniness, he had a button nose and puffy cheeks, and when he took his glasses off to clean them, I saw dark eyes so enormous and soft they reminded me of one of those portraits of children painted on velvet. His hair was youthfully thick and hippishly long, but this seemed to be more a matter of neglect than style.

He picked up the menu and said that this was his first time here, and what should he order?

"I'd stick with these," Robert said, passing over the patchwork wooden bowl of crunchy noodles.

"The water is good," I said.

Neil ordered wonton soup.

Robert told the waiter we'd finished, and added, "It was delicious, thank you," probably because the waiter looked depressed.

"You're a doctor?" I asked Neil.

"A neurologist," he said. "And you?"

I told him I was thinking of going into neurosurgery; meanwhile I worked in advertising.

"You work nearby?"

I told him I worked in the most stressful part of midtown, in the mid–East Forties, where crisis radiated from every building and anxiety lurked around every corner.

Neil said that it was pretty bad here, too, in the hospitalville of the high Sixties and the low Seventies, where sickness and worry prevailed. "What do you think it's like in the Fifties?"

"You know," I said, "butterflies, ponies, freshly baked bread, young lovers."

When Robert said that he had to get back to the hospital, I got up, too.

Neil said, "Do you have to go?"

I did; I had a meeting I could be late for only if I left now.

"Would you . . ." Neil began. "Maybe we could have lunch in the Fifties some time."

"Sure," I said, and I gave him my work number.

Outside, my brother said, "Divorced, one daughter."

I said, "Cute."

"He is cute," Robert said.

. . . . .

Joe, the art director I worked with, was waiting for me in my office. We were already a few minutes late for the meeting, but his "We should go" was all doom and no drive.

The red light on my telephone was blinking, and he didn't object when I said my standard, "I just want to . . ."

I listened to my message; it was "Neil"—hesitation—"Resnick."

I didn't think in French, but the word *frisson* presented itself; I'd never taken Ecstasy, but from what I'd heard I was on two hits.

Joe registered this—possibly his eyes widened a thousandth of an inch—and I acknowledged it with a prolonged blink; from working together we'd achieved the symbiosis of conjoined twins.

We ambled over to the conference room at a quitter's pace. There were empty chairs at the table, but Joe and I joined the Bad Attitudes along the wall.

Gary, our creative director, today's master of ceremonies, stood, marker in hand, by the easel. He was saying, "What is synergy?"

It was unclear whether his question was rhetorical, and no one spoke until he said, "Anybody?"

The room came alive with definitions—"All on the same page";

"Coordination"; "Well-oiled machine"—and Gary wrote each one down on the easel. Then he turned around and shook his head, apparently awed by the brainpower assembled in the room.

Meetings like this usually made me feel the clocks had stopped and all beauty had gone out of the world; now, in my Neil-induced state, the meeting struck me as a musical farce, and I was rapt, even though I didn't like musicals or farces.

I put Gary's "Imagine every department working together synergistically" to the tune of John Lennon's "Imagine."

In his, "Now, how are we going to make it happen?" I heard, *Let's put on a show!*

"Bulletin board?" one gal called out.

"Newsletter," an aspiring suck-up sang.

I added my own voice: "Memos by e-mail!" and a chorus of approval followed.

"Good idea," Joe said, naysayer to naysayer.

. . . . .

When I returned Neil's call, he asked if I would have dinner with him Friday, three nights hence. As he'd eliminated all coyness from our repertoire, I said an immediate, "Okay."

"Really?" he said.

I was hanging up when Joe appeared at my door and asked if I was ready to work on baby wipes.

I repeated the first lines of the soap opera I'd watched when I'd stayed home sick from school: "Like sands through the hourglass, so are the days of our lives."

. . . . .

When I asked my mother about Lev Polikoff, she spoke so softly I had to mash my ear against the receiver.

The information she gave up wasn't worth straining for: Lev Polikoff lived in Lambertville, New Jersey, just across the river from New Hope; he still painted; he made his living as an illustrator.

I didn't realize just how much she did not want to talk about Lev Polikoff until she said, "I should let you go," and hung up first, a first.

In the weeks that followed, the only question I would ask was if she'd spoken to him, and she always had.

. . . . .

Jack had presented Mindy to me with less fanfare than her predecessors; he hadn't, for example, told me how much I'd love her. He'd hardly talked about her at all, which gave me the impression that she was peripheral and ephemeral. But the opposite was true, as I found out when he called to tell me they were engaged.

He asked if I had any objections.

"I have no idea," I said. "I don't know her."

He told me that Mindy was exactly who she seemed to be. "What you see is what you get."

"Okay," I said, "but I've barely seen her."

We agreed to meet at a restaurant around the corner from Mindy's apartment on the Upper East Side, roughly a day's journey from mine in the West Village. The restaurant was elegant and casual, and there at the bar was my elegant and casual brother in jeans, a dark-blue blazer, white shirt, and an exquisite green tie with tiny orange giraffes on it.

"You're getting married," I said, and he said, "I am."

He was drinking a martini, which went with his tie, and he ordered one for me, too.

Placing the drink in front of me, the bartender told Jack that Debbie had called to say Mindy would be a few minutes late.

"Who's Debbie?" I said.

Jack said, "Her P.A."

"Her P.A.?"

"Her personal assistant."

I said, "Will she be your P.A. when you get married?"

He said, "I'll probably be her P.A.'s P.A.'s P.A." Then he swiveled his stool around to face outward so he'd see Mindy as soon as she arrived. I swiveled with him, and noticed a huge arrangement of gorgeous blue flowers. I said, "Do you know what those are called?"

He said, "I'm pretty sure they're called flowers."

Then Mindy walked in, and he went over to her.

They kissed, and he helped her off with what I saw was a real fur coat, one she hadn't found in a thrift shop or in her grandmother's closet. She was very pretty in her work clothes—a pale suit and chiffon blouse—and she walked in high heels with more grace than I did barefoot.

We said hello and held hands for a moment and looked at each other as the sisters-in-law we were to become.

Once we were seated at a table by the window, Mindy apologized for being late and apologized in advance for a phone call she would have to take during dinner; she was in the middle of a big deal. She worked in her family's real-estate business—The Bronstein Group—along with her father and two of her brothers and about a thousand employees.

A waiter told us the specials, noting which he thought Mindy would enjoy, and we ordered.

She caught Jack up on her deal, and I noticed that he was really listening to her, as opposed to pretending to listen or making a show of what a good listener he was.

I asked if she liked her work, and she said, "I love it."

"What do you do, exactly?"

"It's different every day." I could tell by the way she said, "You don't like what you do?" that she already knew.

I explained that I'd sort of fallen into advertising and now I couldn't get out.

As if I were a child trapped in a mine, she said, "We'll get you out," and I heard her "we" not as she and Jack and I, but the entire Bronstein Group, as well as all of their buyers and renters, some of whom were probably celebrities, and all of their independent contractors, some of whom were probably teamsters; her "we" seemed to include everyone who had any power—political, financial, or physical—in Manhattan, on Earth, and in Heaven. She sounded so strong and so sure and so steadfast, I believed I would get out of advertising, and I thought, *This is what Jack loves about her.*

When our salads came, I asked how Jack had proposed. I was really curious because he never said the expected thing, or if he did, it was always with irony, which would be all wrong and even unkind in a proposal.

He turned to Mindy and re-proprosed: "Will you marry me, please?" He spoke without any irony at all, even now, when he could've gotten away with some. "Then I gave her the ring."

I realized I'd been remiss in not asking to see the ring earlier, which seemed to explain in part why I didn't have one myself.

Jack had designed the ring with a jeweler, a diamond set deep into a square-shaped platinum band, and I was trying it on when Mindy's phone rang. She took the call outside.

I held my hand away and said that if it didn't work out with Mindy, he could give me the ring for my birthday.

Jack said, "You really like it?" just as he did after I'd admired one of his screenplays.

"Don't be needy," I said.

When I asked if Mindy was going to change her name, he said no, but he might change his; "I'd keep my maiden name." In a Monty Python voice, high-pitched and English, he said, "Jack Applebaum Bronstein."

I asked if they had a date for the wedding, and they did, almost a year and a half away.

"People will talk," I said.

He was looking out the window at Mindy, and I looked, too. She was pacing the sidewalk. She lit a cigarette. She nodded, she nodded, and then she stopped; her eyes narrowed, her mouth turned down, and, as we watched, she began to argue.

I could see that Mindy was tougher than I was and tougher than Jack; I imagined him on the other side of that call.

Then she spotted us in the window, and she waved her pinky at us.

Jack said, "That's my mogul."

. . . . .

As though sensing my fear of being stood up, Neil called me the day before our date, and the morning of. He asked me to meet him at Jules, which I'd heard of; it had just opened and was impossible to get into—unless, he told me, Jules was the son of a patient of yours.

When my cab pulled up to the restaurant, Neil was waiting outside.

He wore a navy blue duffel coat—the kind with toggles—and was taller than I remembered and ganglier; he held himself like an adolescent, like his body was a rambling mansion he'd inherited and was just now moving into.

"Hi," he said, and he took my hand and led me inside. The hostess ignored Neil until his words, spoken pleasantly, reached her ears: "Would you please tell Jules that Dr. Resnick is here?"

A moment later, Jules appeared. He said, "Hey," to Neil and, "Glad to meet you," to me, and led us through the restaurant, past the many models and the lay beautiful, children all.

I was shaking my head inside, until Neil offered the spectator seat to me and seated himself with his back to the runway.

He said, "Is red wine okay?" and I said it was.

I already knew that Neil was Jewish, like me; like me, he'd gone to public school; like me, he'd grown up in the suburbs, though his was Shaker Heights, outside Cleveland.

When we both ordered the steak frites, I remembered reading a study that showed that the more similar a couple was, the better their chance of staying together.

Neil had gotten a haircut, and was wearing a tie tucked into a V-neck sweater, a look last seen circa 1947 on Main Street, USA, or so I thought. When I complimented him on it, he said that he'd been talked into it at a store I knew to be a hip man's clothier based in London.

I'd liked the ensemble better when it had seemed sincere, but then Neil said that he'd bought it especially for our date and also that he was pretty sure he'd worn exactly the same outfit in junior high. He told me he'd been the dorkiest dork through high school, college, and med school.

I hadn't been cool or popular or even close to cool or popular in high school, and yet no matter what I said I could tell that was how he saw me. When I told him about advertising, he said that he thought that was where the cool kids wound up.

I said that it was, and they were as callow as ever. "The dorks from high school are the people you want to know now."

He said that he'd always just done what he thought was expected of him and was only now figuring out who he was and what he liked to do.

I said, "Like what?" Hovering beside him was a girl so thin she might have faxed herself; her sheaf of friends joined her and folded themselves into the next booth.

"Like books," he was saying, "and movies. And music. I never used to listen to music." Unlike me, Neil favored brand-new music; he named bands I'd never heard of that he was sure I'd love, like the Silver Jews, which he said he'd burn for me.

It took me a minute to understand that he was talking about making a CD. I confessed that I still listened to cassettes, and that many of my favorite songs were decades old: "Tupelo Honey" by Van Morrison; "Mercy, Mercy, Mercy" by Cannonball Adderley; "Knockin' on Heaven's Door" and a dozen other early Bob Dylan songs.

He said, "You have big ears," explaining this was jazz lingo for *discerning listener.* "Bugsy."

I said, "I also like 'You Sexy Thing.' "

He sang the line: "I believe in meerkls since you came along," and I thought, *Here is a man who can sing Hot Chocolate on the first date.*

When our steak frites came, I told him that I liked nothing on Earth better than a french fry.

"Same here," he said. "Did you ever have the fries at the Corner Bistro?"

I had.

Probably the best, he said, were at Pastis, though the fries at the Four Seasons were out of this world.

I thought maybe he was trying to impress me, which was sweet, but I wanted him to know exactly who I was, and I told him: I loved fries anywhere, from the fanciest restaurant to the dingiest diner; I loved them greasy, I loved them greaseless, I loved them fat and white and underdone, I loved them brown and loved them crispy. In my own *Let Us Now Praise Famous Fries,* I spoke as though telling him my most deeply held beliefs, and in a way I was.

He hadn't expected my principled lack of discrimination; maybe it didn't go with his notion of the cool and popular girl who hadn't noticed him in high school. I thought I saw his face say, *This is going to be harder than I thought.*

"Okay," he said, and I heard Cleveland in his voice. "All right then."

We finished our identical meals at exactly the same moment, and I thought, *We will stay together forever.*

A moment later, he turned serious: "I guess Robert told you that I'm divorced."

I nodded.

"And I have a daughter?" He nodded to himself. I couldn't see past his glasses, and, as with our first meeting, I got the impression that he was looking in at himself instead of out at me.

He ordered another bottle of wine. He'd been married for sixteen years, he told me, and divorced for three; Ella was seven.

I admitted that I wasn't good at math.

He told me that his wife was a doctor, too; they'd met as premeds at Yale and had both gone to medical school at Harvard; Beth still practiced in Boston. "You'd like her," he said. "She's very smart." But the marriage had gone from rote to worse, and he said that he'd defended himself against his wife's contempt by receding. "As soon as I heard her voice, it was like a switch flipped my personality off," he said. "Basically, I disappeared."

I'd never been married, but I thought, *I've done that; I've felt that way.* "How long did you disappear?"

"Sixteen years?" he said.

He took a deep breath, and then I heard why: "I had an affair," he said.

I thought of saying, *Taxi!* but he looked too burdened for me to make light of anything.

He took off his glasses; he closed his eyes; he shook his head. He told me that he had made a grave mistake, and I heard it in his voice. I heard that he had spent hours and days, weeks and months, going over it again and again. It was the worst thing he'd ever done, maybe the only bad thing, and I knew he would never do it again. It may sound strange, but his description of his infidelity convinced me of his faithfulness.

I felt in that instant that I was the one who'd had the affair, and I forgave myself for it. I took his hand and looked him right in his velvet-painting eyes, and I said, "What're you reading?"

A moment later, we were back to normal, back to the boyfriend and girlfriend we already seemed to be, and to the husband and wife we seemed on our way to becoming.

He'd just finished reading a new collection of short stories that he loved and I loved, and we loved the same dead writers, too—Hemingway and Fitzgerald but not Faulkner; neither of us had read *Ulysses,* and I said, "Let's never read it," and we swore that no matter what happened between us, we never would.

After our dishes were cleared, he said, "I feel so great with you."

After port, he leaned over and kissed me on the lips.

After he'd paid the check, he led me out to the sidewalk and pulled me against him.

It seemed like the best and most natural thing to bring Neil home with me—if only my friend Kate hadn't said, "Make an effort not to be in the moment." *What?* "Don't sleep with him on your first date." When I'd said, *Are you crazy?* she'd named names.

In the cab, I told the driver, "Two stops."

When I walked into my apartment the phone rang. It was Neil calling me from the cab.

. . . . .

I saw him a few nights later, and a few nights later and a few nights later. He called me at the office every morning and afternoon, and for up to an hour after each call I said yes to everything. Yes, I would proofread another copywriter's copy. Yes, I could go to a focus group during lunch. Yes, Joe and I could meet with the client on Friday.

Joe came into my office and said, "Did you say we'd be ready to meet with the client on Friday?"

"Yes," I said.

"Are you nuts?"

"Yes."

"I told them to forget it," he said.

"Great."

. . . . .

When Neil asked me to go to a play, I tried to act as though many, many men had taken me to many, many plays; meanwhile, I felt as though he'd draped a floor-length ermine cape around my shoulders and handed me a scepter.

In my giddiness, I told the truth: "Sometimes I get claustrophobic at plays."

"We don't have to go, Bugsy," he said.

"No," I said. "I want to." I explained that I'd be okay as long as I had a Life Saver. "I don't know why," I said. "It's like I'll be able to escape through my mouth."

He gave me the name and address of the theater. "I'll be there with bells on," he said.

My brain and nether region reacted as a single entity to Neil: *Yes,* they said. This was a general yes, however, and there was disagreement on the specifics. My brain, for example, wanted me to delay sleeping with him, not on principle but simply on the grounds of, *What's the rush?*

My nether region answered what the rush was.

Once you sleep together, my brain said, *you can never go back to how you were before.*

My brain had a point: Why not prolong this happy stage? There would be years and years of sleeping together.

Mind over body, I didn't clean my apartment or wash my sheets—insurance against bringing Neil home.

. . . . .

Outside the theater, Neil said, "You look beautiful," and from his expression I could see that he really thought so, which made me feel that I was.

I said, "You look nice, too," and he did; he wore a red bow tie and a dark gray suit.

At our orchestra seats, he handed me a roll of cherry Life Savers. We held hands; we tickled each other's arms; we watched the play, or tried to.

Afterward, Neil took me to the white sofas and ottomans in the lobby bar at the Royalton for a late supper.

On my third glass of wine, I told him that I thought it was probably a good idea for us to wait to sleep together. "I think it will be better," I said, though I couldn't remember why. "It will mean more," I said, without conviction.

"I'll wait if you want to," he said. "I can respect your wishes. But I'm ready now."

Back at my apartment, I said, "Sorry for the mess."

My nether region said, *Are you kidding?*

He said, "I don't care."

For a long time, we kissed on the sofa; we lay on the sofa; on the sofa, we took off his bow tie, we took off my camisole, we took off everything.

As a joke, I said, "Another reason I think we should wait . . ."

When we got up to go to my bed-sized bedroom I said that we could either sleep on dirty sheets or strip the bed to the bare mattress and pretend I was a crack whore.

He said, "Crack whore," and I thought I'd never heard anything so romantic.

. . . . .

Adam was the busiest friend I had—by day, he worked in public television, by night he wrote plays—and I was thrilled whenever he called.

After we'd talked for only a few minutes, he said, "What are you taking?"

I told him about Neil.

Adam told me that he'd never heard me sound so happy, and he'd known me since I was twenty-two; we'd worked in publishing together.

"What about when I was with Chris—I didn't sound like I was on drugs?"

"With Chris you sounded like you were strung out on heroin."

Then he told me why he was calling: I'd asked him to tell me if he heard about a job, and he had. "It's a nature series from the BBC," he said. "They need writers to Americanize it."

I admitted that I didn't know anything about science.

He said, "I don't think you have to know anything," and I said, "Sweeter words were never spake."

He said he'd call me when he found out more.

When we hung up, I thought, *I have a new job.*

. . . . .

At some point, with every recent boyfriend, I'd become aware of all the girlfriends who'd preceded me in bed; I'd felt their presence, if only in the form of his expertise. It could be lonely, no matter what my nether region had to say about it.

With Neil, it was just us.

With Neil, I could believe I was the only woman he'd ever slept with, and I knew this wasn't far from the truth.

I am going to teach you everything, I thought. *I will teach you how to be a hundred lovers to me and I will be a hundred lovers to you and we will never need anyone else.*

In sleep, he was already an expert at what you can never teach: He held me all night long, his arms wrapped around me, his chest to my chest.

. . . . .

Neil and I stayed together for nights on end, lost in the Bermuda Triangle of early love.

Then I got a stomach flu. I told him I needed to spend the night alone.

"Do you have diarrhea?" Neil asked. "Loose stools?"

I said, "I'm not talking to you about my stools."

He dropped off ginger ale and made toast for me. He took my temperature. He kissed my forehead and said, "Good night, Bugsy," and I had never felt so cared for.

. . . . .

Adam called and said, "I don't think you want this job."

"Why don't I?"

"It's a political series."

I was about to say, *I thought it was about nature,* but then I realized what he meant.

"The executive producer is happy just changing teatime to coffee break," he said. "The series producer thinks American audiences expect more drama from nature than the English." It was a lot of work to apply for the job, he said; I'd have to write a completely new script for the first episode.

I said, "Bring it on."

He asked if I could do it over the weekend, and I said, "Of course I can."

He sent the tape and script over by messenger. I was happy just looking at my name typed on the address label. I thought of all the times I'd dreaded the question *What do you do?* Now I said aloud, "I work at PBS."

. . . . .

Neil said that he wished he could help—he loved nature programs—but he was spending the weekend with Ella in Boston.

The episode was a day in the life of a pond.

The voice of an Englishman nearly dead with boredom deigned to narrate the program, deadening such dead lines such as, "A spider guards her precious eggs," and, "The water boatman skims the surface in search of prey."

For tranquil scenes, harp music possibly meant for a Japanese tea ceremony was played; for violence, violins that reminded me of the score from *Psycho.*

I called Jack, who suggested I look for the most compelling characters. I liked the water boatman, but he wasn't really on what you could call a journey. The frog was charismatic, but it was hard to forgive him after he'd eaten the eggs the spider had risked her life to produce. The rainstorm seemed like a climax, but of what?

I rewound, I pressed Play, I rewound, I pressed Play, and each time I said, "You can do it!" but I couldn't.

I was back in science class, taking a test I hadn't studied for, choosing (B) just because I thought there wouldn't be three *C*s in a row.

By Saturday night, the script was so marked up that even I couldn't read it, and what I could read made no sense. I decided on (E) None of the above; I erased everything.

Sunday afternoon, I was changing *murder* back to *kill,* when it occurred to me that I'd rather murder myself than press Play again.

I called Kate, who told me that if I couldn't rewrite the first episode I couldn't rewrite the next ten, and I wouldn't want to, and I shouldn't make myself. What I should do, she said, was meet her for wine and fries, and I did.

Afterward, at home, I wrote an apologetic thank-you note to Adam and was sliding it in an envelope with the tape when Neil called.

"How's it going?" he said.

I told him, and he offered to come over and help me with the script.

For a moment I was back in the pond. "Thanks," I said, and, "That's sweet," but my tone said, *No, no, a thousand times no.*

"Maybe you just need a break," he said.

I told him that a break lasting for all eternity wouldn't be long enough to make me want to watch the video again.

"Are you sure?"

I paraphrased Kate: "I couldn't do it and I didn't like doing it and I shouldn't do it."

"Good point," he said. "Can I still come over?"

. . . . .

I couldn't bear to watch the video again, though I imitated the voice-over for Neil. He was reading the script when my mother called.

I can still remember the exuberance in her voice when she said that she was finally getting used to living alone.

"I'm actually liking it," she said. "I'm loving it."

I laughed out loud, I was so relieved.

I think now that must have been the weekend of her reunion with Lev Polikoff.

. . . . .

When my grandmother had her first stroke, Robert drove down to Philadelphia. He called me once she'd been transferred from Emergency to ICU to a regular room in the hospital. He was calm and reassuring: It was a minor stroke, he said.

I said, "How's Mom?"

Robert sounded mystified: "Mom is . . . great."

. . . . .

Neil tried to explain what a stroke was, but all I heard was ". . . blood vessel . . ." and ". . . frontal lobe . . ." until he told me that the kind of stroke my grandmother had was so common that residents abbreviated it to S.O.S.L.O.L.F.O.K.F.—"Same Old Story Little Old Lady Found On Kitchen Floor."

But my grandmother had another little stroke, and then another, and another.

The next time I saw her, at her apartment, she was a little old woman in bed, clutching a white vinyl purse.

In truth, I'd been expecting her health to fail for a long time, and not just because of her age: She'd always regarded people who got sick or died as weak and negligent, which, according to the ironic dictates of fate, would call forth her own demise. After my father's death, when she'd announced, "I exercise and eat right," my mother had grimaced, but I'd thought, *Look out, Steeny.*

I was surprised by how old she looked, but the sight of her was nothing compared to the sound. She said, "Come on in, honey bun," with so much affection I turned around to see if there was a honey bun behind me.

I needed to sit down. The back of my legs found a chair, but the woman occupying my grandmother's body said, "Sit with me."

Both my mother and I sat on the bed, and my grandmother held our hands. "What can I do for you swell kids?" she said. "Would you like tea or coffee? Maybe a glass of sherry?" She offered soup, sandwiches, cake, and ice cream. If she didn't have what we wanted, she said that Laura, the nice woman taking care of her, could run out and pick something up.

My mom said a stiff, "Thank you, I'm fine," and I wondered if her mother's sudden generosity and affection reminded her of all the decades she'd gone without.

"I bet you'd like a scotch," my grandmother said to me.

"I would."

She called for Laura, and said, "You look wonderful, Joyce."

My mother just nodded, as though she got compliments from her mother all the time instead of never.

I said, "You do look great, Mom."

Now she perked up: "Really?"

I said, "You really do." And she did; her face looked less gaunt, her skin pink instead of gray.

"Are you wearing a new lipstick?" my grandmother said.

"No, Mother," she said—coldly, I thought.

"It's pretty," my grandmother said, as oblivious to her daughter's new disposition as her daughter was to hers.

When Laura returned with my scotch, my grandmother said, "I wanted you to put it in a crystal glass," but that was the only sign of the old Steeny.

. . . . .

Afterward, on the elevator, I said, "You didn't tell me."

"What?" my mother said.

"About Grandmom."

She said, "She seems frail, doesn't she?"

"Her whole personality is different."

"She has all those nice leather pocketbooks," my mother said. "Why she's holding on to that vinyl purse I don't know."

"She's nice," I said. "She got nice."

My mother nodded, but either she didn't agree or it didn't matter to her, which seemed as strange and dramatic as my grandmother's transformation.

I said, "You don't see the change?"

"Of course I do," she said. "She feels vulnerable. She's older."

I said, "Does it get on your nerves or something?"

"Of course not," she said. "I think Laura's lovely, don't you?"

. . . . .

Neil and I went away for the weekend; a patient lent him her country house in Connecticut. We rented a car. On the drive, I asked him what he'd wanted to be when he grew up, and without hesitation he said, "Astronaut." He told me that he'd been obsessed with NASA; he'd been transfixed watching the men walk on the moon, and had written letters to all the astronauts.

"Did they write back?"

"Some did." He said he'd have to ask his mom where the letters might be, but then he said, "I'm sure she threw them out."

"Are you serious?"

"She'll let me spend hours looking for them before she admits to it," he said. "Then she'll defend herself by making me feel like an idiot for wanting the letters in the first place."

"Nice," I said. "What about your dad?"

"Let's see," Neil said. "I think the best one is that when the school dentist told me I needed braces, my dad told me to push on my front teeth instead."

"Your dad was a . . . ?"

"Dentist," he said. "No. He was an accountant."

. . . . .

We stopped at an antiques store that had zillions of postcards. Some were just old photographs, posed portraits, that had been made into postcards, and Neil said, "I bet they didn't think they'd wind up in an antiques store someday."

I said, "You never think it'll happen to you."

The owner said, "Anything you're looking for?"

"I like old pictures of animals," I said.

Neil looked at me like he'd never met anyone as fun and zany.

A box was brought down. Old zoos, a pigeon farm, a promenade of ostriches—I bought them all.

In the car, I told Neil that my favorite fashion photograph featured a model named Dovima posing between two elephants. I said that I'd been searching for her long black dress my entire life, though it hadn't done much for Dovima; according to her obituary, she'd gone on to be what *The Times* called "a hostess" in a bowling alley.

When we pulled into the driveway, Neil handed me a giant bag of Life Savers and said, "In case you get claustrophobic with me."

I felt just the opposite and said so. What came to mind was the expression *The wide open,* which an ex-boyfriend had used to describe the Western landscape he missed and longed for.

The house was old and charming with painted floors and a fireplace. We undressed on the way upstairs and got right into the four-poster bed.

When I opened my eyes, I could see outside the window to the apple trees in bloom.

In the last few years, the closest I'd come to cooking dinner for anyone was opening a fresh pack of cigarettes and emptying an ashtray. But I wanted to cook for Neil. Maybe it was because he'd said he'd grown up on frozen dinners and he and his wife had always ordered out. I didn't know, but I got in the car and went to the market for groceries and to the liquor store for wine.

When I got back, Neil was on the phone, and he must've just dialed because he was saying, "May I speak to Ella, please?"

He said, "Okay, then," not exactly into the receiver, and hung up. He tried to make a joke of it, imitating his ex-wife saying, "She's not here," and slamming down the phone.

"She hung up on you?"

He imitated it again.

"I thought you and Beth were on good terms," I said.

"We are, relatively."

I said, "Relative to what?"

"She used to hang up when she heard my voice." He tried to laugh. He told me that they got along better than a lot of divorced couples.

He turned his back to me and pretended to look through a drawer for something. He went into the other room, and then upstairs. I thought of him saying that he'd disappeared for sixteen of the sixteen years he'd been married.

I unpacked the groceries and washed the vegetables. I uncorked the wine and poured myself a big glass.

He came back in the kitchen only when the phone rang and I answered it. I knew his service by then; it was Helen, and she said, "I'm trying to reach Dr. Resnick."

As a joke, I said, "This is Dr. Resnick," and I was glad when Neil laughed.

"Hi," he said into the phone, and, "Okay, put her through," and then: "This is Dr. Resnick."

He was always getting calls from patients because he covered for so many doctors, and one in particular, the forever-traveling Dr. Glatz, whose patients were celebrities of one sort or another and especially demanding.

I didn't mind. I liked listening to Neil talk to patients; I liked how sure he was, and how knowledgeable, and I liked that he was helping someone who needed help.

After he hung up with his last patient, he said, "Sorry," and I said, "No."

He said, "I can't believe you're making dinner for me."

"Me, neither." I lit candles and decorated the table with my new postcards. The chicken was edible and the salad outstanding.

Afterward, we looked through a shelf of videos, and he was thrilled to find *2001: A Space Odyssey*. "We have to watch this," he said.

I said, "It's about space, right? And the future?"

"Uh-huh."

"I have some bad news," I said. "I hate space and the future."

He said, "Please don't say that."

. . . . .

In bed, Neil asked me if I'd ever been close to getting married.

I told him a little about Chris: He'd grown up in Manhattan, gone to Brown, and worked as an advocate for homeless people. I said that we'd been engaged for three weeks when I decided not to go through with it.

"Why?"

"I saw that getting married wasn't going to change anything," I said. "It would just be more of the same."

"Which was . . . ?"

I said, *"Who's Afraid of Virginia Woolf?"*

He said, "So, you don't regret it?"

"He died," I said. "In a car wreck."

"Jesus," he said. "When?"

"About a year later."

"That's so sad," Neil said, holding on to me.

He fell asleep, and for a long time I lay there. Then I got dressed and went downstairs. I poured myself a glass of wine and took it outside to the little porch.

There was a nice moon, not full but fat, and it lit up the apple trees and the petals underneath.

I smoked a cigarette.

What I didn't tell Neil was that I always thought I'd wind up with Chris, even after we'd broken up, even after he'd died.

Adam had gone with me to the funeral. It was crowded, as a young person's funeral almost always is. We sat in the back, where it was hard to see and hard to hear.

I was looking at all the women. I could only see them from behind, but I studied each one, their hair and backs. Their necks and shoulders. Their arms. I found myself thinking, *You? Did he sleep with you?* Here I was at his funeral, overwhelmed not by grief but jealousy.

Reading my mind, Adam told me that whoever these women were they hadn't meant anything to Chris. "They were just keeping your seat warm," he said.

As a procession, we walked to Central Park, past the carousel to the field where Chris had played softball on Sundays. There was a metal can of his ashes, and Adam and I each took some and scattered them on the mound. As a joke, I said, as I had a thousand times, "Tell me the truth: You don't think Chris and I will ever get back together, do you?"

Adam laughed, and so did I; he hugged me, and then I think he knew I was about to cry because he said, "Oh, shoot, I think I got Chris on you," and dusted off my coat.

Adam and I were walking to the Boathouse when a woman stopped us. "You don't know me," she said. "I'm Myla. I was the one after you."

Once she'd gone, Adam said, "See?"

It didn't make any difference.

The part of my brain that made no sense at all didn't believe Chris was dead. He'd switched hospital ID bracelets or charts with another patient. He'd tied sheets together and lowered himself out the window. I looked for him, like he was a fugitive in hiding. A hank of blond hair, a jean jacket, and I'd think, *Chris.*

I'd always thought of him as the one who got away, but right then it stopped being true. I knew that if Chris walked across the moony grass and up to this porch and proposed again I would say no again.

I wondered if he was here—that is, everywhere. I imagined that he was. I imagined him saying, *Who's the guy inside?*

As though he had, I made my voice as kind as I could: "He's the one after you."

. . . . .

After my father's death, my mother had called me every day, then every other day, and then every few days. One Sunday I realized with a pang of guilt that we hadn't spoken in more than a week.

She answered in a voice so husky I said, "Do you have a cold?"

"No," she said. "I feel wonderful."

I told her about Neil, but she was distracted. Finally I stopped talking.

It took her a minute to notice. Then she said, "I'm so glad you have somebody, too."

. . . . .

Once when we were talking on the phone, she said, "That's my Call Waiting." She got flustered, and asked me to hold on, and then she was gone.

I knew it was Lev Polikoff; what I didn't know was whether she'd forgotten about me or decided to let me wait.

She called me back an hour later. "I'm sorry," she said, and I could tell that she was.

. . . . .

I began calling my new-and-improved grandmother as I never had the old one. At first, we'd only talk for a few minutes; I'd call her while I was waiting to go into a meeting or finishing my lunch. She'd ask me about work, and in the beginning I'd say, "It's okay," because I wanted her to think it was.

Once when I called her, she said, "What are you working on until ten at night?"

I said, "I'm trying to write a stupid brochure."

"What's the problem?"

It was hard, I told her, because the brochure wasn't supposed to sound like a person had written it; it had to be authoritative, like the voice of God or Science.

She asked me to read it to her, and I did, even though it was long. I kept stopping, but she said, "Go on," and, "It's not like I've got a dance to go to."

Afterward, trying to compliment me, she said, "I'd never know that was written by a human being."

. . . . .

Adam called to tell me that Steinhardt, the publishing house where we'd met, had been sold, and the editorial department would probably be disbanded. "It's the end of an era."

I said that I thought the era had ended a while ago. I was about to say, *Do we even know anybody who works there anymore?* when I thought of Francine Lawlor, and I said her name aloud.

He complimented me on my memory, but I told him no; Francine had been sending me Christmas cards for the last fourteen years.

While I was on the phone, he looked her up in the *LMP*, the publishing phone directory. "She's still there."

"What is that—twenty years?"

"At least," he said.

I said, "What do you think's going to happen to her?"

He was quiet.

"What?" I said.

He told me he was thinking of the end of "Bartleby the Scrivener." He added, "The Melville story," in case I didn't know.

"What happened to him?"

"He refuses to leave the office," Adam said. "And he's carted off to prison."

I said, "And he lived happily ever after."

He said, "Remember the last line?"

"I read it in college—if I read it."

He quoted: " 'Ah Bartleby! Ah Humanity!' "

"Ah."

Then Adam said, "Aren't you glad I called?"

. . . . .

Neil and I went over to Robert's for dinner, and Jack and Mindy came, too. We sat in the living room while the nanny gave the twins their bath.

Robert made perfect martinis and Naomi passed pretty hors d'oeuvres, bruschetta with tomatoes and pesto.

Neil said, "Did you guys make these?"

Robert said, "I slaved over a hot counter at Zabar's."

I could tell how nervous Neil was, and I didn't blame him. Jack was hanging back; he might as well have been wearing the robes my father had put on for court.

I said, "What's going on with *The Jack Applebaum Show*?"

"Nada," he said. "The producers didn't like the script."

"That's not true," Mindy said. "They wanted him to make changes, and he didn't want to."

"They were idiotic," Jack said.

"So what're you working on?" I asked.

"I'm thinking of starting a production company," he said. He would put projects and people together. "All you really need is a business card, a phone, and an e-mail address."

This sounded scammy to me, but I didn't say so, as I would've if we'd been alone. "So you're like a wheeler-dealer?"

"I'm more of a wheeler-wheeler," he said.

Neil mentioned that he had a patient who was a director and said his famous name.

"Wow," Jack said. "What's he like?"

"Crazy," Neil said.

"Does he have a brain tumor or something?" Jack said.

Neil shook his head—he'd said all he was going to, and I was glad of that at least.

I looked over to see what Robert thought of Neil talking about a patient, but I couldn't tell.

A moment later, the nanny brought Isabelle and Max into the living room to say good night, and Neil asked if we could put them to bed.

Naomi smiled at me.

"Absolutely," Robert said.

Neil and I lay down with them—boy, girl, boy, girl; adult, child, adult, child—and the two of us read to the two of them.

When it was Neil's turn, he used all sorts of voices and sound effects—for monsters he made his voice shaggy, for footsteps he tapped the wall, for wind he whooshed—and the twins loved it.

Right then something happened to me: I looked at Neil from the outside, like he was an alien who had somehow landed in the bed of my niece and nephew.

Then I snapped out of it: I was the alien, sabotaging a sweet moment wherein my boyfriend was trying only to show me what a good father he was. If he was being a ham and a name-dropper, it was only because he wanted the people I loved to like him.

During dinner, Jack described the loft Mindy had found for Rebecca and her new boyfriend to renovate. "It's a penthouse," he said. "A loft with a river view."

I asked if this was the new boyfriend I'd heard about, and Jack said no, a new, new boyfriend. "An engineer," he said. "Nice guy."

I said, "Plus a millionaire."

Mindy said that the space was raw, and it was on an undesirable block in far West Chelsea. But the loft would be beautiful, she said; Rebecca had offered to throw their engagement party there.

Jack said, "Don't make any plans for New Year's."

Under the table, Neil squeezed my hand, and I squeezed back.

I said, "Could I get a raw space on an undesirable block?"

Jack said I could if I was willing to let Aunt Nora stay with me once a week.

During dessert, Neil made a real effort with Jack and finally found an interest they shared—music—and a band they both liked. Neil said that he'd just gotten their new CD, and it was fantastic.

Jack said, "Are you serious?"

Neil said, "Yeah."

"Come on," Jack said. "It sucked compared to their last one."

Neil's face froze in a sneer. "What didn't you like about it?"

"What didn't I like?" Jack said. "It sucked. They sounded like a garage band."

Neil said, "But that was their intent," sounding smug, and for a second I felt the strain of being on his team.

Jack said, "I don't know how much intention counts if the music sucks."

Mindy said, "I like the new CD," which made me love her.

"There you go," Jack said. "Different strokes."

When Jack got up I followed him.

At the bathroom door, I said, "What are you doing?"

"What?"

"Attacking Neil," I said.

"Sophie," he said, "disagreement is the way straight men get along."

"Oh."

"Watch it," he said, "or you'll turn Neil into an even bigger pussy than he is."

"I hate you."

"If you don't mind," he said, "I'd like to make wee wee."

Mindy followed a second later, said, "Sorry," to me, and walked in on Jack.

"Hey," I heard him say. "Bathroom time is private time."

When the two of them came back to the table, Jack said, "Sorry I was an asshole," to Neil.

Neil said, "Don't worry about it."

Mindy said, "He's just a little overprotective."

Robert told the story about my high-school graduation, when Jack caught sight of me kissing my boyfriend and said, "What's he doing to our sister?"

Naomi brought up the importance of napping. "The twins are different children when they don't nap," she said. "And yet a lot of parents don't let their children nap."

Dinner slowed down then, as dinners with Naomi generally did, but on the walk to his apartment Neil said he'd had a great time. "I loved reading to Max and Isabelle," he said, and I heard his whooshing all over again.

He said, "What names do you like for children?"

I was so taken aback that I said, "I like Ella."

He laughed and said, "I can't have two daughters named Ella."

"Albertine?" I said. "And Cleo."

"What about for a boy?"

"George."

He said, "I like George."

We went to Neil's because it was only a few blocks away on West End Avenue. We hardly ever stayed there. The living room was filled with furniture from his parents' basement in Shaker Heights, which was where it belonged.

The only inviting room in the apartment was Ella's. He'd given her the master bedroom, though he went up to Boston on weekends and took her to Cape Cod in the summer. Her room was big and full of light, and he'd decorated it himself with a vanity and ruffled gingham curtains that matched her canopy bed, which was like the one in my childhood bedroom.

Neil's room was small and bare—a brown shag rug, a futon on a platform, a clock on a crate table—a room that made me want to turn out the lights.

In the dark, we kissed. "Naomi is a very, very slow speaker," I said very, very slowly.

Five minutes later, Neil said, "I. Noticed."

. . . . .

In my office, Joe was designing the fulfillment package for all the enthusiastic mothers who checked "YES! Send me my FREE baby wipes."

"Do you realize what we're doing?"

"Of course I do," I said.

"You don't seem to be suffering as much as you should be."

"I'm suffering in silence," I said.

"You're whistling," he said, with real concern. "I heard you whistle."

. . . . .

Over breakfast, Jack told me that Mindy really liked Neil.

"Good," I said.

"I'm sure I would've liked him better . . ." and I waited for him to say, *If he weren't your boyfriend.* Instead, he stopped. "It's just that Mindy's last boyfriend was a doctor. She has a doctor thing," he said. "She's a mediphile." Then he said, "You know who he reminds me of? Who was that friend of Robert's who used to come over wearing pajamas and a bathrobe to study?"

I said, "Ivan Tarsky."

"Ivan Tarsky," he said.

"I loved Ivan Tarsky," I said.

Jack said, "So, what're Neil's friends like?"

I thought of the only one I'd met. What was Jules like? He'd seated us right away. "Nice."

Jack said, "That's good," and he seemed genuinely pleased. He told me how much he liked Mindy's friends and smiled, maybe thinking of the ones he liked most.

"The only thing I will say about Neil," Jack said, "is he seems a little young."

"You only grew up about fifteen minutes ago," I said. "With Mindy."

He said, "I did grow up with Mindy."

"What happened?"

"Beats me," he said. "I was just ready. It was time."

"I feel like that," I said.

He said, "You're just saying that because I said it."

. . . . .

Neil had met a lot of my friends, and I didn't want to ask outright why he hadn't introduced me to his. I waited until we were in bed with the lights out. Then I said, "Let's go out with your friends some night, if you want."

He didn't answer.

I was almost asleep when I heard him say, "I was friends with other couples," he said. "And when Beth found out about Darcy . . ."

I thought, *Who's Darcy?* He'd never told me her name.

. . . . .

"Is Glatz a friend?" I asked, after Neil got off the phone with his second Glatz patient of the evening and came back to the table to finish the dinner I'd made—pork chops in a rosemary marinade and peas with mint.

"Are you kidding?"

I said, "Why do you cover for him all the time?"

He shrugged. "It's a pain in the ass," he said. "And it's not like I get paid for it."

"Can you get out of it?"

Even before he answered, I knew what he was going to say: "Glatz does have some pretty interesting patients, though." Neil mentioned the rock star he'd spoken to—and he sort of laughed and shook his head, like, *Me! Dorky Neil Resnick from Shaker Heights High.*

"Neil," I said, "I got a bad feeling when you told Jack about that patient."

All the pleasure left his face. "Because he's Glatz's patient?"

All I said was, "Name-dropping—" and he nodded, not for me to go on but for me to stop.

He got quiet and busy then, clearing the table and running water. "Can we do these in the morning?" he asked.

"Sure," I said.

"I'm beat," Neil said. "I am beaten down. I'm ready to batten down the hatches."

I didn't know if he'd always free-associated like this, or if I was just noticing it now. It irritated me, and I was triply irritated at myself for being irritated. He was nervous, and I thought, *Why wouldn't he be?* I was acting like the cool girl I myself would have feared in high school. I was acting like my grandmother, the pre-stroke Steeny, who'd looked at all of us like we weren't quite good enough to be related to her.

When I got into bed, he said, "I'm getting on your nerves, aren't I?"

"I don't know why," I said. "It's me. I'm sorry."

"No," he said. "I'm annoying. I know that."

. . . . .

At Jules, Kate said, "You're going to have a baby with this guy." She herself was trying to have a baby, on her own, and she suggested we coordinate our pregnancies.

We'd finished dinner and were having coffee; Neil was outside talking on the phone.

She said, "He seems like such a mensch."

"He is," I said.

But she heard or saw me thinking, *I don't love him the way I loved Chris.* She looked at me. She nodded. She was deciding what to say. "Neil is a good man," she said finally. "He's somebody you could have a family with."

She was saying, *This is your chance.*

Jules stopped by our table and said, "How is everything?"

"Great," I said.

"Great," he said, and went on to another table; faintly I heard their Great-Greats.

When Neil returned, he said, "Sorry," and explained that he'd had to take the call. He was beaming, and I waited for him to say the famous name.

"It was Ella," he said, and to Kate, "my daughter."

Later, in the cab, he told me he couldn't wait for me to meet her.

. . . . .

In bed, I remembered Kate saying, *Neil is someone you could have a family with.*

I pictured Kate at her computer, reading online profiles listing the hair color and hobbies of each potential sperm donor, and with it came the murmurs of absolute authority and undeniable truth, in statistics from *Newsweek*, gossip from the now-married girls I'd avoided in high school, shtetl advice from my grandma Mamie: It was time to stop looking for a soul mate and to be satisfied with a mate, and actually it was past time, Sophie, and here was a perfectly acceptable specimen, not to mention a doctor, not to mention Jewish.

The murmers said, *This is your chance,* and Part Two, *Don't blow it.*

. . . . .

"How's Neil?" my grandmother Steeny asked.

"Fine," I said.

"Are you having fun?"

"Yeah," I said, but I thought of the night before in bed: When I'd tried to tell Neil how to touch me, he'd reminded me of myself trying to hook up my VCR with a poorly translated manual. I said, "But it's more than, you know, fun." I mentioned that we'd talked about children.

"Oh," she said.

"You sound disappointed."

She said, "I'm just sorry you're not having more fun."

. . . . .

My mother mentioned Lev, both to me and my brothers, but only in passing: He'd taken her to the opera; he'd cooked her dinner; he'd painted her portrait.

She herself was taking an art class. When I visited her in June, she'd finished *The House of Mirth* and was halfway through *The Age of Innocence.* She'd started volunteering at the Jewish Home for the Aged, where she was in charge of entertainment and leisure. She'd hired an exercise instructor who got everyone to stand up and raise their hands; as she spoke, she raised her own hands and wiggled her fingers.

On Sunday, we drove downtown to my grandmother's. When we pulled up in front of her building, my mother said, "When should I pick you up? Four?"

"You're not coming up?"

"I'm going to the museum," she said. "Is four good?"

Four was three hours away, which would make my visit the longest in Applebaum-Parker history. I looked at her: *Are you meeting Lev?*

She said, "So, four?"

"Fine."

Laura let me into the apartment and said, "Mrs. Parker will be so glad you're here."

My grandmother was sitting up in bed. "Where's your mother?"

"She went to the museum."

"That's great," she said, which was how I wanted to feel about it.

Robert and his family had visited the weekend before, and my grandmother went on and on about how adorable the twins were.

They were, of course, though I'd never expected my grandmother to see it. I was under the impression that she didn't like children; one of my earliest memories was of her saying, "I don't blame the children; I blame the parents."

I wondered what she'd blamed my parents for, but I didn't dare ask; I was afraid that bringing up the grandmother she'd been might bring her back.

I went to get tea for both of us, and while I was waiting for the water to boil I stood in the living room and looked at the portrait my mother admired. For the first time, I thought of my grandmother's will, and I wondered if she would leave the portrait to my mother.

When I brought the tea in, my grandmother asked again where my mother was, but this time she said, "Where's Joyce?"

"She's at the museum," I said.

"She loves her work there," she said.

I stopped: *Loves?*

"Joyce knows everything about art," she said.

I admit that it occurred to me to ask about Lev Polikoff, as long as we were in the past. It wouldn't be like I was telling on my mother; all I had to do was bring up his name. Instead, I agreed that my mother did know a lot about art. "She's always admiring that portrait."

"Which?"

"Above the yellow sofa," I said.

My grandmother said, "You know, I found that in the attic."

I said, "She really, really loves that portrait."

My grandmother said, "It is a very fine portrait."

. . . . .

My mother was late picking me up. I was waiting in the lobby when Dena's mother walked in.

"Sophie," she said.

"Hi," I said.

I looked for a sign that she was disappointed in me for deserting Dena, or for letting Dena desert me.

"How are you?" I said.

She said, "I get by," and it had the sound of a happy understatement. She told me that her mother lived here and that she herself lived downtown now, too.

"You gave up the house?"

She nodded.

I said, "I loved that house," and I remembered going over there the year after my father died and drinking bourbon with her in front of the fireplace.

"I liked it when the girls lived at home," she was saying. "But it was too big for one person."

It seemed like an extreme way to say that Dr. Blumenthal was never home, though he never was, and maybe that made her extreme.

She saw my reaction. "We got divorced," she said. "Two years ago."

I didn't know what to say; she didn't seem sorry, so it seemed strange for me to say that I was.

"I live near Rittenhouse Square," she said. "You'll have to come visit."

I was nervous about mentioning Dena, but I did: "How's Dena?"

She was fine. She was still working in planning on Roosevelt Island. "She runs the show now."

"Great," I said.

Mrs. Blumenthal said, "Still with Richard," very fast, so I knew not to ask any questions.

I wasn't ready to talk about myself yet, so I asked how Dena's sisters were.

They were married, and each had three children.

"What do they do?" I asked.

"They're raising their children," she said, and I heard that she neither approved nor disapproved. "What about you?"

"I'm still in advertising."

She said, "Oh," her tone matching mine; hers would've been happy if mine had been.

I said, "I'm still waiting for my calling," an expression I never used. It sounded both religious and passive, but my word choice didn't explain the bad feeling I got then: I realized I'd barely thought about my career since meeting Neil.

"Few are called," she said, not unkindly. Then she laughed: "I thought I was supposed to be a doctor's wife."

. . . . .

In the car, I asked my mother if she'd heard about the Blumenthals' divorce.

"No," she said, "but I'm not surprised. I always thought Stevie was cold."

I said, "I like her."

"It takes two to tango."

"Or four or fourteen or forty," I said.

"Excuse me?"

I said, "You said Dr. Blumenthal was a big philanderer."

My mother said, "Some marriages are more complicated than others."

. . . . .

At work and on the street, in the subway and on the bus, in restaurants, drugstores, and dry cleaners, I looked around me and thought, *Few are called.* Almost nobody was. Robert had been called to be a doctor, Francine Lawlor an editor. Adam had always known he wanted to be a playwright. But they were the exceptions. I was like everyone else; I fell into a job, and I worked at it. It didn't seem wrong to want more, but it was wrong to expect it to be delivered.

3.

My grandmother and I had never said we'd loved each other before her stroke because, in fact, we hadn't loved each other; now we said it every time we talked.

I said it partly because I thought she was going to die soon, and that was what I was thinking when Laura called me early one Sunday and told me she was worried. "Mrs. Parker isn't herself."

I assumed that my grandmother had turned back into a witch: "Mean?" I said.

"Mean?" Laura said. "No. She had a bad night. She didn't know who I was this morning."

"Did you call the doctor?"

"He said to keep her comfortable," Laura said. "She doesn't want to go back to the hospital."

"Is my mom there?"

"I've been trying to call her," she said. "The line's busy."

I told her I was on my way.

I wished Neil could go with me, but he was in Boston; I wished Robert could go, but he was at the hospital.

I didn't think Jack would be home; he pretty much lived at Mindy's. I was leaving a message on his answering machine when he picked up, interrupting his recorded voice with his real one.

After I'd told him everything, he said, "Shit. Mindy's cousin has the car."

I was waylaid for a moment—Jack had never lent his car to me—but then I said, "I'm sure I can borrow Robert's."

I waited for Jack to ask if I wanted him to go with me. Instead, he said, "You're going to stop in Surrey for Mom?"

"Yes," I said, and got off the phone fast, so he wouldn't hear my disappointment.

. . . . .

Naomi answered the door and handed me the keys, registration, and the address of the garage where the minivan was parked. She was holding Isabelle, who turned around and said, "Hello, Aunt Thophie," as though for the thousandth time instead of the first.

It sounded so great that I said, "I'm going to ask everyone to call me that."

I watched Naomi make the decision not to ask me what I meant. She said, "I wish I could go with you."

"Me, too," I said.

"But your mom will be there."

. . . . .

It was a hazy day and hot, even for June. I drove as fast as I could. I kept picturing my grandmother alone in her big bed, clutching her white pocketbook and asking who Laura was.

It was noon by the time I got to Surrey. I pulled into the driveway, behind a car I didn't recognize. It was a pale blue sedan with New Jersey plates, and only then did I think of Lev Polikoff.

The back door was wide open, but I didn't go in. I knocked on the metal frame of the screen door.

I waited. "Mom?"

I stood there for a moment; I didn't want to surprise them. I decided to go around to the front of the house and ring the doorbell. I was crossing the lawn when I heard my mother's voice. She was on the screened-in porch. For all my urgency, I stopped. I had never heard her sound so young, incredibly young, younger than I was now. She might have been the twenty-three-year-old Joyce Parker, sneaking behind her mother's back to see her bearded, unmarriageable artist-boyfriend.

I made myself move toward the porch, and I was there sooner than I wanted to be. I walked up the slate steps. I kept my eyes closed as I knocked so I wouldn't have to witness my own intrusion.

I thought I heard whispering, and I did hear a man's voice say, "No."

When I felt the doorknob turn in my hand, I said, "I'm sorry," and, "I tried to call."

My mother's hair was pulled back in a little ponytail; she wore plaid shorts and was barefoot. "No, no," she said. "Don't be silly."

Lev Polikoff had a white beard, and when he stood up I saw that he was no taller than my mother. Together the two of them looked like a fairy tale: Once upon a time, there was a couple who lived in an old can of corn, with an eraser for a bed, a leaf for a blanket, and a fly for a pet.

I heard my mother say, "This is . . ." and falter.

I said, "I'm Sophie," though I realized as soon as I'd spoken that I wasn't the one she was unsure how to introduce.

Lev Polikoff reached for my hand, and I gave it to him. He held on to it while he said my name and then his. His eyes were a calm blue, his eyebrows outstandingly bushy.

I liked him. I liked that he looked right at me and seemed to regard our meeting as important, just as my mother seemed to half pretend that it wasn't happening. He was as still as she was fluttery.

The three of us sat on the egregiously uncomfortable chairs on the porch.

I explained as efficiently as I could why I was there, and I sped up because of how uncomfortable my mother seemed—not just embarrassed, but caught. The word that came to mind was *guilty,* though it was something I sensed rather than saw—until I did see: Lev Polikoff was wearing a wedding band.

I got out of there as fast as I could, and only once I was on the expressway did it occur to me that my mother and I might've driven down together.

. . . . .

My grandmother looked like a withered bird, all beak and bones. I got right into bed with her.

"I heard you had a rough night," I said, rubbing her arm.

She was breathing hard. "I saw Grandpop," she said. "He was sitting right there." She looked over at the wing chair.

"Really?" I said.

"He said, 'What the hell's taking you so long?' and I said, 'I might've asked you the same question.' "

"What did you mean?"

"I meant," she said, "why did he keep me waiting all those years?"

"I'm not following."

"And the whole time my parents saying, 'Well? Well? Why doesn't he ask?' "

I took her hand, but she was too agitated to let me hold it.

"I was in the bathtub," she said, and I could see that she was remembering herself so vividly that she almost was that girl now. "And I thought, *Why not?*"

I said, "Why not . . . ?"

She said, "End it."

"End . . . ?"

"My life," she said. "It was terrible."

"Terrible," I said.

"I didn't know what to do," she said.

She laced her fingers through mine, and we lay like that for a while. Just when I thought she'd fallen asleep, she spoke: "I wrote to his mother." She squeezed my hand. "I wrote her a long letter." She smiled, nodding now, at her victory.

Finally, she did fall asleep. I was pulling my fingers out of hers when my mother walked in. Her face was stricken: She thought her mother had died.

. . . . .

I meant only to drop the keys off at Robert's, but at the door I told him about Lev, and I wound up lying on the sofa.

"What a drag," he said.

Naomi said, "It's going to be hard for your mother."

I nodded. "Hard how?"

Naomi was as loud a breather as she was slow a talker; she inhaled and exhaled exclusively through her nostrils, probably on principle. While she thought of her answer, I imagined myself as her patient and tried to interpret her breathing; I thought, *Boredom? Impatience?* and realized I was projecting.

Finally, Naomi said the obvious: "She spent her life as a wife and mother." Another week passed while she chose her words. "Being a mistress will confuse her identity."

I turned to Robert and said, "Mom is a mistress."

Robert nodded, the sole inheritor of my father's equanimity.

"It's sort of weird even to put *Mom* and *mistress* in the same sentence," I said. "It's like the rabbit and the duck, remember?"

He didn't.

I was referring to a drawing in which you could see either animal, but not both at the same time. I said, "I think it was in *Highlights*," a magazine from our childhood.

"I must have missed that issue," he said. "But ask me anything about 'Goofus and Gallant.' "

. . . . .

When I got home, Neil was asleep on my sofa. I woke him up, saying I needed pizza. We ordered in. Even though I knew I'd soon be naked, I ate as many slices as I could.

In bed, he said, "Do you want to tell me what happened?"

I hadn't told Neil anything important in a long time, and part of me didn't want to now. I was afraid to, afraid that he might be holding my character up to the light and turning it, as I did his.

Who could survive under such a cold eye?

It was the opposite of love, and yet it wasn't love I was opposed to but the murmurs that said, *This is your chance,* which seemed less like the promise of a door opening than the threat of one sealing shut. Judging Neil had been my way of saying that it was up to me to open the door or not, and I would be the one choosing the doors here, and there would be other doors and doors leading to doors. Meanwhile, I'd turned Neil into a door.

It was hard to talk at first, but I told him everything, starting with Lev Polikoff's blue sedan in the driveway. I didn't worry about how childish I sounded. In the morning I could say the adult things that I was supposed to feel; in the morning I would understand it from my mother's point of view. But now I said, "It's just one of those things you don't want your mother to do. You don't want her to do drugs. You don't want her to go out with a married guy."

"I'm sorry," Neil said, and somehow I knew that he wasn't thinking of me, but of what he, the married guy, had done to his own daughter.

"I'm not ready for you to meet Ella," he said. His voice was quiet and slow. He told me that he didn't know how to be a father and a boyfriend at the same time. He wanted to learn, he said, but it would take time.

"Okay," I said.

He was lying on his back beside me, his arms and legs pulled into his sides. I thought of the phrase *The wide open* now not as endless possibility but as the great plains between us. What made me move toward him had nothing to do with him as my boyfriend or us as a couple, but seeing him as him and me as me, just us chickens, two lost longers. I said, "We're not ready."

He nodded, but I wasn't sure he'd heard; he was receding from the contempt he imagined I had for him.

I spoke so low I could hardly hear myself when I said, "Did you love her?"

"I did," he said.

"Who was she?"

"She sang in a band," he said, almost helplessly.

. . . . .

My mother waited eight days to call. "Grandmom's doing much better," she said.

I knew—I'd spoken to my grandmother eight times by then—but I said, "That's good."

She said, "I'm sorry . . ." and her intonation promised more, but then she just said a more finite, "I'm sorry."

I said, "It's okay."

She hesitated. "Lev liked you very much."

"I liked him," I said.

"Did you?" she said, sounding girlish.

I said, "I did," straight back like a man. "But it's sort of 'Other than that, how did you enjoy the play, Mrs. Lincoln?' "

"You mean because he's married," she said softly.

"Right," I said, and I wondered why I was playing Speeding Ticket opposite her Joyride.

She said, "I asked him to take his ring off."

I let this go.

It was because I'd learned about fidelity from her that I said, "I thought you said that marriage was sacred."

For that instant, waiting for her answer, I was a younger woman and she an older one; I was the daughter and she the mother.

She said, "I meant *my* marriage was sacred," but her voice was thin, as though she hoped this was a good enough answer and suspected it wasn't.

"What about his wife?"

"That's really his business," she said. "I don't know if she's mentally ill . . ."

I stopped myself from saying, *Do you think you're Jane Eyre?* Instead, I said, "Do you have any reason to think she's mentally ill?"

"Just that they lead very separate lives."

I would hear this line so many times that it would become what was called a tag line in advertising: Trix are for kids. Just do it. No one can eat just one.

. . . . .

Robert told Jack, who said, "I don't want to think about it."

By then, his whole life was Mindy, Mindy, Mindy, Bronstein, Bronstein, Bronstein.

I'd hardly seen him. Whenever we tried to make plans, he said he had to check with Mindy: "She keeps the book." He'd call me back to say they were busy. They had dinner plans or theater tickets with her brothers and sisters-in-law; her parents had invited them to a silent auction, a black-tie dinner, or a performance to benefit a ballet company, leukemia research, or Israel.

On weekends, they flew up to Martha's Vineyard. Her whole family went—her parents, her brothers and sisters-in-law, nieces, nephews, aunts, uncles, and cousins—as well as the many friends who were like family.

I said, "Don't you guys ever want to be alone?"

The idea seemed never to have occurred to him. "It's a really big place," he said. There were three houses on the property.

"Still," I said.

He and I were having breakfast at the diner around the corner from his apartment; he was only in the city because he and Mindy had a wedding to go to in Scarsdale. He must've been missing the three houses; he drew them on a napkin. My brother was a great artist, and I liked watching him draw; he could make a napkin beautiful.

Unfortunately, as he drew, he talked about the Bronstein multiplex. Forgetting that I didn't care about architecture, he talked about the architecture.

I perked up when I heard him say, ". . . tongue in groove . . ." I thought he was talking about sex, but then he said, "It was built without a single nail."

I went back to dozing with my eyes open until he got to the vanishing pool—vanishing because it seemed to vanish into the ocean.

"Wait," I said. "They're on the ocean?"

He smiled, and tried not to.

"Wow," I said.

He said, "I know."

I said, "How does the pool vanish into the ocean?"

"No edges," he said. "It overflows."

"Sounds wasteful," I said.

He smiled.

"Isn't it hubris to blend your pool with the ocean?" I said. "Icarus-y?"

He had the easy smile of a man who spent his weekends floating in a vanishing pool, and I took advantage of this moment of mirth to bring up the main reason I'd met him for breakfast: "Are you going to visit Mom at all this summer?"

"Isn't she with that guy?"

"Not every weekend," I said.

He said, "I'll see her at Robert's in a couple weeks," meaning the birthday party for the twins.

He pretended to work on his sketch, though it was finished; he was just dotting the beach, grassing up dunes. When I took the sketch from him, he said, "They call it the Shtetl."

. . . . .

I told Neil he didn't have to come to the birthday party, but he said, "Are you kidding?" He loved children's birthday parties.

Robert answered the door. After hello, he told me that Grandma Mamie, my father's mother, was inside.

I'd avoided her since Max's bris, when she'd cornered me in the kitchen and said, "Tell me, Sophie, you don't want to get married?"

Chris had died only a few weeks before, and I'd barely been able to make myself answer. "I don't know if I do."

She'd said, "Tell me, you want to go home alone to a dark apartment night after night after night?"

Now Neil and I walked down the long hall, and there she was, sitting alone, sunk down in the sofa.

I bent down and kissed her. "Hi, Grandma."

"Is that you, Sophie?" she said in my general vicinity. According to Robert, she was nearly blind.

"I hardly recognize your voice," she said. "It's been so long."

"Well," I said, "here I am. And this is my friend Neil."

"Hi," Neil said, bending down. "How do you do?"

She said, "Well, hello," smiling.

She invited both of us to sit on the sofa with her, but only Neil took her up on it; I couldn't bring myself to get that close yet.

I was working up to it when I heard my grandmother say a long and happy, "Oh," and I realized that Neil had told her he was a doctor.

It was probably a coincidence that she looked me right in the eye just then, though it occurred to me that my doctor had cured her blindness.

"We're going to get a drink," I said. "Would you like something?"

"No, no," she said. "Stay here with your old grandma a minute."

"Go ahead," I said to Neil. I took his place on the sofa.

"Well, Sophilla," she said. "A doctor."

"Uh-huh," I said.

"Tell me," she said, "have you met your mother-in-law yet?"

I said, "You're sure I can't get you anything to drink?"

When I stood up, Neil was at my side. "You okay?"

"I guess I am," I said.

We ate hot dogs and chips and I introduced him to Naomi's parents, slow speakers both; I could feel myself getting older as we said hello. Her brother passed by, and his mother explained that he was going to the bedroom to check the score of the baseball game.

There were a dozen children from Max and Isabelle's preschool and as many parents, some of them presumably the anti-nappists Naomi deplored.

Mindy was rescuing a crying child from the Magic Tunnel.

Jack was on all fours, giving Max a pony ride, and whinnied when he saw us.

Neil, excellent sport that he was, offered his own back.

Jack stood. "You know Mom isn't here yet?"

"No," I said.

Naomi peeked out of the kitchen and said, "Sophie? Can you give me a hand?"

"Sure." To Jack I said, "Do I have to?"

In the kitchen, Naomi said, "We just want you to know how much we like Neil," and her "we" reminded me of *We the Jury.*

But Robert, at his subtlemost, cut in and said, "Why don't you have a drink?" and set about making a Bloody Mary.

I said, "Mom isn't here?"

Naomi shook her head and gave me a look as though we two might disapprove together.

"Five more minutes," Robert said, "and I'm lighting the candles."

When he handed me the drink, I saw the face of Robert as a little boy, watching our parents smoke.

I took my Bloody Mary into the bedroom, where Naomi's brother was standing in front of the TV. He'd been in there for a good half-hour, but he said, "I just want to check the score."

I said, "Am I my brother's brother-in-law's keeper?" Then I called my mother.

She picked up on the first ring and said a cheerful, "Hello?"

"Mom," I said. "Where are you?"

She sounded confused: "You called me."

"I'm at Robert's," I said. "At the birthday party."

"Oh, my God," she said, and I was relieved that she'd made a mistake, and hadn't chosen to be with Lev instead of us. He was there, though; in the background, I heard the same game Naomi's brother was watching.

She said, "I thought it was next Saturday," and asked if I could call Robert to the phone, and I did.

During "Happy Birthday," Neil sat with my grandmother, and I stood next to Jack, who sang what might have been an imitation of Dean Martin. After the twins blew out their candles, he said a lounge singer's, "How's your steak?" and, "Anyone here from Jersey?"

Then he said, "I can't believe Mom didn't show up."

It occurred to me that he was angry at her just for having a boyfriend; he saw it as unmotherly. That Lev was married only made her lapse more flagrant, and, lucky for Jack, gave him permission to disapprove.

I said, "She got the dates mixed up," meaning that her absence had nothing to do with her boyfriend, meaning that she was just being the mother we knew and loved and were irritated by.

"I was going to bring Mindy's parents," he said, absorbing nothing I'd said. "They would've come if they didn't have a bar mitzvah to go to."

"What is it with those people?" I said. "Every week a Bronstein gets circumcised or bar mitzvahed or married."

"It's a big family," he said. "They like to get together."

"That's sick," I said.

. . . . .

Steeny moved in and out of coherence. She sometimes seemed to be narrating a dream she was in the middle of. She could repeat herself two, three, four hundred times in a single conversation. She saw my grandfather regularly now; she seemed to commute almost daily to the afterworld, or, I guess, he came here.

I said, "Did he tell you what it was like?"

"I asked him," she said, "and he told me, 'Stop asking so many questions and get over here,' " which was exactly how my grandfather spoke.

When she was lucid, I asked her questions (Did she see herself as different from how she'd been before her strokes? Why had she always favored my uncle?), but her answers—often, "You do the best you can"—weren't the revelations I'd hoped for.

I kept trying, though: "When you used to say, 'I don't blame the children—' "

She interrupted: "I blame the parents."

"What did you mean?"

"I meant, I blame the parents."

"For what, though?"

She said, "Your hair was always so messy," with the sharpness I'd almost forgotten.

. . . . .

For Thanksgiving, my uncle Dan flew into Philadelphia to surprise my grandmother, and my mother joined their bedside feast.

Jack was going to the Bronsteins'.

Neil and I were going to Robert's. I went over early to help baste or stuff, but Naomi had ordered the meal from a kosher place on the East Side. She and her parents had gone to pick it up. Her brother was watching television. The twins were napping. I helped Robert fold laundry.

He seemed quiet, and I asked if anything was wrong.

"Just thinking," he said.

I let fifteen minutes go by. "What are you thinking about?"

He hesitated. "Naomi wants me to talk about my feelings more."

"Wow," I said. "You'd think she got enough of that at the office."

He smiled. It was the only time he'd ever talked to me about Naomi, and he was finished now.

"Maybe you could fake it," I said. "That's what I do with my shrink."

He turned toward the baby monitor; he'd heard the barely audible sound of one twin waking. He told me that we probably had three more minutes of civilization before the monkeys invaded.

I said, "Should I straighten up a little?" There were toys on every table and chair and all over the floor.

He shook his head and mentioned Sisyphus. Three minutes, Robert said, was just enough time to make a perfect martini.

. . . . .

My mother didn't want to come with me to my grandmother's. She forced herself. I said, "Do you want me to drive?"

She said, "Fine," like we were in a fight.

"I'd be happy to," I said.

By then I'd realized that her anger had nothing to do with her mother's transformed disposition or diminished health: Her mother had prevented her from marrying Lev when she'd had the chance.

I wanted to remind her that if she had married Lev there would be no Jack or Robert or me, but it wasn't for me to say.

. . . . .

My mother sat in the wing chair across the room, her whole body turned toward the door, like a sullen teenager. Then she walked out.

I was scratching my grandmother's back. She said, "What's with her?"

I was impressed that she'd noticed, and said I'd find out.

My mother was in the living room, staring not at the portrait but at the teddy bear below.

"I'm going to take a walk," she said, and left.

As usual, I was thinking that this might be the last time I'd ever see my grandmother. As usual, I asked myself what I wanted to say to her. As usual, I said, "I love you."

"I love you, too," she said. "How's Neil?"

"Okay," I said.

She said, "A good man is hard to find."

"You can say that again," I said.

She said, "A good man is hard to find."

I thought, *The old girl hasn't lost her sense of humor;* then she repeated "A good man is hard to find" about ten times. I thought maybe I'd go out for a walk myself when I heard her say, "It's even harder to find a good woman."

"Did you just say, 'It's even harder to find a good woman'?"

She nodded.

I looked at her and said, "You mean . . . ?"

"I mean just what I said."

It was then that I finally said, "Granny, I think it would be really nice if you left that portrait to my mom."

She nodded, and I could tell by the set of her jaw that she'd heard and not liked what I'd said.

For a few minutes I couldn't talk. Then I said, "Why were you so hard on my mother?"

She said, "You want the best for the people you love."

. . . . .

The funeral was small. My uncle Dan cried more than anyone, even me, and I wondered if my grandmother had always been as loving to him as she'd only lately been to us.

Once, years ago, I'd brought up how obviously she'd favored Dan: "Wasn't it hard, Mom?"

She'd said, "It was hard on him, too."

I'd said, "It was hard on the slaveholders, too."

. . . . .

A few weeks after the funeral, I went with her to my grandmother's apartment. We both stopped in the living room and looked at the wall where the portrait had hung.

I assumed that my grandmother had left it to my uncle, and I said, "I'm sorry."

But my mother said that the portrait hadn't been mentioned in the will. "I told Dan he could have it."

I looked at her.

"That's what she would've wanted," my mother said.

I rummaged through the drawers of the night table, desk, and bureau, as I'd always wanted to. My grandmother had kept everything. In one chest, I found every card my brothers and I had made for her, every postcard, every letter, and it occurred to me that even during her tenure as the wicked witch, she'd cared about us more than any of us had imagined. On the nay side of this pretty notion was that she'd also saved coupons for products long since extinct, my grandfather's prescription pads, promotional desk calendars from insurance companies and banks, and a rake for the yard she hadn't had for more than twenty-five years. I counted nineteen hotel sewing kits and twenty-four decks of cards.

I'd waited my whole life to open the rubber-banded jewelry boxes, and I saved them for last. I was thrilled cutting the rubber bands. But there was was nothing inside that I wanted; inexplicably, most of the boxes contained empty beds of cotton.

My mother was holding the white vinyl purse that her mother had clutched in her last months. I said, "What's in there, anyway?"

She pulled out Kleenex after Kleenex.

I sat on the bed beside her.

She kept shaking her head, and finally she spoke: Lev was never going to leave his wife.

"Did he say he would?" I asked.

"He never did," she said.

I thought, *Well, that's good,* but I didn't say it. I said, "Oh, Mom," and she let herself be hugged.

Then she sat up straight and said, "Let's go."

I said, "Aren't you going to take anything?"

She said, "It would just remind me of her."

. . . . .

A few months later, she changed her mind. She hired a moving company, and into our house she installed her mother's apartment—mahogany, brass, chintz, and velvet. On my bureau there now sashayed a china belle wearing a hoop skirt with ruffly pantaloons. My grandmother's teddy bear lounged on Robert's bed, reminiscing about the glory days on her silk sofa.

I asked my mother what time the tag sale started.

She told me that she liked being around her mother's things. "I have fond memories," she said.

Then she told me how good she felt about her work at the Jewish Home for the Aged. She'd arranged for a Girl Scout troop to carol there on Christmas Eve.

I said, "Aren't the Jewish-aged Jewish?"

"Everyone likes carols," she said. In her own defense, she added that many of the residents were deaf, and others disoriented.

. . . . .

I was packing to go back to New York when my mother knocked on my door and handed me an envelope. I recognized Francine Lawlor's handwriting, a script so uniform and legible it might've belonged to the star pupil in a penmanship class. The card was a photograph of a poinsettia overlaid with the words *Seasons Greetings* in gold foil; with a blue ballpoint, Francine had inserted an apostrophe between the *n* and the *s*.

She reported no news, either of Steinhardt or of herself. She'd written only her standard, "Best wishes for a Happy New Year," and signed her full name. I turned the envelope over to see if she still lived in the same apartment in Carteret, New Jersey, and only then did I notice how painstakingly she'd written her return address. Until that moment, it hadn't occurred to me that she'd hoped for a card in return.

. . . . .

When I got back to New York, I called Adam at home, as I rarely did; he wrote on weekends. I said that I was sorry to bother him, and he said, "Dontcha know me, Bert?" his favorite line from *It's a Wonderful Life*. "What's up?"

"I'm worried about Francine," I said.

"I'm sure she's fine," he said.

"What makes you think so?"

"She's a good editor." Then he said that he'd been meaning to call me about a job on a new talk show at PBS: I'd do research on the guests and make up questions for the host. He told me he was sure I'd be good at it. "You ask a lot of questions," he said.

. . . . .

My apartment was overheated, and I couldn't fall asleep with Neil in bed, and I couldn't fall asleep on the sofa. I was thinking about Francine. In my nightmare daydream, I saw her at Steinhardt, in the area where all the editorial assistants worked—the Cave, we'd called it—and it was dark except for her tensor lamp.

. . . . .

The agency Christmas party was huge and awful—a strobe light, a DJ, an open bar—one of those parties where you have to drink and drink just to survive. I noticed Ian because he was so elegant in an atmosphere overflowing with inelegance, because he was so tall and so skinny and so sexy; I noticed him because he noticed me.

He came over to the bar and when he introduced himself it was like a silk shade had been thrown over the glare of the evening. He was from the London office, and his English accent made him both hard to understand and more charming.

If I couldn't exactly hear his words, I could see them. He had *Danger* and *Warning* writ large all over him; he himself looked like a skull and crossbones. I liked talking to him, though, and not just because he was smart and funny, deadpan and reserved. He was exactly the kind of man I'd been drawn to pre-Neil, the kind I'd never be drawn to again.

I leaned back and my elbow missed the bar. "I'm not drunk," I said. "I'm clumsy."

Still, he suggested that food might be in order.

I said, "If anyone needs to eat, it's you."

I felt as safe and relaxed as I would have at home reading a novel about a scoundrel imperiling a naïf; I was radiant with superiority, not over him but over the easy mark I'd been.

. . . . .

On Christmas Eve, I called New Jersey Information and got Francine's number in Carteret.

"Hello," she said, and her voice in that single word reminded me of how pale she was and how pinched.

"Hi," I said. "It's Sophie Applebaum."

"Sophie," she said. Then, nothing. I thought maybe she was stunned to hear from me; I'd never called her.

I said, "I just wanted to wish you a merry Christmas."

"Thank you," she said.

I'd forgotten how hard it was to talk to Francine, and I wished now that I'd planned what I was going to say. "And I wanted to thank you for your Christmas card." *For the last fifteen years.*

"You're welcome," she said.

"So," I said, "I was just wondering how you were."

"I'm fine."

"Great." I waited a moment to give her a chance to ask how I was, but she didn't. "I wanted to tell you how sorry I was to hear about Steinhardt."

"Thank you."

I said, "I guess I wondered if I could help in any way," though I wasn't sure what I could offer.

"Thank you," she said. "I'm doing very well."

As it turned out, after Steinhardt had been sold, Adam had called to ask if Francine would be willing to help his old boss, who was in a real jam; Wolfe needed a top-notch freelance line editor.

I knew it was my turn to talk, but I couldn't. I was thinking, *Ah Adam! Ah Humanity!*

Finally, I got out, "That's good to hear."

She was surprised that Adam hadn't told me. "I thought you were such good friends," she said, and I thought, *You haven't lost your edge, Francie.*

"Well," I said, winding down.

She said, "Wolfe works at Knopf," and I heard pride in her voice.

"That's wonderful, Francine," I said.

"Well," she said, "I should get back to work now. Thank you very much for calling, and happy Hanukkah."

. . . . .

I went to Jack's engagement party alone. Neil had plans with Ella for New Year's Eve. He'd offered to ask Beth about rescheduling but said she wasn't exactly eager to accommodate him, and I knew he wasn't exactly eager to ask.

I'd lived in Manhattan long enough not to be impressed by the word *loft;* as often as not, a loft had the feel of a garage. Rebecca's was in west, west, West Chelsea, close to the river, on a dark street past an auto-glass repair shop that offered free estimates. I buzzed Goldberg, and Goldberg buzzed back. In the elevator I pressed PH for penthouse; in the hall I hung my coat on the long rack.

Then I walked into the white dream the word *loft* inspired.

A jazz band was playing.

It was a big party, a party full of dancing, talking, drinking people—and me. I backed into the kitchen, where women in white shirts and black pants were loading and unloading trays of hors d'oeuvres.

I said, "Can I help with anything?"

"We've got everything under control, I think," a nice woman said. "How about a glass of champagne?" I took one and thanked her.

With my champagne, I stood at the refrigerator and looked at the Before and During pictures of the loft; I tried to act as interested as I would be if I myself were planning a renovation. I made my face say, *Now, how did they do that?*

I wondered why Rebecca hadn't hung the After pictures. Then I realized I was in the After picture, and also in the way of the caterers. I asked, "Do you know where the bathroom is?"

It was down the hall. My studio didn't even have a hall; my studio was a hall.

In the powder-room mirror, my skin had the gray-green pallor I associated with heroin addiction. Imitating an antidrug public-service announcement, I said, "Sophie needs help."

I found it in a small basket of makeup samples. I put on blush. I put on lipstick.

Back out in the world of the party, my mother had just arrived. She seemed shaky, maybe because she'd never driven to New York by herself before, or maybe because she was about to meet the Bronsteins.

"You okay?" I said. "How are you?"

She said, "Great," while her eyes said, *Save me.*

I held her hand, and we walked around. We talked to Robert and Naomi, who was pregnant with their third child and just beginning to show.

The big, beefy Bronstein brothers, the two in real estate and the black-sheep investment banker, introduced themselves and their wives, two of whom seemed to be named Julie.

Mindy came over looking as beautiful as any fiancée ever had. We all kissed and cooed. She was wearing a long black dress with a white sash like the one in the picture of Dovima. It was at that moment that I realized I'd been on the wrong search all along: I'd thought I wanted Dovima's dress when what I really wanted were her elephants.

A moment later, Mindy's parents, Sandy and Ellis, introduced themselves. Sandy wore a spangly dress, and my mother's eyes got spangly looking at her. When my mother got her back up, as happened with only a few women and never with men, she lifted her chin, and she lifted it now.

"I'm so thrilled about Mindy," she said.

Sandy said, "We couldn't be happier about Jack."

All the Bronsteins were standing together now, and father Ellis had his arm around Jack. I knew from Jack that the Bronsteins were rich and powerful, but they were richer and more powerful than I'd imagined: They were a family. That was what Jack wanted. He was willing to go to every bris and bar mitzvah. One Saturday he couldn't go to the movies with me because he was taking Mindy's grandmother to the optician. He would work to be part of Mindy's family as he'd never worked to be part of our family. But then, no one had asked him to.

Rebecca joined us, holding the hand of a man she introduced as her boyfriend, Eugene, who was an even lighter shade of pale than she was. She hugged my mother, whom she called "Aunt Joyce"; she called me "Cousin Sophie," as though we were Quakers at Meeting.

Her mother headed over, looking even more uptight than I'd remembered. I was only a part-time believer in the theory that people became more themselves as they got older, but her face was carved in stone like a commandment: *Thou Shalt Relax.*

"Sophie," she said. "I don't believe it!"

What? I wanted to ask, *What don't you believe?* Instead, I said, "Hi." I'd grown up calling her Aunt Nora, and decided just then that I didn't have to anymore.

I stopped myself from asking where Rebecca's father was, which I realized would've been a theological question at that point; he'd died years before my own father. My mother had dragged us to his funeral, and I remembered that in the car Jack had said, "Uncle David, we hardly knew ye," because the man had never said a word to any of us.

The Bronsteins had already taken a tour of the loft, but Rebecca asked if my mother and I wanted one. Of course we did.

I walked behind Rebecca, a dance therapist who still carried herself like the ballerina she'd been as a child—shoulders back, feet duckish.

As we crossed the living room, I spotted Jack's friend Pete from Martha's Vineyard, standing like an island.

I motioned for him to join the tour; *Come on,* my arm said, and he caught up.

"So, you're in advertising," my former aunt Nora was saying. "Do you love it?"

I thought, *Why would you think I love it?* but said nothing, and she didn't notice. Nora Goldberg did not have big ears, and thus I kept my jazz to myself.

A peek into the powder room, and we were off to the bedroom and the bathroom. Rebecca's mother called the second bedroom her pied-à-terre, and my mother said, "How often do you come in?"

"About once a week." Rebecca was out in the hall, but her mother still lowered her voice when she told mine, "I hope to share it before too long."

It took me a moment to realize that she wasn't talking about the room as a future love nest, but as a nursery for what might be the palest grandchild in the history of the world.

My mother, however, didn't realize. She said, "Are you seeing someone?"

"God, no." Her friend laughed, and then said, "Are you?"

"No, no, no," my mother said, "no." No one knew about Lev, and I saw now how it isolated her. I saw her try to summon up the Joyce Applebaum she was expected to be, but that Joyce Applebaum wasn't on speaking terms with this one; what followed was the emptiness of a credible imitation.

I wish I'd known then and could have told her what was going to happen: Though Lev Polikoff refused to leave his wife, in another year she would get cancer and leave him and everyone else. Piece by piece, my mother would ship her mother's brass and china to her brother. She and Lev would go to flea markets and hunt for blue bottles, which are supposed to be lucky, and he would convince her to hang them in a tree in the backyard.

. . . . .

Rebecca told us that if we wanted to go out on the terrace, we should get our coats. I helped my mother on with hers, an old fur of my grandmother's that was worn down in patches. I said, "I think you might be molting."

In a low voice, Pete said, "Play nice." Over his corduroy suit, he wore a red down jacket patched with silver duct tape.

We went out to the terrace, and when I saw the Hudson spread before us I said an involuntary, "Jesus."

Rebecca said, "I know," and she said it as though the dazzling view belonged to me, too.

"Well," I said, "I guess you kids won't be having that New York real-estate dream anymore."

Rebecca said, "What?" a muted version of how she'd spoken to me when we were younger.

"You know," Eugene said, "you find a door that you never noticed and it leads to a terrace or a huge room or even to a whole other apartment that turns out to be yours, too."

"I never had it," she said.

I said, "It's actually a nice dream."

My mother said she was cold and going in, and then Rebecca and her mother and Eugene said they were, too.

I told them, "I'm right behind you," but I wasn't.

Pete stayed on the terrace with me. After a few minutes, he said, "You don't really love advertising, do you?"

"Nope," I said. I told him that I was applying for a job as a researcher in public television, but I was also thinking of becoming a cartoonist, a songwriter, an underwater photographer, a peace activist, and a zookeeper for a really good zoo, the kind animals would have to apply to get into.

I was going to go from career to career and I wouldn't stop until I found one I loved. I was going to be the career version of a serial monogamist.

We stood at the railing, and I was glad he was there. No one was easier not to talk to than Pete, with whom I'd spent many happily quiet hours clamming and fishing and swimming; he spoke only when he had a really good joke to make or a truly interesting thing to say, or when he saw that I was about to get creamed by a wave. I thought that no one would appreciate this view more than Pete, until he turned around and faced the party instead. Then I remembered that Pete wasn't himself anywhere but Martha's Vineyard. Everywhere else, he was just waiting to go back.

"What's the matter?" I said. "Our stars aren't bright enough for you?"

Un-Petely, he said, "How much do you think this place cost?"

I thought of the current slogan for the New York lottery: "All it takes is a dollar and a dream," I said. "And another, I don't know, one-point-five million dollars?"

For a second I got a pang of envy—the unPHairness!—but then I reminded myself that this loft doubled as Nora Goldberg's pied-à-terre.

Pete was shivering—Pete, a man who took an annual swim with his Newfoundland in the Atlantic on Christmas Day. I thought maybe talking about Martha's Vineyard would warm him up; I said, "Remember all those little silver fish we saw that time?"

"No," he said.

"On Lucy Vincent Beach?" I said. "They were jumping out of the water."

He didn't remember because he'd seen thousands of little fish hundreds of times, and because it didn't mean to him what it had to me. "Soph," he said, "little fish only jump out of the water when a big fish is chasing them." Then he said, "You're not cold?"

I was, but I shook my head.

He said, "I'll see you inside," and in he went.

With so much sky and so much river, you couldn't help seeing the big picture. It was what you already knew, but crowding into the subway or rushing to a movie, you only saw it for a second, and close up. Now I took a good long look. I'd always heard you couldn't see stars in Manhattan because of all the lights. But here they all were. Here was my night in shining armor.

THE WONDER SPOT

SETH TALKS ME INTO going to a party in Brooklyn. He says that we can just drop by. I tell him that a party in Brooklyn is a commitment. It takes effort. It's like a wedding: You can't just drop by.

"We can just drop by," he says again, and he gives me a look that means, *We can do anything we want.*

This will be our first party as a couple.

He says, "It'll be fun."

My boyfriend is a decade younger than I am; he is full of hope.

We drive to Brooklyn in his old Mustang convertible, with the top down. Because of the wind and because I'm on the side of Seth's bad ear, we can't really talk—or I can't. But he tells me that we're going to Williamsburg, the section of Brooklyn that's been called the New Downtown. After the party we can walk around and have dinner at a restaurant his friend Bob is about to open there. Bob has offered to let us try everything on the menu-to-be if we'll help him name the restaurant; the finalists are the Shiny Diner, Bob's, and the Wonder Spot. "Start thinking," Seth says, and I do.

Across the bridge and into the land of Brooklyn, we go under overpasses and down streets so dark and deserted you know they're used only to get lost on, and I get a pang for Manhattan, where I am never farther than a block from a bodega, never more than a raised arm from a cab. But then we turn a corner and—*Lights! People! Action!*—we park.

Walking to the party, I tell Seth about the Williamsburg I've already been to, the one in Virginia. I expect him to have heard of it—

he's from Canada and knows more about the United States than I do—but he hasn't. I tell him that I was five or six at the time, and I didn't understand the concept of historical reenactment; I thought that we'd just found a place where women in bonnets churned butter and men in breeches shoed horses. I tell him the real drama of the trip: I lost the dollar my father had given me for the gift shop.

I'm having such a good time that I forget about the party until we're on the elevator up. I say, "Maybe we should have a code for 'I want to go.' "

He starts to make a joke but sees that I'm serious and squeezes my hand three times. I okay the code.

The elevator door opens right into the loft. I was counting on those extra few seconds of hallway before facing the party, the party we are now part of and in, a party with people talking and laughing and having a party time. I think, *I am a solid, trying to do a liquid's job.*

I am only a third joking when I squeeze Seth's hand three times. He squeezes back four, and before I can ask what four means, our hostess is upon us. She is tall and slinky, with ultra-short hair and a gold dot in one of her perfect nostrils; I feel every pound of my weight, every year of my age, until Seth tells her, "This is my girlfriend, Sophie."

I smile up at this ghosty-pale sweetie-pie man o' mine.

As soon as our hostess slinks off to greet her next arrivals, I say, "What does four mean?"

"It means, 'I love you, too,' " he says.

I want to be happy to hear these words—it's the first time we've squeezed them—but I feel so close to him at this moment, I say the truth, which is, "I feel old."

He puts his coat around my shoulders and says, "Is that better?" and I realize that I've spoken into his bad ear.

I nod, and we move deeper into the party. He introduces me as his girlfriend to each of the friends we pass, all of whom seem happy to meet me, and I think, *I am his girlfriend, Sophie; I am girlfriend; I am Sophie, girlfriend of Seth.* I'm fine, even super-fine, until he goes to get a glass of wine for me. Now I look around, trying to pretend, as I always do at parties, that I could be talking to a fellow partygoer if I wanted to, but at the moment I'm just too captivated by my own fascinating observations of the crowd.

The women are young, young, young, liquidy and sweet-looking; they are batter, and I am the sponge cake they don't know they'll become. I stand here, a lone loaf, stuck to the pan.

It is at this moment that I see Vincent—only from behind, and it's been years, but I know it's him.

I've told Seth almost nothing about my ex-boyfriends. Now he'll meet the one who told me my head was too big for my body.

When Seth returns with my wine, he says, "Still cold?" and he rubs my shoulders.

A small crowd gathers around us—the drummer in Seth's band, and his entourage—girlfriend, brother, and girlfriend of brother. They try to talk to me, and I try to talk back. One of the girlfriends, I'm not sure whose, works in public radio. Since I'm a public-radio lover, I can keep this conversation going, program to program, until she asks what I do.

I say that I do research for a PBS talk show but add that what I love doing better than anything at the moment, and what I am getting damn good at, is practicing the lost art of the silhouette. I mime cutting, which leads to an almost post-nuclear silence.

But the girlfriend who works in public radio says, "People?"

"And animals," I say.

"That sounds fun."

I say, "It's stressful," and she laughs, and we are insta-friends.

Then we girlfriends go back to them boyfriends. I plant myself beside Seth like a fire hydrant, my back to where I imagine Vincent to be.

But he's not; he's right across the room, his arm slung like a belt around the hips of a girl who I can tell right away is a model. She has the long, straight hair I used to wish for, and sky-high thighs I can see through her mesh stockings.

Just like the bad old days, Vincent doesn't seem to recognize me. Then he does.

I inadvertently squeeze Seth's hand, and he smiles without looking at me, like we have a secret language, and I wish we did.

I watch Vincent steer his girlfriend toward us.

He's grown his hair long and now sports a Lucifer-style beard and mustache. Plus, he's wearing a shirt with huge pointy collars jutting out like fangs over his jacket.

When he reaches us, I say, "Happy Halloween."

"Hello, Sophie," he says, Dr. Droll.

I say, "Seth, this is—"

Vincent interrupts and introduces himself: "Enzo."

"Enzo?" I say.

He doesn't answer, and I remember his New Jersey friends calling him Vinnie and his firm correction: "Vincent."

Vinnie-Vincent-Enzo pulls his model front and center and says, "This is Amanda."

"I'm Sophie." Then I get to say, "This is my boyfriend, Seth."

"Hi." She is both cool and chirpy, an ice chick. "We know each other," she says about the man I've just introduced as my boyfriend, and she kisses him—just his cheek, but so far back that her pouty mouth appears to be traveling neck- or ear-ward.

I stare at her, even while I am telling myself not to. I fall under the spell not of her eyes but her eyebrows, which are perfectly arched and skinny and make me aware of my own thick and feral pair; mine are a forest and hers are a trail.

When I blink myself out of my trance, Vincent is saying, "Whenever anyone would say, 'Small world,' Sophie used to say, 'Actually, it's medium-sized.' "

I say, "I was about eleven when I knew Vincent."

Then, like the hostess my mother taught me to be, I say, "Vincent"—I correct myself—"*Enzo* is a musician, too."

"I used to be," he says, and names the best known of the bands he played in, though I happen to know it was only for about fifteen minutes. Then he asks Seth, "Who do you play with?"

Seth says the name of the band, and I can tell Vincent's impressed and doesn't want to be; he fast-talks about starting up a start-up—an online recording studio, a real-time distribution outlet, a virtual music label. He goes on and on, Vincent style, grandiose and impossible to understand.

I say, "Basically, you do everything but teach kindergarten?"

Vincent says, "There is an educational component."

Seth squeezes my hand three times.

"Oh, shoot," I say, looking at my wrist for a watch I'm not wearing, "we have to go," and I love the sound of *we,* and I love that it's Seth who wants to go, and I love that we are going.

Vincent says they're headed to another party themselves. He kisses both my cheeks—what now must be the signature Enzo kiss—and he looks at me as though he cares deeply for me, a look I never got when we were together, a look that Seth notices, and I think, *Phew! Seth will think another man loved me; he will think I am the lovable kind of woman, the kind a man better love right or somebody else will.*

Vincent says, "You look great, Sophie," and I think of saying, *Whereas you look a little strange,* but I just say, "See you, Vinnie."

A few more pleasantries, and Seth and I are on the elevator, just the two of us, pressing 1.

I say, "Good thing she was just a model." I am giddy, talking fast, and happy. "I think that would've been really hard if she were a supermodel."

Seth looks at me, not sure what I mean.

Out on the street, I say, "How do you know her, by the way?" and instantly regret how deliberately offhanded I sound.

"I don't really know her," he says. "She came up to me after a show a few weeks ago."

I think, *Came* up *to you or* on *to you?* but I give myself the open, amused look of a bystander eager to hear more about one of life's funny little coincidences.

"She asked me if I would help her celebrate her half-birthday," he says, and his tone tells me I would be crazy to think he'd ever be interested in her.

Unfortunately, now I am crazy, and I have to stop myself from saying a tone-deaf and tone-dumb, *So you're saying you didn't eat her half-birthday cake?*

Suddenly I feel like I'm Mary Poppins, floating with an umbrella and a spoonful of sugar into the city of sexual menace, population a million models with ultra-short and long straight hair and pouty mouths and thighs you can see through mesh stockings.

From there I go straight to, *This will never work. He has models coming on to him after his shows. He'll be forty-nine when you're turning sixty. He is young and hip, and you don't even know the hip word for* hip *anymore. You belong at home in bed with a book.*

I remind myself that this is what I always say and what I always do. As soon as I'm in a relationship, I promote fear from clerk to president, even though all it can do is sweep up, turn off the lights, and lock the door.

I am so deep in my own argument that I almost don't hear Seth say, "Sophie."

He stops me on the pavement and turns me toward him. His face practically glows white; he is a ghost of the ghost he usually looks like.

He says, "When did you go out with him?"

"So long ago he had a different name."

"Beelzebub?"

I tell him that Vincent was still in purgatory when I knew him.

"But it was hard for you to see him with somebody else, tonight?"

"No," I say, a little surprised.

He nods, not quite believing. "But the thing you said about her being a model?"

"Models are always hard," I say. "And it was hard to see her necking with your cheek."

After I've said this, I want to say that I don't usually use the word *neck* as a verb; it's a fifties word, my mother's word, but he is shaking his head and I can see he is not thinking about how old I sound or look or am.

"Obviously he still has a thing for you," Seth says, and shakes his head and swallows a couple of times, like he's trying to get rid of a bad taste. "The way he looked at you."

My *phew* gives me an Indian burn of shame. "That look was for Amanda's sake," I say, and I know it's true. For a second, I am an older sister to my younger self. "If she brings it up later, he'll tell her she's crazy."

"Very nice," Seth says, and his voice tells me that he doesn't want to hear any more about Vincent and Amanda, he doesn't care about them, and that he's wishing he didn't care so much about me.

It scares me. But then I get this big feeling, simple but exalted: *He's like me, just with different details.*

His eyes are closed, and I think maybe he's picturing me with Vincent or other men he assumes I've slept with or loved. Maybe he's telling himself that he's too tall or doesn't hear well enough.

Usually he pulls me in for the hug, but now I do it. I pull him in and we stay like this, his chin on my head, my face on his chest.

I find myself picturing Amanda at another party with Vincent and feeling sorry for her. It occurs to me that if I were as beautiful as she is, every passing half-birthday would be harder to celebrate. But mostly I am just glad I am not her and glad we are not them and glad just to be out here on the curb, breathing the sweet air of Williamsburg and postcolonial freedom.

We are quiet for a while, walking. I begin to see where we are now. We pass the Miss Williamsburg Diner. Little bookstores I could spend my life in. We pass a gallery with mobiles hung above a reflecting pool.

Then we're standing in a parking lot, outside of what Seth tells me is Bob's restaurant. I'm saying that living in Manhattan gives you a heightened appreciation of parking lots when Seth takes something out of his pocket and puts it in my hand. It's a dollar. "For the gift shop," he says. "Don't lose it now."

With my dollar hand, I squeeze Seth's about thirty-seven times, telling him everything I feel.

He says, "What does that mean?"

I say, " 'I'm hungry.' "

What I feel is, *Right now I am having the life I want, here outside the Shiny Diner, Bob's, or the Wonder Spot, with my dollar to spend and dinner to come.* We will try everything on the menu. Then we will drive through Brooklyn and cross the bridge with the Manhattan skyline in front of us, which looks new to me every time I see it, and we will drive right into it. We'll find a parking space a few blocks from my apartment on Tenth Street, and we'll pick up milk and tomorrow's paper. We will undress and get into bed.